In our Bestselling Author Collection, Harlequin Books is proud to offer classic novels from today's superstars of women's fiction. These authors have captured the hearts of millions of readers around the world, and earned their place on the *New York Times, USA TODAY* and other bestseller lists with every release.

As a bonus, each volume also includes a full-length novel from a rising star of series romance. Bestselling authors in their own right, these talented writers have captured the qualities Harlequin is famous for—heart-racing passion, edge-of-the-seat entertainment and a satisfying happily-ever-after.

Don't miss any of the books in the collection!

BESTSELLING AUTHOR COLLECTION

New York Times and *USA TODAY*
Bestselling Author

LINDA
HOWARD

ALMOST FOREVER

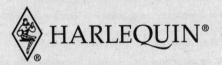

HARLEQUIN®

TORONTO • NEW YORK • LONDON
AMSTERDAM • PARIS • SYDNEY • HAMBURG
STOCKHOLM • ATHENS • TOKYO • MILAN • MADRID
PRAGUE • WARSAW • BUDAPEST • AUCKLAND

Recycling programs
for this product may
not exist in your area.

ISBN-13: 978-0-373-38989-6

ALMOST FOREVER

Copyright © 2010 by Harlequin Books S.A.

The publisher acknowledges the copyright holders
of the individual works as follows:

ALMOST FOREVER
Copyright © 1986 by Linda Howington

FOR THE BABY'S SAKE
Copyright © 1994 by Christine Rimmer

This edition published by arrangement with Harlequin Books S.A.

For questions and comments about the quality of this book
please contact us at Customer_eCare@Harlequin.ca.

® and TM are trademarks of the publisher. Trademarks indicated with
® are registered in the United States Patent and Trademark Office, the
Canadian Trade Marks Office and in other countries.

www.eHarlequin.com

Printed in U.S.A.

CONTENTS

ALMOST FOREVER

New York Times and *USA TODAY*
Bestselling Author

Linda Howard

LINDA HOWARD

says that whether she's reading them or writing them, books have long played a profound role in her life. She cut her teeth on Margaret Mitchell and from then on continued to read widely and eagerly. In recent years her interest has settled on romance fiction, because she's "easily bored by murder, mayhem and politics." After twenty-one years of penning stories for her own enjoyment, Ms. Howard finally worked up the courage to submit a novel for publication—and met with success. This Alabama native is now a multi-*New York Times* bestselling author.

Chapter 1

Anson Edwards sat alone in his big plush office, his fingers steepled as he weighed the strengths of his two lieutenants, wondering which of the two would be best to send to Houston. His own strength was his ability to analyze quickly and accurately, yet in this instance he didn't want to make a snap decision. His opponent—Sam Bronson—was an enigma, a man who played his cards close to his chest; it wouldn't do to underestimate him. Instinct told Anson that an overt takeover attempt on Bronson's metal alloy company would fail, that Bronson was wily enough to have hidden assets. Anson had to discover what those assets were, and their value, before he could realistically expect victory in his attempt to take Bronson Alloys under Spencer-Nyle's corporate umbrella. He knew that he could take control simply by offering much more than the company could possibly be worth, but that wasn't Anson's way. He had a responsibility to the stockholders of Spencer-Nyle, and he wasn't reckless. He would do what was necessary to take Bronson, but no more.

He could set a team of investigators on the job, but that would alert Bronson, and if Bronson were given any sort of warning he might be able to take evasive action that could drag into months. Anson didn't want this; he wanted things to be over quickly. The best bet would be one man, a man whom he could trust in any situation. He trusted both Rome Matthews and Max Conroy completely, but which man would be the best one for the job?

Rome Matthews was his handpicked, personally trained successor; Rome was tough, smart, fair, and he set out to win at everything he did. But Rome had a formidable reputation. He was far too well-known in business circles, and Houston was too close to Dallas for Anson to hope that no one would know him. Rome's very presence would trigger alarm in the business community.

Max Conroy, on the other hand, wasn't that well-known. People tended not to take him as seriously as they did Rome; it was those male-model looks of his, as well as the lazy, good-humored image he projected. People just didn't expect Max to work as hard at something as Rome would. But there was steel in Max Conroy, a ruthlessness that he kept skillfully disguised. That famous affability of his was only a pose; he kept the almost fearsome intensity of his character under strict control. Those who didn't know him were always completely fooled, expecting him to be more playboy than executive.

So it would have to be Max, who would have a better chance of quietly gathering information.

Anson picked up a file again, leafing through the pages of information about key personnel with Bronson Alloys. Nothing could be learned from Bronson himself; the man was wary, and a genius. But a chain was only as strong as its weakest link, and Anson was determined to find Bronson's weak link.

He came to the photograph of Bronson's assistant and

paused. Bronson appeared to trust his assistant completely, though there was no hint of romance between them. Anson frowned as he studied the photograph; the woman was a pretty, dark-eyed blonde, but no great beauty. There was a reserved expression in her dark eyes. She had been married to Jeff Halsey, the heir of a wealthy Houston family, but they had divorced five years ago. She was thirty-one now and hadn't remarried. Anson checked her name: Claire Westbrook.

Thoughtfully he leaned back in his chair. Would she be vulnerable to Max's seductive charm? It remained to be seen. Then he tapped the photograph in sudden decision. Claire Westbrook just might be the weak link in Bronson's chain.

Claire slipped through the double doors onto the terrace and walked to the waist-high fieldstone wall that separated the terrace from the flower garden. Resting her hands on the cool stone, she stared blindly at the garden, not seeing the masses of blooms that were highlighted by strategically placed lights. How *could* Virginia invite Jeff and Helene, knowing that Claire had accepted an invitation? She'd done it deliberately, of course; she'd been gloating at the shock that Claire hadn't been able to hide when her ex-husband arrived at the party with his beautiful, pregnant wife.

Tears burned at the back of Claire's eyes, and she blinked to control them. She thought she could have handled an accidental meeting with aplomb, but she was stunned by Virginia's deliberate cruelty. She and Virginia had never been close friends, but still, she'd never expected this. How ironic that Claire had accepted the invitation only at the urging of her sister, Martine, who thought it would do her good to get out of the apartment and socialize! So much for good intentions, Claire thought wryly, controlling the urge to cry. The episode wasn't worth crying over, and it had taught her a lesson:

never trust any of your ex-husband's old girlfriends. Evidently Virginia had never forgiven Claire for being Mrs. Jeff Halsey.

"Did the smoke and noise become too much for you, too?"

Claire whirled around, startled by the words spoken so close to her ear. She'd been certain no one else was on the terrace. Determined not to let anyone know she'd been upset, she lifted one eyebrow in casual inquiry.

The man was silhouetted by the light coming through the double glass doors behind him, making it impossible to see his features, but she was certain she didn't know him. He was tall and lean, his shoulders broad beneath the impeccable cut of his white dinner jacket, and he was so close to her that she could smell the faint clean scent of his cologne.

"I apologize. I didn't intend to startle you," he said, moving to stand beside her. "I saw you come out here and thought I'd enjoy some fresh air, too. We haven't been introduced, have we? Maxwell Benedict."

"Claire Westbrook," she murmured in return. She recognized him now; they hadn't been introduced before, true, but she'd seen him when he had arrived at the party. It was impossible not to notice him. He looked like a model, with thick blond hair and vivid eyes; Claire remembered thinking that a man with a face like his should be short, just to keep the scales balanced. Instead he was tall and moved with a casual masculine grace that drew every feminine eye to him. Despite the chiseled perfection of his face, there was nothing effeminate about him; his looks were wholly masculine, and whenever he looked at a woman, his gaze was full of male appreciation. Pretty women weren't the only ones singled out for the megaton force of his charm; every woman, young or old, plain or pretty, was treated with a mixture of courtesy and appreciation that melted them, one and all, like a snowball in hot summer sunshine.

If he expected her to melt right along with the rest, she thought wryly, he was in for a disappointment. Jeff had taught her some hard lessons about handsome charming men, and she remembered every one of them. She was safe even from this man, whose charm was so potent that it was almost a visible force. He didn't even have to flirt! His spectacular looks and flashing smile stunned, his crisp-edged British accent intrigued, and the quiet baritone of his voice soothed. Claire wondered if his feelings would be hurt when she failed to be impressed.

"I thought you seemed upset when you came out here," he said suddenly, leaning against the wall with total disregard for the condition of his crisp white evening jacket. "Is anything wrong?"

My goodness, all that and he was perceptive, too! Claire shrugged, putting lightness in her tone when she answered, "Not really. I'm just not certain how to handle an awkward situation."

"If that's the case, may I be of any assistance?"

His offer was calm, polite and coolly controlled. Claire paused, vaguely intrigued despite herself. She had expected him to smooth and sophisticated, but that element of control she sensed in him was out of the ordinary.

"Thank you, but it isn't a major problem." All she had to do was somehow make a graceful exit without anyone noticing that she was in full retreat. It wasn't Jeff; she was long over him. But the baby that Helene carried was a reminder of a pain that she'd never gotten over, of the baby she'd lost. She'd wanted her baby so badly….

Behind them the double doors opened again, and Claire stiffened as Virginia rushed toward her, gushing false sympathy. "Claire, darling, I'm *so* sorry! I really had no idea Jeff and Helene would be here. Lloyd invited them, and I was as horribly surprised as you. You poor dear, are you very upset? After all, we all know how crushed you were—"

Maxwell Benedict straightened beside her, and Claire sensed his acute interest. Hot color burned in her cheeks as she broke in before Virginia could say anything more. "Really, Virginia, there's no need to apologize. I'm not upset at all." The casual coolness of her voice was utterly convincing, even though it was a complete lie. She had died a little inside when she'd heard that Helene was pregnant, and the sight of Jeff's wife, so glowingly lovely and so proudly pregnant, had twisted her heart. She was still haunted by a sense of loss; that was the one pain she couldn't seem to conquer.

Virginia hesitated, disconcerted by the total lack of concern Claire was showing. "Well, if you're certain you're all right…I had visions of you crying your heart out, all alone out here."

"But she isn't all alone," Maxwell Benedict said smoothly, and Claire started as his warm arm slid around her shoulders. Automatically she began to move away, but his fingers tightened warningly on her bare shoulder, and she forced herself to stand still. "Nor is she crying, though I'd be delighted to offer her my shoulder if she felt so inclined. Well, Claire? Do you think you want to cry?"

Part of her disliked the easy way he'd used her first name, when they had only just met, but another part of her was grateful to him for giving her this opportunity to keep her pride and not let Virginia guess that her ploy had been successful, after all, though not in the way she'd planned. Tilting her head up to him the way she'd often seen her sister Martine do when intent on charming someone, Claire gave him her most brilliant smile. "I think I'd rather dance."

"Then dance you shall, my dear. Excuse us, won't you?" he said politely to Virginia, ushering Claire past their disappointed hostess and back into the house. After the relative peace of the terrace, the party seemed that much more crowded and noisy. The alcohol fumes and the crush of bodies stifled her, but the music from the stereo rose above the clash of conversation and laughter, and they joined the group of people who were trying to dance in the middle of the room. Space was so limited that swaying in one spot was really all that could be done. Claire started to suggest that they forget about dancing, but he clasped her hand in his and drew her to him with his other arm, and she decided to dance this one dance. He wasn't holding her close despite the press of the crowd, and again she sensed the strict control that seemed to govern his actions. Perhaps she'd misjudged him, she mused. Just because his face was as precisely sculpted as that of a Greek idol, she'd automatically assumed that he was nothing but a shallow playboy, but a playboy wouldn't have that cool control. Perhaps it was his British reserve that she sensed.

"How long have you been in the States?" she asked, necessarily moving closer to him in order to be heard.

A rather whimsical smile curved his beautiful mouth. "How could you tell I'm not a native Texan?"

She chuckled. "A lucky guess."

"Actually, I have a hybrid accent. When I go home for holidays or vacations, my family constantly complains that I talk too slowly."

He hadn't answered her original question, but she let it go. It was too noisy for conversation, anyway. She let her mind drift back to her present situation, and she considered ways of handling it that would be the least awkward for all of them. She certainly didn't want to embarrass either Jeff or Helene; they had been as victimized by Virginia's petty vengeance as Claire.

Just as the dance ended, someone called his name. Claire took advantage of his distraction to say politely, "Thank you for the dance, Mr. Benedict," and walk away, while he was effectively trapped by the woman who had demanded his attention. Her mouth quirked in wry humor. It must be hell for him to have women constantly yapping at his heels; poor man, he probably suffered terribly…when he wasn't taking full advantage of it.

Out of the corner of her eye, Claire saw Virginia watching her closely, and conducting a sotto voce conversation with another woman, who was also eyeing her with intense curiosity. Gossips! She decided at that moment to defuse the situation by confronting it head-on. With her head high and a smile on her face, Claire walked up to Jeff and Helene.

Just before she reached them, she saw Jeff stiffen and an expression of alarm cross his face; he'd noticed the glitter of her eyes and probably wondered if she was going to cause a scandal with one of the passionate scenes that he remembered so well. With determined effort Claire kept the smile pasted to her lips. She had obviously made a mistake in avoiding anything except the most casual companionship with men in the five years since their divorce—her mother and sister thought she still pined for Jeff, and evidently Jeff shared that opinion, along with Virginia and the rest of their social circle. She didn't know what to do about that now, except try to be casual and polite, to show that it really meant nothing to her at all.

"Hello," she said brightly, addressing herself mostly to Helene. "I think Virginia invited the three of us to provide the entertainment for the evening, but I'm not willing to play her game. Shall we spoil her fun?"

Helene was quick; she put a smile in place. "I'd like to spoil her *face*; but by all means, let's be civilized."

As other people drifted close enough to hear what they were saying, Claire launched into a gay account of a recent shopping trip when everything had gone wrong. Helene countered with her own tale of hazardous encounters while shopping, and by that time Jeff had recovered enough to contribute by asking after Claire's parents and her sister's family. It was so civilized that she wanted to laugh aloud, but at the same time strain began to tighten her throat. How long would they have to keep this up? Pride was one thing, but standing here chatting with Helene, who was even more beautiful in her pregnancy, was almost more than she could bear.

Then a warm hand touched the small of her back, and she glanced up in surprise as Max Benedict appeared at her side. "I'm sorry I was detained," he apologized smoothly. "Are you ready to leave, Claire?"

He made it sound as if they had other plans, and Claire was desperate enough to seize the opportunity of escape. "Yes, of course. Max, I'd like you to meet Helene and Jeff Halsey."

He took over, all suave courtesy as he murmured his name, inclined his head over Helene's hand and shook Jeff's. Claire almost laughed at the dazed look in Helene's winsome blue eyes. She might be happily married and very pregnant, but that didn't make her immune to Max Benedict's charm! Then he glanced at his watch and murmured, "We really must go, dear."

"Go" was exactly what Claire wanted to do. With an effort she kept a smile on her face as she listened to Max say all the polite things; then his hand applied a steady pressure on her back as he walked with her to the bedroom, where she'd put her small evening bag. She dug it out from under a tangle of other bags, lacy shawls, a few unglamorous raincoats and several mink jackets. He stood in the doorway waiting for her. He didn't say anything, and Claire wasn't able to read anything in his expression. Why had he rescued her? It had certainly been a deliberate action on his part, but she couldn't think of any reason why he should have made the effort. After all, they were complete strangers; the brief conversation they'd had on the terrace hadn't been enough to qualify them as even casual acquaintances. She was more than a little wary of him, and all her defenses sprang into place.

But first there was an exit to make, and getting out of there took priority over everything else right then. What better way to do it than on the arm of the most breathtaking man whom she'd ever seen? Handsome, charming men had a few uses, after all; they weren't much on permanency, but they were great for making impressions.

A curiously cynical smile touched his perfectly carved lips, as if he'd read her mind. "Shall we?" he asked, holding out his hand.

She left the party on his arm, but as soon as the door was closed behind them she stepped away from his touch. The streetlights spread their silvery light over the lawn and the tangle of cars parked in the driveway and along the street, obscuring the faint stars that blinked overhead. The spring night was warm and humid as the young season celebrated its birth with an exuberant burst of heat, determined to banish the last of the winter chill. A bird chirped shyly in a tree, then fell silent as their footsteps on the sidewalk disturbed it.

"Did the bitch set that up deliberately?" he asked in such a calm, cool voice that for a moment Claire wasn't certain she'd heard the steel in his tone. She glanced up and found his face undisturbed by any hint of temper, and decided that she'd been mistaken.

"It was awkward, but not tragic," she finally said, unwilling to share with this stranger even a hint of what it had actually cost her. She'd never been able to let anyone see what went on inside her mind; the more something hurt, the more she retreated behind a meaningless smile and blank, immovable remoteness. It was a trait that, when she'd been a child, had infuriated and frustrated her mother, who had been determined that her youngest daughter would follow in the footsteps of her other daughter, who was bright and beautiful and talented and could melt stone with her sunny laughter. But the more she tried to force Claire out of her backwardness, the more Claire had retreated, until eventually Alma West-brook had given up.

Suddenly aware from the silence that had fallen between them that her thoughts had wandered again, Claire stopped on the sidewalk and held out her hand. "Thank you for your help, Mr. Benedict. It was nice meeting you." Her tone was polite but final, making it clear that she considered the evening at an end.

He took her hand but didn't shake it. Instead his fingers clasped hers lightly, warmly, a touch that didn't demand anything. "Will you have dinner with me tomorrow night, Claire?" he asked, then added, "Please," as if he sensed the refusal that she'd been about to make.

She hesitated, vaguely disarmed by that "please," as if he didn't know that he could have the company of almost any woman he wanted, whenever he wanted. Almost. "Thank you, but no."

His eyebrow lifted slightly, and she saw the glitter of his vivid eyes. "Are you still carrying a torch for your ex-husband?"

"That's none of your business, Mr. Benedict."

"You didn't say that a moment ago. I rather thought you were relieved by my interference in something that is now none of my business," he said coolly.

Her head lifted, and she took her hand from his. "Payback time, is it? Very well. No, I'm not still in love with Jeff."

"That's good. I don't like rivals."

Claire looked at him in disbelief, then laughed. She didn't want to dignify that last statement by challenging him; what did he think she was, the biggest fool alive? She had been, once, but not again. "Goodbye, Mr. Benedict," she said in a dismissive tone and walked to her car.

When she reached out to open the car door, she found a lean, tanned hand there before hers. He opened the door for her, and Claire murmured a quiet thank-you as she got in the car and took her keys from her bag.

He rested one arm on the roof of the car and leaned down, his turquoise eyes narrowed and as dark as the sea. "I'll call you tomorrow, Claire Westbrook," he said, as cool and confident as if she hadn't already dismissed him.

"Mr. Benedict, I've tried not to be rude, but I'm not interested."

"I'm registered," he replied, amusement twitching at his mouth, and despite herself Claire found herself staring at his lips, almost spellbound by their seductive perfection. "I've had all my shots, and I'm reasonably well mannered. I'm not wanted by any law-enforcement agency, I've never been married, and I'm kind to children. Do you require references?"

A warm laugh bubbled past her control. "Is your pedigree impressive?"

He squatted in the open door of the car, smiling at her. "Impeccable. Shall we discuss it over dinner tomorrow night?"

There was a small, curious softening inside of her. Without allowing herself to dwell on it, she'd realized for some time that she was lonely. What harm could there be in having dinner with him? She certainly wasn't going to fall in love with him—they would talk and laugh, enjoy a nice meal, and perhaps she would make a friend.

She hesitated a long moment then gave in. "All right. Yes, thank you."

He laughed outright now, his white teeth gleaming. "Such enthusiasm! My dear, I promise I'll be on my best behavior. Where shall I pick you up, and at what time? Eight?"

They agreed on the time, and Claire gave him directions to her apartment. A moment later she was driving away, and by the time she stopped at the first traffic signal, her brow was furrowed in consternation. Why had she agreed to go out with him? She'd sworn to avoid his type like the plague, yet he'd neatly worked around her defenses and made her laugh, and she found herself liking him. He didn't seem to take himself too seriously, which would have made her run at top speed in the opposite direction. He'd also shown kindness in coming to her rescue....

He was far too dangerous to her peace of mind.

By the time she let herself into her apartment, she had decided to cancel the date, but as she closed the door and locked it, the empty silence of the rooms rushed at her, overwhelming her. She had refused to get a cat, feeling that would be the crowning symbol of her aloneness, but now she wished that she had some sort of pet, anything, to welcome her home. A cat or a dog wouldn't care if she never quite measured up to expectations. A full belly, a warm bed and someone to scratch it behind the ears was all a pet would expect. Come to think of it, she thought tiredly, that was all humans needed. Food, shelter and affection.

Affection. She'd had the food and shelter, all the material trappings of an upper-middle-class childhood. She'd even had affection, but it had been the absentminded, exasperated crumbs of the doting love that her parents had given to Martine. Claire couldn't even blame them; Martine was perfect. Some sisters might have lorded it over a shy, gawky younger sister, but Martine had always been kind and patient with Claire and even now worried about her. No matter how busy Martine was with her thriving law practice, her popular, outgoing children and her equally busy husband, she always made time to call Claire at least twice a week.

Still, something inside Claire had always shriveled at her parents' obvious preference for Martine. She could remember staring at herself in a mirror as a child and wondering what was wrong with her. If she had been ugly or possessed a nasty disposition, at least then she would have been able to find some reason for not being quite good enough to please her parents. But even though she hadn't been as beautiful as Martine, she'd still been a pretty child, and she'd tried so hard to please everyone, until she'd realized that her best wasn't going to be good enough and began to withdraw. That was what was wrong with her: she simply wasn't up to par. Martine was beautiful; Claire was merely pretty. Martine was a sunny, outgoing child; Claire was prone to unexplained bouts of tears and shrank from people. Martine was talented, a marvelous pianist and an outstanding art student; Claire refused to study any sort of music and often hid herself away with a book. Martine was brilliant and ambitious; Claire was bright but didn't apply herself. Martine married a handsome, equally ambitious young lawyer, went into practice with him and had two gorgeous, happy children; Claire had married Jeff—the one time in her life she'd ever pleased her mother— but the marriage had fallen apart.

Now, from a distance of five years, Claire had a very clear view of her marriage and the reasons it had failed. Most of it had honestly been her fault. She had been so terrified of failing to live up to what she thought everyone expected of her as Mrs. Jefferson Halsey that she had dashed around trying to be the perfect social hostess, the perfect homemaker, the perfect sport and had spread herself so thin that there had been almost nothing left over for Jeff. At first he'd tolerated it; then the gulf between them had widened and his eye had begun wandering...and settled on Helene, who was beautiful, older than Claire and marvelously self-assured. Only Claire's unexpected pregnancy had prevented a divorce right then. To his credit, Jeff had been tender and kind to Claire, even though her pregnancy had been the end of his relationship with Helene. He loved Helene, but Claire was his wife and carried his child, and he refused to devastate her by asking for a divorce.

Then she had miscarried. He waited until she had recovered physically then told her that he wanted out. Their divorce had probably disappointed half of Houston in its lack of acrimony. Claire had known that it was over before she'd ever lost the baby. They divorced quietly, Jeff married Helene as soon as it was legally possible, and within a year Helene had presented him with a son. Now she was pregnant again.

Claire washed her face and brushed her teeth, then got into bed and picked up her book from the night table, trying not to think of the baby she'd lost. That was the past, as was her marriage, and really, the divorce had been the best thing that had ever happened to her. It had forced her to wake up and take a good look at herself. She had been wasting her life trying to please everyone else, rather than herself. She was going to *be* herself, and for the past five years, she had been. On the whole, she was content with the life she'd made for herself. She had a good job; she read when she liked and as much as she liked. She listened to the music she preferred. She was really closer now to Martine than she'd ever been before, because Claire no longer felt threatened by her older sister. She was even on better terms with her parents…if only her mother would stop pushing her to "find a nice young man and settle down."

Claire didn't go out a lot—she couldn't see any point in it. She wasn't inclined to settle for a lukewarm marriage based on common interests, and she wasn't the type to inspire red-hot passion. She had learned control and how to protect herself with that control. If that made her cool and unresponsive, that was fine. Better that than to leave herself open to the devastating pain rejection brought.

That was the life she'd chosen and deliberately built for herself; why, then, had she accepted a dinner date with Max Benedict? Despite his sense of humor, he was still a playboy, and he had no place at all in her life. She should politely but firmly break their date. Claire closed her book, unable to read it, after all; Maxwell Benedict's handsome face kept swimming before the print. Her brown eyes were troubled as she turned out the lamp and pulled the sheet up to cover her. Despite all the warnings of her instincts, she knew that she wasn't going to break the date.

Max sat in his hotel room, his feet propped on the coffee table and a pot of coffee at his elbow. His brow was furrowed with an intense frown as he read one of the thick reports he'd received in the mail. One lean forefinger stroked his left eyebrow as he read; his reading speed was phenomenal, and he had almost finished. Absently he reached for the coffeepot, and the frown turned impatient as he realized that the pot was nearly empty. He replaced the pot on the tray and pushed it aside. Coffee! He'd become addicted to the stuff, another American habit that he'd acquired.

Swiftly he finished the report then tossed it aside. His eyes narrowed to slits. Anson had picked up hints that another company was after Bronson Alloys. That was a disturbing development in itself, but even more alarming were the rumors that this company had ties to China. If the rumors were true, then word had somehow gotten out that Bronson had developed an alloy that was lightweight and almost indestructible, superior to the alloy used for spy planes. So far, the alloy itself was only a rumor—nothing had been announced, and if anything had been developed, Sam Bronson was keeping it to himself. Still, the rumors were persistent.

He didn't like it. Any move by another company would force him to make his own move, perhaps before he was ready, which would increase the chance for failure. Max didn't intend to fail. He despised failure; his personality was too intense and fiercely controlled to accept anything less than total victory in whatever he attempted.

He picked up the report again and thumbed through it, but he allowed his thoughts to drift. The woman, Claire Westbrook…she wasn't quite what he'd expected. Anson had thought that she might be the weak link, and Max had coolly expected that he could charm her as effortlessly as he did every woman. It hadn't worked out that way. She was cool and calm, almost too controlled, and unresponsive. Even though she had eventually accepted his dinner invitation, Max had the impression that she'd done so for her own reasons.

His eyes narrowed. From the time he'd reached puberty, the female sex had practically been at his feet. He appreciated women, enjoyed them, desired them, but women had come easily for him. This was the first time a woman had looked at him with a cool, blank expression then turned away in total disinterest, and he didn't like it. He was both irritated and challenged, and he shouldn't feel either of those responses. This was business. He would use his charm to get the needed information without a qualm—corporate war was just that: war, despite the outward civility of three-piece suits and board meetings. But seduction had never been a part of his plan, so his unwilling attraction to her was doubly unwelcome. He couldn't afford the distraction. He had to concentrate on the job at hand, get the information in a hurry and make his move.

He knew his nature was intensely sensual, but always

before, his physical needs and responses had been controlled by the power of his icy intellect. He was master of his body, not the other way around. That was part of his character; nature had given him both a towering intelligence and a sexual appetite that would have taken control of a man of lesser intellect, but he was brilliant, and his mental capacities were so intense and focused that he controlled his physical needs and never unleashed the driving power of that portion of his nature. His unwilling attraction to Claire Westbrook both angered and disconcerted him. It was totally out of place in this situation.

She was pretty, but he'd had women who were far more beautiful. She hadn't responded to him or flirted or in any way indicated that she was attracted to him. The only unusual thing about her were her eyes, huge and velvety brown. There was no reason for him to be thinking about her, but he couldn't get her out of his mind.

Chapter 2

The shrilling of the telephone startled Claire out of sleep the next morning, and her soft mouth curved in a wry smile as she rolled over to lift the receiver and stop the intrusive noise. "Hello, Martine," she said, her voice husky with sleep.

There was a short pause, then Martine laughed. "I wish you wouldn't do that! How did you know?"

"I thought you might call this morning to check up on me. Yes, I went to Virginia's party, and no, I wasn't the belle of the ball."

"You're answering my questions before I ask them," Martine said in fond exasperation. "Did you enjoy yourself anyway?"

"I'm not the social type," Claire hedged, sitting up in bed and stuffing a pillow behind her back. She didn't mention meeting Max Benedict or that she was having dinner with him. Martine would ask a thousand questions and become all excited over something that was basically unimportant. Claire didn't expect the dinner date to be the beginning of a fabulous romance. Max could have any woman he chose, so he wasn't likely to settle for anything but the best. This was just a dinner date, nothing more or less, an evening out with a man who was new in town and didn't know many people. It was probably a respite for him to meet a woman who didn't chase him.

Martine sighed. Experience had taught her that if Claire didn't want to talk about something then no amount of prying or badgering could change her mind. For someone so retiring and unassuming, Claire was stubborn. Because Martine loved her sister and recognized how vulnerable and sensitive Claire was, she refrained from badgering her and instead gracefully changed the subject, laughing as she recounted a horrendous piece of mischief that her eight-year-old son had gotten into that morning.

They chatted for a few moments then said goodbye. Claire hung up the receiver and lay back on the pillows, her dark eyes reflective as she stared at the ceiling. Her thoughts kept going back to Max Benedict, and his features formed in her mind; she saw his eyes, vivid turquoise, but the shade of turquoise kept changing. Sometimes they were more green than blue, sometimes more blue than green, and twice she had seen a flash of something in his eyes that had startled her, but she hadn't recognized it. It was as though she'd seen a shadow in the sea that was gone in an instant and left behind only the swirling, breathtaking turquoise waters, yet reminding the observer of the dangers of the sea. Perhaps he had dangers hidden in his depths, hidden behind the beauty that nature had given him. All human beings had hidden depths, of course, but some people were deeper than others, and some very shallow, but all had their private defenses. Did he use his appearance as a barrier, deflecting interest with his looks the way a mirror turns back the sun?

He was surprisingly controlled; perhaps some people

wouldn't see that, but Claire was more sensitive than most. She recognized control because she had had to learn it. As a child, she had seethed with pent-up emotion, a wild flood of love and devotion just waiting to be given to someone who would love her for herself. She had thought Jeff was that person, and she had released the torrent of passion, driving herself to be the perfect wife for him, only to fail again. Now she no longer waited for that one person. She had been hurt, and she refused to let anyone hurt her ever again. She had locked her emotions and passions away and was more content without them.

But how would those turquoise eyes look if that cool control were banished and passion heated their depths? How would he look while making love?

Claire sat up, pushing away the disturbing mental image. It was Saturday. She had chores to do. She pulled off her nightgown and let the wisp of silk fall across the bed, and for a moment her eyes enjoyed the contrast of the pink silk lying on the white eyelet lace of the comforter. She loved pretty things. That part of her personality was carefully hidden away and protected, but it was expressed in her preference for exquisite lingerie, in the harmonious colors that she gathered around her. Her bed was white, the carpet a soft color, and around the room were touches of rose and jade. The bath towels that she bought were thick and lush, and she enjoyed the feel of them on her skin. So many things delighted her: fresh rain on her face, or the warm sunshine; a ray of light through a jar of plum jelly; the translucent beauty of a green leaf in spring; the plush texture of carpet beneath her bare feet. Because she hung back, she saw more than the people who hurried through life.

She had slept late, so she had to hurry through the housekeeping and laundry that she did every Saturday in order to allow herself enough time to do her hair and nails. She was restless and on edge, all because of a man with vivid sea-colored eyes and sunshine in his hair, and that response was unusual enough to bring all her instinctive defenses springing into place. She would have to be on guard every moment, against herself more than Max. The weakness was hers, the same weakness that had let her believe that Jeff loved her as much as she loved him, because that was what she had wanted to believe. Jeff hadn't misled her; she'd misled herself. *Never again.*

Even so, pride wouldn't allow her to look anything but her best when she went out with Max, and she took a long time over her makeup. Her features were delicate, with high cheekbones and a wide, soft mouth—blusher brought color to those cheekbones, and lipstick made her mouth look even softer. Smudged eyeliner and smoky shadow turned her dark eyes into pools of mystery. After putting up her honey-blond hair, leaving a few tendrils curling loosely at her temples, she slipped pearl-drop earrings in her ears and stared at her reflection in the mirror. The old-fashioned hairstyle suited her, revealing the clean lines of her cheek and jaw, the slenderness of her throat, but she looked disturbingly solemn, as if secrets were hiding behind her eyes.

She was ready when the doorbell rang at exactly eight o'clock and had been ready long enough to become nervous; the peal of the doorbell made her jump. Quickly, before her nerve failed her, she opened the door. "Hello. Come in, please. Would you like a drink before we go?" Her voice was calm and polite, the voice of a hostess doing her duty without any real enthusiasm. Instinctively Claire moved a little away from him. She'd forgotten how tall he was, and she felt dwarfed.

His pleasant expression didn't waver as he held his hand out to her, palm up. "Thank you, but we haven't time. On such short notice, I had to take reservations that were somewhat earlier than I'd planned. Shall we go?" His outstretched hand was steady and unthreatening, but the gesture was a command. Claire had the distinct impression that he had noticed her withdrawal and was demanding her return. He wanted her to step within reach of his hand, his touch, perhaps even place her hand in his in a gesture of both trust and obedience.

She couldn't do it. The small confrontation took only a moment, and she ended it when she stepped away to get her bag and the waist-length silk jacket that went with her oyster-colored silk chemise. It wasn't until she turned around and found herself staring at his chest that she realized he hadn't let the moment end. She froze.

He plucked the jacket from her hands and held it up for her to slip her arms into the sleeves. "Allow me," he said in his cool, precise voice, so devoid of any real emotion that Claire wondered if her reaction had been an overreaction, that his out-held hand had been a mannerly gesture rather than a subtle command. Perhaps if she had gone out more, she wouldn't be so wary and skittish now; Martine had probably been right in urging her to become more socially active.

She let him help her with the jacket, and he smoothed the small collar, his touch brief and light. "You look lovely, Claire, like a Victorian cameo."

"Thank you," she murmured, disarmed by the gentle, graceful compliment. Suddenly she realized that he had sensed her agitation and was trying to put her at her ease, using his almost courtly manners to reassure her, and the odd thing was that it worked. He was controlled, unemotional, and she liked that. People who acted on the urges of their emotions and glands were unreliable.

His hand was on the small of her back, resting there with a slight warm pressure, but now it didn't disturb her. She relaxed and found that she was looking forward to the evening, after all.

His choice of car further reassured her. She would have been suspicious of a flamboyant sports car, but the sedate, solidly conservative black Mercedes-Benz wasn't the car of someone who was attracted to flash and glitter. He was dressed as conservatively as a banker, too, she noticed, glancing at his gray pin-striped suit. It was wonderfully cut, and his lean, elegant frame gave the suit a look of dash and fashion that it wouldn't have possessed on any other man, but it still wasn't the peacock attire of a playboy.

Everything he did put her more at ease. He carried on a light, casual conversation that put no pressure on her; he didn't use innuendos or sly double meanings or ask any personal questions. The restaurant he'd chosen was quiet, giving the impression of privacy but not intimacy. Nothing he did was in any way meant to impress her; he was simply dining out with a woman, with no strings attached, and that was immensely reassuring.

"What sort of work do you do?" he asked casually, dipping an enormous Gulf shrimp into cocktail sauce before biting into it with frank enjoyment. Claire watched his white even teeth sink into the pink shrimp, her pulse speeding up in spite of herself. He was just so impossibly handsome that it was difficult to refrain from simply staring at him.

"I'm a personal assistant."

"In a large company?"

"No. Bronson Alloys is small, but growing rapidly, and we have outstanding prospects. It's a publicly held company, but I work for the major stockholder and founder, Sam Bronson."

"Do you enjoy your work? Being an assistant seems to have lost all its attraction for a lot of people. The push is to be an executive, with an assistant of your own."

"Someone has to be the assistant," Claire said, smiling. "I don't have either the talents or the ambition to be an executive. What company are you with? Will you be in Houston permanently?"

"Not permanently, but I could be here for several months. I'm investigating certain properties for investment."

"Real estate?" Claire asked. "Are you a speculator?"

"Nothing so dashing. Basically what I do is make feasibility studies."

"How did you come to be transplanted from England to Texas?"

He gave a negligent shrug. "Business opportunities are more plentiful over here." Max studied her smooth, delicate face, wondering how she would look if any real warmth ever lit her dark eyes. She was more relaxed now than she had been, but there was still that lack of response from her that both irritated and intrigued him. So long as he kept the subject impersonal and made no move that could be interpreted as that of an interested male, she was relaxed, but she withdrew like a turtle into its shell at the least hint of masculine aggressiveness or sexuality. It was as if she didn't want anyone to be attracted to her or even flirt with her. The less masculine he was, the better she liked it, and the realization angered him. What he wouldn't give to force her out of that frozen nunnery she'd locked herself into, to make her acknowledge him as a man, to make her feel some sort of passion!

Claire looked away, a little rattled by the cold, unreadable expression in his eyes. For a moment his face had lost its expression of suave pleasantness and taken on the hard, determined lines of a Viking warrior. Perhaps that was the ancestry that had given him his golden hair and sea-colored eyes, rather than an Anglo-Saxon heritage.

What had she said to bring that expression to his face? It had been only a polite question; she'd been so careful not to step over the bounds she'd set for herself, saying nothing that could be construed as reflecting a personal interest in him.

"Last night," he said abruptly. "That was deliberate viciousness, wasn't it? Why?"

Claire's head jerked around, the only sign she gave that she was disturbed by the change of subject. Her dark eyes went blank. "Yes, it was deliberate, but nothing came of her efforts. It isn't important."

"I don't agree." His crisp accent bit off the words. "You were upset, though you carried it off well. Why was that little scene staged?"

She stared at him, that blank look still in her eyes, as if a wall had been erected in her mind. After a moment he realized that she wasn't going to answer him, and a powerful surge of anger shook him, made him want to grind his teeth in frustration. Why was she so damned aloof? At this rate he'd never get close enough to her to get any of the answers he needed! He wanted this damned thing over with—with business out of the way, he could concentrate on Claire and his irritating attraction to her. He had no doubt that if he were able to devote himself fully to her, he would be able to get behind those barriers to the woman. He had never yet failed to get a woman he wanted; there was no reason why Claire should be his first failure. She might be the most challenging woman of his experience, though, and the thought quickened his interest.

How could he gain her trust if she retreated every time he advanced? A small frown furrowed his brow as he studied her openly, trying to read her mind. If she retreated, then she must feel threatened by him, yet he hadn't done anything to warrant that reaction. Most women were attracted to him on sight, gravitating to him like a compass needle to the magnetic north pole, but Claire made an obvious effort to keep a certain distance from him. In a flash of insight Max realized that it was his looks that made her so wary, and his frown deepened. She had seen the playboy persona and felt threatened by it;

she was probably determined not to become another one of his women. Bloody hell! She would run like a frightened rabbit if she realized that her reaction was attracting him far more surely than a blatant play for him. Max was accustomed to being pursued by women; a woman who retreated from him brought out the primitive male urge to chase fleeing prey.

She was soft, tender prey, he thought as he watched a delicate tinge of color sweep over her cheeks. She was disconcerted by the way he was staring at her, but he liked looking at her. She had a gentle, intelligent face, and he kept getting caught by those enormous dark eyes, as velvety as melted chocolate. Her coloring was exquisite, like delicate china. Did she have any idea how enormously appealing her dark eyes were? Probably not. Her ex-husband's wife was a real beauty, but if he'd been given the choice between the two women, Max would unhesitatingly have chosen Claire. He'd been stunned by the courage and dignity with which she'd handled the situation at the party the night before. How many other women would have kept their poise under those circumstances? Watching her coolly, deliberately, he knew that he wanted her.

He'd have her, too, but first he had to get past those damnable barriers.

"Talk to me," he said softly. "Don't treat me as everyone else does."

Startled, Claire looked at him, her eyes widening. What did he mean? How did everyone else treat him? "I don't understand," she finally murmured.

His eyes were green ice, with no hint of blue in them. "It's poetic justice, my dear. My face makes me a target, a sexual trophy to be nailed on the wall above the bed, figuratively speaking, of course. Most women have no interest in me other than as a stud. I could be brainless for all the concern they have in me personally. I enjoy the sex, yes—I'm a healthy man. But I also enjoy conversation, music and books, and I would damn well prefer being considered as a person as well as a warm body."

Claire was stunned, so stunned that she forgot the alarm that had been racing up and down her spine as he had stared at her with such cold ferocity. "But I'm not—that is, I haven't been chasing you," she stammered.

"No, with you it's the opposite. You took one look at me and decided that with this face I can't possibly be anything more than a playboy, letting myself be used as a living ornament in any woman's bed."

She was aghast; that was exactly what she'd thought at first, and now she was ashamed of herself. Claire was unusually sensitive, and because she was so easily hurt she went out of her way to keep from hurting anyone else. The idea that she had so casually labeled this man as pretty but useless appalled her. She had other reasons for wanting to keep her distance from him, but he didn't know them—to him, it must seem as if she had simply written him off as being shallow and immoral, without getting to know him at all. He was angry, and he had every right to be.

"I'm sorry," she apologized in a soft, earnest voice. "It's true that I did think you were a playboy, but it's also true that I realize I'm not in your league."

He leaned forward, his eyes narrowed. "What do you mean by that? Just what is 'my league'?"

Claire dropped her eyes, unable to meet that piercingly bright stare, and found that his hands were in her line of vision. They were lean, aristocratic hands, beautifully fashioned, but strong for all that. Was the man like his hands?

"Claire," he prompted.

At last she looked up, her face composed, as usual, but her

eyes revealed some of her vulnerability. "You're far more so-phisticated than I, of course, and far more beautiful. I'm sure women chase you unmercifully, but the other side of the coin is the fact that you can probably have any woman you want. I really don't want to be your next target."

He didn't like her answer at all; his facial muscles didn't move, but still his displeasure was a definite chill brushing across her skin.

"Then why did you come out with me? I realize I was being a trifle persistent, but you allowed yourself to be persuaded."

"I was lonely," she said, then looked away again.

At that moment the waiter appeared with their dinner, and the interruption gave Max time to control the explosion of fury in his mind. Damn her to hell! So she accepted his invitation only because she was lonely? Evidently he rated above tele-vision, but only just! He wondered savagely if his ego could take much more.

When they were alone again, he reached across the table and caught her hand, holding her delicate fingers firmly when she automatically tried to draw away. "You aren't a target," he said tersely. "You're someone I met and liked, someone who looked at me without any hint of speculation about how well endowed I am or how bloody versatile I am in bed. Do you think I don't get lonely, too? I wanted to be able to talk to you. I want a *friend*. Sex is something that can be had whenever I take the urge."

There was color in her face again, as if she were faintly em-barrassed, but suddenly there was a twinkle in her eyes. He'd seen it briefly the night before, and its reappearance caught his attention, made him realize how really lovely she was with that light dancing in her dark eyes. "Do they *really*?" she asked in a scandalized whisper.

He felt a bit disoriented, as if he'd just had a blow to the head. A moment before he'd been angry, but now he found himself completely bemused by the teasing humor of her expression. He shifted his grip on her hand and rubbed his thumb across the back of her fingers, absently savoring the feel of her soft flesh. "Ladies have become incredibly bold. It's disconcerting to meet a woman and five minutes later find her hand inside my trousers."

She laughed, and he felt himself become warm. At last he was gaining some ground with her! That was the way—she was lonely and badly needed a friend, while all her defenses were set up to deflect any romantic or seductive move. She wanted a friend, not a lover. Max didn't agree with her choice, but he would have to go along with it for now or risk frightening her away.

"Could we be friends?" he asked gently, determined to act with restraint. Claire simply wasn't like the women he had pursued with single-minded intensity; she was softer, more sensitive, with secret dreams in her eyes.

Claire's lips still held a little smile. Friends? Was it possible to be friends with a man who was as sleek and beautiful as a cheetah? And why would he want to be friends with her? She was nothing out of the ordinary, while he was completely unordinary. Yet perhaps he really was lonely. Claire understood loneliness. She had chosen it as the safest course in life, but there were still times when she longed for someone to whom she could talk without guarding all but her shallowest layers. It wasn't that she wanted to unburden her heart; it was the simple, everyday conversation of friends that she needed so badly. She had never had that even with Martine, dearly though she loved her. Martine was so courageous and outgoing that she couldn't understand the hurts and fears of someone who lacked that courage. Nor had Claire ever been able to confide in her mother, because she had always feared and flinched from the inevitable comparison with Martine. Even when there was no comparison, fear of it had kept Claire silent.

"You could help me look for an apartment tomorrow," he suggested, drawing her back from her thoughts. "A week in a hotel is straining my tolerance."

His tone was testy, and Claire smiled at his accent, more clipped than usual. "I'd be happy to look with you. Do you have anything in mind?"

"My dear, I don't know anything about Houston. I'm totally in your hands."

"Buy a newspaper tomorrow and circle the apartments that you like best, and we'll drive around to see them. What time would you like to start?"

"As early as it's convenient for you—after all, I'm at your mercy."

She doubted that he was ever at anyone's mercy, but a light, happy feeling was swelling in her. His eyes were a warm, brilliant turquoise now, and his smile would have turned the head of a statue. She wasn't proof against his charm, and suddenly it didn't worry her.

Their food had been cooling in front of them, and they both realized it simultaneously. As they ate, Claire began to watch him with growing amazement. How could someone so lean eat so much? His manners were faultless, but nevertheless the amount he ate would have done a stevedore proud. His metabolic rate had to be high, because his movements were characterized by an indolent grace; he didn't burn off calories with nervous energy.

She said as much, and he smiled at her. "I know. My mother used to scold me for eating too much in company. She said it made it appear as if they kept me in a dungeon on starvation rations."

"Do you have a large family?"

"There seem to be hundreds of us," he said blithely. "Aunts and uncles and cousins by the score. In the immediate family, I have one brother and three sisters, and eight assorted nieces and nephews. My father is dead, but my mother still rules us all."

"Are you the eldest?" Claire asked, fascinated by his large family.

"No, my brother is the eldest. I'm second in line. Is your family a large one?"

"No, not really. Just my parents, and my sister Martine and her family. There are cousins in Michigan and an aunt who lives in Vancouver, but the relationship isn't close."

"A large family has its advantages, but there are also times when it closely resembles a zoo. Holidays are chaos."

"Do you go home for all the holidays?"

He shrugged. "Sometimes it isn't possible, but I pop over on the odd weekend."

He made it sound as if it were only a matter of getting in a car and taking a half-hour drive, instead of "popping over" on a transatlantic flight. She was still marveling at that when he turned the conversation to her job. He asked interested questions about the sort of work done at Bronson Alloys, the market for special alloys and the uses for them. It was a fairly complicated subject, and Claire had studied intensely when she'd first gotten the job as Sam Bronson's assistant, trying to understand the processes and the practical applications of Sam's metallurgical genius. She knew her ground well but had to make a special effort to keep abreast. The ease and rapidity of Max's understanding was amazing; she could talk to him as naturally as if he also worked in the field, without having to pause continually for complicated explanations.

Then they began talking about real estate, and the way Max explained it, it sounded fascinating. "You don't actually buy the real estate yourself?"

"No. I act as a consultant, investigating properties for people who are interested buyers. Not all property is suitable for investment or expansion. There are the geological considerations, first of all—some land simply isn't stable enough to support large structures. There are other variables, of course: the depth of the water table, any bedrock, things that effect the price effectiveness of locating a building on that particular plot of ground."

"You're a geologist, too?"

"I'm a gatherer of facts. It's like putting a puzzle together, with the difference that you have no idea what the finished product will look like until it *is* finished."

They lingered over coffee, still talking, and gradually Claire realized how hungry she'd been for simple conversation, for the sharing of ideas and opinions. He was extraordinarily intelligent, but he didn't parade his mental capabilities about for anyone to admire; his intelligence was simply there, a part of him. For her part, Claire had always been unusually studious, losing herself in the varied worlds offered by books, and she was both astonished and delighted to discover that one of his favorite writers was Cameron Gregor, a wild Scotsman whose books were horribly difficult to find and who was her own favorite.

They argued fiercely for almost an hour over which book was Gregor's best. Claire forgot her reserve, leaning toward him with her eyes shining, her face lit with pleasure. After a while Max realized that he was arguing for the sheer pleasure of watching her, not because of any real difference of opinion. When passion brightened her face, she was almost incandescent. Jealousy began to eat at him, because all of that fire was for *books*, and none for him.

Finally he held up both hands, laughing. "Shall we stop trying to change the other's mind and dance instead? We've totally ignored the music."

Until that moment Claire hadn't even realized that a band was playing, or that the dance floor was crowded with people swaying to the slow, bluesy tunes. A saxophone was crying pure mournful notes that almost brought tears to her eyes; it was her favorite type of music. He led her to the dance floor and took her in his arms.

They danced well together. He was tall, but her heels brought her up to a comfortable height, allowing her to nestle her head just under his chin. He knew just how to hold a woman, not so tightly that she couldn't maneuver and not so loosely that she was unable to follow his lead. Claire gave a quiet sigh of pleasure. She couldn't remember enjoying any evening more. The firm, gentle clasp of his fingers around hers told her that she was in capable hands, and still there was the sense of control about him that reassured her. Unconsciously she breathed in the faint scent of his cologne, so quiet that it was just barely there, and beneath that was the warm, musky scent of his skin.

Somehow it felt right to be in his arms, so right that she failed to notice her reaction, the way the rhythm of her heartbeat had increased just a little. She felt pleasantly warm, even though the restaurant was cool and her shoulders bare. They laughed and talked and danced together, and she hated for the evening to have to end.

When it did end, he walked her to the door of her apartment and unlocked it for her, then returned the key to her. "Good night," he said in an oddly gentle tone.

She lifted her head and smiled at him. "Good night. I enjoyed the evening very much. Thank you."

That breathtaking, whimsical smile tugged at the corners of his lips. "I should be thanking you, my dear. I'm looking forward to tomorrow. Good night again, and sleep well." He bent and pressed a light kiss on her cheek, his mouth warm and firm; then the brief pressure was lifted. It was a kiss as passionless as that of a brother, asking nothing of her, not even response. Smiling at her, he turned and left.

Claire closed and locked the door, a smile still on her lips. She liked him, she really liked him! He was intelligent, humorous, widely traveled, and remarkably comfortable to be with. He had been a perfect gentleman toward her—after all, he'd as much as told her that he could have sex any time he wanted it, so perhaps she was a welcome change for him. She was a woman who *wasn't* after him. There was no pressure to perform, no sense of being pursued because of his startling physical beauty.

While they'd been dancing, Claire couldn't help noticing that other women had followed him with their eyes, sometimes unconsciously. It was true that some women stared at him openly, with curiosity and even hunger evident in their expressions, but even those who would never think of leaving their own escorts hadn't been able to keep from looking at him periodically. His golden good looks drew the eye like a natural magnet.

Even her own. Lying in her bed, pleasantly tired and relaxed on her silk sheets, she kept seeing his face in her mind's eye. Her memory was a loop of film spliced to run endlessly, and she replayed every changing expression she'd seen, from anger to humor and every nuance in between. His eyes were green when he was angry, blue when he was thoughtful, and that vivid, wicked turquoise when he was laughing or teasing.

Her cheek tingled warmly where he'd kissed it, and sleepily she pressed her fingers to the spot. Sharp curiosity and a sense of regret pierced her—what would it have been like if he'd kissed her mouth, if there had been passion in his touch instead of the cool pleasantness with which he'd ended the evening? Her heart leaped at the thought, and her lips parted unconsciously. She wanted to know the taste of him.

Restlessly she turned on her side, forcing the thought away. Passion was one of the things she'd forced out of her life. Passion was dangerous; it made sane people suddenly turn into unreasonable maniacs. Passion meant a loss of control, and a loss of control ultimately led to terrible vulnerability. She was sometimes lonely, she admitted to herself, but loneliness was better than leaving herself open to the sort of devastating pain she'd barely survived once before. And she *was* afraid. That was another, more difficult thing that she admitted, lying there in the darkness. She lacked the self-confidence with which Martine faced every morning. She was afraid to let anyone get too close to her, because she might not be all they had expected, and she didn't know if she could bear the pain of rejection.

It was far better to be friends rather than lovers. Friends didn't risk as much. Friendship lacked the intimacy that necessarily gave lovers the sure, deadly knowledge of where and how to inflict the most hurt when the relationship went bad.

And friendship was what Max wanted, anyway. If she threw herself at him, he would probably turn away in disgust. He didn't want passion, and she was afraid of passion. Daydreams—or nighttime fantasies—about him were a waste of time.

Chapter 3

Until she answered the telephone the next morning and heard his voice, Claire hadn't realized just how much she had been looking forward to seeing him again. Her heart gave a little leap of joy, and her eyes closed for the briefest moment as she listened to his cool, deep voice, and his clipped, exceedingly British upper-class accent that delighted her ear. "Good morning, Claire. I've realized that we didn't set a time for me to pick you up today. What would be good for you?"

"Noon, I think. Have you seen any likely prospects in the paper?"

"I've circled three or four. Noon it is, then."

It disturbed her that just the sound of his voice could affect her. She didn't want to miss him when he wasn't there, didn't want to look forward to seeing him again. Just friends. That was all they were going to be, all they could be.

But when she dressed, she once again found herself paying far more attention to her hair and makeup than usual. She

wanted to look good for him, and the realization caused a
small pain deep inside her chest. There had been times before
when she'd hovered anxiously before her mirror, wondering
if she would come up to par, if the Halseys would approve of
her, if Jeff would look at her with desire in his eyes again.

The situations weren't the same at all—at that time she'd
been desperately trying to hold together a disintegrating
marriage, and now she was simply going to spend the day with
a friend, helping him look for an apartment. If Max made her
heart beat faster, that was something she would have to ignore
and never, never let him see.

Telling herself that was one thing, but schooling her
features to reveal only a pleasant welcome when she opened
the door to him was another thing entirely. She'd seen him in
a formal white dinner jacket and in a severely conservative
gray suit and had thought at the time that nothing could make
him look any better, but in casual clothes he was almost breathtaking. His khaki pants, crisp and neat, outlined his lean hips
and belly. The emerald green polo shirt he wore had a double
impact: it revealed the surprising muscularity of his arms and
torso, and intensified, darkened, the shades of green in his eyes
until they were the color of some paradise lagoon. Those eyes
smiled down at her, and deep inside her something stirred.

"I'm ready," she said, picking up her lemon-yellow garden
hat. It matched her yellow-and-white striped sundress, which
Martine had persuaded her to buy more than two years ago,
insisting that the sunny color suited her. Claire had to admit
that Martine's taste, as usual, was impeccable. She didn't
wear the dress often, preferring more businesslike attire, but
the morning was so bright and warm that nothing else had
seemed suitable.

He put his hand on her bare arm, his lean fingers gently
curving around her elbow. It was only a polite gesture, but

Claire felt her skin tingle under his touch. An instinct of self-protection told her to move away from him, but it was only a small voice, easily swamped by the disturbing rush of warmth generated by the light touch of his hand. Just walking beside him gave her pleasure.

He opened the car door for her, and when she was seated, he leaned down to tuck her skirt out of the way, another of his casually courteous gestures that disturbed the even rhythm of her pulse. Thank God he didn't have any romantic interest in her! If she responded to him this strongly when he was merely being polite, what would it be like if he were making an effort to charm her? With an almost helpless fear, she realized that she wouldn't stand a chance against him.

Lying on the seat between them was a newspaper, folded open to the ads for apartments for rent, and several of them had been circled. Max pointed to the first one. "This seems suitable. Are you familiar with the area?"

Claire picked up the newspaper and glanced at his choices. "Are you certain you want to look at these?" she asked doubtfully. "They're terribly expensive."

He gave her an amused glance, and Claire looked up in time to see it. She flushed suddenly. If she'd thought about it, she would have realized that he had no need to worry about money. He wasn't flashy, but the signs were there for anyone to read. He dressed well—his clothing was tailored instead of bought off the rack. All the trappings of wealth were there, from his Italian shoes to his impossibly thin Swiss wristwatch, as well as being evident in his speech and manner. Perhaps he wasn't rich, but he was certainly comfortable—companies must pay dearly for his services. She'd made a fool of herself by fretting about what he could afford to pay for an apartment.

"If I must travel so much, the people who pay me must be prepared to keep me in comfort," he said with a chuckle in his voice. "I need privacy, but enough space to entertain when it's necessary, and the apartment must be furnished, as I refuse to cart my furniture about the country."

She gave him stilted directions to the first apartment he'd circled, her cheeks still warm. He began to tell her amusing tales of the pitfalls he'd encountered when he first came to the United States, laughing at himself, and gradually Claire began to relax. She had a horror of making social gaffes, a fear that had been born in the early days of her marriage when it had seemed as if everyone was pressuring her to "live up" to her newly acquired position as Jeff Halsey's wife. As one of *the* Halseys, even by marriage, she'd been expected to be socially perfect. Even the smallest mistakes had been so terribly public that every social function had become an exercise in endurance for Claire.

But Max didn't let her retreat into her shell. He talked to her easily, without letting awkward silences fall between them. He sprinkled small questions through his conversation, compelling her to answer them and in that way contribute, until the last traces of embarrassment had faded and she was smiling naturally again. He watched her carefully, gauging her reactions. He'd be damned if he would let her draw back behind those cool, blank barriers of hers. He had to teach her to trust him, to relax in his company, or he would never be able to get any information from her. This damned takeover irritated him. He wanted it out of the way so he could concentrate on Claire and discover more about the woman behind the defenses. He was becoming obsessed with her, and that knowledge irritated him, too, but he couldn't simply shrug it away. Her cool, distant manner attracted him even while it drove him mad with frustration. She had a habit of drifting away in her thoughts, those deep brown eyes revealing secrets that he couldn't read and she wouldn't share with him. His reaction to her confused him. He wanted to make love to her until all the shadows in her eyes were gone, until she burned for him, until she lay warm and helpless beneath him, her skin dewy from the heat and violence of his possession…and he wanted to protect her, from everything and everyone except himself.

She didn't want him in either capacity, as lover or protector. She wanted him only for companionship, which was almost as exciting as warm milk.

The first address he'd marked was a group of condominiums, turning their bland identical faces to the street. They were new and expensive, but they were nothing more than brick growths on the Texas soil. Claire glanced at Max, unable to imagine him living there. He surveyed the condos; then his aristocratic brows climbed upward. "I think not," he said mildly and put the car in reverse.

Absurdly pleased that she had been right in her estimation of him, Claire picked up the paper and studied the addresses of the other apartments he'd marked, trying to place them. Houston had grown so rapidly that she wasn't certain where two of the apartments were, but one address she did recognize. "I think you'll like the next one better. It's an older building, but the apartments are very exclusive."

Once again, she was right. Max looked pleased when he saw the mellowed building with the wrought-iron gate at the entrance and the brick-paved courtyard. There was private underground parking for the tenants. Max stopped the car before the office and came around to open the door for Claire. His fingers were warm on her elbow as he helped her from the car; then his hand moved to the small of her back. Claire didn't even try to move away; she was becoming used to his touch, to his more formal European manners.

Even in his casual clothing, Max had an air of authority that commanded the attention of the apartment manager. The man bubbled over with enthusiasm, showing them about the vacant apartment, pointing out the old-fashioned charm of the oak parquet floors and the high, arched ceilings. The windows were wide and tall, flooding the apartment with light, but the rooms were rather small, and Max politely thanked the man for his time.

When they were in the car, Claire said casually, "You do believe in being comfortable, don't you?"

He laughed aloud. "I'm fond of the creature comforts, yes. Being cramped is one of the things I hate most about hotels. Does that make me horribly spoiled?"

She looked at him. The bright sun was caught in the golden cap of his hair, framing his head in a gilt halo. He was relaxed, smiling, his vivid eyes sparkling, but still there was something about him, perhaps a natural sense of arrogance bred into him by the same aristocratic ancestors who had given him that hard, lean, graceful body and sun-god face. She had no doubt that he was spoiled; probably from the day of his birth, women had been dashing about to satisfy his smallest whim. What truly surprised her was that he had the ability to laugh at himself, as if he accepted his looks and the attention they brought him but didn't take them too seriously.

He reached out and took her hand. "What are you thinking? You're looking at me, but you've drifted away."

"That you *are* incredibly spoiled but rather nice in spite of it."

He threw back his head on a shout of laughter. "Aren't you worried that such lavish compliments will go to my head?"

"No," she said serenely. A warm sense of happiness was filling her again, making the bright spring day take on an incandescent glow. She let her hand lie in his, content with the touch.

"Direct me to the next apartment on the list while I still have a healthy ego."

The third apartment was being sublet by an artist who was taking a sabbatical on a Greek island. The decor was understated and sophisticated, from the black slate tiles in the entry to the light-colored walls and the tracks of indirect lighting overhead. The rooms were large; Claire's entire apartment would have fit easily into the enormous living room. Max wandered into the bedroom to inspect the bed, and Claire knew that he was pleased. His tastes were sophisticated, but never avant-garde. The almost spare luxury of this apartment would appeal to him.

"I'll take it," he said easily, interrupting the manager's spiel. "Are the papers ready to sign now?"

They were, but there was the matter of references. Max squeezed Claire's shoulder, smiling warmly at her. "While I take care of this, will you look about the place and decide what extras I'll need to buy, other than linens?"

"Of course," she agreed, wryly aware that now she was spoiling him, too. He had been polite and logical in his request, but the simple fact was that he'd expected her to agree to do that chore for him. If she hadn't been there, he would have done it himself, but she *was* there, and therefore available to do his bidding. Max went with the manager down to the office, and Claire took inventory of the apartment, making note of what he would need.

She was bemused by the luxury that he took for granted. Her background was in no way deprived. She was the product of an upper-middle-class upbringing, used to a certain amount of luxury herself. And she had been married for almost six years to a wealthy man and had lived in the center of the lap of luxury, yet she had transplanted herself without problem into a four-room apartment that could best be described as cozy. Having refused alimony, not wanting the link of financial dependence to tie her to Jeff, she had found a job and begun living on a budget, and not once had she missed the money that had enabled her to buy anything that took her fancy. Max's income was obviously far larger than hers, but still his attitude was an aristocratic expectation that his comfort be assured.

Sometime later he found her standing in the middle of the bedroom, her shoes off, her stockinged feet sunk into the thick dove-gray carpet. Her eyes were open, but that dreamy far-away look was in them again, and he knew that she was unaware of his presence. She was motionless, the tiniest of smiles on her face as she drifted in her thoughts. He stopped, watching her, wondering what dreams pleased her so much and if she wore that same look of contentment after lovemaking, when everything was quiet and dark and the frenzied heat had passed. Had she worn that look for her ex-husband or for another man? The sudden twist of jealousy in his gut was unwelcome and left a bitter taste in his mouth.

He crossed the room and put his hand on her arm, determined to draw her away from those dreams and back to him. "All finished with the paperwork. Are you ready to go?"

She blinked, and the dreams vanished from her eyes. "Yes. I was just enjoying the room."

He looked down at her bare feet. "Especially the carpet."

She smiled. "The colors, too. Everything blends together so nicely."

It was a mellow room, large and well lit, with the soothing gray carpet and pale-blue walls. The bed was covered with a thick comforter, and a large ceramic urn in the corner held an enormous philodendron. The bed was oversize, piled high with pillows. It was perfect for a tall man, and more than roomy enough for two people. He looked at the bed then at Claire as she bent down to slip on her shoes. He would have her in that bed before this was finished, he promised himself.

She gave him the list she'd made of what he would need to buy. He read it briefly then folded it and put it in his pocket. "We've certainly made short work of this—we have most of the afternoon left. Would you like to have a late lunch or an early dinner?"

She thought of inviting him home to eat dinner with her but hesitated; she had never before invited a man to eat at her apartment. The apartment was her place of privacy, and she had been reluctant to share it. But she didn't want the day to end, and somehow she didn't mind the thought of his presence in her home. "Why don't we go back to my apartment?" she offered a bit nervously. "I'll cook dinner. Do you like orange-glazed chicken?"

"I like food," he stated, glancing at her as they left the apartment and wondering at her obvious unease. Was cooking dinner for him such an ordeal? Both the invitation and the occasion were casual yet something about it bothered her. A woman with her social experience should be completely relaxed with such a simple evening, but nothing about Claire was as it should have been. He wondered if he would ever understand what went on in her mind.

The telephone began ringing as they entered her apartment, and Claire excused herself to answer it.

"Claire, guess what!" her mother said enthusiastically. Claire didn't even attempt to guess, knowing from experience that her mother wouldn't pause long enough to allow an interruption, and she was right. Alma rushed headlong into her next sentence. "Michael and Celia are being transferred to Arizona, and they've stopped to visit on the way through. They'll only be here this one night, and we're having a family cookout. How soon can you be here?"

Michael was Claire's cousin from Michigan, and Celia was his wife. Claire was fond of them both, but she had already invited Max to dinner, and she couldn't just throw him out now, even though Alma took it for granted that Claire would drop everything and rush right over. "Mother, I was just about to cook dinner—"

"Then I've called just in time! Martine and Steve are already here. I tried to call you earlier, but you were out."

Claire took a deep breath. She didn't want to tell her mother that she was entertaining, because she never did so, and Alma would immediately attach far greater significance to it than it warranted, yet she didn't see any way out of it. "I have company. I can't just rush over—"

"Company? Anyone I know?"

"No. I've invited him to dinner—"

Immediately Alma's maternal curiosity switched on. "Who?"

"A friend," Claire said, trying to evade any further questions, but knowing it was a hopeless maneuver. She looked up to see Max grinning at her, his turquoise eyes twinkling. He signaled that he had something to say, and she interrupted Alma's barrage of questions before her mother could get up speed. "Hold on just a minute, Mother. I'll be right back." She covered the mouthpiece with her hand. "My cousins have arrived from Michigan, and they'll only be here overnight, so Mother wants me to come over for a cookout," she explained.

"And you have already invited me to dinner," he finished, coming close to her and taking the phone out of her hand. "I have the perfect solution."

"Mrs. Westbrook," he said into the phone, "my name is Max Benedict. May I offer a solution and invite myself to your cookout, if it wouldn't be too much of an imposition on you? Claire really would like to see her cousins, but she has me on her hands, and she's too well mannered to withdraw her invitation to dinner, and I'm too hungry to do the polite thing and take myself off."

Claire closed her eyes, not having to hear the other half of
the conversation to know that Alma had completely melted at
the sound of Max's deep, smooth voice and that seductive
English accent. Part of her was amused, but another part of
her went into a panic at the thought of taking Max to meet
her family. Everyone in her family was outstanding in some
way, and she tended to fade into the background, overshadowed by their more exuberant personalities. Max perceived
her as quiet—if he saw her with her family, he would realize
that mousy was a more accurate description, and suddenly she
knew she couldn't bear that. Something in her would die if
he compared her to Martine, then looked back at her as if wondering what had gone wrong with the family genes.

"Thank you for taking pity on me," Max was drawling. "I'll
have Claire there shortly." He hung up the phone, and Claire
opened her eyes to find him watching her intently, as if wondering why she was so reluctant to attend her family's impromptu outing. "Don't look so frightened," he advised,
winking at her. "Perhaps I don't have on my best bib and
tucker, but I'll be on my best behavior."

There was still a residue of terror in her eyes as she turned
away. "It isn't you," she confessed, trying to make light of it.
"Family gatherings tend to overwhelm me. I'm not at my
best in a crowd." That was a massive understatement, she
thought, resigning herself to the bleak hours ahead of her.
"Excuse me while I change clothes and—"

"No," he said, reaching out to take her hand and effectively
halting her flight. "You look wonderful as you are. You don't
need to change clothes, brush your hair, or freshen your
lipstick. Waiting will only make you more nervous." He
watched her thoughtfully, wondering at the sudden urge he
had to protect her, but there it was. There was something
about her that made him want to gather her close and keep

everything hard and hurtful away from her. The realization that he wasn't being completely honest with her gave him a tight feeling in his chest—what would happen when she found out who he really was? Would she withdraw completely from him, her soft, dark eyes becoming cold and remote? A chill ran down his back at the thought, and he knew he couldn't let it happen. Somehow, some way he had to engineer the takeover without alienating Claire.

His eyes were narrowed and brilliant as he watched her, and Claire felt uneasiness grow in her. He saw too much, read her too well. The realization that she was so vulnerable to him frightened her, and instinctively she withdrew behind a quiet, polite, blank wall as he led her back out to the car, his hand still clasping hers in what would have been a comforting grip if she had noticed it, but she paid no attention to his touch. Her mind was already constructing painful scenarios in which Max fell in love with Martine on sight and spent the entire afternoon staring at her with an adoring expression in his turquoise eyes. He would be in pain, too, because Martine wouldn't return the emotion. Martine was deeply in love with her husband and never seemed to be aware of her devastating effect on the male sex.

Claire automatically gave directions, and too soon Max was turning into the driveway of her parents' home. The drive was already crowded with her father's BMW and her mother's small Buick, Steve's Jeep, and a loaded-down blue van with Michigan license plates. Max parked his car off to the side, under a tree. Claire stared blindly at the roomy Tudor-style house where she had grown up, almost paralyzed with dread of what was to come. Everyone would be in the large backyard, under the enormous chestnut trees; it was too early in the year for the pool to be uncovered, so the children would be running wild on the grass instead of swimming. The adults would be sitting lazily in the chairs grouped under the trees, and her father would be guarding the steaks and hamburgers slowly smoking on the grill. It would look like suburban heaven, but everything in Claire shrank from the ordeal of walking across the grass toward the small group, knowing that everyone would be avidly staring at the handsome man walking beside her, wondering why on earth he was with someone as ordinary as she, when he could obviously have any woman he wanted. Oh, God, she couldn't do it.

Max opened the car door, and Claire got out. The shouts and laughter of children at play came from the backyard, and he grinned at her. "That sounds like home. My nieces and nephews are hellions, every one of them, but there are some days when my sanity slips away and I miss their chaos. Shall we?"

His hand was warm on her back, and now she was aware of his touch, because he'd put his hand between her shoulder blades, and his fingers were resting on her bare skin, revealed by the low back of the cheery yellow-striped sundress. As they walked through the gate and came in view of her family, seated beneath the trees just as she'd pictured them, his thumb rubbed gently across her spine, and the sensation fractured the icy dread that had gripped her stomach. She was helpless against the surge of warmth that washed through her, tightening her nipples and making her breasts feel heated and full. That small touch had thrown her completely off balance. All her defenses had been raised against the dread of having Max meet her family and compare her to them, and she'd been totally unprepared to deal with the way she responded to him despite the caution of her common sense.

Then they were surrounded by her family, and Claire heard herself making the introductions automatically. Alma was practically beaming at Max, her beautiful face aglow with enthusiasm, and Claire's father, Harmon, was both dignified

and warm as he greeted his new guest. There were hugs and
kisses as Claire greeted Michael and Celia, conflicting excla-
mations, the noise of the children as Martine's two rowdy
youngsters, followed closely by Michael's two children,
charged into the group to hug and kiss Claire, who was their
favorite aunt. Martine, who was unbelievably gorgeous in a
dazzling white knit top and white shorts that hugged her lithe
figure and exhibited the golden length of her long, perfect
legs, began good-naturedly trying to bring some sort of order
to her children. Celia did the same, but it was several minutes
before things settled down. Through it all, Claire was aware
of Max standing closely beside her, smiling and chatting with
that incredible charm of his that already had everyone eating
out of his hand.

"Have you known Claire long?" Alma asked, smiling at
Max, and Claire tensed. She should have known that Max
would be grilled on his life from birth to present. It was her
own fault—since her divorce from Jeff, she'd stubbornly
resisted the efforts of her family to plunge her back into the
social scene, so it was out of character for her to show up with
a man in tow. Virginia's party had been the only party she'd
attended in years, except for small family get-togethers, and
Claire had no doubt that Martine and Alma had discussed at
length the fact that she'd finally given in to Martine's urgings.
Their curiosity over Max would be running high.

His eyelashes had drooped over his brilliant eyes, as if he
were a little drowsy. "No, I haven't," he said, his tone gentle
and faintly amused. Claire wondered if she were the only one
who heard that amusement, and she darted a quick look at her
mother. Alma was still smiling, and she wore that slightly
dazed expression Claire had seen before on women's faces
when they saw Max for the first time. Suddenly Claire
relaxed, no longer worried about any interrogation Max might

face from her family; she sensed that he was perfectly at ease, as if he'd expected to be questioned.

"Max is new in town, and I've been showing him around," she explained.

Both Alma and Martine gave her intensely pleased looks then glanced at each other as if congratulating themselves for a job well-done in finally getting Claire out of her shell. Now that she was older, Claire often found this silent communication between her mother and sister amusing, though when she was a child it had intimidated her, making her feel left out. Her lips twitched in a smile—really, there was something comforting in knowing your family so well that you could almost read their thoughts. Martine looked back at Claire and saw her sister's amusement, and a sunny smile broke over her lovely face. "You're doing it again!" she said, laughing.

"What's that?" Steve asked, leaning toward his wife.

"Claire's reading my mind again."

"Oh, she's always done that," Alma said absently. "Harmon, dear, the steaks are on fire."

Claire's father calmly sprayed water on the flaming charcoal. "What type of work are you in, Mr. Benedict?" he asked, keeping an eagle eye on the coals in case they flamed up again.

"Investments and real estate."

"Real estate? That's a volatile profession."

"Speculating in real estate certainly is, but I'm not in that area of the business."

"When we get settled in Arizona, I'm going to begin studying for my real estate license," Celia put in. "It's a fascinating career, and now that the children are both in school I want to get back into it. I worked in a real estate office in Michigan," she explained to Max. "I was planning to get my license then, but two babies persuaded me to put it on hold until they were older."

Martine leaned forward, her dark blue eyes sparkling as she leveled them on Max. "Do you have any children, Mr. Benedict?" she asked sweetly, and Claire closed her eyes, wavering between horror and a bubble of laughter. Martine didn't believe in tact when she was engaged in protecting her younger sister, and right now that protection took the form of digging all the information she could from Maxwell Benedict.

Max threw back his golden head and laughed, a deep, rich sound that made Claire open her eyes. "No children, and no wives, either present or past, to the despair of my mother, who thinks I'm a disobedient reprobate for not providing her with grandchildren as my brother and sisters have done. And please call me Max, if you'd like."

After that, everyone was eating out of his hand. Though she'd seen it before, Claire was still amazed at his talent for striking just the right note. His relaxed laughter and the fond references to his family had assured everyone that he was perfectly normal, not a con man, an ax-murderer or a heartless womanizer who would take advantage of her. Sometimes Claire thought that her family must consider her an absolute nitwit, incapable of taking care of herself, and she couldn't think what she'd ever done to deserve that opinion. She lived quietly, she worked and paid her bills, she never got into any trouble, and she handled the varied crises at work with serene aplomb, but none of that seemed to matter to her family. One and all, they seemed to think that Claire "needed looking after." Her father wasn't quite as obvious as Alma and Martine, but he still had a habit of regularly asking her if she needed any financial help.

Max lightly touched her arm, bringing her thoughts back to the laughing, chattering group, and his turquoise eyes were warm as he smiled at her. He never lost pace with the conversation swirling around them, and he promptly removed his hand, but that small touch told her that he was aware of her.

The afternoon was a revelation to Claire. Max was friendly and relaxed with her family, but he wasn't bowled over by Martine's classic golden beauty, as most men were. He was there with Claire. He sat beside Claire while they were eating at the redwood picnic table, he joined Claire in entertaining the restless children after they had been fed, and soon he was romping on the grass with all the aplomb of a man who was accustomed to being swarmed by his energetic nieces and nephews. Claire watched him playing with the children, this beautiful, elegant man who seemed to care not at all that his golden hair was tousled, or that his pants were now stained with grass. The setting sun made a gilt halo of his hair and caught the brilliant sea-colored sparkle of his eyes, and as she looked at him Claire felt her heart swell until it was almost on the point of exploding, and everything went dim for a moment.

I don't want to love him, she thought in despair, but it was already too late. How could she not love him? His laughter as he rolled on the grass, wrestling gently with the four giggling, shrieking youngsters, undermined her defenses far more quickly than any attempt at seduction would have.

She was still in a state of shock when Max drove her back to her apartment that night. It was almost ten o'clock, as everyone had been reluctant to let the day end.

"I like your family," Max said as he walked her to the door, rousing her from her thoughts.

"They liked you, too. I hope all those questions didn't make you uncomfortable."

"Not at all. I'd have been disappointed if they hadn't been interested in your well-being. They love you very much."

Startled, Claire paused with the key in her hand. Max took the key, unlocked the door and reached in to turn on the light then ushered her inside with his hand on her back. "They think I'm an idiot and can't do anything by myself," she blurted.

"That's not what I saw," Max murmured, cupping her bare shoulders in his warm hands. Claire's pulse suddenly throbbed, and she glanced down to hide the response that she couldn't control. "If you think your family is overprotective, I shudder to think how you'd react to mine. My entire family is so incredibly nosy that I sometimes think the mob would have more finesse."

She laughed, as he'd meant her to, and the way her face lit suddenly made his loins throb. He clenched his teeth, restraining himself from grabbing her and grinding his hips against her soft curves. "Good night," he said, bending to press his lips against her forehead. "May I call you tomorrow?"

"Again? I mean, of course, but I thought you'd be tired of my company."

"Not at all. I can relax with you. If you have other plans…?"

"I don't," she said hurriedly, suddenly terrified that now he wouldn't call at all. The thought of a day without seeing him made her feel bleak.

"Then have lunch with me. Is there a restaurant close to your office?"

"Yes, just across the street. Riley's."

"Then I'll meet you there at noon." He touched her cheek briefly then left. Claire locked the door behind him, her eyes filling with unexpected tears and her throat clogging. She was in love with him, with a man who, by his own admission, wanted only the refuge of an undemanding friendship. What a stupid thing for her to do! She had known, by her unusual response to him, that he was a danger to her and the quiet, uncomplicated life she'd built for herself. By not making any demands at all, he'd taken far more than she would ever have offered.

Chapter 4

When Claire entered the office, she saw at once that Sam had spent the night there again. File drawers were open, the lights were on, and a pot of old coffee was scorching on the warming pad of the coffee maker. Wrinkling her nose, she poured out the old coffee and put on a fresh pot, then set about restoring order to the office. The door of Sam's office was closed, but she knew that he would either be sprawled on the sofa or slumped over his desk. He spent a lot of nights in the office whenever he was working on a new alloy; his delight was in the development of new metals, not in the day-to-day routine of running the business he'd founded. For all that, he was a cagey businessman, and nothing escaped his attention for long.

When the coffee was finished, she poured a cup and carried it through to Sam's office. He was asleep at his desk, his head resting on his folded arms. A legal pad crowded with numbers and chemical symbols lay beside him, and five Styrofoam cups with varying levels of cold coffee was scattered around the desk. Claire set the cup of steaming coffee on the desk and crossed to the windows to open the curtains, flooding the office with light. "Sam, wake up. It's almost eight o'clock."

He woke easily, yawning and stirring at her voice. Sitting up, he yawned again and rubbed his face, eyed the fresh cup of coffee with appreciation and drank half of it. "What time did you say it is?"

"Eight."

"Almost five hours' sleep. Not bad." Five hours' sleep was really a lot for him—he often functioned on less. Sam was something of an enigma, but she was fond of him and intensely loyal. He was lean and gray haired, and his face had lines that told of hard living sometime in his fifty-two years, making her suspect that he had quite an interesting past, but he never talked about it. She knew little about him other than that his wife had died ten years before and he still mourned her, having no interest in remarrying. Her photograph still sat on his desk, and Claire had seen Sam look at it with an expression of such pain and longing that she'd had to turn away.

"Have you been working on something new?" she asked, nodding toward the legal pad.

"I'd like to make that new alloy stronger, but so far all I've done is make it brittle. I haven't hit on the right combination yet without making it heavier, too."

The challenge was to develop a metal that was both strong and light, because the heavier a metal was, the more energy was required to move it. The advanced metal alloys had practical applications more far-reaching than simply making a long-lasting I-beam for construction; the sophisticated alloys were used in space and opened up new opportunities in land travel. After an alloy was developed, ways had to be found to produce it cheaply enough that industry could use it. When Claire had first begun working, it had seemed like a routine job to her, like working in any steel mill, but she'd soon discovered her error. The security was tight and the research fascinating.

She loved her job, and that morning she was especially grateful for it, because it took her mind away from Max and gave her some breathing space. He had occupied both her time and her thoughts since she had first met him Friday night, overwhelming her with his sleek sophistication and wry good humor, inserting himself into her life so neatly and firmly that even in her sleep she couldn't quite escape from him. Claire had slept badly the night before, waking to tell herself over and over that she didn't love him, she *couldn't* love him, but then her traitorous mind would form his image in her thoughts, and her body would react wildly, growing warm and heavy, and she was afraid. Loving him was both reckless and foolish, especially for a woman who prized the secure, even tenor of her life and never again wanted to risk the pain of loving. It was even more foolish because Max had told her from the outset that he only wanted to be friends. How awkward it would be if he guessed that she was just like all the others, mooning over him like a starstruck teenager! Goodbye friendship, goodbye Max.

Sam called her into his office late that morning to take letters, but dictated only a few. Leaning back in his chair, he steepled his fingers and peered at her over them, frowning. Claire sat quietly, waiting. Sam wasn't frowning at her; he was lost in his thoughts and probably didn't even see her. At last he roused himself and got to his feet, groaning a little as his stiff muscles protested. "Days like this remind me of my age," he growled, rubbing his lower back.

"Sleeping at your desk reminds you of your age," Claire corrected, and he grunted in agreement.

"I heard some rumors over the weekend," he said, walking to the window to look down at the roof of his laboratory.

"Nothing concrete, but in this case I tend to believe them. Some foreign interest seems to be interested in buying up some of our stock. I don't like that. I don't like it at all."

"A takeover?"

"Could be. There's no active trading in our stock, no sudden surge in demand or price, so the rumor could be groundless. Still, there is something else that makes me uneasy. Another rumor is also circulating, about the new titanium alloy I'm working with now." His lined face was taut with worry.

They stared at each other in silence, both aware of the implications. Sam had developed an alloy so superior to its predecessors in strength and lightness that the possibilities for its use were so far-ranging they were almost beyond belief, though he still wasn't satisfied with the production process. That was still in the experimental stage, and security had been especially tight on its development. By necessity the lab people knew about it, though Sam was the only one in possession of all the information, and the people in production also knew about it. Information, once leaked, took on a life of its own and spread rapidly.

"This is too sensitive," Claire finally said. "The federal government wouldn't allow a foreign-held company to buy access to this alloy."

"I've always tried to stay independent," Sam mused, staring out the window again. "This research should have been classified, and I knew it all along, but I was too much of a maverick to do the sensible thing. I thought we were too small to attract notice, and I didn't want the hassle of government security clearance. It was a mistake."

"Are you going to contact the government?"

He thrust his fingers through his gray hair. "Damn, I hate to! I don't want all that going on right now, distracting me. Maybe…"

Sam was a maverick all right, with his unorthodox genius and his impatience with boundaries and restraints. Claire watched him, already knowing what his decision would be. He would wait and watch. He wouldn't allow the alloy to fall into the wrong hands, but he was going to conduct his research in private for as long as possible.

"Any takeover attempt right now would probably fail. We have some property that has skyrocketed in value, but it hasn't been appraised in years. An offer wouldn't take that into account."

"I'll have it reappraised," Claire said, making a note.

"Tell them to rush it. I hope it'll be enough to keep us safe. I just want time to finish my research before I turn this over." He shrugged his broad shoulders, looking tired. "It was good while it lasted, but I've known for some time that we were getting too close to an important breakthrough. Damn, I hate to complicate things with bureaucratic nonsense!"

"I suspect it isn't nonsense, but you just hate for *anyone* to tell you what you have to do, bureaucrat or not."

He scowled at her, a look that Claire met with complete serenity, and a moment later the scowl faded into wry acceptance. That was one of the things she liked most about Sam. He had the ability to see the truth and accept it, even when it was something he didn't like. Whatever blows life had dealt him, he'd learned from every one of them. He was a genius, locked into his creative dreams, but he was also a cautious, scrappy street fighter. Sam would never be a nine-to-five button-down executive; paperwork and corporate decisions, as important as they were, didn't interest him, and he did them only out of duty. His ambition, his life, was in his laboratory.

Despite the distractions of the morning, Claire was always aware of the passage of time, bringing her closer and closer to lunch, when she would see Max again. At last it was time to leave, and she grabbed her purse and darted out of the office. Her flesh was burning and her heart was pounding as she crossed the street, and she took several deep breaths in an effort to calm herself. This would never do. This was a simple lunch date between friends, nothing more. She didn't dare let it appear to be anything else.

Max stood up as she wove her way through the maze of crowded tables. She was flushed from hurrying, and his eyes dropped momentarily to her mouth, parted because of her rapid breathing. Her lips were wide and soft, and his senses jolted. He wanted to taste her, not restrict himself to those chaste, monumentally unsatisfying pecks on her cheek or forehead. He wanted to strip off her clothes and *taste* her, from her head all the way down to her pink toes, with a hungry urgency that threatened to shred his self-control. Damn her, he couldn't get her out of his mind, but he didn't dare make a move on her. She was so skittish that she would retreat from him again, and he wouldn't be able to get any information from her at all. He didn't have a lot of time, anyway, and he was hampered by not knowing exactly what he was looking for, but Anson was certain that Bronson would have hidden assets, and Anson Edwards's hunches were never wrong.

The trouble was that when he looked at Claire, it was difficult to remember that business was supposed to be his primary reason for being in Houston. The entire thing was beginning to leave a bad taste in his mouth. Corporate maneuvering was one thing, but he didn't like the idea of involving Claire, of using her. Only his loyalty to Anson Edwards kept him on this particular job, and for the first time Max felt that loyalty wavering. He didn't want to waste his time searching for information; he wanted to fold Claire in his arms and hold her so tightly that there could never be any distance between them again. A sharp longing knotted his insides as she finally reached his table and he stood to welcome her, but he schooled his features to reflect only the light, casual friendliness she seemed to prefer.

"Busy morning?" he asked, leaning down to kiss her cheek before seating her. His gesture was smooth and casual. He probably kissed every woman he met, Claire told herself painfully, but that didn't stop the surge of warmth that suffused her body.

"It's a typical Monday. Everything was in perfect order when I left Friday afternoon, but over the weekend it somehow turned into chaos."

A waitress appeared with the menus, and they were silent while they made their selections. They ordered, and Max turned his attention back to her. "I moved into the apartment this morning."

"That was fast!"

"All I had to relocate was my clothing," Max pointed out, amused. "I've stocked the pantry and bought new sheets and towels—"

The waitress whisked up with their coffee, sliding the cups and saucers in front of them with practiced ease. Riley's was famous for fast service, and today the waitress was outdoing herself. They tried several times to begin a conversation, but each time they were interrupted as their coffee cups or water glasses were refilled. The restaurant was crowded and noisy, and the clatter of plates and glasses was incessant, forcing them to raise their voices in an attempt to be heard.

"Claire! And Mr. Benedict! I'm so glad to run into you here!"

Max politely got to his feet, and Claire turned to see who had addressed them. The pretty brunette beaming at them was Leigh Adkinson, a member of the Houston social stratosphere to which Claire had belonged when she'd been Mrs. Halsey. Leigh was cheerful and lacking in malice, but they had been acquaintances rather than friends, and after Claire's divorce she'd almost completely lost contact with all of the old crowd. She could count on one hand the number of times she'd talked with Leigh in the years since her divorce, but there Leigh was, smiling at her as if they were the best of friends. And how did Leigh know Max? she wondered.

"Do you remember me, Mr. Benedict? We met at Virginia's party Friday night," Leigh chattered.

"Of course I remember. Won't you join us?" He indicated an empty chair, but Leigh shook her head.

"Thank you, but I have to run. I know it's short notice, but I wanted to invite you to a dinner party I'm giving Saturday night. Actually, it begins as a dinner party at my house then we're moving it to the Wiltshire Hotel for dancing in the ballroom. Tony's kicking off his candidacy for the governorship. Please say you'll come, both of you. I noticed at Virginia's party how well you dance together!"

Max glanced at Claire, his eyebrows uplifted. "Claire?"

She didn't know what to say. Leigh had somehow assumed that they were a couple, but that wasn't the situation at all. Perhaps Max would prefer taking someone else to the dinner party, if he wanted to attend at all.

"It isn't a fund-raising dinner," Leigh said, laughing. "It's a party for friends. You've been hiding yourself away for far too long, Claire."

Claire hated it when anyone made it sound as if she'd buried herself in deep mourning after her divorce, which wasn't what had happened at all. She stiffened, withdrawing from them, and a refusal began forming on her lips.

Max put his hand on hers, stalling her. "Thank you, we'd love to attend."

"Oh, good. We're having an early dinner, at seven. Claire knows where we live. I'll see you Saturday, then. Bye!"

Max resumed his seat, and silence fell briefly between them. "Are you angry that I accepted for both of us?" he asked, forcing her to look at him.

"I'm embarrassed. Leigh assumed that we're an item, and you were too polite to tell her the truth."

His eyebrows arched, and suddenly the languid, cosmopolitan gentleman was gone, and in his place was a man with cool, almost ruthless eyes. "Do you really think I'd care about being polite if I didn't want to attend? I can be a bloody bastard on occasion."

Claire felt mesmerized, staring into his turquoise eyes and suddenly seeing someone else, but abruptly the ruthlessness was gone, and in its place was the familiar calm control, making her feel as if her mind and eyes were playing tricks on her.

"Why don't you want to go?" he probed.

"I don't belong to that social set any longer."

"Are you afraid you'll see your ex-husband again?"

"I'm certainly not interested in socializing with him and his wife!"

"You don't have to socialize with them," Max persisted, and Claire felt the steely purpose in him. "If they're there, simply ignore them. Divorce is too rampant nowadays for it to be practical to split friends and acquaintances into warring factions."

"I'm not at war with Jeff," Claire denied. "That isn't the issue at all."

"Then what *is* the issue? I'd like to take you to the dinner party and dance with you afterward. I think we'd have fun, don't you?"

"I'm monopolizing your time—"

"No, dear," he interrupted gently. "I'm monopolizing yours. I like being with you. You don't have emotional fits all over my jacket. I freely admit to being selfish, but I'm comfortable with you, and I like being comfortable."

Claire gave in, knowing that for her own emotional safety she should stay as far away from him as possible, but she simply couldn't. She wanted to be with him, see him, talk to him, even if only as a friend, and the need was too strong to be controlled.

After lunch he walked her across the street. While they had been eating, the sky had rapidly filled with dark clouds, promising a spring shower. Max glanced up at the sky. "I'll have to run to beat the rain," he said. "What time are we having dinner tonight?"

Claire turned to stare at him in disbelief. "Dinner *tonight?*" Three nights in a row?

"Unless you have other plans. I'll be the chef. After all, it'll be the first meal in my new apartment. You don't have other plans, do you?"

"No, no other plans."

"Good. Strictly casual tonight, too, so you can relax. I'll collect you at six-thirty."

"I'll drive," she said hastily. "That way you won't have to leave in the middle of cooking."

He gave her a cool, deliberate look. "I said I'll collect you. You're not driving home alone at night. My mother would disinherit me if I allowed such a thing."

Claire hesitated. She was beginning to learn how determined Max was to have things his way. He was unyielding once he'd made up his mind. Behind the pose of sophisticated indolence was pure steel, cold and unbreakable. She had glimpsed it a few times, so briefly that she had never been quite certain of what she'd seen, but she was too intuitive not to sense the strength of the man behind the image.

Max tilted her chin up with his finger, bringing his charm into play as his eyes twinkled at her. "Six-thirty?"

She glanced at her wristwatch. She was already late and didn't have time to argue over such an unimportant detail. "All right. I'll be ready."

He was an expert at getting his way, she realized some ten minutes later. If charm didn't work, he used that cold authority that appeared without warning, and vice versa, but usually the charm would be enough. How often had anyone refused him, especially a woman? Probably not in this decade, Claire thought ruefully. Even as wary as *she* was of handsome charmers, she hadn't been immune to him.

She rushed home after work, alive with anticipation. Quickly she showered and shampooed and was just beginning to blow-dry her hair when the telephone rang.

"All right, spill your guts," Martine drawled when Claire answered the phone. "I want to hear all about that gorgeous man."

When Claire thought about it, she realized that it was nothing less than a minor miracle that Martine had curbed her curiosity for as long as she did, instead of calling Claire at work.

Claire paused, and a tiny frown pulled at her brow. What did she know about Max? That he had three sisters and a brother, was from England, and dealt in real estate. Her family already knew that much, from the adroit answers he'd given them the day before. She knew that he had expensive tastes, dressed elegantly and had impeccable manners. Other than that his life was a blank. She remembered asking him questions, but oddly enough, she couldn't remember his answers. She didn't even know how old he was.

"He's just a friend," she finally answered, because she didn't know what else to say.

"And the *Mona Lisa* is just a painting."

"In essence, yes. There's nothing between us except friendship." He'd never even kissed her, except for those sexless pecks on the cheek and forehead, and it wasn't that he didn't know how to go about it. He simply wasn't interested.

"Ummm, if you say so," Martine said, her skepticism evident. "Are you seeing him again?"

Claire sighed. "Yes, I'm seeing him again."

"Aha!"

"Don't 'aha' me. We're *friends*, without the capital *F* that Hollywood uses so meaningfully. You saw him, so I'm sure you won't have any trouble imagining how he's chased. He's tired of it, that's all, and he feels comfortable with me because I don't chase him. I'm not after a hot romance."

On the other end of the line, Martine raised her expressive eyebrows. She readily believed that Claire wasn't after a hot romance, but she didn't for one minute believe that Max Benedict was seeing her sister merely because he was "comfortable" with her. Oh, he was probably used to being chased, all right, and every hunting instinct man possessed would have been aroused when Claire looked right through him as if he were sexless. Martine knew quite a lot about men, and one look had told her that Max was pure male, more predatory than most, smarter than most and possessed of a sexuality that burned so vividly she wondered how Claire, who was so unusually sensitive to other people, could fail to see it. But perhaps Claire was too innocent to recognize that energy for what it was. Even though she'd been married to Jeff Halsey, there had always been a certain distance to her, a dreaminess that separated her from other people.

"If you're certain…"

"I'm certain, believe me."

She finally got off the phone with Martine and glanced anxiously at the clock. It was almost six. She hurriedly finished drying her hair, but she didn't have time to do anything with it except leave it loose. He'd said to dress casually, so she pulled on beige linen pants and topped them with a loose blue sweater with a deep neckline and a shawl collar. Was that too casual? Max was always so well dressed, and he had the English sense of formality. Another look at the clock told her that she didn't have time to dither over her clothes; she still had to do her makeup.

Just as she pulled a brush through her hair one last time, the doorbell rang. It was six-thirty exactly. She picked up her bag and hurried to open the door.

"Ah, you're ready, as usual," he said, and fingered the collar of her sweater. "You'll need a jacket. The rain has turned chilly."

Tiny raindrops glittered on his tweed jacket and in his golden hair as he leaned against the doorframe, waiting for Claire to get a jacket. When she rejoined him, he draped his arm over her shoulders in a friendly fashion.

"I hope you're hungry. I've outdone myself, if I do say so." His smile invited her to share his good humor, and when he hugged her into his tall body as they walked, she was content to lean against him. To be that close to him was a painful pleasure that she knew she should resist, but for the moment she simply couldn't pull away. She felt the heat of his body, the strength of the arm that lay so casually over her shoulders, and smelled the warm, clean scent of his skin. Her eyes closed briefly on the longing that welled inside her but she pushed it away. It would do no good to pretend, even for a moment, that the way she felt could ever come to anything—all it would bring her was pain. She was destined to be Max's *buddy*, and that was all the arm around her shoulders signified.

"I hope you like seafood," he said as they entered his apartment. The gilt-edged mirror over the Queen Anne table reflected their movements as he took her jacket from her and shrugged out of his then hung both in the small coat closet in the foyer. Attracted by the mirror, Claire watched him in its reflection, noticing the grace of his movements in even that small chore.

"This is Houston. The Gulf is at our back door. It would be unpatriotic or something not to like seafood."

"Shrimp in particular?"

"I love shrimp in particular." She licked her lips.

"Would that include shrimp creole?"

"It would. Are we having shrimp creole?"

"We are. I got the recipe in New Orleans, so it's authentic."

"It's hard for me to imagine you puttering around in a kitchen," she said, following him into the narrow, extremely modern kitchen, where everything was built-in and at his fingertips. A delicious spicy aroma filled the air.

"I usually don't but when I develop a taste for a certain dish, I learn how to prepare it. How else could I have shrimp creole when I'm in England for a visit? It's a certain thing my mother's cook has never prepared it. Then again, I had to learn how to do Yorkshire pudding for the same reason—different continent. The table is already set, will you help me carry all this through?"

It was difficult for her to believe that he had moved into the apartment only that morning. He seemed so at home there, and the apartment itself bore no signs of unpacking. Everything was in place, as if it had all been waiting for him, and he'd simply strolled in. The table was perfectly set, and when they were seated, Max uncorked a bottle of white wine and poured it into their glasses. The wine was crisp and clean, just what she wanted with the spicy shrimp creole and wild rice. They were relaxed together, and Claire both ate and drank more than she usually did. The wine filled her with warmth, but pleasantly so, and after dinner they both continued to sip the wine while they cleaned up the dinner dishes.

Max didn't insist that she leave the dishes for him, and that amused her—he wasn't *that* domesticated. He saw no reason why she shouldn't help him. It was difficult for two people to maneuver in the narrow kitchen, and they were continuously bumping into each other, but even that was pleasant. The brush of his body against hers gave her such secret pleasure that a couple of times she deliberately didn't move out of his way. Such behavior was uncharacteristic of her, because it bordered on flirtatiousness, and Claire had never been a flirt. She wasn't good at it, like Martine. Martine could smile and bat her eyelashes and make teasing little innuendos, but Claire wasn't at ease with sexual games, even when they weren't meant to be taken seriously.

The wine had relaxed her even more than she had realized. As soon as they sat down in the living room, she felt her muscles begin to turn into butter, and she sighed drowsily. She took another sip of the golden wine, and Max took the glass from her hand to set it on the coffee table.

"I think you've had your limit. You're going to go to sleep on me."

"No, but I *am* tired," she admitted, leaning her head back. "It was a busy day, even for a Monday."

"Anything unusual?" He sat down beside her, his eyes shielded by lowered lashes.

"You might say that. Sam—that's Mr. Bronson, my employer—heard a rumor that we may be the target of a takeover attempt."

"Oh?" His attention was focused on her, his body tense despite his relaxed pose. "How did he hear that?"

"Sam has remarkable sources and remarkable instincts. What bothers him the most is the possibility that a foreign company may be behind it."

His face was expressionless as he reached behind her and

began kneading the muscles of her neck and shoulders, his fingers making her give a quiet *mmmm* of pleasure. "Why is that particularly disturbing?"

"Because Sam is in the process of developing an alloy that could have far-reaching possibilities, especially in space," she murmured, then heard her own words echoing in her ears, and her eyes popped open. "I can't believe I told you that," she said in horror.

"Shh, don't worry. It won't go any further," he soothed, resuming the massaging motion. "If the production of the alloy is that important to national security, why isn't it classified? That would protect him from a takeover by a foreign company."

"Sam is a maverick. He doesn't like rules and regulations or the strict supervision he knows would come with government intervention and protection. He wants to perfect the alloy first, do all of his research and experimentation at his own speed, under his own rules. He'll go to the government, of course, if the rumor turns out to be true. He won't let the alloy go to another country."

Spencer-Nyle had been buying stock in Bronson Alloys, but very quietly, in small amounts. Anson wasn't quite ready to make his move, but if Bronson had also heard the rumor that foreign interests were backing a covert takeover, that gave the speculation a certain credence and Spencer-Nyle might have to step in sooner than Anson had planned. The danger was that now Bronson would be on the alert for any movement of his stock, and Claire had confirmed that Bronson worked best on his own. He wouldn't welcome a takeover by Spencer-Nyle any more than he would by a foreign interest. The company, though publicly held, was his baby, and Sam Bronson was known as a tough, gritty fighter. Max made a mental note to call Anson after taking Claire home.

He eased Claire down on the couch, stretching her out

full-length on her stomach. "What're you doing?" she asked, her eyes widening.

"Just rubbing your back," he said, keeping his voice low and soothing. He used the strength of his hands to find the kinks left by tension, and silence fell between them, except for the gentle sound of Claire's sighs. Max noticed her eyelids drooping again, and a smile tugged at his chiseled lips. She was actually going to go to sleep on him. That had never happened to him before, at least not this early in the evening. Women had gone to sleep in his arms, after the loving, but Claire seemed totally unaware of his sexuality. Even when their bodies had brushed in the kitchen, while they were cleaning up, she'd given no sign that she noticed it; it was as if she didn't even know sex existed.

He looked down at her, her honey-blond hair spread out across the couch, her lips soft and relaxed, those enormous, velvet-brown eyes closed. His hands looked big against her slender back; if he put his thumbs together on her spine, his spread fingers would reach around to the sides of her breasts. He could feel the fragile cage of her ribs beneath the soft fabric of her sweater and the even softer silk of her skin. She was asleep, in more ways than one—he wanted to wake her up and take her to bed, then wake her up sexually. He wanted to make her aware of him, so that she never again looked at him with that maddening distance in her eyes. But not yet. Not quite yet. He couldn't take the chance of frightening her off until he had found out all he needed to know for that bloody damned takeover. But then…then he would move, and Claire Westbrook would find out what it was like to be a woman in his bed.

His hands trembled as he looked down at her, and for the first time he wondered what she would say when she discovered his true identity. She would be angry, of course—he couldn't imagine her *not* being angry—but he thought he could handle her anger. It was the thought that she might be hurt that disturbed him. He didn't want to hurt her in any way. He wanted to hold her, make love to her, *cherish* her, damn it! It was insupportable that he might lose the trust he had so slowly earned from her, that she would no longer give him any of her slow smiles or quiet company. He'd met no other woman like Claire, no one so gentle or remote. He never knew what she was thinking, what dreams went on behind those dark eyes. Max was extraordinarily acute where women were concerned. Only Claire eluded him, and every smile, every thought, she gave him was like a treasure, because it allowed him closer to the secret woman behind her aloof facade.

Tenderness filled him as he watched her. She really was exhausted; if he couldn't take her to his bed, then she needed to be in her own. Gently he woke her, enjoying the way she blinked her dark eyes at him in confusion. Then she realized where she was, and a blush of mortification spread over her cheeks. "I'm sorry," she apologized, scrambling to her feet. "I didn't mean to fall asleep."

"Don't worry about it—you were tired. What are friends for? I'd have let you sleep on the couch, but I thought you'd be more comfortable in your own bed." They walked to the foyer, and he held her jacket for her. He was quiet on the drive back to her apartment, and Claire was still too sleepy to be interested in talking, either. It was raining again, a slow drizzle that kept the streets wet, and the chill made her huddle deeper into her jacket.

He checked her apartment while she watched, knowing that he would get that arrogant look if she suggested that he didn't need to do it. "I'll call you tomorrow," he said, coming back to her and cupping her chin in his hand.

"Yes," she agreed softly, feeling that each hour until she saw him again would seem a year long. "Max?"

He lifted a brow at her hesitant tone, waiting.

"What I said about the alloy…"

"I know. I promise, I won't say a word about it. I understand how sensitive that information can be." It was a promise he felt safe in giving, since he had no need to discuss the alloy with anyone. Anson already knew about it. Their problem now was the possibility—no, the probability—that a foreign interest, almost certainly unfriendly, was working behind the scenes to gain that technology through a takeover using a domestic company as a front. Bronson would move swiftly to protect his company from such a threat, and in doing so also protect it from other takeover attempts.

She looked so incredibly soft and sleepy, her defenses down. He tilted her chin up and bent to kiss her lightly, his mouth closing over hers before she realized he wasn't going to give her another brotherly peck on the cheek. He kept the contact light and swift, but almost immediately she stiffened and backed away from him, that damned blank look coming over her face. He dropped his hand and stepped away from her, as if he hadn't noticed anything, but a primal rage burned in his gut. Damn her, someday soon he'd make her see him as a man!

"I'll call tomorrow," he said again. "I have to investigate a few details, so I'll be busy until early afternoon, but I'll call you before you leave work." Without waiting for her agreement, he let himself out and walked away.

Chapter 5

"Claire, dear, I don't see why you're being so stubborn about this," Alma argued gently. "It's just a small party to repay some social favors, and I'd like for you to come. Your father and I would both like you to come. We don't see enough of you. Martine and Steve will be there."

Knowing it was useless, because when Alma used that gentle voice it meant that she'd dug in her heels and wasn't budging an inch, Claire tried again. "Mother, I don't like going to parties."

"Well, I don't like giving them. They're too much trouble, but I do it because it's expected and helps your father."

Which meant that Alma was doing her duty, Martine and Steve were doing their duty by showing up as the supporting cast, and Claire, as usual, was failing to come up to par, by refusing to do her part. Claire winced inside.

"You can leave early, I know you have to work tomorrow," Alma soothed, reading her victory in Claire's silence.

"And bring Max Benedict with you—from the rumor flying around town, Harmon and I think we should be better acquainted with him."

"What rumor?" Claire asked, horrified.

"That things look pretty serious between you. Really, you could at least have warned me, so I wouldn't have to act as if I knew what everyone was talking about."

"But we *aren't* serious! We're just friends." Claire had repeated that statement so often that she was beginning to feel like a parrot who knew only one phrase.

"You haven't been seeing him regularly?"

Only every day, but how could she tell Alma that without it sounding as if there was a passionate romance going, when it wasn't a romance? It was…well, it was almost like a partnership. They provided each other with companionship, simple, undemanding companionship. "I've seen him, yes."

"Leigh Adkinson saw you having lunch with him on Monday, Bev Michaels saw you having dinner with him on Tuesday, Charlie Tuttle saw you with him last night in a mall, shopping. Every day! That's pretty regular, dear. Now, I'm not pushing you—let the relationship develop at its own pace. But, really, it would be so much more comfortable if Harmon and I were better acquainted with him."

"I'll be at the party," Claire said quietly. She might as well capitulate and get it over with, because Alma wasn't about to give up.

"With Max."

"I don't know. I haven't talked to him about today. He may have a date."

"Oh, I don't think so," Alma chuckled. "Thank you, dear. We'll see you both tonight."

Claire hung up, biting her lip in consternation. What a way to begin the morning! Alma's call had come mere seconds before Claire's alarm clock had gone off. Well, her mother might be certain that Max didn't have a date, but Claire wasn't. Max was too much of a man not to have a love life, and since he didn't have that sort of relationship with Claire, nor did he seem interested in developing one, it followed that he would be seeing other women. If not tonight, then soon. A rest from strenuous pursuit was one thing, but a healthy man wouldn't let it go on too long. Max had a man's needs, and Claire had seen how women followed him with their eyes.

He couldn't have made it more obvious that he wasn't physically attracted to her. He hadn't kissed her again after that brief kiss on Monday night. As light as it had been, it had sent tingles of electricity shooting all through her body, and she had had to force herself to step away from him, to keep him from seeing how it had affected her. That one small touch and she had been ready to throw herself at him, just like all those other women. She had cried herself to sleep that night, certain she'd made a fool of herself and that he would never come near her again, but he'd called her the next day as promised and didn't seem to have noticed what had happened. Perhaps she had covered it well enough that he didn't suspect.

It didn't seem possible that it had been only a week since she'd met him. She had seen him every day, usually twice a day, when he met her for lunch, and after work, too. She sometimes felt as if she knew him better than she'd ever known anyone before, even Jeff, but at times Max was like a stranger. If she looked up quickly…she would occasionally catch him watching her with an unreadable expression in his eyes. If crossed, he could be a hard man, but he always kept himself under strict control, and it was that control that made her trust him.

She thought of not even asking him to go to her mother's party. She could go by herself, stay long enough to be polite then plead tiredness and go home early. That would satisfy Alma. But it would also mean that Claire wouldn't see Max that day, and emptiness filled her at the thought. Before she could talk herself out of it, she pushed herself up on the pillows and punched out his number on the telephone.

It rang only once before he answered it, his voice deep and a little husky with sleep. As always, Claire's heart gave a tiny leap at hearing him speak.

"It's Claire. I'm sorry to wake you," she apologized.

"I'm not sorry you woke me," he said and yawned. "I had planned to call you as soon as I woke, anyway. Is something wrong?"

"No, nothing like that. Mother just called. She's giving a cocktail party tonight and insists that I be there."

"Am I invited?" he asked with that smooth, cool self-confidence that often amazed and disconcerted her. Max was always so certain of what he was about. It was as if he knew Alma had insisted that Claire invite him and as if he was equally aware that Claire, being herself, would find it difficult to ask him. The more he seemed to see inside her mind, the more Claire tried to keep him from doing just that. She was in love with him; he wasn't in love with her. If he knew that…he would pity her, and he would also stop seeing her.

"You don't mind?"

"I like your family. Why should I mind?"

"People are talking about us."

"I don't give a bloody damn what people say," he said calmly then yawned again. "What time is the party?"

"Seven."

"Of course. Everything starts at seven. I'm going to be a bit tight on time, darling. I have to go out of town today, and I'll be shaving it down to a whisker if I drive all the way to my apartment, then to your apartment, then to your parents' house. Would it inconvenience you terribly if I simply got ready at your apartment? It would save almost forty-five minutes in driving time."

Her heart gave that stupid little leap again at the thought of his using her bathroom to shower in and then dressing in her bedroom. "No, it wouldn't be a bother," she managed to say. "It's a good idea. What time will you be here?"

"About six. Will that give you time?"

"Yes, of course." She would have to hurry, but she thought she could make it. It usually didn't take her long to get ready, and she had time to wash her hair before going to work. That would help.

"I'll see you tonight, then."

It was a horribly busy day; Alma's phone call had set the tone for the entire day. No matter how she hurried, Claire seemed to be a step behind all day long—even routine tasks developed aggravating complications. Part of her job was to shield Sam from unnecessary interruptions, which meant that she had to handle them herself, and there were some things that simply couldn't be put off to the next day. She worked through lunch, trying not to wonder where Max was and wishing that she were with him, wherever he was.

It was midafternoon when the emergency reappraisals arrived by special delivery, and a slow smile moved across Sam's face when he read them. With a gesture of supreme satisfaction he tossed the reports on his desk and leaned back in his chair, linking his hands behind his head. "Even better than I'd hoped," he told Claire. "The real estate values have quadrupled in the past year. We're safe, and I was really beginning to sweat it. Trading has picked up in our stock, though no pattern has developed yet. Someone's definitely after this company, but they're not going to get it. Take a look at that reappraisal."

Claire read through the documents, amazed at the way the value of the land had skyrocketed. Once again Sam's instincts had been right. It was really uncanny, the way his long shots all seemed to pan out. He had bought that land as a hedge against inflation, and now the land would probably be what saved the company from an unfriendly takeover attempt, and Sam wouldn't have to entangle himself in government regulations before he was finished with his research.

Of all days, she was almost twenty minutes late leaving work. It was fifteen to six when she let herself into her apartment, and she pulled off her clothes as she dashed to the bedroom. She jumped in and out of the shower, and had just dried off and pulled on her robe when the doorbell rang. She pressed her hands to her clean face, wishing that she had at least had time to put on her makeup, but there was nothing she could do about that now.

"I had to work late," she stammered in explanation when she opened the door to Max. "Let me get fresh towels and the bathroom is yours."

He carried a fresh suit and shirt and a small traveling kit. A shadow of beard darkened his jaw, but his smile was relaxed. "Don't worry, we'll be on time," he assured her, following her into the bedroom. He placed his clothing on the bed and carried the kit into the bathroom while she got fresh towels for him. Coming back out of the bathroom, he shrugged out of his suit jacket and tossed it across the bed, then began tugging at his tie. Her breath caught in her chest, and she turned away to sit down at her dresser, picking up a brush and pulling it through her hair without having any realization of what she was doing. She tried not to watch him, but the edge of her mirror caught him, and there was no way she could look away. He pulled his shirt free of his pants then unbuttoned it and pulled it off. For all his leanness he was unexpectedly muscular, his torso roped with long, smooth muscles that rippled when he moved. Dark brown curls grew across his chest, fascinating her with the discovery that his body hair was dark instead of blond, though she should have guessed, because his brows and lashes were dark brown, creating a striking contrast with his golden hair and framing his brilliant eyes.

To her relief he didn't take his pants off, though she wouldn't have been surprised if he had. Max was probably very comfortable with being nude in front of a woman, and he had no reason to be ashamed of his body. He was beautiful, even more beautiful than she'd dreamed, his body rippling with fluid strength that was usually hidden by his clothing.

He took his fresh pants off the hanger and took them into the bathroom with him. It wasn't until she heard the shower start that Claire recalled the need to hurry. She forced herself to begin applying her makeup, but her hands were shaking and she botched her eye makeup twice before she got it right. The shower stopped, and her mind immediately supplied a picture of Max standing there naked, drying himself on her towels. Hot color surged into her cheeks. She had to stop thinking about him! She was making a nervous wreck out of herself, when she should be concentrating on getting ready.

"Bloody hell!" he muttered clearly, then raised his voice. "Claire, I forgot my razor. Do you mind if I borrow yours?"

"No, go ahead," she called back. He was shaving; she would have time to dress before he came out. Jumping up, she got out fresh underwear and pulled it on, not taking the time to savor the sensation of cool silk on her skin as she usually did. She smoothed hosiery on her legs, not daring to hurry with that task or she would put a run in the delicate fabric. Now, what to wear? She opened the closet door and hurriedly surveyed the contents—she didn't have that many dresses suitable for a cocktail party. The water had stopped running in the bathroom; he would be out any moment. She jerked a cream-colored jersey dress off the hanger and pulled it over her head just as the bathroom door opened. Hidden in the folds of material, her face flamed red at the spectacle she was making of herself, with her head and upper torso fighting to emerge from the garment, while her lower body was exposed in only skimpy panties, a garter belt and hosiery. Turning her back on him, she tugged the dress into place and began fumbling with the back zipper.

"Allow me," he said, his voice very close. His warm hands brushed hers aside, and he efficiently pulled up the tab of the zipper then hooked the tiny hook at the top. His hands dropped. "There."

Keeping her face averted, she muttered a stiff thanks and returned to the dresser to repair the damage she'd just done to her hair. He was whistling under his breath as he finished dressing, and for a moment she envied his casual attitude, which was a measure of how accustomed he was to that type of situation. She leaned toward the mirror to apply her lipstick and saw him unzip his pants to tuck in his shirt. Her hand was shaking, and she had to take extra care with the lipstick to keep from smearing it.

Then he appeared in the mirror, standing behind her and bending down to check his hair, an abstract frown on his face. "Is everything in place?" he asked, standing back for her inspection.

She had to look at him then, and her eyes drifted over him. Again his charcoal-gray suit was ultraconservative but extremely well tailored. He knew what looked best on him; with his looks, trendy clothes would have made him too over-powering, like a neon light. The plain, unadorned clothes he chose enhanced rather than challenged his golden Viking beauty. Perhaps the lean, high-cheekboned beauty of his face had a Celtic origin, but there was something, perhaps that touch of ruthlessness that she had sometimes sensed in him, that made her think again that many generations back he might have had a Viking ancestor who had gone raiding on English shores and left behind a reminder of his visit. "No, you're perfect," she finally said, and he couldn't guess how much she meant those words.

"Let me look at you." He took her hand, drew her from the chair and turned her for his inspection. "You're just right—wait, you need earrings."

She'd forgotten them. Quickly she slipped pearl-drop earrings into her ears, and Max nodded, checking his watch. "We have just enough time to get there."

Perhaps it was just a small cocktail party, but the driveway was already choked with cars when they arrived at her parents' house. Alma and Harmon were both popular and outgoing, drawing people to them with the magnetism of their personalities. Inevitably Claire felt herself tensing as she walked up to the door with Max close beside her.

The door opened before they reached it, and Martine stood laughing at them, resplendent in an emerald-green dress that showed off her beautiful figure and made her glow with color. "I knew you'd be here," she said in triumph, hugging Claire. "Mom has been in a dither that you wouldn't come."

"I told her that I would," Claire said, reaching deep inside herself for the composure that she kept like a shield between herself and others, even her family.

"Oh, you know how she has to fret over something. Hello, Max, you're looking as beautiful as ever."

He laughed, a deep sound of true amusement. "You really must work to get over that shyness."

"That's what Steve tells me. Oh, here come the Waverlys.

I haven't seen Beth in ages." She waved past them to the approaching couple.

"Is there anything I can do to help?" Claire asked.

"I don't know. Ask Mom, if you can find her. She was in the den, but that was five minutes ago, so it's anyone's guess where she is now."

Max put his hand on her waist as they walked into the crowded living room, and Claire immediately felt the impact of everyone's eyes as they turned to survey the new arrivals. She knew their thoughts, knew that everyone had heard the rumors and was looking them over, trying to decide if the rumors were true.

"You did make it!" Alma beamed, sailing across the room to kiss Claire's cheek. She turned that thousand-watt smile on Max, whose mobile lips twitched into a devilish grin. Before either Alma or Claire could guess what he was about, he took Alma in his arms and kissed her lips, then did it again. Alma laughed, but she was blushing when he released her.

"Max, what are you doing?" she exclaimed.

"Kissing a pretty woman," he replied blandly, the tone of his voice belied by the wicked twinkle in his eyes. He reached out and brought Claire back into the circle of his arm. "Now Claire and I are going to find something to eat. I'm starving, and she didn't have time for dinner, either."

Claire felt frozen as she walked beside him to the kitchen, feeling the eyes boring into her back like knife blades. He'd kissed Alma twice, which meant that he'd kissed her mother more than he'd kissed her. She had stood to the side, envying the brilliant, easy charm that both Max and Alma possessed, wishing that she had the gift of laughter. Martine could do it, too, have people eating out of her hand within moments of meeting them. All her life she'd been surrounded by beautiful, charming people, but none of that magical self-assurance had rubbed off on her.

The breakfast bar in the kitchen was crowded with hors d'oeuvres and finger sandwiches, and Max raided it shamelessly, but Claire only nibbled at a sandwich. Automatically she replenished the trays as Max depleted them and finished the condiment tray that Alma had been in the middle of preparing before she had rushed off to greet her guests. Alma rushed back into the kitchen, her glowing smile bursting over her face when she saw that Claire had completed the preparations. "Bless you, dear. I completely forgot what I was doing. You always did keep your common sense. I can't count the times Harmon has told me to slow down and think before I do something, but you know how deep an impression it's made."

Claire smiled quietly at her mother, thinking that she did love her very much even though it had never been easy, growing up in the shadow of a beautiful mother and an equally beautiful sister. Both Alma and Martine were warm and outgoing people, without an ounce of maliciousness. It wasn't their fault that Claire had always felt overshadowed by them.

She picked up the heavy tray, and Max promptly relieved her of the burden. "Show me where you want it," he said firmly when Claire turned to him with her brow raised in question. "You're not to try to carry these trays yourself." He looked at Alma as she began to lift one of the trays, and the cool warning in his eyes made her drop her hands and step back.

"Masterful, isn't he?" Alma whispered to Claire as they followed Max's broad shoulders back into the living room.

"He has set ideas on what's proper," Claire said in understatement.

Max carried all the trays in, then became immersed in a conversation with Harmon, Steve and several other men. Periodically his eyes sought out Claire, wherever she was in the room, as if reassuring himself that she wasn't in need of him.

Claire sipped on a margarita and surreptitiously checked

the time, wondering when they would be able to leave. The cocktail party wasn't as bad as she'd feared, but she was tired. The pressure of the hectic day, the hectic *week*, was telling on her. Bracing herself, she tried to concentrate on the conversation around her.

Someone turned on the stereo, but since Harmon was an ardent blues fan, the selection was limited. The smoky, mournful wail of a saxophone lured several people into dancing. Claire danced with Martine's law partner, then with her father's best friend, then with an old friend from school. She was on her second margarita when it was taken from her hand, placed on the table, and Max turned her into his arms.

"You're tired, aren't you?" he asked as they swayed to the low music.

"Exhausted. If tomorrow weren't Friday, I don't think I could make it."

"Are you ready to leave?"

"More than ready. Have you seen Mother lately?"

"She's back in the kitchen, I think. The nation's dairy farmers would be in ecstasy if they could see the amount of cheese that has been consumed tonight," he said dryly.

"You ate your share, I noticed."

His mouth quirked. "I burn off the calories."

Sighing, she stepped back from his embrace. "Let's find Mother. I think we've stayed long enough to be polite."

Alma was indeed in the kitchen, dicing cheese into another heap of small squares. She looked up when they entered, and a mixture of dismay and resignation crossed her features. "Claire, you can't be leaving!" she protested. "It's still early."

"I know, but tomorrow's a working day." Claire leaned forward to kiss her mother's cheek. "I've enjoyed myself. Really."

Alma looked at Max for reinforcement. "Can't you get her

to stay a little longer? She has that stubborn look, and I know she won't listen to me."

Max's arm went around Claire's waist, and he, too, bent to kiss Alma's cheek. "That isn't a stubborn look—it's a tired look," he explained easily, employing his charm as he smiled at Alma, pacifying her. "It's my fault. I've had her out every night this week, and the lack of sleep is catching up with her."

It worked, but then, Claire had never doubted him. Alma was beaming at him. "Oh, all right, take her home. You must come back—we haven't really had a chance to get to know you."

"Soon," he promised.

It was a silent drive back to Claire's apartment, but when she offered him coffee he came inside with her. After making the coffee and carrying the cups into the living room, they sat on the couch and sipped quietly. Claire kicked off her shoes, sighing in relief and wiggling her toes.

Max's gaze was on her slender feet, but his mind was on other matters. "What happened that you had to work late today?"

"Everything. It was just one of those days, and it didn't help that Sam was so edgy. He's almost certain there's going to be a takeover attempt, and soon—there's been increasing trading in our stock. Even though he has an ace in the hole, the waiting and wondering are nerve-racking."

"What's his ace in the hole?" Max asked, his voice sleepy, almost disinterested.

It was a new situation for Claire, actually being able to sit down and discuss her day at work with someone. She had never talked about her day before—she couldn't remember if anyone had ever asked. Small talk was a subtle sort of intimacy, letting someone into her mind by sharing the details of her life with them, and she had always instinctively kept to herself. But it was so easy to talk to Max. He listened, but he didn't make a big deal of it.

"Real estate," she said, smiling a little. His lashes lifted to reveal a lazy gleam of interest. "I thought that might interest you."

"Ummm," he said, an indistinct sound of agreement.

"Sam invested in some property that has quadrupled in value. The reappraisal came in today, and it was even better than he'd hoped."

"Land values can do that. They go up and down like a roller-coaster. The trick is to buy just before the price bottoms out, and sell just before it goes over the top. The value must really be astronomical to be enough to protect him against a takeover." He sat up more alertly and finished his coffee.

"I'll get you a refill," Claire said, getting up and going into the kitchen before he could refuse. She reappeared almost immediately with the pot, and Max watched her walk toward him, her slender body moving gracefully. She looked so quiet and restrained, but he knew what was beneath that ladylike dress. He'd seen the satin panties, the shockingly sexy garter belt and filmy hosiery. A garter belt, for God's sake! His body jolted with response now just as it had then, and he clenched his teeth. He'd had a difficult time keeping his mind off her underwear and his hands off her body. He kept seeing her with that dress over her head, baring her slender hips and legs to his view. The need to take her to bed was growing out of control, fed by frustration that she was so unaware of him as a man and by anger that she would freeze up on him if he tried to change the situation. He wasn't accustomed to abstinence, and he didn't like it one damned bit.

Claire picked up the conversation where they had left off, sitting down beside him again. "I wouldn't call the land value astronomical, but we're a small enough company that it doesn't have to be. Anyone making a bid for the company is going to come short by several million dollars."

He jerked his thoughts back to what she was saying. Damn it, she was practically handing him the information he needed on a silver platter, and he couldn't keep his mind on the conversation. He wanted very much to stretch her out on the couch and lift that dress over her head again, to run his hands over her and feel the softness of her skin, but that would have to come later.

"How much was the appraisal?" he asked. He watched her closely, wondering if she would answer him. It was a bold move, asking outright for the information he needed, but she had already given him the major part of it, and the actual appraisal would only fill in the details. He kept his face carefully blank, hiding his intense interest in her answer.

"In the millions."

Damn, that *would* make a difference! "What did they do? Find oil on it?" he muttered.

She laughed. "Close."

Mingled satisfaction and relief filled him; the job was done. It hadn't taken long, and had been relatively easy. The difficult part had been restraining himself from making a move on Claire and scaring her off, but now the job was out of the way and he could concentrate on her. She could try hiding behind that shell of hers, but he was free to pursue his own interests now, and Claire was his interest. He wanted her. He had no doubt that he would have her. He was a master at seduction, and no woman had ever resisted him for long when he made the effort to charm her into his bed. But with Claire, he'd been handicapped by his professional concerns, forced to restrain himself. She was already accustomed to his company, and she had come to accept his casual touches. It wouldn't be long before she was also accepting the most intimate touches between a man and a woman.

His hunger, his *need*, for her were becoming more urgent.

It wasn't just the physical need for release, though that was strong enough—he wasn't accustomed to celibacy. No, his strongest need was the primitive urge to bind her to him *now*, before she found out the truth, but he found himself uncharacteristically hesitant, his usual self-assurance fading. What if this wasn't the right time? What if she rebuffed him? What if she retreated completely? He would have lost even her friendship, and to his surprise he wanted her friendship very much, as much as he wanted her physically. He wanted all of her, her mind as well as her body.

She smothered a yawn, and he laughed, reaching out to massage her shoulder, the light touch filling him with pleasure. "You need to be asleep. Why haven't you told me to leave?"

Claire curled up on the couch, tucking her feet under her, and sipped her coffee contentedly. It was so peaceful, sitting there together and drinking their coffee, making desultory conversation. Her heart was beating in that slow, heavy way it did whenever she was with him, and in that moment she was happy. "I'm comfortable with you," she replied, and knew that she was lying. Her nerves were alive and acutely tuned to him, her senses assailed by his nearness. She could smell him, feel his warmth, look at him, and her flesh ached to be even closer to him. How foolish she was to love too fast, too much, but it was out of her control and perhaps had been from the very beginning.

He reached out and took her hand, folding her fingers in his and rubbing his thumb over her silky skin. "Claire," he said in a quiet voice, drawing her gaze to him. Her eyes were dark pools, soft and velvety. "I want to kiss you."

He felt the way her hand jerked in his, and he tightened his grip just enough to hold her. "Do I frighten you?" he asked, amused.

Claire looked away from the laughter in his face. "I don't

think it would be a good idea," she said, her voice going stiff. "We're just friends, remember, and—"

He got to his feet, laughing at her as he pulled her up and took the coffee cup from her free hand to set it down. "I'm not going to bite you," he said and kissed her.

It was a light, swift touch, exactly the way he had kissed her before. "There, did that hurt?"

His vivid eyes were dancing. He was teasing her, and she relaxed. She had thought that he meant a different kind of kiss, and she didn't dare let him kiss her deeply. She wasn't certain of her control—if he kissed her with any degree of passion, she felt that she would explode in unbridled response. He wouldn't have any doubt then about the way she felt. He was too experienced, had been with too many women who were desperate to hold him, not to recognize the same lovesick symptoms in her. It was far better that he tease her rather than feel sorry for her.

Then he kissed her again.

It was an admirably restrained kiss, but it lingered, and he opened his lips over hers. Automatically she parted her own lips to adjust the fit. His taste filled her mouth, his lips firm and warm. Pleasure rose in her, and for a moment she almost melted against him, almost raised her arms to twine them around his neck. Then panic twisted her stomach. She didn't dare let him know, or she would never see him again! Swiftly she turned her head away, breaking the contact of their mouths.

He pressed his lips to her temple, and his strong hands rubbed up her back in a long, slow sweep. He didn't want to push her too far. Just for a moment she had responded to him, and the taste of her had gone to his head like a potent wine. His body was responding strongly to her nearness. He didn't dare hug her to him the way he wanted, because there was no way he could hide his arousal. Reluctantly he let her go, and she immediately took a protective step away from him, her face set in a blank mask. Suddenly he was determined not to let her retreat, as she had done so many times before. He was a man; he wanted her to see him as one. "Why are you so uneasy whenever I touch you?" he asked, tipping her chin up with his finger so she couldn't hide her face from him. She was too good at hiding her thoughts, anyway, and he needed every little clue he could get. He wanted to be able to see her face, her eyes.

"You said you wanted to be friends," she replied stiffly.

"Friends aren't allowed to touch?"

His whimsical tone made her feel as if she were making far too much of things, and perhaps she would have been—if she hadn't felt far more for him than just friendship. But she was in love with him, and even his most casual touches tormented her with mingled pleasure and longing.

"You told me that you wanted a friendship without sex."

"Surely not. I don't believe I've taken leave of my senses." Gently he rubbed his thumb over her bottom lip. "What I said was that I was tired of being pursued simply as a sexual trophy."

Claire was both astounded and alarmed. Had she so completely misread the situation? He was looking down at her with amusement, and she began to tremble. "Don't look so frightened," he soothed, moving his hand down to stroke her bare arm. "I'm attracted to you, and I'd like very much to kiss you occasionally. Is that so alarming?"

"No," she stammered.

"Good, because I intend to continue kissing you." His lashes veiled his eyes, allowing only a thin glittering line of turquoise to show, but Claire sensed his burning triumph and satisfaction, and she became even more uneasy. It was just like those times when she had glimpsed something ruthless in him, as if he weren't what he seemed at all. It didn't help that his look of triumph was immediately gone, because it left her feeling disoriented, not knowing anything for certain.

He bent and kissed her again, then left, and Claire stood staring at the door long after it had closed behind him. He seemed to have decided that he wanted more than simple friendship from her, and she didn't know how to protect herself. She was without any emotional defenses and so terribly vulnerable to any hurt he might give her. She loved him, but she felt that she didn't know him at all.

Chapter 6

MAX placed a call to Dallas as soon as he got back to his apartment, wanting to pass along the information Claire had given him as soon as possible. He knew that Anson would take action on it first thing in the morning; by Monday, the takeover would be in motion. His job wasn't finished, of course—he would have to oversee the transfer of ownership and negotiate the endless details that were always so important to the anxious personnel of the acquired company, but the major hurdle had been cleared. Max Benedict could become Max Conroy again, and he could turn his attentions on Claire.

Claire. She was the most complex, elusive woman he'd ever known. She kept herself hidden away, not letting anyone get close enough to really know her, but that was about to change. The irritating restraint he'd placed on himself was at an end. He would take it slow with her, gradually getting her accustomed to his touch. As torturous as this past week had been, it had had a positive side in that she was already used to his company. She was relaxed with him, and despite his frustration, the undemanding companionship he'd shared with her had had its own charm. Claire wasn't a chatterbox, and the time he spent with her had been punctuated by peaceful silences. He wanted her more than he'd ever wanted any other woman, and he didn't know why.

She wasn't the most beautiful woman he'd ever known. She was quietly pretty, with a fragile bone structure and eyes as dark as midnight pools, eyes that were full of dreams. She wasn't voluptuous—her body was almost reed slender, yet undeniably feminine. There was a softness to Claire that he found very appealing. He wanted to take her in his arms and make love to her, get behind the blank wall that she kept between herself and other people; he wanted to know her thoughts, what she felt, what dreamworld she drifted away to when those dark eyes turned shadowy and faraway.

Added to that, he liked her as a person. Max was passionately fond of women in general, but his intense sexuality sometimes got in the way of friendship—a woman was in his bed before they had a chance to know each other as people. The restraints that had been necessary in his relationship with Claire had allowed liking and friendship to grow. He liked talking to her; she was thoughtful and never malicious, and she wasn't uncomfortable with occasional silences. It would be extremely pleasant to wake up next to Claire, to spend lazy mornings with her, reading the newspaper and lingering over breakfast, talking if they felt like it and simply being silent if they didn't.

There had been only one other woman he had *liked* in the same manner, and he thought about her for a moment. Sarah Matthews, his friend Rome's wife: she was incredibly gentle, and incredibly strong. Max had been on the verge of loving her, and in fact did love her for the very special person she was, but she had made it plain from the beginning that Rome was the only man in the world for her, and the way Max felt about her had never grown into the area of intimacy. Now she and Rome were his closest friends, and their marriage was stronger than ever, more passionate than ever.

He would like to have that with Claire.

The thought jolted him. He kicked his shoes off and stretched out on the bed, staring at the ceiling. The scenario he had just imagined had a powerful charm to it, too powerful. Claire tugged at something in him. He wasn't certain that he liked what he felt, but he was completely certain that he had to do something about it. Claire Westbrook was going to be his.

The next night he took her to the symphony, which she loved, and afterward they ate at a tiny Japanese steakhouse. Claire had been nervous at first, and because she was nervous she became quieter, more remote, but the music had helped to relax her. Max seemed just as he always had: cool and controlled, watching the world with lazy amusement. She felt safe when he was like that.

She had slept restlessly the night before, her imagination picturing again and again the way he had kissed her, what he had said, like a loop of film on a projector that ran continuously. Every time she woke it was to find her heart racing with excitement, her body warm and yearning for him. She'd had no lovers since the divorce. She had drawn so deeply into herself, trying to build strength and recover from the shattering emotional blow of losing her baby and watching her marriage disintegrate, that there had been nothing left, no passion to give to a man. But without her being aware of it, time had worked its healing process, and she was alive again. Her nature was warm, passionate, and she trembled inside with need whenever she remembered his mouth on hers.

It hadn't even been a passionate kiss, but she had wanted to lace her arms around his neck and stand on tiptoe to press herself against him. She had wanted to lose herself in him, to give him everything that she was. It was a primitive, unconquerable urge, the need to lie in his arms, to mate, an urge that was inborn. Just as strong was the need to protect herself, and the two needs were warring inside her. Claire's capacity to love was so enormous that she was instinctively wary, backing away from any threat to her emotions. Because she loved so deeply, she was acutely vulnerable to him. He had the power to hurt her so badly that she might never recover.

The safe thing to do would be to run, to simply stop seeing him. She had lain in her bed and turned the idea over and over in her mind, but when morning had come she had admitted to herself that she couldn't do it. She loved him, and perhaps he was coming to care for her a little. There had been something hot and a little frightening in his eyes before he'd masked his expression, an almost predatory look of hunger. A man didn't look like that if he wasn't interested. That look gave her hope.

Now she came out of her thoughts to find him watching her with wry amusement, and color tinted her cheeks. Had he been able to tell the direction of her imaginings?

"You aren't eating at all. You're dreaming," he said, taking the fork from her hand and placing it on the mat. "Shall we go?"

On the drive home he asked quietly, "Claire, I didn't intend to make you uneasy with me. I apologize for putting you in a difficult spot. If you aren't attracted to me, I understand. We'll simply continue being friends—"

"Oh, please," she sighed, interrupting him. "Do you honestly believe I'm not attracted to you?"

He glanced sharply at her then returned his attention to his driving. "You've made it fairly obvious that you don't want me to touch you. In fact, at first you didn't want to have anything to do with me at all. I all but begged to get you to accept me as a friend."

She was silent. She couldn't tell him that she had been afraid of his charm, afraid that she would fall in love with him, because she'd done exactly that. Finally she turned her head to look at him, his perfect profile etched in silver against the darkened window, and her heart gave that funny little leap that she'd come to expect. Was he asking her to believe that dreams came true? It was hard for her to trust, to let anyone get behind the emotional barriers that protected her from hurt. She didn't think she was the type who could recover from one heartache after another, bouncing right back to take another try at true love, trusting that eventually everything would work out. Claire loved too deeply; it took her too long to recover from heartbreak.

She wasn't a gambler, but she didn't see that she had much choice. She couldn't walk away from him now. Her heart had known it almost from the beginning, and now she acknowledged it in her mind. She had to try again; she had to reach out or despise herself for the rest of her life. Max was worth the risk, and perhaps she might win.

"I'm very attracted to you," she finally said, her voice so soft that he wasn't certain he'd heard her. His head jerked around, his eyes narrowing, and she steadily met his gaze.

"Then why have you held me away?"

"It seemed safer," she whispered, tightly knotting her hands together in her lap.

His chest expanded as he drew in a deep breath. They were near her apartment building, and nothing more was said as he parked the car. The silence extended, then he reached out and gently drew her into his arms. She didn't see his head coming down, but she felt the warmth of his body close to her, the controlled strength of his arms wrapping around her, and then his mouth was on hers. Her head tilted back to fully accept him, and her lips parted softly, her response slow and tender. He took her mouth in the same way, taking his time about it, not bruising her soft flesh. The way was open for his tongue, and he probed her mouth, feeling the quiver of her body at the deepening intimacy of the kiss. He held her closer, arching her to him, and another quiver ran along her body at the sweet, heated pleasure of feeling her breasts pushing against his chest. A small groan rose in his throat. With a sure, experienced motion he covered her breast with his hand.

Her hands clenched his sleeves, her fingers shaking. Max lifted his mouth from hers and began nuzzling her jawline, seeking the delicate fragrance of her skin. He tasted her flesh as he went, discovering some of the soft places that had been driving him wild for a week: the small hollow below her ear, the length of her neck, the ultrasensitive hollow above her fragile collarbone. And all the time her small, firm breast nestled in his palm, the nipple already peaked, inviting a more intimate touch.

"Put your arms around me," he said, his voice one of quiet demand. He wanted to feel her clinging to him, all weak with wanting. She fit into his arms as if no other woman had ever been there; he wanted it to be the same way for her. He wanted her to hold him, feel how perfect it was, their two bodies pressed together. Slowly her fingers released his sleeves, and her arms slid upward. One twined around his neck and the other around his shoulder. A shuddering breath eased out of her.

Slowly he massaged her breast, taking care not to hurt her or to scare her by losing control and grabbing at her. His own breathing didn't sound quite steady, and he knew that he had to stop or lose control. He wasn't accustomed to celibacy, and since he had met Claire, his only lovelife had been in his imagination. Reluctantly he eased away from her, his body on fire with a burning hunger that bordered on violence. He would have to get himself under control before he dared make love to her. She was so soft, so fragile; he didn't want to take the chance of hurting her, and he was very much afraid that he would.

"It's time to call a halt to this, while I still can," he admitted ruefully, his sharp, knowing gaze taking in the dazed look of passion on her face. Delight filled him that Claire wasn't a cold woman, merely a deeply reserved one, and she was finally responding to him.

His words recalled her from the warm, drifting world of physical pleasure where he had carried her, and she sat up straighter, her glance darting away from him, her hands going up to smooth her hair, as if by tidying herself she could deny what had just happened. Max took her hand and carried it to his lips. "Don't," he whispered.

He got out of the car, walked around to open the door for her and helped her out, his hand under her elbow as she maneuvered the long skirt she'd worn to the symphony. His arm went around her waist as they entered her apartment building and remained there during the short elevator ride to her floor. Some of Claire's distress at herself began to fade. His attentiveness was doing something to her, slowly making her feel more certain of herself, and it was like the first hesitant flutterings of a butterfly's new wings.

He checked her apartment then came back to her. The usual lazy, good-humored smile was on his lips, but his eyes were vivid and intent as he bent down to kiss her again. "I won't stay, not tonight. I want you to be comfortable with me, and frankly, my self-control is wavering. I'll see you tomorrow night. How formal is Mrs. Adkinson's dinner party?"

Claire remembered Leigh's inclinations well. "Very."

"White dinner jacket?"

He had been wearing a white dinner jacket when she had met him exactly a week ago, and her senses gave a brief whirl as she recalled the way he had looked, with the lights caught in his golden hair like a halo, his eyes as brilliant and glowing as gemstones, the white jacket molded to his broad shoulders. She hadn't been the same person since that night.

"That would be perfect," she said. He didn't know how perfect.

He kissed her again and left, and Claire went through the motions of getting ready for bed, but her mind was drifting, floating, recalling every sensation, every moment of his kisses, his touch on her breast. Her natural human need to be touched had been suppressed for a long time by her driving need to prove to herself that she could be independent, but now her body was aching and burning as it came alive after being dormant for so long. She lay in bed, and she dreamed of him.

The gown she wore to Leigh's dinner party the next night was almost nine years old, but she had seldom worn it before, and it was one of those simple styles that couldn't be dated. It was black velvet, with only a little fullness to the skirt, and the bodice hugged her lovingly. It wasn't particularly lowcut, revealing only a hint of the beginning curve of her high breasts, but it was held up only by two thin straps, leaving her shoulders and back bare. Jet earrings dangled from her ears, and she wore no other jewelry. Her mirror told her that she had never looked better, and her fingers loved the soft, lush feel of the velvet. All her senses seemed to be more alert, and she was achingly aware of her own body in its casings of silk and velvet. When she opened the door to Max, his pupils expanded until the black almost swallowed the sea-colored irises, and the skin seemed to become taut across his cheekbones. Tension hummed from his body.

But if he thought of reaching for her, he controlled the

impulse. "You're lovely," he said, his eyes never leaving her, and she felt lovely.

Claire enjoyed the dinner party more than she had expected, even though her pleasure was dimmed by the presence of Virginia Easley. It would be a long time before she'd forget Virginia's maliciousness in inviting Claire and Jeff to the same party. Max felt Claire's slight stiffness and glanced at her in question. Then he saw Virginia, too, and his eyes narrowed. "Don't let her bother you. She isn't worth the effort."

Leigh Adkinson sailed up to greet them and hug Claire, exclaiming how glad she was to see Claire again. Max stood close to Claire, a little behind her, his presence like a solid wall of strength in case she needed him. He had met several of the other guests at Virginia's party, so people drifted over to speak to him and Claire, but most of the guests were strangers to him. For a time he and Claire merely stood still, like royalty holding court, surrounded by people who hugged and kissed Claire and told her how much they had missed her. The women would glance slyly at him, waiting for an introduction, but there was no hint of flirtation in his manner. As he had before, he made it perfectly clear that he was with Claire and had no intention of straying from her side.

Virginia came up, all smiles and dripping sweetness. "Rumors about you two are all over town," she cooed. "Why, I hear you're practically *living* together! I'm so proud that you met at my party!"

Claire's smile went brittle, and Max stepped forward, his hand touching her arm. He pinned Virginia with a narrowed, deadly look that made her smile fade, and a waiting silence descended over the guests nearest them. "Rumors have a way of turning on those who repeat them," he said in a tone laced with contempt. He was furious, and he had no compunction about letting others see it. "Especially jealous bitches who lack both breeding and manners."

Virginia went pale, then beet red. Leigh, sensing a budding scandal, came up to hook her arms through both Max's and Claire's. "There's someone you just have to meet," she chattered gaily as she led them away. Her quick action defused the situation, and the party resumed its normal buzz of conversation. After dutifully introducing them to someone, she darted away to make certain Virginia wasn't seated close to them at the table.

Except for that one scene, it was an enjoyable dinner. Claire found that she wasn't as upset as she would have expected. She was with Max, and that was the most important thing. When she remembered how difficult she had found dinners like this when she was married to Jeff, she wondered at the difference. She had proved to herself that she was capable of managing her own life, and somehow it no longer seemed so important if she accidentally picked up the wrong fork.

The woman on Max's other side leaned across to get Claire's attention. "Do you still play tennis? We miss you at the club, you know."

"I haven't played in years. I was never any good at it, anyway. I didn't keep my mind on the game."

"Dreaming?" Max teased.

"Exactly. My mind wanders," she admitted, laughing at herself.

"I concentrate as hard as I can, and I'm still not any good," the other woman admitted with a chuckle. Claire couldn't remember her name but had often seen her at the country club where the Halseys had belonged. The woman sipped her wine then set the glass down, but it caught the edge of her bread plate and toppled over, sending her wine splashing over Max's white jacket.

The woman blushed crimson. "Oh, Lord, I'm so sorry. Now you see why I'm not any good at tennis. I'm too clumsy!" She grabbed her napkin and began trying to blot the wine from his jacket.

"It's only a jacket," he soothed, his face calm. "And you're drinking white wine, so it won't stain. Please, don't let it upset you."

"But it's all over you!"

He took the woman's hand and kissed it. "It isn't important. Claire and I will stop by my apartment on the way to the hotel and I'll change."

His manner was so unruffled that it reassured the woman, and the meal continued without further mishap. When dinner was finished, he quietly made his excuses to Leigh, and he and Claire left.

"I always had a horror of spilling my wine on someone," she mused in the car. "It never happened, but I was always terrified that it would."

He was philosophical about it, and there was a slight smile on his lips. "I poured my wine in a lady's lap on one occasion. Her dress became transparent when wet, so it was truly memorable. Then, too, I've dandled my nieces and nephews when they were babies, and everyone knows what complete barbarians babies are, no shame or manners at all, so in comparison wine is definitely preferable."

At his apartment, he went into the bedroom to change while Claire checked her appearance in the gilded mirror in the foyer, reapplying her lipstick and tucking a strand of hair away from her face. Max took only a moment, reappearing in a stark black evening jacket that intensified his golden beauty. Looking at him, Claire caught her breath. Dressed all in black, except for the snowy expanse of his tucked dress shirt, he was overpoweringly male. His eyes drifted over her as she returned the tube of lipstick to her tiny evening bag. "We're a matched pair," he said.

Claire glanced down at her black gown as she preceded him to the door. "Yes, we are. Perhaps it was a happy accident at that."

He paused with his hand on the door handle, giving her another appreciative look. Releasing the handle, he turned to face her, tilting her chin up with his hand. His lips brushed lightly over hers. Then he lifted his head and their eyes met, hers wide and dark, his brilliant, narrowed. He kissed her again, molding her lips with gentle pressure. She responded, returning the kiss, standing quietly before him. As if he were cupping a fragile flower, he put both hands on her face, his thumbs meeting under her chin, and continued to kiss her with long, slow, leisurely kisses, their tongues meeting in play. His taste filled her mouth, and with a sigh of pleasure Claire put her hands on his shoulders.

He murmured something unintelligible, moving his hands from her face and putting his arm around her to pull her closer. With that utter assurance of his, he put his free hand on her breast, the warmth of his fingers heating her through the velvet of her gown.

She trembled, and shivery desire began to grow inside her. Lifting herself up on her toes, she pressed against him, needing to feel his hard body and the strength of his arms enfolding her. Their mouths clung together, the contact hungry, his tongue thrusting into her mouth. His hand delved inside her bodice and cupped her naked breast, his thumb rubbing over the sensitive nipple and sending heated sparks racing along her nerves. She whimpered a little, unprepared for the sudden flood of passion that swept over her flesh. Her body arched against him, and she felt his hardness, and suddenly they both exploded with need, fierce and uncontrolled.

His mouth ground into hers, his lips hot and firm, his arms

straining her to him so tightly that she couldn't take a breath. Her senses spun wildly, overwhelmed by the sudden excess of pleasurable messages that were ricocheting along her nerves. She could feel his steely strength in the muscles of his shoulders, taut under her clenched fingers. He was boldly, obviously, aroused, his flesh pushing against her. An insidious weakness began to creep through her bones and muscles, and deep inside her there was heat and a burning, writhing need.

She hadn't expected this wild hunger in him, or in herself, and she was helpless to stop it. She hadn't been prepared for the intensity of his touch, or the way in which she was responding to him, as if her body had taken charge, and she could no longer control it. He moved his hands down to cup her buttocks and bring her against him in a movement so blatantly sexual that she couldn't stop the moan of pleasure that broke from her throat. She loved him, she wanted him, and nothing else mattered.

"Claire," he muttered, his breath rasping as it left his chest. The thin strap had drooped off her right shoulder, letting her bodice slip, and he brushed the strap completely down until her breast was exposed. He stared down at her naked flesh, and she felt seared by his gaze. His face was hard, taut, like that of a man on the verge of agony. She was a doll in his grasp, completely helpless against his strength, as he bent her back over his arm and arched her breast up for his mouth. He wasn't gentle now; his mouth closed hotly over her nipple, suckling at her and making her cry out.

His hand was under her skirt, smoothing over her thighs, her bottom, between her legs. A thin, wordless cry broke from her lips, but it wasn't a cry of protest. She was beyond protesting. His touch intensified the torrent of sensation inside her. She felt afire, literally molten with need, and he was wild with the need to get at her. His hard fingers closed on her panties and garter belt and jerked them down with one movement, tugging them off. Then she felt the hard edge of the table behind her, and he lifted her onto it. His hand was there now, touching her intimately, stroking and rubbing and probing, doing things to her that pushed her intolerably close to the edge. She cried out again, clutching at him, so empty and aching that she couldn't stand it any longer and tears seeped out from under tightly closed lids.

"Claire," he said again, his voice no longer recognizable. It was rough, raspy, and as her name left his lips, he was tearing at his clothing. In a fever, he pushed her skirt to her waist then spread her legs and put himself between them. For a frozen moment in time she felt the shock of his naked flesh against her, then he drove into her, and her body jolted from the impact. She ceased to exist as a person; she was only heat and need, her bare legs wrapped around his waist, her arms around his shoulders, crying out and twisting to meet his thrusts. He caught her mouth with his, and her breathing stopped, taken away by his wildfire. The pressure and aching need were building inside her, and it was more than she could stand. It was going to kill her, shatter her into a thousand tiny pieces.

"Max, stop," she moaned, tearing her mouth from his. "I can't…I can't bear it."

His teeth clenched, and an animal sound rose from his throat. "I—can't stop. Not now, not now—"

The need exploded, and she did shatter, her body heaving in his arms. He held her and surged into her and met his own shattering, blind with the unbridled fury of what had just happened between them. Claire was limp in his arms, drooping against him, her head on his shoulder. He let his own head drop, resting on the curve of her neck and shoulder, her sweet, female scent rising to his nostrils as he gulped in air. Her skin was fevered, and he felt the way she was shaking, like a leaf in a storm.

It was a long time before either of them could move, could gather enough strength to do anything except cling to each other for support. Then she began to move, trying feebly to free herself from him, to pull her bodice up and cover her naked breast. She kept her head down, her face averted, unable to face him. She couldn't believe that she had acted like an animal in heat, moaning and writhing against him, out of control and lost to every thought except the need to satisfy her body.

"Stop it!" he ordered in a fierce whisper, finally stepping back from her, but instead of being freed she found herself swept into his arms, held high against his chest. He carried her swiftly through the darkened apartment and into the bedroom, with only the small light from the foyer to show him the way. Without bothering to turn on a light even then, he laid her on the bed and stood over her as he tore out of his clothes, popping buttons from his shirt in his haste to get out of it. He was naked before she could control her quaking limbs enough to get off the bed, and by then it was too late. He bent to pull the gown off her, leaving her bare on the satin comforter. The satin was cool on her overheated skin. Then he was on her, and in her, and she was no longer aware of the coolness beneath her. He was slower this time, the urgency gone, his body moving against her with long, slow movements that rubbed his hair-covered chest against her breasts, and she began to move with him.

She hadn't realized that such a degree of sensuality even existed, but he revealed to her a new side of her nature, the potential of her woman's body for pleasure. And he reveled in her, holding her and kissing her endlessly, taking her to the peak of pleasure, letting her rest then doing it again before it all became too much for him, and he began surging wildly as he reached for his own sweet madness.

She lay in his arms, and he smoothed the sweat-dampened hair back from her face. He took small kisses from her lips, her cheek, her temple. "I've been going half-crazy, wanting you," he muttered rawly. "I know this was too fast, that you weren't ready for it, but I don't regret it. You're mine. Don't try to run away from me, love. Stay with me tonight."

She was incapable of running from him, her strength gone, her legs like water, and at the moment she couldn't think of why she should want to run. He pulled the comforter back and put her between the sheets, resting her head on the pillow. He lay beside her, his body warm and hard, his arm draped over her waist, and exhaustion claimed them. Claire went to sleep right away, sinking into the enveloping blackness and welcoming it. She didn't want to think, didn't want to dream. She just wanted to sleep....

She woke in the darkened room and lay staring through the darkness at the blank ceiling. Max still slept beside her, his breathing deep and easy, his strong body relaxed. Until that night she hadn't realized just how strong he was, but now her body ached in ways that testified to his strength. For all his sophistication and cosmopolitan manners, he made love savagely, as if civilization hadn't touched him. Perhaps his smooth urbanity was only a veneer, and the real man was the one who had taken her with primitive urgency.

And perhaps she wasn't the woman she had always thought herself to be. If he had been wild, so had she. If he had been hungry, so had she.

He had asked her to stay, but she didn't know if she could face him in the morning. Every instinct in her wanted to find a place that was quiet and private, where she could come to terms with this new part of herself. A lifetime of reserve hadn't prepared her for the wildness that had surged within her. It frightened her that he had such power over her. She hadn't known that this could be a part of love.

Moving slowly, her body protesting, she slid out of the bed and groped around on the floor until she found the crumpled velvet heap of her gown. At the door she paused, looking back at his barely visible form on the bed, but he still slept deeply. Tears welled in her eyes; was it wrong to leave him now? What would happen if she woke beside him in the morning light, without the shield of darkness to protect her from the possibility that he might see too much? She wanted to creep back to his side and curl up in his arms, but she turned away.

"Come back here."

His voice was low, rough with sleep. She stood there with her back to him. "It's better that I leave now," she whispered.

"No, I won't let you." She heard the rustle of the bed as he left it; then he was behind her, his naked body hot against her back. His arms circled her waist, and the gown slipped from her fingers to the floor.

"Have I frightened you?" he asked, his mouth against her neck. "Is it because I hurt you?"

Her head moved slowly from side to side in denial. "You didn't hurt me," she said.

"I was on you like a rutting bull, love, and you're so soft." His lips moved to her shoulder and found the tender hollow there. His hot breath wafted over her skin like a caress, and she felt her breasts tighten in automatic response. "So delicate. Your skin is like silk." His hands were on her breasts now, and her head dropped back against his shoulder, her eyes closing as delight spiraled in her again.

"Come back to bed," he urged softly. "I know you're uneasy, but everything will be all right. I promise. We'll talk in the morning." Sometime during the next day he would tell her who he really was, and he was glad that this night had happened. It bound her to him, gave him an advantage in handling her. She would be angry, of course, but he didn't think it would be anything he couldn't handle.

She went to him, allowing herself to believe that it really would be all right. And a small while later, lying beneath him with the now-familiar fire burning inside her, she forgot why she had ever been uneasy.

The shrill ringing of the telephone woke her. Beside her, Max uttered an obscenity and sat up in the bed, reaching for the receiver to halt the intrusive noise. Bright sunlight filled the room, and she pulled the sheet higher under her chin then closed her eyes again. She didn't feel quite ready to face the morning yet, and she wished the phone hadn't rung.

"It's too bloody early in the morning to be funny," Max snarled into the receiver, running his fingers through his tousled hair. He listened a moment then said, "I don't give a damn what time it is, whenever I've just woke, it's too early. What is it?"

When he hung up the phone a few minutes later, he cursed under his breath before rolling over to look at her. Claire opened her eyes and stared at him, uncertainty plain on her face.

"I have to go to Dallas," he said, putting out his hand to finger her hair. "This morning."

She swallowed and tried for a casual tone. "It must be urgent—this is Sunday."

"It is. Bloody hell, what timing! I wanted to spend the day with you. We badly need to talk about what's happening between us, and there are some other things I wanted to tell you, but now they'll have to wait."

"It can wait," she whispered.

Chapter 7

But could it? After hurriedly taking her home, Max had left, and Claire hadn't heard from him since. She hadn't really been surprised when Sunday passed without a call; his business in Dallas must have been urgent to require him on a Sunday, but she had expected to hear from him on Monday. In such a short length of time he had insinuated himself so deeply into her life and her heart that now things didn't feel right without him. She hurried home after work on Monday, afraid that she might miss his call, but her telephone sat in silence, and the longer the silence stretched, the more she became convinced that something was wrong. She didn't know what it might be, but there was a sense of unease growing inside her. What was it that he had wanted to talk about? She knew it had to be important; his expression had been too serious, even a little grim. But it had all gone unsaid, and it shouldn't have—whatever it was, that had been the time for it, and now that time had passed.

She slept badly, too worried to rest, her awakened body reminding her of the pleasure he had given her, the things he had taught her. It was amazing that she had been married to Jeff for years without learning that she could go mad with desire, that a man's touch could turn her into pure molten need. No, not just a man. One man. Max.

Why didn't he call?

Lack of sleep left shadows under her eyes the next day, and when she looked in the mirror, the sense of impending doom intensified. She stared at the fathomless dark pools of her eyes, trying to see beyond them into the woman she was, deep into herself where she sensed these things without really knowing what they were. Had he found her lacking somehow? Had she been clumsy? Had he been appalled to find that she was just like all the others, easy to bed and easy to forget? Had he done just that, forgotten her?

But he had been wild to have her, so wild that he hadn't even taken her to the bedroom, hadn't even removed their clothing. A hot blush colored her cheeks at the memory. In the foyer, of all places, like savages in evening clothes. Her reserve had been shattered, his control destroyed, and they had merged together with primitive force. It had to mean something to him.

But he was so sophisticated, while in many ways she was not. Had that night been normal for him? Was it nothing to him but more of the same?

There were no answers in the mirror.

It was after lunch when the call came at work, and Sam spent a long time in his office. When he came out, he was pale.

"I've just been notified of a takeover attempt," he said quietly.

Claire looked up at him, waiting.

"It's Spencer-Nyle, in Dallas."

It was an enormous corporation, spreading out into diverse

fields, and the chairman of the board was legendary for his crafty moves. Sam and Claire looked at each other, knowing that it was really only a matter of time. Had the takeover attempt been by anyone closer to Bronson Alloys in size, they would have had a good chance to fight, but Spencer-Nyle could swallow them whole and never even strain. Sam might win the first round, because of the real estate values, but the war would go to Spencer-Nyle.

"They can't be foreign-backed," Claire said, shocked and puzzled.

"No. It seems we were being threatened on two fronts, but I didn't see it. I was too worried about keeping my research secure."

"When will they make their offer?"

"That's up to them, but I'd better use however much time we have left to strengthen our position."

"Can we possibly win?"

"Anything is possible." He grinned suddenly. "If we put up such a fight that the takeover would be more trouble than we're worth, they might pull out of it."

"Or you could find a white knight."

"White knight or hostile takeover, the end result would be the same—the company would belong to someone else. I suppose I could give in gracefully, but hell, I've always liked a good fight. Let Anson Edwards and his team of hatchetmen work to get us."

Now that the moment was actually there, Sam seemed to relish the thought of a fight. Claire wondered a moment at his mentality—he actually enjoyed conflict. But there were people who thrived on challenge; Martine was one of them. Put a mountain in front of her and she climbed it, it was as simple as that. Claire preferred to go around it. She approached a challenge head-on only when the other paths were blocked.

There was a lot to be done. The board of directors had to be notified, and proper action had to be discussed. Until a firm offer was received, they had little to go on. As the principal stockholder and chairman of the board, Sam's opinion carried a lot of weight, but he was still answerable to the board.

The phone rang off the hook. Claire worked late and was even grateful that the pressure kept her mind off Max, at least a little. She was almost afraid to go home, afraid that he wouldn't call and she would have to spend another night with that silent telephone. At least this way she didn't know.

But eventually she had had to go home, so she put on some music to fill the apartment with noise. Odd, but the silence had never bothered her before; she had welcomed it, enjoying the peace and solitude after the hectic pace of her job. Max had changed that, had turned her interests outward, and now the silence grated on her nerves. The music abolished the quiet outside but couldn't touch the stillness inside.

He wasn't going to call. She knew it, sensed it.

Had she been only the last warm body in a long line of warm bodies in his bed? Was that all she had been to him, a challenge, so that once she capitulated the challenge was gone? She didn't want to think that; she wanted to trust Max completely, but more and more she remembered those tiny jarring moments when she had seen the hardness beneath his perfect manners, as if the cosmopolitan gentleman were only a veneer. If that were so, then the image he projected was just that, an image, and she didn't really know him at all. Several times she had thought that, but now she was terrified that it was true.

Max brooded in his office, wishing that he could call Claire, but things were in motion now, and it would be in the best interests of both sides if he had no more contact with her until the takeover was settled. To see her now would put her in an awkward position, possibly subject her to undeserved hostility. Damn Anson for calling him back so soon, before he had a chance to talk to her and explain things! He wasn't worried about making her see reason; he was very experienced, and he knew the power of the weapon he had over her, the power of sensuality. Beneath that aloof, ladylike exterior was a woman who burned for his touch, whose own sensuality exploded out of control during his lovemaking. No, he could handle Claire's anger. What worried him was the pain and confusion she must be feeling because he had seemingly walked out of her life after that unbelievable night they had shared. He didn't want anything or anyone to hurt her, but he was very much afraid that he had, and that thought caused a tightening in his chest. Damn this bloody takeover to hell and back! It wasn't worth hurting Claire.

The senior vice president, Rome Matthews, entered his office. It was late and they were both in their shirt-sleeves, and they were friends as well, so Rome didn't bother with the formality of knocking.

"You've been glaring at that file for the past hour," Rome commented. "Is something bothering you about Bronson's?"

"No. We won't have any trouble," Max said, assured on that point, at least.

"You've been edgy since you got back from Houston."

Max leaned back in his chair and hooked his hands behind his head. "Isn't Sarah waiting for you?"

Rome's black eyes glittered the way they did when he was on to something, and he had the determination of a bulldog. Sprawling his big frame in an office chair, he watched Max through narrowed eyes. "Well, I'll be damned," he drawled. "You're acting just like I did when Sarah used to drive me crazy. God, I love it! It's poetic justice. You, my friend, have woman trouble!"

Max scowled at him. "Funny, is it?"

"Hilarious," Rome agreed, a wolfish grin lighting his hard, dark face. "I should've guessed sooner. Hell, you were in Houston a week. Something would have been seriously wrong if you *hadn't* found a woman."

"You have a perverted sense of humor," Max said without heat, but also without smiling.

"Who is she?"

"Claire Westbrook."

Because Rome had studied the file on Bronson Alloys, he knew the name and knew her connection with the company. He also knew that the vital information needed for the takeover to be successful had come from her. One brow lifted. "Does she know who you are?"

"No," Max growled, and Rome gave a soundless whistle.

"You're in trouble."

"Damn it, I know that!" Max got to his feet and paced the expanse of his office, shoving his fingers through his hair. "I can handle that, but I'm worried about her. I don't want her hurt by this."

"Then call her."

Max shook his head. A call wouldn't work, he knew that. He had to be where he could hold her, soothe her with his touch, reassure her that what was between them was real.

"You're going to be back in Houston in a couple of days. Anson is really pushing this. She'll have to know then who you are."

"I intend to tell her before anyone else knows." Frowning, he stared out the darkened window at the myriad lights and angles of the Dallas skyline. He wanted to be with Claire now, lying in bed with her and stroking the intoxicating softness of her skin. He wasn't sleeping well, wanting her, tortured by his aching loins. If he had had difficulty getting her out of his mind before, it was damned impossible now.

Claire tried to eat the sandwich she had brought for lunch, but it was tasteless, and after a few bites she rewrapped it in cellophane wrap and tossed it into the garbage can. She hadn't had much appetite, anyway. The office was empty. Sam was at lunch, as was almost everyone else. It was Friday, almost a week since she had seen Max or heard from him. A small eternity. She had stopped expecting the call, but something inside her was still marking time. Two days. Three. Four. Soon, a week. Eventually it would be a month, and perhaps someday the pain would be a little duller.

The most important thing was to keep her time filled, to stay busy. She began typing a stack of letters. Correspondence had doubled this week in direct relation to the notification Spencer-Nyle had given that it was interested in Bronson Alloys. It really couldn't have happened at a better time, she told herself—it left her less time to brood.

It was amazing how happy Sam seemed to be. He was preparing for this like a football coach preparing his team for the annual game against an arch rival, with almost unconcerned enthusiasm. He was actually enjoying it! The stockholders were coming out pretty well, too. The price of the stock had shot up as soon as the news got out.

Sam had been doing some research into Spencer-Nyle in general, and Anson Edwards in particular, and had come up with an impressive array of articles on the man. His desk was littered with them when Claire carried the letters in to leave them for his signature. A business magazine lay open on his desk, folded to an article on Spencer-Nyle, and Claire curiously picked it up. A color picture of Anson Edwards was on the first page. He didn't look like a corporate shark, she thought. He was trim and nondescript, with no outstanding features, the sort of man who blended into a crowd, except for the sharp intelligence obvious in his eyes.

The article was surprisingly interesting and went into some depth. She carried the magazine back to her desk to finish reading it. Then she turned the page, and Max's face stared up at her.

She blinked, stunned, and tears blurred her eyes. She closed her eyes, willing the tears away. Just a picture of him stirred up a whirlwind of pain and memories and aching love. If only she knew what had happened!

Opening her eyes, she looked at the picture again. There was another picture beside it of a dark man with penetrating dark eyes, and beneath both photos was the caption: "Roman Matthews, left, and Maxwell Conroy, are Anson Edward's hand-picked lieutenants, and corporate America generally considers Spencer-Nyle to have the nation's best team of executives."

They had his name wrong. He was Maxwell Benedict, not Maxwell Conroy. Her hands shook as she held the magazine, her eyes skimming to find the text concerning him. There it was. She read it then reread it, and finally the truth sank in. He was Maxwell Conroy, not Benedict at all, and he had romanced her so intensely in hopes of getting information about Bronson Alloys from her. Perhaps he'd even planned to snoop in her papers, but that hadn't been necessary. She had *given* him the information he needed. She had a vivid memory of herself talking to him, trusting him, never dreaming that he was a spy for another corporation! After he had what he wanted, he had left. It was that simple, and that terrible.

Slowly, painstakingly, Claire reread the entire article, some tiny part of herself hoping against hope that she had misunder-stood, but the second reading was even worse, because the details she had skipped the first time only supported the facts. Maxwell Conroy was an Englishman who had emigrated first to Canada, where he had been employed at a branch of Spencer-Nyle and had swiftly climbed the corporate ladder. He had been transferred to the Dallas headquarters four years ago, gained American citizenship, and was acquiring a reputation for engineering lightning-fast takeovers, moving in and taking control before the target company could be warned and devise any sort of defense.

She felt numb all over, as if paralyzed. Even her face was still, and it was an effort to blink her eyes, to swallow. Lightning-fast takeovers. He moved in; he took control; he walked away. Yes, he had done exactly that. She hadn't had a chance. He had played her like the expert he was, reeling her in so gently that she hadn't even realized she'd been hooked. She thought of her gullibility in swallowing that line he'd fed her, about how tired he was of being pursued as a sexual object, how he just wanted a friend. She had actually believed it! How had he kept from laughing in her face?

She couldn't have been much of a challenge to him, she thought, cringing inside at how stupid she'd been. She had fallen in love with him almost immediately and fell into bed with him the first time he'd made the effort. He hadn't had to make love to her, she thought painfully. She had already told him about the land reappraisal. That must have been the icing on his cake, to see how easily he could topple her into bed.

Her eyes were dry, burning, and her throat hurt. She realized that she was breathing in quick, hard rasps, and a hard chill shook her. Betrayal burned like acid inside her.

The magazine had slipped from her cold, numb fingers, and she sat there in numb shock. That was how Sam found her when he came back from lunch.

Her face was white and still, and she didn't seem to see

him, even though she was looking straight at him as he came in the door. Sam frowned, walking toward her. "Claire?"

She didn't answer, and he squatted down in front of her, lifting her hand in his and chafing her cold fingers. "Claire, what's wrong? Has something happened?"

Her lips barely moved, and her dark eyes were black as she stared at him. "Sam, I've betrayed you."

Slowly, like someone who was old and feeble, she leaned down and picked up the magazine. With great care she leafed through it until she came to the article on Spencer-Nyle and folded the pages back to Max's photograph. "I've been seeing him," she whispered, pointing to him. "But he told me his name was Max Benedict, not Max Conroy, and he…he knows about the property."

Sam took the magazine from her, his face set, and Claire wondered if he hated her. He should; he'd probably fire her on the spot, and it was nothing less than what she deserved. She had cost him his company with her stupidity, her incredible, inexcusable stupidity.

"How did it happen?" he murmured.

She told him, sparing her pride nothing. Max had made a fool of her, and she had fallen for every word he'd said. Tears began to slide down her pale cheeks, but she didn't notice them. Sam reached out and held her hand, and when it was over he did something incredible. Gently he took her in his arms and held her head to his shoulder. His tenderness, when he should have hated her, when he should have railed at her, broke what little control she had left, and sobs began tearing from her throat. She cried for a long time, rocked in Sam's arms, and he stroked her hair and whispered soothing words to her until at last her body stopped shaking from the force of her crying, and she raised her wet, tear-swollen face from his shoulder.

"I'll get my things and leave," she whispered, wiping her face with the heel of her hand.

"Why?" Sam demanded calmly.

"Why?" she echoed, her voice cracking. "Sam, I've lost you your company! You can't possibly want me around now—I've proved that I can't be trusted."

"Well, now, that's where you're wrong," he said, taking his handkerchief out of his pocket and offering it to her. "It's true that the property was our ace in the hole, but it's also true that if Spencer-Nyle really wants us, we don't have a prayer. They're just too big, too powerful. The best I hoped to do was make them pay more than they'd wanted to. As for trusting you—" he shrugged "—I'd say you're the most trustworthy employee I have. You made a mistake, and I think you'd walk over live coals to keep from making another."

"I don't see how you can possibly forgive me, because I'll never forgive myself." She dried her eyes then knotted the handkerchief in her hands.

"You're only human. We all make mistakes, some of them more serious than others. Examine your mistake from another point of view. Will any jobs be lost because of what you told Conroy? Probably not. Spencer-Nyle will need our expertise; they won't run in a whole new set of employees. Did your mistake affect the outcome of the takeover attempt? I don't think so. I think they have us, one way or the other, and to tell you the truth, I almost feel relieved. The only thing that's changed is the timetable." A ghost of a smile touched his hard mouth, and his eyes took on a certain faraway look. "I wish that the mistakes I've made were no more serious than that."

"He used me," she whispered.

"That's his loss," Sam said. "He'll be back, Claire—this is his baby. He'll be here, negotiating, supervising the takeover.

You're going to have to see him, work with him. Can you handle that?"

Part of her said no, shrinking from the idea of seeing him again. How could she bear to look at him, knowing that he had used her, lied to her, betrayed her, and knowing deep inside that she still loved him, because love didn't die easily for her? But if she ran, where would she run to? She had to have a job, and running wouldn't change anything. She would still have to face herself in the mirror in the morning; she would still carry inside herself the knowledge that it had all been a lie.

She should have known better. How could she ever have been blind enough to really think a man like Max would be interested in her? He would want someone sleek and sophisticated and beautiful, someone who wore experience like a luxurious mink on smooth, suntanned shoulders. Her only attraction for him had been that she gave him an inside contact in Bronson Alloys.

But she had loved him and trusted him.

She had spent the past five years slowly and painfully rebuilding her life, her sense of worth and self-respect. If she ran now, it would all be for nothing; she would be a rabbit, hiding from herself. No, not again. Never again. She would *not* let Max Benedict—no, Max *Conroy*—destroy her.

"Yes, I can handle it," she told Sam.

"Good girl," he said, patting her shoulder.

She got through the day…and the night. The night was the worst. At least during the day she was distracted by the necessity of doing her job, but at night there was nothing, and she was alone with herself. She lay awake, as she had done every night since Max had left, trying to marshal her strength for the grueling days that lay ahead. She tried to plan the future, because she knew that, despite Sam's effort to cheer her up, there would be changes made at Bronson Alloys. Sam would almost certainly leave management entirely and devote himself to his research. That would suit him—he was happier in his laboratory, anyway. Where would that leave her? Would he need a secretary then, even taking for granted that he would want her if he did? Would the new CEO want her for a secretary? Would Spencer-Nyle allow her to work in any position where she would have access to sensitive information? After all, she had already proved herself untrustworthy! All a man had to do was pay attention to her and she would tell everything she knew! She thought bitterly that they would be justified in taking that position.

Alma called over the weekend, inviting Claire and Max to dinner. Claire accepted, but calmly told Alma that she hadn't seen Max lately. It was inevitable that then Martine would call, trying to find out what had happened.

"I tried to tell you and Mother that there wasn't anything serious between us," Claire pointed out. How true that was! But her voice was even, almost casual, and she was proud of herself.

"But he acted so...so wild about you. He hardly took his eyes off you. Did you have a fight or anything?"

"No, no fight. There was just nothing there." On his part, at least. It was just like Martine that she had hit on the crux of the entire situation: Max had been *acting*, and he was so good at it that he had fooled everyone.

Late Sunday night, just as she was finally dozing off to sleep, the telephone rang. Sleepily she propped herself on her elbow and reached for it, thinking it would be a wrong number. None of her family ever called that late, and Claire wasn't the type to think that every late-night call meant an emergency. "Hello," she sighed, pushing her tangled hair out of her face.

"Claire. Did I wake you, darling?"

She froze, horrified, that familiar deep voice with the crisp-edged accent making chills run down her body. She didn't think, she simply reacted, replacing the receiver in its cradle so gently that it didn't even click. A soft whimper rose in her throat. How dare he call her after what he'd done? Was he back in Houston? Sam had warned her that Max would be back, but she hadn't thought that he would have the arrogance to call her.

The ringing began again, and she reached out to turn on the lamp, staring at the telephone with pain and indecision etched on her face. She had to cope with him sometime, and perhaps it would be better to do it over the phone rather than in person. It was cowardly of her, but she had endured a lot of pain; she wasn't certain how much more she could take, and pride demanded that he not know how badly he'd hurt her. If she broke down in front of him, he would be able to see how horribly foolish she'd been.

"Hello," she said again, picking up the phone and making her voice brisk.

"The connection must have been bad," he said. "I know it's late, darling, but I need to see you. May I come over? We have to talk."

"Do we? I don't think so, Mr. Conroy."

"Damn it, Claire—" He stopped, realizing what she had called him. "You know," he said, his voice changing as tension edged into it.

"Yes, I know. By the way, the connection wasn't bad. I hung up on you. Goodbye, Mr. Conroy." She hung up again, as gently as before. Crashing the receiver down would be too mild to even begin to express the way she felt, so she didn't waste the effort. She turned off the lamp and made herself comfortable on her pillows again, but her former drowsiness was gone, and she lay awake, her eyes open and burning. The sound of his voice reverberated in her mind, so deep and smooth and so well remembered that it hadn't been necessary for him to identify himself. She had known who it was, from the first word he'd said. Had he really thought he could take up where he'd left off? Yes, probably so. She had been such a pushover for him the first time that he wouldn't have foreseen any difficulty in seducing her again.

Why did she still have to love him? It would be so much easier if she could hate him, but she couldn't. She was hurt and angry and betrayed—she had trusted him, only to have that trust thrown in her face. But she didn't hate him. There wasn't a night that she didn't cry for him, that her body didn't ache with an emptiness that wouldn't go away. Well, if she couldn't hate him, she could at least protect herself by never, never letting him get close enough to hurt her again.

In his apartment, Max cursed viciously and threw the telephone across the room in a rare fit of violence. The instrument jangled crazily then lay on its side with the receiver beside it. Damn it. *Damn it!* Somehow she'd found out who he really was and probably put the worst possible connotation on it. He'd intended to tell her that night rather than walk into the offices of Bronson Alloys the next day and hit her with it cold, but at least then he would have been with her, able to hold her and love her out of her anger. Now it would be hell getting through her door again. She'd probably slam it in his face.

The telephone began a raucous beeping to signal that it had been left off the hook, and he swore again, stalking over to pick it up and crash the receiver down on the button. This damned job had been nothing but trouble. It had brought Claire into his life, but it had also been between them from the start, and now he had to get the merger negotiations out of the way before he could approach her again. He sat down, frowning at the carpet. He missed her more than he'd ever missed anyone in his life.

She looked up from the computer when the office door opened, and her heart stopped. Max stood there, flanked by two men who carried bulging briefcases. His face was expressionless, his turquoise eyes guarded. There was no point in playing games, so he said bluntly, "I'd like to see Sam Bronson."

Claire didn't betray her feelings by even a flicker of emotion. "Yes, Mr. Conroy," she said neutrally, as if there were nothing unusual in his presence there, as if she had never lain naked in his arms and burned with desire. She got to her feet without another glance at him and knocked briefly on Sam's door, then entered and closed it behind her, leaving Max and his associates to wait. She came out after a moment. "Go in, please," she said, holding the door open for them.

His gaze lingered on her face for a fraction of a moment as he passed her, and there was something hard and threatening there, something that frightened her. She kept her face blank; he might have been a stranger to her. When the door closed behind them, she sat down at her desk again and clasped her shaking hands to still them. Seeing him had been like taking a knife in the chest, a sharp, brutal pain that almost doubled her over. Odd, but she'd forgotten how handsome he was, or perhaps that had been blanked out. The lean, chiseled planes of his face had stunned her anew, and underlying that was the memory of how he'd looked in the throes of passion, his hair damp with sweat, his eyes burning in his taut face. He'd braced himself above her, and the muscles in his torso had rippled with power—

Stop it! she ordered herself, biting down on her lip hard enough to bring blood. Wincing, she grabbed a tissue and blotted the tiny drop of blood away. She couldn't let herself keep thinking about him. There was no point in it, no use in tormenting herself with memories of that one night. She had a job to do, and if she concentrated on it she just might get through the day.

But the day was a nightmare. She was called in to take notes, and it was almost more than she could bear to sit so close to Max, feeling his eyes on her as she scribbled page after page. Sam was a hard-nosed negotiator, and he was determined to win everything he could. An emergency meeting of the board of directors was called, and the office hummed with activity.

Finally they went out for lunch. As soon as the office was empty, Claire collapsed into her chair, her eyes closed in relief. She hadn't known how hard it would be to see him again. He hadn't said a personal word to her, but she had been vividly, painfully aware of him.

She heard a sound at the door and hastily opened her eyes. Max stood there with his hand on the knob. "Get your bag and come with us," he said curtly. "You haven't had lunch, either."

"I brought my lunch, Mr. Conroy, but thank you for the invitation." She kept her voice even as she uttered the careful courtesy, her face a blank wall that hid her thoughts. His mouth tightened, and she knew that her answer had angered him. Without another word he turned and left the office.

It was a lie that she had brought her lunch. She put on a pot of fresh coffee and ate a pack of crackers that she found in her desk, telling herself that she had to start eating better. She wasn't going to let herself lapse into a decline like some Victorian maiden. She was going to get through this somehow.

Her first instinct was to quit her job and get as far away from Max as she could. She wanted to be safe; she wanted to get her emotions back on an even keel and forget about him, if that were possible. She even typed up a letter of resignation, but when she reread it, she knew that she couldn't do that and deleted it. She wasn't going to let this take command of her life. She was going to continue just as she always had. She would get on with the everyday business of living. She wasn't going to run. Running and hiding was a childish reaction. It wouldn't be easy, facing Max and doing her job without letting him see how he affected her, but she really had no choice if she wanted to face herself in the mirror every morning.

She had changed a lot in the past few years, changes that hadn't been easily attained. She was more self-confident now. She would never be as bold and eager for new experiences as Martine, but she had found a quiet inner strength that she'd learned to trust. No matter what it took, or how painful it was, she was going to do her job and ignore Max Conroy as best she could.

They came back from lunch, and the negotiations resumed. Max somehow maneuvered things so that he was sitting next to her while she took notes, forcing her to concentrate on getting the notes right and not letting him know how his nearness affected her. Whenever she glanced at him, she would find his eyes on her, narrowed and intent, and she knew that he wasn't going to let the subject of their relationship drop gracefully. She stopped looking at him even when he spoke. That was the only way she could keep her composure—to pretend that he didn't exist.

Max watched her, trying to read her expression, but her quiet face was a total blank. If she had been aloof before, she was totally unreachable now, and her distance from him made him furious. She was ignoring him, and that was the one thing he didn't intend to allow. He was hampered now by the job at hand, but it wouldn't last forever. When it was finished, he was going to smash down those damned defenses of hers and never let her build them again.

Chapter 8

It took two long weeks for the negotiations to be hammered out. It was a hard fact for Spencer-Nyle to accept, but Sam Bronson still had a card they couldn't trump: himself. He was, in effect, the most valuable asset of Bronson Alloys. It was his genius, his instinct, his research, that produced the alloys. They were trying to buy the man as much as the company, and Sam knew it, they knew it, and they knew he knew it. To keep the man, they had to keep him happy, and keeping him happy meant making concessions. The job security of his employees was guaranteed; no one would be brushed aside in the usual house cleaning that came with a takeover. Benefits were sharply increased and raises were given, and even though the overall structure of the company would be changed, the employees would be happy because they would be very well taken care of.

Yet in the end Max still managed to work out an agreement that cost Spencer-Nyle less than what Anson had feared. He did it with cool, relentless negotiating, not giving in on anything he thought was excessive, and inch by inch working Bronson into a position they both found acceptable. He had to give Bronson credit—the man was as tough as nails, fighting as hard as he could for his company, even though the end had been inevitable from the first.

And Claire was there every day, calmly taking notes, her very presence controlling the tempers that threatened to flare. There was something about her cameo-smooth features and velvety dark eyes that made people control their anger and their language. Max watched her closely without appearing to, so hungry for just the sight of her that he couldn't stop himself. He hadn't tried to call her again. Not only would she probably accuse him of trying to get information from her, but he preferred to wait until he could devote himself completely to making her see reason. Time would work in his favor to blunt the edge of her anger. He watched her closely, incessantly, trying to read the thoughts behind that smooth blank face. She had to be furious with him, but there was no hint of it in her speech or actions. She was as remotely polite with him as she would be with a stranger, as if he meant nothing to her, as if they had never made love with frantic, explosive need. After a week Max decided that he would rather have her scream curses at him—anything—than treat him with that immense indifference. He could handle anger and tears; it was her mental distance that frustrated him to the point of madness.

Claire knew that Max watched her, though she never reacted to it in any way. The only way she could function was to push all her pain and sense of betrayal into a small part of her mind and lock them away. She didn't think about them; she didn't agonize over what might have been. She had survived the destruction of the life she'd built once before, and she was determined to do it again. The end of every day marked a small victory for her: a day that she had gotten through without breaking down. She couldn't wallow in self-pity. She had to complete the task she'd set for herself, getting through the days one at a time. She couldn't guess how long the negotiations would continue, so she didn't try to make plans or look forward to the day when Max was gone. It could be days, or weeks, or even months, if he remained to oversee the changeover to Spencer-Nyle ownership.

Sam hadn't discussed Max with her, and he acted as if he had forgotten that she had been involved with him. In actuality, there was little chance for them to talk—it seemed there was never a spare minute, and someone was always in the office. Max and his associates were going over the books, which meant they were constantly underfoot, and Sam, like Claire, guarded his words.

The final meeting was long and exhausting, the boardroom filled with stale air and the stench of old coffee. Tempers were frayed and voices hoarse from hours of talking. Claire took notes until her fingers cramped, and her back felt as if it were breaking in two from sitting for so long. The odors in the closed room made her stomach roll threateningly, so she hadn't been able to eat lunch when sandwiches and fresh coffee were brought in. All she wanted was to escape into the fresh air and listen to the silence. Late in the afternoon a thunderstorm hammered the city, washing the streets with a deluge of rain. Sam, with an understanding glance at Claire's pale face, got up and opened the window to let in a gust of cool, fresh, rain-sweetened air. The heavy purple clouds had completely covered the sky, and the streetlights came on as premature dusk settled over the city. With the breaking of the storm there seemed to come a break in the negotiations; everyone was tired and sleepy, and the pounding of the rain against the windows had a soporific effect. Points that had

been crucial just that morning no longer seemed so important—what was important was reaching agreement, getting it
over with and going home.

At last it was done, and they wearily shrugged into their
coats, shaking hands and smiling. Claire gathered her notes
together, thinking of the chores she had to do before her day
was ended. Quietly she slipped from the boardroom and
walked to her office—she planned to type the final agreement
that night. She was exhausted, her body aching, but she
wanted to finish the documents while her notes were still
fresh. The contracts would be needed first thing in the
morning, so it was either do them immediately or come in to
work early. She elected not to put the chore off. It was much
more peaceful now than it would be tomorrow morning. The
building was empty, except for the weary men who had ne-
gotiated the details of the takeover. There would be no phone
calls, no interruptions, no series of small crises to handle. All
she had to do was finish her work and leave.

She had barely begun typing the documents when the
office door opened. She glanced up inquiringly, and an expressionless mask slipped over her face when she saw it was Max.
Without a word she went back to work.

He strolled with indolent grace to her desk and leaned his
arm on top of her computer terminal. A frown knitted his brow
as he saw what she was doing. "That doesn't have to be done
tonight," he said.

"I have to do it now, or come in early in the morning." She
kept her gaze on her work. Why didn't he go away? His
presence made her tense and started that dull ache in her heart
that she had briefly forgotten.

"Let it wait." It was a crisp command, and he reached
down to push the power button on to the terminal. The screen
went blank, wiping out everything she had put into the

machine. "You're exhausted, Claire, and you haven't had anything to eat today. I'm going to take you to dinner, then we're going to talk. You've put me off long enough."

She looked at him now, sitting back in her chair and raising cool eyes to his. "I can't think of anything we could talk about, Mr. Conroy. I don't have any more corporate secrets you'd be interested in."

Dark fury washed over his face. "Don't push me," he said in a voice like splintered ice. "I've let you hold me off for two weeks now, but that's at an end."

"Is it?" she asked indifferently and reached to turn on the terminal again. "Excuse me, I have work to do." She couldn't let herself respond to him, couldn't react to him in any way, or she would slide out of control. For the past two weeks she'd been holding on by a thread; it wouldn't take much to snap it.

Max turned the computer off again, punching the button with controlled violence. His eyes were blue-green fire, burning like lasers. "You're coming with me. Get your bag— and don't turn on this bloody damned machine again," he snarled as she reached for the button.

Claire stared straight ahead at the blank screen. "I'm not going anywhere with you."

His eyebrows lifted. "Do you want me to force you? You forget that you're an employee of Spencer-Nyle now."

"I've forgotten nothing, but my job doesn't require me to associate with you away from the office. I've gotten very particular of the company I keep." She faced him calmly, determined never to let him see the desolation inside her. Staring at him, she saw an entirely different man from the one she had thought she knew. He wasn't the epitome of a controlled, reserved, rather old-fashioned Englishman, after all. He was a fire behind mirrors that reflected the image he chose, a ruthless, determined man who let nothing stop him.

His facade was that of an even-tempered and sophisticated man of the world, civilized to his fingertips, but it was a lie. He was an elegant savage, a shark cutting through opalescent seas, dazzling people with his beautiful image before he attacked.

He was very still, his eyes glittering the way they did when something displeased him. His mouth was a grim white line. "I know you're angry, but you'll still listen to me if I have to carry you to my apartment and tie you to the bed."

"I'm not angry," Claire pointed out, and she wasn't. She hurt too much to be angry. She could feel a tiny trembling beginning deep inside her as her exhaustion grew, and she knew she couldn't handle this scene right now. "As you pointed out, I'm your employee now. If you don't want me to work tonight, I won't. But I won't go anywhere with you, either. Good night, Mr. Conroy." She reached for her bag and stood, and Max lashed out, catching her arm in a grip that bruised.

"Don't call me Mr. Conroy," he said evenly.

"Why? Is that an alias, too?"

"No, and neither is Benedict—that's my middle name."

"How appropriate. Benedict Arnold was a spy, too."

"Damn you, I didn't spy," he rasped. "There were no papers gone through, no conversations taped. You *gave* me that information without any urging on my part."

Her dark eyes didn't even flicker. "You sought me out at Virginia's party because you knew I worked here."

"That's not important! Yes, I deliberately introduced myself to you. It was possible that you had some helpful information about Bronson Alloys." He shook her lightly. "What does that matter?"

"It doesn't, not at all." She glanced down at his hands, and her voice was cold. "You're hurting me."

He released her, something shadowy moving in his eyes

as he watched her rub her upper arms. "That was business. It has nothing to do with us."

"How nice for you, to be able to put areas of your life in tidy little compartments and not let them touch! I'm not like that. I think that if a person is dishonorable in one thing, he will be in another."

"Don't be so damned unreasonable—"

"That was quite a blitzkrieg you put on," Claire interrupted, her voice rising as she felt her control slipping. Fiercely she groped to regain it. "Does Anson Edwards know what a prize he has in you? Has any woman ever resisted you when you turn on the heat? I fell for it completely, so you can give yourself a pat on the back. Poor man," she breathed, her eyes burning. "So handsome that women only treated you like a body without a soul, you were tired of meaningless sex and wanted someone to be a real friend. I must have the word 'fool' stamped on my forehead, because you knew just what line to feed me. You turned on the charm, forced yourself into my life and got the information you wanted, then waltzed out again. Fine. I was a fool once, but don't expect me to be a fool again! I'm not really stupid—I don't have to have my face rubbed in it!" Breathing hard, she turned away, rubbing her forehead with a trembling hand. Perhaps she was stupid, at that; she hadn't learned all that much from Jeff's betrayal. It had made her cautious, but not cautious enough. In the end she'd walked back into the vicious trap of loving a handsome, charming man who could have anyone he wanted and had dreamed the fool's dream that he might love her in return.

"I didn't 'waltz out'!" he yelled, glaring down at her. Max rarely lost his temper. It was seldom necessary; he usually got what he wanted without having to put out that much effort, simply by using his charm and sensuality. But his reactions to Claire had been extreme from the beginning, and the cold contempt in her eyes triggered something fierce inside him. "I was called back to Dallas. You should know. You were in bed with me when the call came!"

The little remaining color washed out of her face, and she gave him an uncontrolled look of such naked pain that he halted. "Claire…" he began, reaching out for her, but she recoiled from him so violently that she bumped into the edge of the desk and sent papers flying.

"How kind of you to remind me," she whispered. Her eyes were black in her paper-white face. "Get away from me."

"No. It was good between us—I want to have it again. I won't let you push me out of your life."

She was visibly shaking, and he wanted to put his hands on her to support her but didn't dare. All of a sudden her icy reserve had shattered before his eyes, leaving a woman who was almost staggering with pain. The realization struck him like a blow to the chest, taking his breath. She wasn't an aloof, controlled woman, a little unfeeling, a challenge to his male sexuality. She put a buffer between other people and herself in an effort at self-protection because she felt too much and was too easily and too deeply hurt by life. He hadn't understood her at all, casually counting on his sex appeal and charm to smooth things over as he'd always done, and so intent on getting her into bed that he'd overlooked all of the small signals she'd given him. God, what had he done to her? How deeply had he hurt her to put that look on her face?

"You don't have any choice about it," she said jerkily. "Do you really think I'd be stupid enough to trust you again? You lied to me, and you used me. It was all in a good cause, though, so that makes it all right in your eyes. The end justifies the means, right? Please, just leave me alone."

"No," he said harshly, feeling a sudden, intense twist of pain in his gut at the thought that he might have lost her forever. He couldn't accept that; he *wouldn't* accept that! For reasons he couldn't analyze, Claire had become increasingly precious to him, filling his thoughts during the day and his dreams at night. The night he'd spent with her had made him want more, a lot more.

"I'd say you're going to have to, at least for now," Sam interrupted from the doorway, his voice as cool as the look in his eyes. "Stop badgering her. She's worn out."

Max didn't move a muscle except to turn his head to look at Sam, but suddenly there was something wild about him, a fine tension in his lean, deceptively muscled body, his eyes icy and lethal. "This doesn't concern you," he said, and he was every inch the predatory, aggressive male, with the primitive instinct to fight whenever another male approached the woman he'd marked as his.

"I'd say it does. After all, it was my company that you took, using the information Claire gave you."

Max froze, then looked sharply at Claire. "He knows?"

Dumbly she nodded.

"Claire told me right away," Sam said, leaning against the door. "As soon as she realized who you were. Her sense of honor is too strong for corporate games. She wanted to quit right then, but I talked her out of it." At Max's lifted brow, he added, "I knew she'd never let herself make that mistake again."

Claire couldn't stay and listen to them talk about her. She felt exposed and raw, her deepest secrets laid out for the world to examine and chuckle over. A small sound of distress escaped her as she walked past Max, keeping her head averted.

"Claire!" He moved swiftly, catching her arm again and pulling her to a halt. Desperately she wrenched at her arm, trying to twist it from his grip, but he caught her other arm and held her still in front of him. Biting her lip, she stared fixedly at the knot of his tie and struggled for control. Why did he have to hold her so close? She could feel his warmth, smell the exciting male muskiness of his skin. His nearness reminded her of things she would have to forget in order to survive. Her body felt the touch that had driven her to such feverish heights of pleasure and reacted wildly, independent of her control. Her nipples hardened, wanting the touch of his hands, his mouth; her legs quivered, wanting to wrap about his hips, and the emptiness in her wanted to be filled.

"Let me go," she whispered.

"You're not in any shape to drive. You haven't eaten all day, and you look as if you might faint at any moment. I'll drive you home," he insisted.

"I wouldn't go with you to a dogfight," she said, using her last ounce of defiance. His grip slackened, and she pulled free, taking the chance to walk out of the office without him. It might be the only opportunity she had, and she was too upset to tolerate any more. Another minute and she would be weeping, completing her humiliation.

Her hurried steps carried her out of the building and to the parking lot. It was still raining lightly, but gusts of wind battered her, and flashes of lightning in the low-hanging purple clouds lit the darkness with momentary brilliance. The storm intensified the darkness, making the efforts of the street-lights seem ineffective. Her heels tapped sharply on the wet pavement as she ran to her car. She reached it and stopped to unlock it and only then heard the footsteps behind her. Cold terror washed down her spine, and tales of rape and robbery flooded her mind. Grasping her keys like a weapon, she whirled to face any assailants, but there was no one close to her. On the other side of the parking lot Max walked to his car and got in, and Claire sagged with relief.

Her hands were shaking as she opened the car door and slid behind the wheel, cautiously locking the door again. What if it had been a mugger or a rapist? How many articles had she read that warned women against going to their cars alone at night? She'd been foolish to let her emotions push her into a dangerous situation, and she drew a deep breath. She had to get control of herself.

She was still shaky, and the rain made the streetlights reflect dizzyingly on the wet streets. She drove with extra care, not wanting to risk an accident. She didn't notice the car behind her until she turned down the street to her apartment building and the other car turned, too. Nervously she peered into the rearview mirror, trying to tell what kind of car it was, but the headlights were right in her eyes, and she couldn't see anything. Was she so on edge tonight that she was becoming paranoid? Quickly she found a parking place and pulled into it, deciding to wait until the other car had gone on before she got out.

But the other car slowed and pulled into the empty parking space beside her. It was a black Mercedes, and the man driving it had golden hair that gleamed like a halo in the silvery artificial glow of the streetlight.

Still shaking, Claire leaned her head on the steering wheel. He was determined to talk to her, and she was beginning to realize that he didn't give up once he'd decided to do something. How had she ever thought him civilized? He was as ruthless as any Viking, and she feared him as well as loved him because he would destroy her if she didn't find a way to keep him at a distance, to protect herself with indifference.

He tapped on the window, and she jerked her head up.

"It's raining harder," Max said, his voice muffled through the glass. The rain beaded and ran down the windshield, emphasizing his words. "Let's go in, dear. You're going to get soaked if you wait much longer—I think a new storm is coming in."

She flinched at the endearment, amazed at how easily it

rolled off his tongue. How many other women had been fooled by his glib lies?

He wasn't going to give up and go away, and she was too tired to sit out in the car indefinitely. Gathering her wavering strength, she got out of the car and carefully locked the door, then hurried up the sidewalk without looking at him.

He stretched out his arm and opened the door for her and was right beside her in the elevator. Claire clutched her keyring, keeping it ready. Damn him, why wouldn't he give up? What did it matter to him, anyway?

Catching her wrist firmly, he relieved her of the keys and opened the door, stepping inside to turn on the lights and pulling her in with him. He released her wrist to close the door, and tossed her keys onto the small table that stood by the door, her catchall table that she had found in a flea market and refinished. Fixedly she stared at the table; it wasn't a Queen Anne, like the one in his foyer. She remembered the way he had lifted her onto that elegant Queen Anne table and moved between her thighs, and for a moment she thought she really might faint, after all. Her legs felt wobbly, and there was a faraway roar in her ears. She sucked in a deep breath, hoping the extra oxygen would steady her.

"Sit down," Max said roughly, propelling her toward the couch. "You look dead white. Are you pregnant?"

Stunned, she stared helplessly at him, sinking down onto the cushions as her legs folded beneath her. "What?" she gasped.

"You haven't eaten. You're pale. You've lost weight, you feel ill." He enumerated all the things that had been haunting him since that explanation had first blasted into his mind. "Did you think I wouldn't notice that Sam opened the window for you this afternoon? Why would you tell him and not me?"

"I haven't told him anything," she protested, thrown off balance by his line of questioning. "I'm not pregnant!"

"Are you certain? Have you had your period this month?"

For the first time that night color flooded her cheeks. "That isn't any of your business!"

His face was grim as he stood over her. "I think it is. I didn't protect you that night—*any time* that night—and I don't think you're on the pill. Are you?" Her expression was answer enough. "No, I didn't think so."

"I'm not pregnant," she repeated doggedly.

"I see. You're simply on a diet, is that it?"

"No. I'm exhausted. It's as simple as that."

"That's another symptom."

"I'm not pregnant!" she yelled, then buried her face in her hands, aghast at her loss of control.

"Are you certain?"

"Yes!"

"All right," he said with sudden calm. "I apologize for upsetting you, but I wanted to know. Now sit there while I get something for you to eat."

The last thing she wanted was something to eat. She wanted him to get out of her apartment so she could fall facedown on her bed and sleep. But she couldn't chase him out, because her legs were lead weights, and suddenly it wasn't worth the effort of getting up. She sat there staring blankly in front of her, wondering how she could have been so stupid as not to have considered the possibility of a pregnancy, but the truth was that it hadn't entered her thoughts at all. Nature had assured her that she wasn't pregnant, but she hadn't thought of it even then. It was a good thing, because she wasn't sure she could have borne the added stress. What if she had been pregnant? Would it have been all right this time? Would she have held her own baby in her arms? Max's baby, with golden hair and eyes like the sea. Suddenly pain shot through her, because it wasn't to be, and she wished it could have been.

She was so completely exhausted that to continue sitting upright was asking too much of her body. With a quiet little sigh she sank back against the cushions of the couch, her eyelashes sinking down as if pulled by a force she couldn't withstand. With the suddenness of a black curtain dropping down, she was asleep.

When Max came back into the living room with a tray loaded with a selection of sandwiches, a glass of milk for Claire and a cup of coffee for him, because he was hungry too, he was braced to receive all her hurt accusations, but he was also ready to stay there all night, if necessary, to explain his side of it and convince her that they had something special between them. Then he saw her curled against the cushions, one arm folded in her lap and the other hanging to the side in that limp way that indicated deep sleep. Her hand was lying palm upward, her fingers curled slightly, and he stared down at the peculiar, innocent vulnerability of her open palm, so soft and pink. Memory seared him. Sometime during the night they had spent together, during one of those frantic, greedy matings, he'd taken her hand and carried it down his body, and every muscle in him had jerked in reaction to her gentle fingers closing around him. He jerked now in reaction to the memory, his body growing hard and sweat popping out on his brow.

He swore soundlessly and set the tray down, bringing his surging appetite under iron control. Now wasn't the time to seduce her, assuming that he could even get her to wake up. He looked at the tray of food, then at Claire, sleeping so deeply. She needed both food and rest, but evidently her body had taken over and given sleep the highest priority. The kindest thing now would be to let her sleep, even though it meant postponing that talk once again.

Bending down, he gently slid his arms around her, one under her knees and the other around her back, and lifted her easily. Her head fell sideways against his shoulder, her gentle breath warming his flesh through his shirt, and he stood still for a moment with her clasped in his arms, his eyes almost closed as he drank in her nearness, the softness of her body in his arms and the faint, elusive sweetness of her skin. Until then he hadn't realized quite how much he'd missed her, but now the delicious agony of holding her again almost made him groan aloud. She fit into his arms in a way no other woman ever had. Max had held many soft, trembling bodies against him and beneath him, but now he couldn't recall any of the others. Only Claire. She made him feel oddly complete, and the thought disturbed him, because that meant he was incomplete without her.

He carried her into the bedroom and eased her down onto the bed. She was so soundly asleep that she didn't even murmur but lay exactly as he'd placed her. With the expertise of a man who had undressed many women, Max removed the short lightweight jacket she wore, then pulled her blouse free of the skirt. It was a thin silk blouse, and beneath it he could see the lacy edge of her camisole, reminding him of the marvelously sexy underwear she wore. Reminding him? He wiped his perspiring forehead. His problem was forgetting.

Reaching beneath her, he unbuttoned and unzipped her skirt then worked the garment down her legs. She wasn't wearing a camisole, but a full-length slip, all silk and lace. His hands began a fine trembling as he pulled off her shoes and set them aside. He didn't dare go any farther. Not only would she not appreciate being stripped naked, but he was suddenly afraid that his control would snap if he continued. He thought of the satin and lace garter belts she wore, and the filmy underpants, and his body flooded with heat. Bloody hell! He swore furiously, silently, forcing himself to his feet. Her penchant for sexy underwear was likely to give him a fetish.

With effortless strength he lifted her and turned the cover back, then placed her between the sheets. She looked so tired, he thought, pushing back a strand of hair from her temple. Her face was pale and strained, with dark shadows under her eyes, but it was a relief to know that it was only exhaustion instead of the strain of early pregnancy that had put those marks there. He had never before lost control like that, not only of his body, but of his mind. He had always made certain that his partner was protected and been more than willing to assume responsibility if she hadn't taken care of it herself. Then, and only then, would he unleash his sexuality, lose himself in the sensual pleasures of the flesh. But with Claire, he hadn't even thought of it. He had had only one thought, to penetrate, and had been blind to everything else. Even now he was stunned by the driving urgency he'd felt, the simple and powerful animal instinct to mate that had taken control. He didn't like the feeling. He'd always thought that the power of his mind could control the lusty appetites of his body. His icy, superlative intelligence had *always* been in control…until Claire had responded to him, and the restraints he'd been placing on himself had shattered under the violent surge of desire.

He hadn't even had the control, the consideration, to take her to bed. He had simply lifted her onto the table in the foyer, pushed her velvet skirt to her waist and thrust into her. She was such a delicate woman, as finely made as the finest porcelain, and he'd taken her with all the finesse of a conquering warrior. The only thing that kept him from being completely disgusted with himself was the memory of her response, the way she had clung to him, twisted against him, the little whimpers in her throat as she met his thrusts, the way she had cried out and the sweet inner clenching that had signaled her peak of satisfaction. Behind her distant manner was a capacity for passion that overwhelmed him and made him hunger for her. He wanted her all for himself.

Realizing that he was shaking with the need to take her again, he turned away from the bed while he still could. Where Claire was concerned, his self-control was almost negligible.

He went into the living room, wolfed down several of the sandwiches and drank the pot of coffee he'd made, not worrying about the effect of the caffeine on his system so late at night. A deep frown furrowed his brow as he considered the situation with Claire.

Until that night he hadn't doubted his ability to talk her around eventually. Never in his life had he been denied anything he really wanted. Nature had given him an enormous advantage in coupling his face and body with a superior intellect. But for the first time he wasn't certain that he would win. He had seen behind Claire's shield and, for the first time, seen the vulnerability of the real woman and realized the necessity for that shield. She felt too much, loved too deeply, gave herself too completely…and betrayal would strike a crippling blow at that too-tender heart.

Whatever happened, he had to make certain that she couldn't hide from him, and he knew her well enough to realize that would be her first form of defense. She would do whatever she could to put distance between them, mentally if not physically. Time was on her side. Soon he would have to return to Dallas, and they would be separated by more than two hundred miles. He would be traveling to other cities, putting even more distance between them. He considered his options, and a plan formed in his mind. The thing to do was to take her to Dallas with him—the problem was in getting her there.

He cleaned up after himself then went into the bedroom to check on her, to assure himself that she was really all right. She was still sleeping soundly, and a healthy pink color was beginning to return to her cheeks as she rested. Thoughtfully he looked at her alarm clock, then picked it up to make certain the alarm was turned off. Let her sleep as long as she needed. He wrote a short note and propped it on the clock, then let himself out of the apartment. He had plans to make, and it wasn't too late at night to set them in motion.

A faint grin relieved the grimness of his expression as he drove through the rainy Houston night. It wouldn't hurt Rome to be jarred out of a sound sleep by a telephone call. After all, it had been Rome's call three weeks before that had pulled Max out of the bed he'd been sharing with Claire. Fate had a way of evening things out.

Chapter 9

When Claire woke the next morning she felt rested for the first time in weeks, and she lay in drowsy relaxation, waiting for the alarm to go off. The minutes ticked by without the alarm, and finally she opened a curious eye to check the time. The first thing she noticed was that the room was very light for so early in the morning, and the second thing she noticed was that it was almost nine-thirty. "Oh, no!" She hated being late to anything, even by a few minutes, and she was more than a few minutes late. She should have been at work an hour-and-a-half ago!

She scrambled out of bed, still a little disoriented from sleeping so long, and stared down at herself in confusion. Why was she wearing a blouse and slip instead of a nightgown? Then memory flooded back, and her face heated. Max! She'd gone to sleep on the couch. Max must have put her to bed. At least he hadn't stripped her; she couldn't have borne that. It was bad enough that he'd handled her so easily while she'd been asleep, undressing her and putting her to bed as if he had every right to be so familiar with her. She would have preferred that he let her sleep on the couch.

But that explained why she had slept so late—he hadn't set her alarm. She looked at the clock then noticed the note beside it. She didn't even have to pick it up to read it; the handwriting was a series of bold slashes written with a strong hand. *Don't worry about being late. You need the rest. I'll handle it with Bronson—Max.*

She grabbed the note and crumpled it with a despairing cry. That was just what she needed, for him to "handle" it with Sam! What would he say? That he'd left her in bed, and she was so tired that he was going to let her sleep late? Sam would have to pull one of the other secretaries in to handle the office, and the reason why she was late would spread through the office like wildfire.

Her stomach rumbled, and she realized that she was both very hungry and very grungy from having slept in her clothes and makeup. She was already so late that she would gain nothing by hurrying to work. She decided to take her time. After a long shower, a shampoo and a leisurely breakfast, she would feel better. She wouldn't go to work looking thrown-together; she would be professional if it killed her.

It was almost noon when she walked into the office, but her stomach was pleasantly full, her hair washed and pulled back into an attractive chignon, and she wore her favorite dress, a navy-blue blouson with white piping. Her efforts to bolster her spirits had worked, or perhaps it was the extra sleep she'd had. For whatever reason, she felt almost calm. There was indeed another secretary at her desk, a young woman who had been with the company only a few months, and whose eyes widened with surprise when she saw Claire. "Miss Westbrook! Are you feeling better? Mr.

Bronson said you fainted last night and wouldn't be working today."

Bless Sam for covering for her! Claire said calmly, "I'm feeling much better, thank you. I was very tired, nothing else."

She relieved the young woman and sent her back to her own job. When she sat down at her desk, Claire felt more normal, as if things were settling back into their rightful place. Then the door to Sam's office opened, and someone stood there watching her. It wasn't Sam—she had never felt that tingle of awareness sweep over her from Sam's gaze. Without looking at Max, she gathered her notes on the documents that needed typing.

"Leave those," he ordered, coming to stand behind her. "I'm taking you to lunch."

"Thank you, but I'm not hungry. I've just had breakfast."

"Then you can watch me eat."

"Thank you, no," she repeated. "I have a lot to do—"

"This isn't personal," he interrupted. "It concerns your job."

Her hands stilled. Of course. Why hadn't she thought of that? Sam would no longer need a secretary, so she would no longer have a job. The guarantees that applied to the others could hardly be expected to apply to her. She raised shocked eyes to Max, trying to cope with the idea of being so abruptly unemployed. There were other jobs, of course. Houston was a boomtown, and she would find other work, but would she enjoy it so much and would it pay so well? Though her apartment wasn't an expensive one like Max's, it was nice and in a good section of town. If she had to take a large cut in pay, she wouldn't be able to afford it. For a terrible moment she saw herself losing not only her job but her home.

Max reached down and pulled her to her feet. His eyes were gleaming with the success he'd had in putting his plan into motion. "We'll go to Riley's. It isn't quite noon, so we should get a good table away from the crowd."

Claire was silent as they left the building and crossed the street. It was a hot spring, with the daytime temperatures already climbing into the low nineties, and though the sky was a deep, clear blue now, the forecast was for more thunderstorms in the afternoon. Even on the short walk to Riley's her navy-blue dress began to feel too warm. Worry ate at her. How much notice would she be given? Two weeks? A month? How long it would take to move Sam completely into research?

They just beat the lunch crowd at Riley's and got one of the secluded booths in the back. Claire ordered a glass of iced tea, earning a hard look from Max. "You might eat a little something—you've lost weight, and you had precious little to spare."

"I'm not hungry."

"So you said. The point is, you should eat even though you aren't hungry to gain back the weight you've lost."

Why did he keep harping about her weight? She had lost only a pound or two, and she had always bordered on thinness, anyway. She had other things to worry about. "Are you firing me?" she asked, keeping her expression blank.

His eyebrows lifted. "Why should I fire you?"

"I can think of several reasons. The most immediate is that my job is being phased out, since Sam won't need a secretary in research, and whoever takes over as CEO will probably bring his own." She met his gaze squarely, her dark eyes fathomless and a little strained, despite her efforts to keep all expression from them. "There's also the fact that this would be a good opportunity to get rid of a bad security risk."

Swift anger darkened his eyes. "You're not a bad security risk."

"I leaked confidential information. I trusted the wrong person, so I'm obviously a terrible judge of character."

"Damn it, I—" He interrupted himself, glaring at her from narrowed, brilliant eyes. "You aren't being fired," he finally continued in a clipped voice. "You're being transferred to Dallas, to Spencer-Nyle headquarters."

Stunned anew, she opened her mouth to say something then closed it when nothing came to mind. Transferred! "I can't go to Dallas!"

"Of course you can. It would be foolish of you to refuse this opportunity. You won't be executive secretary to the CEO, of course, but there will be a substantial increase in salary. Spencer-Nyle is much larger than Bronson Alloys and pays its employees well."

Panic edged into her eyes, her voice. "I won't work for you."

"You wouldn't be working for me," he snapped. "You'll be working for Spencer-Nyle."

"In what capacity? Shoved into a closet sorting paper clips, so I can never get my hands on any valuable information?"

He leaned over the table, rage turning his eyes dark green. "If you say another word about being a security risk, I'll take you over my knee wherever we happen to be, even if it's the middle of the street—or in a restaurant."

Claire sank back, warned by the look and the barely controlled ferocity in his face. How had she made the colossal mistake of thinking him civilized? He had the temperament of a rampaging savage.

"Now, if you're through with the sarcastic remarks, I'll give you your job description," he said icily.

"I haven't said I'll take the job."

"It would be foolish of you to turn it down. As you pointed out, your job at Bronson Alloys will no longer be there in a short while." He named a figure that was half again as much as she was currently making. "Can you afford to turn down that much money?"

"There are other jobs in Houston. My entire family is here. If I moved to Dallas, I'd have no one."

His jaw tightened, and his eyes went even darker. "You could visit on weekends," he said.

Claire sipped at her tea, not looking at him. It *would* be foolish to turn down that much money, even though it meant moving to Dallas, but her instinct was to turn it down, anyway. If she relocated to Spencer-Nyle's headquarters she would be in Max's territory, seeing him every day, and he would have authority over her. It wasn't a decision she could make immediately, even though logic said she should jump at it.

"I'll have to think about it," she said with the quiet stubbornness that her family had learned to recognize.

"Very well. You have until Monday."

"That's just three days, counting today!"

"If you decide not to take the job, another person will have to be found," he pointed out. "Your decision can't be very complicated—you have to relocate or join the unemployment lists. Until Monday."

She saw no sign of relenting in his eyes, even though three days seemed like no time at all to her. Claire didn't hurry toward change; she liked to do things gradually, becoming used to changes by slow increments. She had lived all of her life in or near Houston, and to move to another city was like asking her to change her entire life. Things were difficult enough now without being lost in a totally new environment.

Max's prime rib was served, and he devoted himself to it for a few minutes while Claire nursed her tea and turned the idea of moving over and over in her mind. At last she pushed it away. She couldn't decide now, and she had other things she wanted to ask him.

"What did you tell Sam?"

He looked up. "Concerning what?"

"Last night. The fill-in secretary said that Sam told her I'd fainted and wouldn't be working today."

"Embellishment on his part. When he asked me this morning what the hell I was doing following and harassing you last night, I told him to mind his own bloody damn business and that it was a good thing someone made certain you got home safely because you collapsed."

"I didn't collapse."

"Really? Do you remember when I undressed you?"

She looked away, her cheeks heating. "No."

"I didn't cheat. I don't take advantage of unconscious women. When I make love to you again, you'll damned well be awake."

She had noticed that the more irritated he was, the more crisp his accent became, and he was practically biting off his words now. "If I don't go to Dallas," she whispered, getting up from the booth, "it will be because of you, because I can't stand being near you." Then she walked off before he could say anything, fleeing back across the street to the relative safety of the office.

Max watched her go, his face stiff. He hadn't thought that she would reject the job offer, but now it seemed that she might, and he was afraid that if he lost track of her now he might lose her forever. Damn it, after all the strings he had pulled, she *had* to take the job!

Rome hadn't been pleased by the late phone call the night before. "Damn it, Max, this had better be good," he'd growled. "Jed is cutting teeth and raising hell about it, and we'd just gone to sleep after getting him settled."

"Kiss Sarah good-night for me," Max had said, amused by Rome's grouchiness.

Rome told him where he could go and how he could get there, and in the background Max had heard Sarah's laughter. "This is important," he'd finally said. "Is there a job opening in the office? Any job?"

They worked so well together that Rome hadn't wasted any

time asking unimportant questions, like for whom, and why. They trusted each other's instincts and plans. Rome had been silent for a moment, his steel-trap brain running through the possibilities. "Delgado in finance is being transferred to Honolulu."

"Good God, what strings did he pull to get that?"

"He understands money."

"All right, who's taking his place?"

"We've been talking about bringing Quinn Payton in from Seattle."

Max had been silent in his turn. "Why not Jean Sloss in R and D? She has a degree in business finance, and she's done a damned good job. I think she's executive material."

By that time Rome had seen a pattern in all this moving around. "Who do you suggest to replace Jean Sloss? I agree that she deserves a promotion, but she's good enough that replacing her won't be easy."

"Why not Kali? She'd love to work in R and D, and it would be a chance for her to eventually move into a managerial position. She knows the company."

"Damn it, she's *my* secretary!" Rome had roared. "Why don't you move your own secretary?"

Max had considered that, but didn't think Claire would take the job. On second thought, being Rome's secretary would be too close and make working difficult, too. "Forget Kali, then. Caulfield, the general office manager…what's his secretary's name? Her qualifications are good, and she's ambitious. Carolyn Watford, that's it."

"I'm taking all this down. We're not in the habit of playing musical offices. Who takes Carolyn Watford's place?"

"Claire Westbrook."

After a long pause of silence Rome had said, "I'll be damned," and Max had known he didn't have to make any further explanations.

"I'll see what I can do. It won't be easy, moving this many people around on such short notice. When can I let you know?"

"Sometime before lunch tomorrow," Max had said.

"Hell!" Rome had snorted, and hung up, but he had been on the phone before ten o'clock with the all-clear. Rome Matthews was a mover and a shaker; when he decided something would be done, it was better not to stand in his way, and Anson Edwards generally gave him a free hand.

Max hadn't considered that he would have more trouble convincing Claire to move than Rome had had in shaking up an entire office, but he should have known. He had made enough mistakes in dealing with her, mistakes that had come back to haunt him, that he should have been expecting it. If he could just get her to Dallas, he would have plenty of time to convince her that he wasn't a complete bastard after all. If it took time to rebuild her trust in him, he was willing to take that time. He had hurt her, and the knowledge was eating away at him. It had been true when Claire accused him of compartmentalizing his life. He hadn't allowed for the possibility that Claire would think he had used her solely for the purpose of getting that information. Now he couldn't get her to listen to him, and he had the cold feeling inside that even if she did, she wouldn't believe him. He had destroyed her trust in him, and only now was he realizing how rare and precious that trust was.

Claire did her usual Saturday morning chores, finding comfort in the routine while she tried to get her thoughts in order and make a logical decision. She scrubbed and waxed the kitchen floor, cleaned the bathroom from top to bottom, did her laundry, and even washed the windows, trying to burn up the anger that consumed her. With a shock she realized that she was not just angry, she was furious. She was usually calm—she couldn't even remember the last time she had been truly angry, so angry that she wanted to throw something and scream at the top of her lungs. Damn him, how *dare* he! After using her as callously as he had, now he actually expected her to uproot herself and change her entire life, agree to move to another city and in doing so throw herself into continuous contact with him. He had said she wouldn't be working for him, but she would be in the same building, in the same city, and he had made it plain that he didn't consider things over between them. How had he said it? "When I make love to you again, you'll be awake." *Again*. That was the key word.

His gall made her almost incoherent with anger, and she muttered to herself as she cleaned. It was odd, but she couldn't remember being angry when Jeff had left her for Helene. She had been tired and grief-worn over the baby, and bitterly accepting that Jeff should want someone else, but she hadn't been angry. Only Max had touched her deeply enough to find the core of passion inside her. He brought out all the emotions and feelings she had spent a lifetime controlling and protecting: love, fierce desire, even anger.

She still loved him; she didn't even try to fool herself on that score. She loved him, she burned for him, she wanted him, and the flip side of the coin was her deep anger. It was nature's decree that for every action there should be a balancing reaction, and that was also true of emotions. If she hadn't loved him so deeply, she would have been able to shrug away his betrayal and accept it as a lesson in trusting the wrong person. But because she loved him, she wanted to shake him until his teeth rattled. She wanted to scream at his arrogant assumption that she was his for the taking, and she wanted to show him just how wrong that assumption was.

She could tell him to keep his job, turn her back on him, and walk away—that would show him that he couldn't use her and expect her to fall back into his bed whenever he beckoned. That would show him that she was perfectly capable of living without him…or would it? Wouldn't it instead be admitting that he had hurt her so badly that she *couldn't* face seeing him every day? She had to admit that joining the unemployment line when she had the offer of a good job was a drastic, illogical move. He would know how much he had hurt her, and her pride demanded that she put up a good front. It was somehow essential to her self-esteem that she prevent him from knowing that his betrayal had hurt her so deeply that the wound was still bleeding.

But what other choice did she have? If she went to Dallas, she would be playing right into his hands, dancing to his tune like a marionette on a string.

Claire straightened from her dusting, her mouth set firmly and her eyes deeply thoughtful. What she had to do was not allow Max to be a factor in her decision at all. This was her job, her financial future, and she shouldn't allow anger to cloud her judgment. Even if she went to Dallas, she wouldn't *have* to dance to Max's tune; when it came down to it, she was a woman, not a marionette. The choice, and the decision, were hers.

Looking at it like that, from a logical point of view, she knew that she would take the job. Perhaps that would be the best way of putting up a good front. If she went on about her life as normal, it would seem as if Max hadn't made such a disastrous impact on her heart, and only she would know the truth.

Once the decision was made it was as if a weight had lifted. The difficult part would be telling her family, and Claire chose to tell Martine first. That afternoon she drove out to Martine's house in the suburbs, a ritzy location that accurately reflected Martine's and Steve's dual success. Martine's house wasn't cool and picture-perfect, though. It reflected Martine's warmth and outgoing personality, as well as her joy in her children. A tricycle was parked next to the first step, and a red ball lay under a manicured shrub, but most of the cheerful tangle of toys was in the fenced backyard that surrounded the pool. Because it was a warm, sunny Saturday, Claire directed her steps toward the back. As she rounded the corner of the house, the tapping of her heels on the flagstones warned Martine of someone's presence, and she lazily opened her eyes. Just as Claire had expected, her sister was stretched out on a deck chair, lazing in the sun in a diminutive white bikini that had to make Steve choke whenever he saw it. Even wearing no makeup and with her golden blond hair pulled back in a haphazard ponytail with an ordinary rubber band, Martine was gorgeous and sexy.

"Pull up a chair," she invited lazily. "I would hug you, but I'm slimy with suntan oil."

"Where are the children?" Claire asked, sinking onto a deck chair and propping her feet up. The sun did feel good, all hot and clean, and she turned her face up to it like a flower.

"Skating party. It's Brad's best friend's birthday. It's an *all-day* skating party," Martine said gleefully. "And Steve is playing golf with a client. This may be the only day I have alone again until both children are in college, so I'm making the most of it."

"Shall I go?" Claire asked teasingly.

"Don't you dare. With our schedules, we don't see enough of each other as it is."

Claire looked down, thinking of the decision she'd made that morning. She was only now beginning to realize how close-knit her family was, without living in each other's pockets. Moving away from them was going to be a wrench. "What if you saw even less of me? What if I moved to Dallas?"

Martine shot upright in the deck chair, her blue eyes wide and shocked. "What? Why would you move to Dallas? What about your job?"

"I've been offered a job in Dallas. I won't have my job here much longer, anyway."

"Why not? I thought you and Sam got along like a house on fire."

"We do, but Sam—the company has been taken over by Spencer-Nyle, a conglomerate based in Dallas."

"I've been reading about the possibility in the papers, but I had hoped it wouldn't happen. So it's final, then? When did it happen, and what does that have to do with you, anyway? They certainly aren't going to get rid of Sam. He's the brains behind Bronson Alloys. Aren't you going to stay on as his secretary?"

"The final agreement was signed yesterday." Claire looked down at her hands, surprised to see that her fingers were laced tightly together. She made a conscious effort to relax. "Sam is going completely into research, so he won't need a secretary any longer."

"That's bad. I know how much you like him. But it's also good that you've already had a job offer. What company is it?"

"Spencer-Nyle."

Martine's eyes widened. "The corporate headquarters! I'm impressed, and you must have impressed someone else, too!"

"Not really." Claire took a deep breath. This wasn't getting any easier, so she decided to just get it said. "Max Benedict's real name is Maxwell Conroy, and he's a vice president with Spencer-Nyle."

For a full five seconds Martine merely stared at Claire with a stunned expression. Then hot color flooded her cheeks and she surged to her feet, her fists clenched. She seldom swore, but it was due to choice, not lack of vocabulary. She used every bit of that vocabulary now, pacing up and down and damning Max with every invective she could think of, and inventing new combinations when she ran out of the ones she already knew. She didn't need to hear all the details to know that Claire had been hurt. Martine knew Claire well, and she was fiercely protective of her sister, as she was of everyone she loved.

When Martine showed signs of running down, Claire interrupted quietly. "It gets more complicated. I gave him confidential information that he needed for Spencer-Nyle to engineer the takeover. That was why he was down here, and that was why he was showing so much interest in me. I blurted it all out like an idiot."

"I'll tear his face off," Martine raged, beginning to pace up and down again like a caged tigress. Then she stopped, and a peculiar expression came over her face. "But you're going to Dallas with him?"

"I'm going to Dallas for the job," Claire said firmly. "It's the only logical thing I can do. I'd have to be an even bigger idiot than I already am if I deliberately chose unemployment over a good job. Pride won't keep the bills paid."

"Yes, it is the logical thing to do," Martine echoed, and sat down. She still had that peculiar expression on her face, as if she were trying to think something through and it didn't quite tally up. Then a slow smile began to crinkle the corners of her eyes. "He's transferred you so you'll be with him, that's it, isn't it? The man is in love with you!"

"Not likely," Claire said, her throat going tight. "Lies and betrayal aren't very good indicators of love. I love him, but you already knew that, didn't you? I shouldn't love him, not now, but I can't turn it on and off like a faucet. Just don't ask me to believe that he ever saw anything in me except the means to an end."

"But when I think about it, he always watched you… Oh, I can't describe it," Martine mused. "As if he were so hungry for you, as if he wanted to absorb you. It gave me the shivers, watching him watch you. The *good* shivers, if you know what I mean."

Claire shook her head. "That isn't likely, either. You've seen him," she said, feeling her body tense up again. "He's beautiful. It stops my breath to look at him! Why should he be interested in me, except for the information he needed?"

"Why shouldn't he? In my book he'd be a fool if he didn't love you."

"Then a lot of men have been fools," Claire pointed out wearily.

"Fiddlesticks. You haven't *let* them love you. You never let anyone get close enough to really know you, but Max is more intelligent than most men. Why *wouldn't* he love you?" Martine asked passionately.

It was hard for Claire to say, almost impossible. Her throat tightened. "Because I'm not beautiful, like you. That seems to be what men want."

"Of course you aren't beautiful like me! You're beautiful like *yourself!*" Martine came over to Claire and sat down on the deck chair with her, her lovely face unusually serious. "I'm flamboyant, but that isn't your style at all. Do you know what Steve once said to me? He said that he wished I were more like you, that I would think before I leaped. I punched him, of course, and asked what else he likes about you. He said that he likes your big dark eyes—he called them 'bedroom eyes'— and I was about ready to do more than punch him! Blue-eyed blondes like me are a dime a dozen, but how many brown-eyed blondes are there? I used to die with envy, because you only had to turn those dark eyes on a man and he was ready to melt at your feet, but you never seemed to know that, and eventually he gave up." Suddenly Martine caught her breath, her eyes widening. "Max didn't give up, did he?"

Claire was staring at her sister, unable to believe that beautiful Martine had ever found anything about her to be jealous of. Distracted, she said, "Max doesn't know those two words are ever used together." Then she realized what she had just admitted, and she flushed. She wasn't used to talking so frankly to anyone, even her sister, but she was learning some things about herself that she'd never suspected before. Was it true that she held people away from her, that she didn't let them get close enough to care? She hadn't looked at it from that angle before; she had thought that she was keeping a distance between herself and other people so *she* wouldn't care, without considering the person who was being held at arm's length.

"Max won't leave me alone. He insists that it isn't over. He was called back to Dallas," she explained steadily. "By the time he returned to Houston, I had already found out his real name and what he was doing here. He called, but I refused to go out with him again. So now I've been transferred to Dallas."

"To his own territory. Smart move," Martine commented.

"Yes. I know all that. I know how he reacts to challenges, and that's all I am to him. How many women do you suppose have ever refused him?"

Martine thought, then admitted ruefully, "You probably stand alone."

"Yes. But I have to have a job, so I'm going." Even as she said the words, Claire wondered if there had ever been anything else she could have done. "What would you do in my place?"

"I'd go," Martine admitted, and laughed. "We must be more alike than you think. I know I'd never let him think that he'd made me run!"

"Exactly." Claire's dark eyes turned almost black. "He makes me so angry I could *spit!*"

Martine raised a militant fist. "Give him hell, honey!" Seeing the anger in Claire's face made Martine want to dance around the yard. Too often Claire held her emotions in, hiding her vulnerabilities from the rest of the world. Even when she had lost her baby, Claire had been pale and quiet. Only Max had ever jostled her out of her composure. Claire might not think that Max cared for her at all, but Martine had seen Max watching her sister, and thought Claire was seriously underestimating the strength of his attraction to her. There was no doubt that he loved a challenge—he had that sort of fire in his eyes, that self-confident arrogance. But Claire didn't realize that she was an ongoing challenge, with her silences and perceptions, and the depths of her personality. If Martine read him correctly, Max would be fascinated by the complexity of Claire's character. And, damn him, if he hurt Claire again, he'd have to answer to Martine for it!

Claire felt as if she had made a momentous decision, but she was calm, even though the thought of changing her life so completely was a wrenching one. She had lived in her quiet, cozy apartment for five years, and it hurt to think of leaving, yet she knew that she had made the only logical choice. It was just that she preferred changes to come slowly, so she could adjust to them, rather than in a confusing rush.

She sat in silence that night, looking around and trying to accustom herself to the idea of a new apartment, a different city. She wasn't in the mood for either television or music, and she was too disturbed to find refuge in a book. There were plans to be made, work to be done—she had to find another apartment, get the utilities turned on, pack…say goodbye to her family. Martine already knew, but Alma would be the difficult one. It wouldn't really be goodbye, but it would be the end of easy access to her family. The distance between them would be great enough that she couldn't just get in the car and drive over whenever the whim took her.

Her doorbell rang, and she answered it without thinking. Max filled the doorway, looking down at her with a peculiarly intense glitter in his eyes. Claire tightened her hand on the doorknob, not stepping back to allow him entrance. Why couldn't he leave her alone? She needed time by herself to get accustomed to the sweeping changes she was making in her life.

The glitter in his eyes intensified as he realized that she wasn't going to invite him inside. He put his hand on hers and gently but forcefully removed it from the doorknob, then stepped forward, crowding her back into the apartment. He shut the door behind him. "Are you sitting here brooding?" he asked shortly, glancing around the silent apartment.

Claire moved away from him, her face closed. "I've been thinking, yes."

Strong habits had been established in the short time they had been together—Claire went automatically to the kitchen and put on a pot of coffee, then turned to find him leaning in the doorway, still watching her in a way that made her want to check all her buttons to make certain they were fastened. She would have to brush past him to get to the living room, so she opted for retaining the relatively safe distance between them and remained where she was. "You might as well know," she said, throwing the words into the silence between them. "I've decided to take the job."

"Is that what you've been brooding about?"

"It's a major change," she replied coolly, using every ounce of self-control she possessed. "Didn't you have any doubts when you relocated from Montreal to Dallas?"

Curiosity sharpened his gaze even more. "Ah, yes, I've been meaning to ask you about that. Exactly how did you discover my last name?"

"I read a magazine article on Spencer-Nyle. It had a picture of you."

He strolled into the kitchen, and Claire turned away to get two mugs out of the cabinet. Before she could turn around again, he was behind her, his arms braced on the cabinet on

either side of her, effectively trapping her. "I had intended to
tell you that morning, when we woke up," he said, bending
his head to take a little nip at her ear. Claire sucked in her
breath and twisted her head away, both alarmed and angered
by the way his slightest touch made her pulse race. He ignored
her movement of rejection and nuzzled her ear again, continu-
ing his explanation whether she wanted to hear it or not. "But
that phone call interrupted everything, and by the time I got
back to Houston, you'd already found out, damn my luck!"

"It doesn't matter," she protested tightly. "What could you
have said? 'By the way, dear, I'm an executive with a company
that has targeted your company for takeover, and I've been
using you to get information'?" She mimicked his clipped
accent and saw his hands clench on the cabinet in front of her.

"No, that wasn't what I would have said." He pushed
himself away from her, and Claire turned, clutching the coffee
mugs to her chest, to find him staring at her with barely restrained violence in his eyes. "I wouldn't have said anything
at all until you were in bed with me. Trying to reason with
you has turned out to be a waste of time."

"Oh?" she cried. "I think it's terribly *un*reasonable of you
to think you could just waltz back into my life and pick up
where you'd left off, after what you did!" She slammed the
mugs down onto the cabinet, then stared at them in horror.
What if she'd broken them? She never lost her temper, never
screamed or threw things or slammed them down, but now it
seemed as if her anger was so close to the surface that Max
could bring it out every time he spoke to her. She was reacting
in a way that was totally unlike herself. Or maybe, she thought
grimly, she was simply discovering facts about herself that
she'd never before suspected. Max had a talent for drawing
intense reactions from her. Grimly she sought control again,
taking another calming breath. "Why are you here?"

"I thought you might want to know more about the job before you made your decision," he muttered, still looking furious. He admitted to himself that he was lying. He had wanted to see her—he had no other reason.

"I appreciate the thought," Claire said, as distant as the moon. She poured coffee into both mugs and extended one to him, then took a seat at her tiny kitchen table, which was just big enough for two. Max took the chair opposite her, still scowling as he drank his coffee.

"Well?" she prompted a few minutes later, when he still hadn't said a word.

His frown deepened. "You'll be secretary to the general office manager, Theo Caulfield. The departments of payroll, insurance, general accounting, data processing, maintenance, office supplies and equipment, as well as the secretarial pool, are all under his control, though each department has its own manager. It's a demanding job."

"It sounds interesting," she said politely, but she was being truthful. A job that diverse had to be interesting, and challenging.

"You'll need to work late occasionally, but the extra hours won't be excessive. You have two weeks to get settled. I would give you a month but the office is in an uproar with a lot of transfers, and you're needed on the job." He didn't add that he was the reason the office was in an uproar. "I'll help you look for an apartment. You helped me, so I owe you a favor."

Claire's face stiffened at the mention of his apartment; it was only an expensive prop, a part of his hoax. That apartment had given him the appearance of stability and permanence. "No, thank you. I don't need your help."

His face turned dark, and he set his mug down with a thump. "Very well," he snapped, getting to his feet and hauling her up with a strong grip on her arm. "You're determined not to give an inch, not even to listen to my side of it. Be safe, behind those walls of yours, and if you ever think of what you might be missing, think of this!"

His mouth was hot and strong. His arms crushed her against him, as if he couldn't get her close enough. His tongue went deep, reminding her.

Claire whimpered, tears burning her eyes as the wanting curled in her again, as hot and alive as it had ever been.

Max pushed her away, breathing hard. "If you think that has anything to do with business, you're a damned fool!" he said harshly and slammed out of the apartment as if he couldn't trust himself to stay a minute longer.

Chapter 10

To her surprise, Claire was too busy during the following two weeks to feel much anxiety over her move to Dallas. Finding an apartment wasn't easy—she spent hours inspecting and rejecting, getting lost time and again in the unfamiliar city but somehow having fun doing it. Alma, once she'd gotten over the shock of one of her daughters moving out of her immediate reach, threw herself into the apartment search with all her typical zest and spent days touring Dallas with Claire, ruthlessly hunting out any potential trouble spots in an apartment. Claire let her mother go on, amused by that overflow of energy. It was odd that the older she became, the closer Claire grew to her family. At some point, their beauty and self-confidence had ceased to intimidate her. She loved them and was proud of their accomplishments.

Even Martine was dragged into the apartment hunting, and together they made a list of the most suitable locations then began narrowing the choices. Claire didn't like the ultramodern condos, despite their conveniences, and though she hadn't really considered a house, in the end it was a tiny, neat house that won over the apartments. The rent was remarkably reasonable because of its size. Getting it ready for Claire to move in became a major family project. Claire and her father repainted the rooms in white to make them seem larger, while Alma and Martine bought material and sewed curtains to fit the odd-size windows. Steve put new dead-bolt locks on the doors and locking screens on the windows, then sanded and polished the old-fashioned wooden floors. Brad and Cassie, the children, romped in the postage-stamp yard and appeared periodically with demands for sandwiches and Kool-Aid.

On the day she moved in the entire house was in chaos, with the movers carting furniture and boxes in, while she and Alma and Martine tried to put everything in some sort of order. Harmon and Steve kept out of the decision-making, simply standing by to provide muscle if needed. Claire was headfirst in a box of books when a cool voice said from the door, "Would another pair of hands be welcome?"

Claire straightened abruptly, her face still as she tried to deal with the way the sound of his voice affected her. For two weeks Max had been as polite as a stranger, and she had been tormented by a lingering sense of loss. The tumult of moving, with its mingled moments of hilarity and frustration, and her pure physical exhaustion from so much work, had buffered her somewhat from her thoughts, but there were still far too many moments when she wished she had never found out the truth about him, that the hurt and anger would all just go away. The distance between them the past two weeks had hurt, too, though she had tried to ignore it. Why had he shown up now, strolling into the middle of the overflowing mess with that indefinable grace of his?

Harmon groaned, straightening from his task. "Another

strong back is just what we need! Take the other end of this table—it weighs a ton."

Max picked his way over the cluttered floor to help Harmon lift the table and put it where Claire had directed. Alma sailed out of the kitchen, and a glowing smile broke over her face when she saw Max. "Oh, hello! Did you volunteer, or were you kidnapped?" she asked, going over to hug him.

"I volunteered. You know what they say about mad dogs and Englishmen," he said, smiling as he returned Alma's hug.

Claire turned back to the box of books she'd been unpacking, a tiny frown darkening her eyes. She hadn't told Alma all the circumstances behind her move to Dallas, but neither had she thought that her family would be having any further contact with Max. Perhaps Martine had revealed some things, but Claire didn't know and didn't want to ask. Would Alma have been so friendly to Max if she had known the truth? This could be a little awkward—they knew Max as Max Benedict, but he was really Max Conroy. Should she let them continue thinking that was his name or reintroduce him? What could she say? "Conroy is Max's real last name; he just uses Benedict as an alias occasionally." She thought that Miss Manners probably hadn't ruled on this particular situation, so she decided to say nothing.

He fit in easily with her family, joking and conversing as effortlessly as he had before. They didn't know that this congeniality was a disguise for the driving power of his true personality. She watched him, but didn't talk to him except to answer direct questions and she sensed that he was watching her, too. She'd thought that he'd given up, but now she remembered telling Martine that he wasn't even familiar with the term. He hadn't given up—he'd simply been waiting. He calmly wrote down her unlisted telephone number, copying it off the telephone, and when he looked up to find her watching him, he lifted an eyebrow in silent invitation for her to make an issue of it. Claire simply turned away to continue her chores. Attacking him now over a telephone number would make her look like an ungrateful wretch after he'd worked tirelessly most of the day, helping her get settled.

It was late when everything was put in its place, and everyone was yawning widely. Rather than attempt the long drive back to Houston that night, her family had elected to stay in a motel and drive back the next morning. Somehow Claire found herself waving goodbye to them from her new porch, with Max standing beside her as if he belonged there.

"Why did you come here?" she asked quietly, watching the taillights disappear down the street. The warm night sounds of chirping insects and the rustle of leaves in the trees from a slight breeze surrounded them, where only a moment ago there had been laughter and noisy yawns and enthusiastic cries of "Bye! Take care now. I'll call you tomorrow!"

"To help you with your things," he said, holding the screen door open for her as she reentered the house. She didn't trust his bland tone for a minute. "And to make certain that you're comfortable. Nothing more sinister than that."

"Thank you for your help."

"You're welcome. Is there any coffee left in the pot?"

"I think so, but it is probably undrinkable by now. You drink too much coffee, anyway," she said without thinking, going into the kitchen to pour out the stale coffee. He stopped her as she was beginning to make a fresh pot.

"You're right. I don't need any more coffee," he said, taking the pot out of her hand and placing it in the sink. Grasping her elbow, he pulled her around to face him. "What I need is this."

His other arm went around her waist, bringing her up against him, and he bent his head. His mouth closed over hers, and the hot, heady taste of him filled her. He kissed her with deep, greedy hunger, until a painful hunger of her own began to coil in her body. Both angered and alarmed by the desire he could arouse so effortlessly, she jerked her mouth from his and pushed against his shoulders, feeling the heavy muscles beneath her palms.

To her surprise he let her go easily, releasing her and stepping back. Satisfaction was plain in his eyes, as if he'd just proved something to himself. He must have felt her response; for a brief moment she hadn't been able to prevent herself from melting against him, her body seeking his.

"I wish you hadn't come," she whispered, her dark eyes locked on him. "Why involve yourself with my family? How do I tell them that you aren't Max Benedict, after all?"

"You don't have to tell them anything—they already know. I've explained it to your mother."

Shocked, Claire stared at him. "What?" she stammered. "Why? When did you tell her? *What* did you tell her?"

He answered readily enough. "I told her that the takeover of Bronson Alloys by my company has complicated our relationship, but that I transferred you to Dallas so we would still be together and could work out the problems."

He made it all sound so simple, as if he hadn't abandoned her as soon as he'd gotten the information he wanted! It was true that he hadn't been expecting the phone call that had forced him to return to Dallas, but it was also true that he hadn't made any attempt to contact her after that until the actual mechanics of the takeover had put him back in Houston. Now, in his typical high-handed fashion, he believed that all he had to do was move her to Dallas and the "complications" would be settled.

Her expression was so troubled, for once so easily read, with all her doubts and hurt there for him to see, that he had to fight the urge to pull her against him and shelter her in his arms. Max had never known failure with a woman he wanted; they came easily into his arms and his bed, and they had always been so easy to read. It was ironic that Claire, the one woman he couldn't easily understand, should be the woman he wanted more intensely than he'd ever dreamed he would want a woman. He couldn't tell what she was thinking—her defenses were too strong, her personality too complex. Yet every glimpse he had of the inner woman only made him hungrier to find out more about her, to get deeper into her mind. Looking at her now, with her clothes grimy from the day's labors, her hair straggling down from its topknot, her face free of makeup and her velvety dark eyes full of pain and uncertainty, Max felt something jolt in his chest.

He was in love with her.

The realization stunned him, though now that he recognized it for what it was, he knew that the feeling had been there for some time. He had labeled it as attraction, desire, even challenge, and it was all of those, and more. Of all the women in the world, he hadn't loved any of the soft, willing beauties who had shared his bed and would have done anything for him. Instead it was a difficult, aloof, yet extraordinarily vulnerable woman who made him feel as if he would explode with joy if she smiled at him. He wanted to protect her, he wanted to discover all the hidden depths of her character, he wanted to lose himself in the unexpected and shattering passion she had to offer.

Claire moved away from him, rubbing the back of her neck tiredly and not seeing the arrested expression on his face. "How did you explain your change of name?"

It took a minute before he could gather himself and make sense of what she had asked. "I told her the truth, that I had been looking for certain information and didn't want Bronson to know my true identity."

Claire thought Alma was so charmed by Max that she would be prepared to believe anything he said. "What did she say?"

An appreciative smile quirked Max's mouth as he remembered exactly what Alma had said. That lady did have a way with words, though he could hardly tell Claire that her mother had said, "If you hurt my daughter, Max Benedict, or Conroy, or whoever you are, I'll have your guts for garters!" Claire didn't seem to realize how fiercely protective her entire family was of her.

"She understood," was all he said, watching Claire as she retreated even more, continually expanding the distance between them. She was so wary!

"I'm sure she did," Claire sighed.

Impatiently Max closed the gap between them, his quick strides carrying him to her side. Claire looked up, startled by his sudden movement, then gave a soft cry as he put his hands on her waist and lifted her up so her eyes were level with his. "Yes, your mother understood—it's a pity you don't!" he muttered, then put his mouth on hers.

There was a tiny, despairing cry deep inside her mind. How could she keep control of herself if he kept kissing her? Especially kisses like these, deep, hungry kisses, as if he couldn't get enough of her taste. His lips released hers and slid down to her throat, nipping at her skin as they went. He held her so firmly that his hands were hurting her, and she didn't care. Her eyes closed firmly, and tears welled beneath her lashes.

"Why do you keep doing this to me?" she cried rawly. "Do you just chase anything that runs? Did it hurt your pride that I told you to leave me alone?"

He raised his head; his eyes were burning green fire. He was breathing harshly. "Is that what you think? That my ego is so enormous I can't stand for a woman to turn me down?"

"Yes, that's what I think! I'm a challenge to you, nothing more!"

"We burned each other up in bed, woman, and you think it was nothing more than gratifying my ego?" He put her on her feet, infuriated that she continually put the worst interpretation on his actions.

"You tell me! I don't know you at all! I thought you were a gentleman, but you're really a savage in a tuxedo, aren't you? Your instincts are to win, regardless of how ruthless you have to be to get what you want!"

"You know me pretty well, after all," he snapped. "I go after what I want, and I want you."

Claire shivered, alarmed by the hard expression on his face. Swearing under his breath, he took her in his arms again, holding her head against his chest, his fingers threading into her soft hair. "Don't be afraid of me, love," he whispered. "I won't hurt you. I want to take care of you."

As what? As a mistress? She shook her head blindly, the motion limited by the way he held her to his chest.

"You'll trust me again, I promise." He murmured the words against her hair, and his hands slid down to stroke her back. Claire found that her hands were clenched on his shirt and that she was clinging instead of trying to push him away. "I'll make you trust me, love. We'll get to know each other. We have the time. There will be no more masks between us."

He bent his head and kissed her again, and this time Claire's self-control wasn't strong enough to keep her from responding. Blindly she rose on tiptoe, straining against him, her mouth opening under the probing of his tongue. She kept making foolish mistakes where Max was concerned, and the latest one was the idea that she would be able to keep him at a distance. Shaking with love and pain that mingled into a tangled knot, she let the pleasure sweep through her, because there was nothing she could do to stop it. His hand was on the buttons of her shirt, and there was nothing she could do to stop that, either. She trembled, waiting in an agony of anticipation for his touch, her body craving his heat and strength. Then his fingers were on her, sliding inside her opened shirt to cup her naked, swelling flesh, and electricity shot from her hardened nipples straight to her loins.

"I know you're tired, but I'm not a noble, self-sacrificing gentleman," he said harshly, lifting his head to look at her. "If you don't stop me now, I won't be leaving tonight at all."

She couldn't deny it, even to herself. He was giving her one last chance to reconsider. For a moment she almost pulled his head back down to her. Then common sense asserted itself, and she pushed at his arms until they fell away from her. Her fingers trembled, and she couldn't look at him as she fumbled with the buttons of her shirt until at last she was covered again.

"Thank you," she said, meaning it. She felt exposed and vulnerable, because only his self-control had given her the chance to reconsider—she had had none at all, and he knew it.

He had offered, but that didn't help the frustration raging through his body. He glared down at her. "Don't thank me for being a bloody stupid fool," he said, his tone savage with temper. "I have to get out of here before I change my mind. Be ready at six-thirty tomorrow night. I'm taking you out to dinner."

"No, I don't think—"

"That's right," he interrupted, catching her chin in his hand. "Don't think, and above all, don't argue with me right now. I want you so much that I'm hurting. I'll be here at six-thirty. If you want to go out, be dressed. If not, we'll stay here. The choice is yours."

She shut her mouth. His mood was dangerous, his eyes glittering. He kissed her again, hard, then stalked out of the house.

When he was gone the house echoed strangely. She locked

the doors and checked all the windows to make certain they were secure, then showered and got ready for bed. The furnishings were all familiar, and the bed was the one she had slept in for five years, yet she lay awake staring into the darkness. It wasn't the unfamiliarity of her surroundings, but her thoughts that prevented her from sleeping. Why had he given her the chance to stop? He'd said that he wasn't noble or self-sacrificing, but then he had made a self-sacrificing offer. He could have taken her to bed, and they both knew it. He had wanted her; there hadn't been any secret in the way he had pushed against her, letting her feel his arousal. So why had he given her that last opportunity to stop?

Pain squeezed her chest. Who was the biggest fool? Him for giving her the chance to stop, or herself for taking it? He had hurt her, and he had made her so angry that she had wanted to throw things at him, but none of that had stopped her from loving him. She wanted to cling to her anger, to use it as both a weapon and a defense against him, but she could feel it ebbing away from her and leaving her vulnerable to the truth. She loved him. No matter what happened, even if he wanted her only for a brief affair, she loved him. With that acknowledgment she felt her last defenses crumble inside her.

Nothing was working out the way she had planned. She hadn't intended to go out with Max again; she had intended to do her job and ignore him, but he hadn't given her a choice about that. He was taking over again, and with her defenses down she was helpless to do anything about it. All her intentions had gone down the drain with her anger. She could no longer make any plans or form any intentions. All she could do was face the fact that she loved him, and take each day as it came.

Claire was so nervous that she kept dropping the pins she was using to put up her hair. It was her first day on a new job, and Max was taking her out to dinner. She needed to concentrate on the job, but she kept thinking of Max. He simply wouldn't leave her head.

A pin flew from her trembling fingers again, and she muttered an impatient "damn!" as she leaned down to retrieve it. She had to calm down, or the day would be a disaster.

Finally she got her hair securely pinned, and with a frantic glance at the clock she put on the jacket that matched her gray skirt, grabbed her purse and left the house at a run. She wasn't certain how long it would take her to drive to the Spencer-Nyle building in the early morning traffic, so she had cautiously allowed an extra fifteen minutes, then used most of that picking up hair pins. What an impression it would make to be late on her first day!

But she made it with five minutes to spare, and a smiling receptionist directed her to Theo Caulfield's office on the fifth floor. A tall, dark man with a face like granite paused in passing, his dark eyes on Claire. She felt his gaze and glanced at him then quickly looked away. He was vaguely familiar, but she was certain she'd never met him. There was an almost visible force about him, and the receptionist became obviously nervous when she realized that the man was listening.

"Are you Claire Westbrook?" he asked abruptly, moving to Claire's side.

How had he guessed, unless he was Theo Caulfied? She looked up at him, feeling dwarfed by his powerful build despite the three-inch heels she wore, and hoped that he wasn't her new boss. He couldn't be a comfortable man to work with. Because he made her nervous, too, she reacted by hiding behind her usual mask of composure.

"Yes, I am."

"I'm Rome Matthews. I'll show you to your office and introduce you to Caulfield. Good morning, Angie," he said to the receptionist as he led Claire away.

"Good morning, Mr. Matthews," the receptionist said faintly to his back.

His name was familiar, too. Claire darted another look up at that hard, almost brutally carved face and remembrance shot through her. His picture had been beside Max's in that article she'd read, when she had discovered Max's true identity. He was executive vice president and Anson Edwards's right-hand man, his chosen successor. How did he know her name, and why was he personally escorting her to her office?

Whatever his reason, he wasn't inclined to make explanations. He asked polite questions, whether she liked Dallas, had she gotten settled yet, but she could feel him watching her. His hand was on her elbow, and she was surprised by the gentleness of his touch.

"Here it is," he said, drawing her to a halt and reaching out to open a door. "You'll have your hands full, you know. Your predecessor had to be on her new job today, so you'll be training yourself."

Claire thought of running while she still could, but a man came out of the inner office on hearing their voices, and she was trapped. To her relief Theo Caulfield was an ordinary man, middle-aged and thin, without the intimidating force of Rome Matthews. He, too, seemed nervous at the other man's presence and visibly relaxed when the short introductions were performed and the executive vice president took himself off to his own office.

To her relief her duties were fairly routine, and she settled in quickly. Theo Caulfield was quiet and meticulous, but not fussy. She missed Sam, but he was far happier in his laboratory than he had ever been in an office. Perhaps the takeover had been best for him, as well as for the company.

* * *

Max called her just before the day was over—the only time she had heard from him—to tell her to dress casually for dinner. Claire hurried home to her little house, afraid that he would take it as a signal that she wanted to stay in if she weren't ready when he arrived. How casual was casual? She opted to play it safe with a plain skirt and blouse and flat heels, and was waiting to open the door before he could knock.

"Where are we going?" she asked, eyeing his slacks and open-neck silk shirt.

"We're having dinner with some friends of mine," he said, drawing her to him for a quick kiss. "How did it go today? Any trouble settling in?"

"No, it wasn't difficult. It's mostly the routine work of an assistant."

Max asked her several questions about her day, distracting her. She was still unfamiliar with the city, so she wasn't concerned with where they were going until she noticed they were in a residential section. "Where are we?" she asked.

"We're almost there."

"Almost *where?*"

"At Rome's house. We're having dinner with him and his wife, Sarah."

"What?" Claire asked faintly. "Max, you can't just take me to someone's house when they haven't invited me!" And Rome Matthews's house, of all people! She wasn't comfortable with him; he was the most overpowering man she'd ever seen.

He looked amused. "They *have* invited you. Sarah told me that if I didn't have you with me tonight, not to come myself." There was an unmistakable note of affection in his voice. He turned into the driveway of a sprawling, Spanish-style house, and Claire tensed.

He put his hand on her back as they walked up the brick

walk to the front door, and if it hadn't been for that pressure at her back, Claire would have turned around and left. He rang the bell, and in a moment Rome Matthews opened the door himself.

Claire stared, almost not recognizing the high-powered executive in the man who stood there, clad in tight-fitting jeans that molded his powerful hips and legs, and a red polo shirt. His face was infinitely more relaxed, and there was amusement in his dark eyes. Even more amazingly, he held a chubby toddler in one strong arm and a tiny elfin girl in the other. Somehow Claire hadn't imagined him as a family man, especially one with young children. Then her eyes were drawn to the two children, and she gasped. "They're beautiful," she whispered, automatically reaching out her hands. The children both had their father's black hair and eyes and olive complexion, with the gorgeous rosy cheeks that only young children have. Two pairs of wide inquisitive dark eyes stared at her. Then the baby gave a chuckle and launched himself out of his father's arms, straight into hers, his fat hands outstretched.

"Thank you," Rome said, his amusement deepening, and Claire flushed. She cuddled the little boy to her, loving the feel of his sturdy, wriggling little body. He smelled of baby powder, and she wanted to bury her face in his fat little neck.

"Here you go sweetheart," Max said, holding out his hands to the little girl, and with a giggle she, too, abandoned her father. She hugged Max around the neck and kissed his cheek. Max settled her comfortably on his arm and carried her into the house, keeping his other hand at Claire's back.

"The little tank you're holding is Jed," Rome said, reaching out to tickle his son. "The flirt around Max's neck is Missy. She's three, and Jed is almost one."

Claire was gently rubbing the baby's back, and he had nestled down against her as if he'd known her all his life. He was incredibly heavy, but his weight felt good in her arms. "You darling," she crooned to him, kissing his soft black hair.

Max looked up from the game he was playing with Missy, and his eyes flickered as he watched Claire playing with the baby.

A low laugh reached them, and Claire turned as a slim, delicate woman with white-blond hair came into the room. "I'm Sarah Matthews," the woman said warmly, and Claire looked into the most serene face she'd ever seen. Sarah Matthews was lovely and fragile, and when her husband looked at her it was with an expression in his dark eyes that made Claire want to turn away, as if she had witnessed something terribly intimate.

"Sarah, this is Claire Westbrook," Max said, his hand warm on Claire's arm.

"You have beautiful children," Claire said sincerely, and Sarah beamed with pride.

"Thank you. They're quite a handful. Your arrival has given Rome a rest," Sarah replied, slanting a teasing look at her husband. "They're always wild when he first gets home, especially Jed."

At that moment Jed was lying adoringly against Claire, and Rome laughed at his son. "He can't resist a pretty woman. He's the biggest flirt ever born, except for Missy."

Missy was perfectly content in Max's arms, and Claire noticed the tenderness with which he handled her, and the calm capability. She had noticed his skill with children before, soon after they had met. It had been while he was playing with Martine's children at the cookout that she had fallen in love with him. It had been that simple, that easy and that irrevocable.

"Enjoy the peace," Sarah advised, breaking into Claire's thoughts, and Jed chose that moment to lift his head from Claire's shoulder and look down at the scattered toys on the floor. With a grunt he pushed himself out of her arms. Claire gave a gasping cry and grabbed for him, and Rome did the same, leaping to snag his son out of the air. Sighing, he placed the baby on the floor. His attention completely on his toys, Jed toddled over to the red plastic truck he'd selected.

"He has no respect for gravity, and no fear of heights," Rome said wryly. "He's also as strong as a mule. There's no holding him when he decides he wants down."

"He scared me to death," Claire gasped.

"He's been scaring me since he learned to crawl," Sarah said with a chuckle. "Then he started walking when he was eight months old, and it's been even worse since. All you can do is chase after him."

It was impossible to believe that such a delicate woman had given birth to such a sturdy little boy who showed every sign of inheriting his father's size. The children resembled Sarah very little, except for Missy's delicate stature, and something in the shape of her soft mouth.

It was such a relaxed household, filled with the high-pitched giggles of happy children, that Claire forgot to be intimidated by Rome. Here he was a husband and a father, not an executive. It was evident that Max was a close friend who visited often, because the children climbed over him as enthusiastically as they did over their father, and he not only tolerated it, he seemed to enjoy it.

The children were fed and put to bed, then the adults sat down to dinner. Claire couldn't think when she had enjoyed an evening more; she didn't even shrink when Rome teased her. "I had to check you out this morning," he said, his hard mouth quirked in amusement. "Sarah was dying of curiosity."

"I was not! Max had already told me all about you," Sarah told Claire. "It was his own male curiosity Rome wanted to satisfy."

Rome shrugged lazily, smiling as he looked at his wife.

Claire wondered what Max had said about her, and why he would talk about her, anyway. She glanced at him and blushed when she found him watching her intently.

It was late when Max drove her home, and Claire was sleepily curled in the corner of the seat. "I really liked them," she murmured. "I can't believe he's the same man who terrified me so this morning!"

"Sarah tames him. She's so incredibly serene."

"They're very happy together, aren't they?"

Max's voice roughened a little. "Yes. They've gone through some rough times. If they hadn't loved each other so much, they wouldn't have made it. Rome was married before and had two children, but his wife and sons were killed in an automobile accident. He was terribly scarred by it."

"I can imagine," Claire said, pain grabbing at her. She had never even held her child—it had been gone almost before she had been able to do more than dream of its existence. What would it have been like to have had two children taken from her in such a tragic way? She thought of the way Jed had nestled against her, and tears burned her eyes. "I miscarried. Right before my divorce," she whispered. "And losing the baby nearly killed me. I wanted it so badly!"

Max's head jerked around, and he stared at her in the dim, flickering glow of the streetlights they passed. An almost violent jealousy filled him because she had been pregnant, and it hadn't been with his child. He wanted her to have his baby; he wanted his children to be *her* children. She was a natural mother, so loving with children that they instinctively clung to her.

When they reached her house, he went inside with her and quietly locked the door behind him. Claire watched him, her dark eyes becoming enormous as he came to her and caught her hands in his.

"Max?" she whispered, her voice shaking.

His face was both tender and wild, and his eyes glittered. He put her hands around his neck, then drew her close to lie full against him.

"I'm going to take you to bed, love," he said gently, and a hot tide of pleasure surged through her body at his words. She drew a deep breath and closed her eyes, the time for protests gone. She loved him, and now she realized exactly what that meant; she loved him too much to preserve any distance between them.

He carried her to her bed, and this time he was slow, gentle, taking his time to kiss her and caress her, arousing her to fever pitch while he kept tight control over his own body. Then he eased inside her, and Claire cried out as he filled her. Her nails dug into his back; her hips arched wildly toward him. Max's control broke, and he gave a hoarse cry as he grasped her hips and began driving into her. That same wild, ungovernable need exploded between them, just as it had the first time. They couldn't get enough of each other, couldn't get close enough. Their joining was as elemental as a storm, and as violent.

In the silent aftermath Max held her close, his hand on her stomach. It had happened again, and he couldn't regret it. This woman was his; he could never let her go. She was tender and loving, sensitive and vulnerable and easily hurt. He would gladly spend the rest of his life protecting her from those hurts, if she would only stay with him.

Claire watched with wide, unfathomable eyes as he rose on his elbow and leaned over her. He was very male, and never more so than when he was nude, the power of his body exposed. She put her hand on the brown tangle of hair that covered his chest, stroking gently. What was he thinking? He was serious, almost stern, his sea-colored eyes narrowed to brilliant slits, and he was so beautiful that he took her breath away.

"I may have made you pregnant tonight," he said, his fingers sliding over her stomach. Claire inhaled slightly, her eyes widening. His hand slid down even farther to touch her intimately and explore her in a way that shot rockets along her nerves, making her arch and twist against his fingers. He leaned even closer, his mouth finding hers. "I want to make you pregnant," he groaned, the thought so erotic that his body was hardening again. "Claire, will you have my baby?"

Tears streaked silvery trails down her cheeks. "Yes," she whispered, reaching up to hold him with both hands as he rolled onto her. He thrust deeply into her, and they stared into each other's eyes as they made love, moving together and finding incredible magic. If she could have his child, she would never ask anything more of life. She moved under him. She felt; she loved; she experienced; and she cried.

He lay on her, still deep within her, and kissed away her tears. Incredible contentment filled him. "Claire," he said, holding her face still in his hands, "I don't think anything but marriage will do."

Chapter 11

Claire felt as if her heart had simply stopped beating. Everything inside her went still, waiting for that moment when time would begin again. She couldn't breathe, couldn't speak, couldn't move. Then, with a little jolt, her heart resumed its function, freeing her from the temporary paralysis. "Marry?" she asked faintly.

"My mother will be in ecstasy if you make an honest man of me," he said, tracing her lower lip with his finger. "She's quite given up on me, you know. Marry me, and have my children. I find that I want that very much. When I saw you holding Jed tonight, I thought how perfect you look with a baby in your arms, and I want it to be my baby."

There was nothing about love in his proposal, but Claire found that there didn't have to be. She could accept the fact that he didn't love her. She would take whatever he offered her and do anything she could to make him happy with his decision. Perhaps she should have more pride than to settle for anything less than love, but pride wouldn't gain her anything except an empty bed and an empty life. Happily ever after was a fairy tale, after all.

"All right," she whispered.

His shoulders relaxed almost imperceptibly, and he eased away from her to lie beside her, hugging her against him. His free hand absently stroked her satiny shoulder, and his handsome face was thoughtful. "Does this mean you've forgiven me?"

She wished he hadn't asked that; it touched on a wound that hadn't healed, reminded her of pain that still lingered. She didn't want to think of the past, not now, when she had just agreed to take a step into the future, a step that terrified her with its enormity. If Max were just an ordinary man perhaps she wouldn't feel so uncertain, but Max was extraordinary in every way, and she was filled with doubts that she would ever be able to satisfy him.

"It seems I have to, doesn't it?"

"I never intended to hurt you. I wanted only to get the business part of things over with, so I could concentrate on you. I've wanted you pretty desperately from the first," he admitted wryly. "You wreck my self-control, but that's obvious, isn't it?"

Her head found the hollow of his shoulder, nestling there comfortably. "Why is it obvious?"

He gave a short laugh. "Bloody hell, you can't believe I normally go about attacking women on a table in the foyer? You kissed me back, and I went mad. I couldn't think of anything but being inside you. It was like being picked up by a storm, unable to do anything but go along for the ride."

It had been like that for her, too, an explosion of the senses that obliterated everything else in the world except that moment, this man. The memory of that first lovemaking would make her blush for the rest of her life, because she hadn't known she was capable of such passion. Since then she had come to expect that inner burning whenever he touched her.

She sighed, suddenly so tired that she could barely keep her eyes open. Max kissed her then untangled himself from the bed and got up. Claire opened her eyes, watching him in bewilderment as he sorted out his clothing and got dressed.

"If you weren't half-asleep already, we'd make wedding plans," he said, bending over to tuck the sheet around her naked body. "But you're tired, we have to work tomorrow, and all my clothes are at my apartment, so it's best that I leave."

There would be a thousand-and-one problems to work out, some small and some not so small, but she couldn't think of them now. She was drowsy, her body satisfied, and though she was disappointed that he wouldn't be spending the night with her, she realized that it wasn't practical. He kissed her, his hand stroking over her body in blatant possessiveness.

"I hope you like big weddings," he murmured.

Her lashes fluttered. "Why?"

"Because I have hundreds of relatives who would die of terminal dudgeon if they weren't invited to my wedding."

She chuckled, snuggling deeper into the bed. Max kissed her again, so reluctant to leave her that he considered saying to hell with work and climbing back into bed with her. She was so warm and rosy and relaxed, and he knew it was from his lovemaking. There was nothing quite like the feeling of certainty that he had left her satisfied, and his emotions ran the gamut from pride to possessiveness to wonder. Under all that lay his own bone-deep satisfaction. Beneath her cool, self-possessed mask was a passionate nature. Other people saw only the mask, but she burned for him with a sweet fire that left its scorch marks on his heart and branded him as hers.

She was asleep, her breathing soft and even. With one last

look at her, Max quietly turned out the light and left the bedroom. Soon they would be sharing a bedroom and a name, and his ring would be on her hand.

When she woke the next morning, Claire had the confused feeling that it had all been a dream, a wonderful, impossible dream. Had Max actually asked her to marry him, or had her imagination conjured up the fantasy? Then she moved, and the startled realization that she was naked brought back clear memories of the night before. He had made love to her; then he'd asked her to marry him, and she had agreed. Panic twisted her stomach. What if it didn't work out? What if they got married and he decided that she didn't suit him, after all? What if she failed to satisfy him, just as she had failed with Jeff? What if he already regretted asking her? Men sometimes said things in the heat of passion that they later wished had never been said.

The phone rang beside her, startling her, and she almost dropped the receiver as she grabbed it. "Yes? Hello?"

"Good morning, love," Max said, his voice warm and intimate. "I wanted to make certain you didn't oversleep. I forgot to turn on your alarm when I left last night."

Even though he couldn't see her, a deep blush covered her body, and she pulled the sheet up high under her chin. "Thank you," she said, not hearing the uncertainty in her voice.

Max paused. "We'll go tonight to pick out the rings, shall we? Are you going to call your parents today, or wait until the weekend when you visit them?"

Claire closed her eyes on an almost painful surge of relief—he hadn't changed his mind. "I'll call them. Mother wouldn't forgive me if I kept it a secret until the weekend."

He chuckled. "It's the same with my mother. I'll call her in a moment, and she'll be on the phone for the rest of the day calling everyone in the far-flung family. How soon do you think we can manage the deed? Poor Theo. He's just gotten you, and now he'll have to find another assistant."

"Another assistant?" Claire echoed in surprise.

"Of course. You can't continue to be his assistant after we're married. We'll decide tonight on a date for the wedding, and you'll know when to turn in your notice. I'll see you at work, love. Take care."

"Yes, of course," she said, still holding the receiver after he'd hung up and the dial tone was buzzing in her ear. Slowly she hung up, a frown pulling at her brow. She was expected to give up her job when they were married?

She fretted about it while she showered. On the one hand, she could see that it wouldn't work for both of them to be employed by Spencer-Nyle, and as his salary was far more than hers, it was logical that she should be the one to quit. On the other hand, she had struggled for years to establish her own independence, and it was important to her own sense of self-worth that she continue to support herself, or at least feel as if she were making a contribution to their lives. It wasn't just that Max expected her to quit Spencer-Nyle; Claire had the feeling that he expected her to quit working completely, and the thought made shivers of alarm race down her spine.

What sort of life would they have together? She didn't even know if she could expect him to be faithful. Women melted around him—how could a man not be tempted when he was surrounded by constant opportunities to wander? Given that, she would be incredibly foolish to stop being self-supporting. She only hoped he would be sensible about it.

She didn't have time to call Alma that morning, but found time at lunch and sat chewing her lip, listening to the ringing on the other end of the line. At last she hung up, both relieved and disappointed that Alma wasn't at home. She didn't know how she felt about marrying Max, either. Part of her was ecstatic because she loved him so much. Another part was plain terrified. What if she couldn't make him happy? He was so intelligent and sophisticated and supremely self-confident. He made Jeff look like a lightweight, and Jeff had turned from her to someone more poised and polished.

Max was waiting in the office for her when she returned from lunch, and a warm, intimate smile touched his chiseled mouth when he saw her. "There you are, darling. I'd hoped to take you to lunch, but I couldn't get clear in time. Was your mother pleased?"

Claire glanced at Theo's office, relieved to see that he hadn't returned from lunch. "I just tried to call her, but she wasn't at home. I'll call her tonight."

He put his hands on her waist and drew her to him for a quick kiss. "*My* mother was all but dancing on the table," he said in amusement. "By now half of England knows."

He was in a good mood, his eyes sparkling like sunlight on the ocean, and she felt her heart give that little jolt again. Uneasily she watched the door, trying to draw back from him. "Should you be in here?" she asked, worried. "What if someone saw you kiss me?"

He actually laughed. "Is it supposed to be a secret that we're getting married? I told Rome this morning, and he's already called Sarah to let her know. Then I told Anson, who asked if I couldn't have proposed to you in Houston, rather than rearranging the entire office to empty a position for you. So you see, it's already common knowledge. The news will have gone around the office at the speed of sound."

Claire flushed, staring at him in mortification. "You *made* this job me?" And did the entire office know that he'd brought her to Dallas for himself?

"No, love, the job is a legitimate one. I simply made it available by promoting and shifting some people who, incidentally, are all thrilled with their new positions." Gently he touched her pink cheek. "You don't have any reason to feel embarrassed."

He kissed her again then reluctantly let her go. "Have you been thinking about the type of ring you would like?"

She hadn't, and surprise was plain on her face. "No, not really. I think I'd like a plain wedding band, though." The rings Jeff had given her had been encrusted with yellow diamonds, and she had never really cared for them. The stones had been so large, almost ostentatious, as if they were only what was expected of the Halseys. She had returned them to him after the divorce and never missed them.

He watched her, wondering what memories had caused the brief sadness that darkened the soft brown of her eyes. "Whatever you want," he promised, wishing that he would never see sadness on her face again. For a brief moment she had drifted away in her thoughts, leaving him behind, and he resented even a minute when she wasn't with him.

Max was at her house that night when she finally got Alma on the phone, and he lounged across from her, smiling as he listened to the conversation. Alma laughed, then she cried. Then she had to speak to Max, who assured her with quiet sincerity that he would take care of Claire. When he gave the phone back to Claire, she gave him a look of gratitude for being so understanding with Alma.

"Have you set a date?" Alma asked excitedly.

"No, we haven't had time to talk about it. How long will it take to arrange a church wedding?" Claire listened then turned to Max. "How many of your family do you think will attend?"

He shrugged. "At an offhand guess—seven hundred, give or take a hundred."

"Seven hundred?" Claire gasped, and on the other end of the line Alma gave a small shriek.

"I've mentioned that I have a large family. That also includes friends—Mother will be able to give us a list in a week or so." He motioned for the telephone, and Claire gave it to him again. "Don't panic," he said soothingly to Alma. "Perhaps it would be easier if we were married in England. How many people would we have to transport?"

Claire tried to think of how many people would be invited to her wedding. Her family was small, but there were friends of the family who would have to be included. But if they were married in England, how many of them would be able to attend? And if they were married in Texas, how many of his family and friends wouldn't be able to make a transatlantic trip? Suddenly the wedding was assuming horrendous proportions.

"Accommodations aren't a problem," Max was saying soothingly, so Claire guessed that Alma was having hysterics at the thought of moving the family, lock, stock and barrel, to England. "There are plenty of spare bedrooms scattered around the family. The church? Yes, the church is large enough to handle a wedding of that size. It's an enormous old rock pile." He listened a moment, then laughed. "No, I don't care where we're married. England or Texas doesn't matter to me, so long as I get Claire and it doesn't take an eternity to do it. How long? Six weeks is my limit."

Even sitting across from him, Claire heard the loud protest that Alma was making. Max merely said patiently, "Six weeks. I'm not waiting any longer than that. Claire and I will visit this weekend, and we'll make our plans."

Claire stared at him in horror as he hung up with an air of patent satisfaction. "Six weeks?" she echoed. "It's impossible to put on a wedding for more than seven hundred people in six weeks! That takes months of planning!"

"Six weeks, or I'll carry you before a judge and do the deed. I'm being generous, at that. My inclination is to marry you this weekend, and it's damned tempting. The only thing is, a lot of people would never forgive us."

He flashed her a brilliant smile, standing and holding his hand out to her. Claire put her hand in his, and he pulled her to her feet and into his arms, kissing her long and hard. "Don't worry. Between your mother and mine, this wedding will be perfect. Nothing would dare go wrong."

To Claire's consternation, he didn't take her to one of the small jewelry stores she'd anticipated. Instead she found herself seated in a luxurious salon while the manager brought trays of glittering jewels for her inspection. What on earth was Max thinking about? Surely he didn't think he had to compete with Jeff Halsey in the material things he could give her? Claire knew that Max was certainly not poor; his salary was far more than comfortable, but it didn't make him a millionaire. He didn't have to compete with Jeff in anything, because he had Jeff outclassed in everything.

But there the rings were, waiting for her to make a selection. "What I really want is a plain simple old-fashioned wedding band," she said, frowning slightly.

"Certainly," the manager said politely, starting to take away the tray of diamonds and emeralds and rubies.

"No, leave that," Max instructed. "We'll look these over again while you're bringing the tray of wedding bands."

Claire waited until the manager was out of hearing then turned to Max. "I prefer a wedding band, truly."

He looked amused. "Darling, we'll have our wedding bands, and don't look so surprised. Of course I intend to wear a ring. I've waited long enough to be married. I'm not going to waffle about it. But this is for your engagement ring."

"But I don't need an engagement ring."

"Strictly speaking, no one *needs* any sort of jewelry. An engagement ring is just as old-fashioned and traditional as a wedding band, a symbolic warning to other primitive and marauding males that you aren't available."

Despite her misgivings Claire couldn't keep herself from smiling in answer to the twinkle in his eyes. "Oh, is that what you're doing, warning off other primitives?"

"One never knows what caveman instincts lurk beneath a silk shirt."

Claire knew. She looked at him, and her breath caught as she remembered the wild sensuality behind his calm mask. Most people would never realize just how primitive he really was, because he disguised it so well with his lazy, good-humored manner. He was tolerant, so long as he could get his way with charm and reason, but she sensed the danger in him.

"That was supposed to be a joke," he said lightly, touching her cheek to dispel the look she was giving him. "Take another look at these rings, won't you, before the poor man gets back with that other tray."

She did look at them then shook her head. "They're too expensive."

He laughed—he actually laughed. "Love, I'm not a pauper. Far from it. I promise you that I won't have to go in debt for any of these rings. If you won't choose, I'll do it for you."

He bent over the tray, eyeing each ring carefully. "I really don't care for diamonds," Claire tried, seeing that he was determined.

"Of course not," he agreed. "They wouldn't suit you, not even with that sexy black velvet gown of yours. Pearls are for you. Try this ring." He plucked a ring from its velvet bed and slipped it on her finger.

Claire looked down at it, and a feeling of helplessness came over her. Why couldn't it have been a truly hideous ring that she would have hated on sight? Instead it was a creamy pearl, surrounded by glittering baguettes, and it looked just right on her slender hand.

"I thought so," he said in satisfaction as the manager returned with a tray of wedding bands.

Claire was silent as they left, still trying to come to terms with the changes this wedding would bring in her life, had already brought even though they weren't married yet. Max put his arm around her and held her close, as if trying to shield her from the worries that darkened her eyes.

"What is it, love?" he asked, following her into the tiny house that she liked so much, but which had turned out to be only a temporary stopping place in her life.

"There are so many problems, and I'm not certain how to deal with them."

"What sort of problems?"

"The wedding for one thing. It seems impossible, with so much to be done and the distance involved, the problems of transportation and housing and getting everything coordinated. The cake, the dresses, the tuxedos, the flowers, the receptions. Not only that, I've been divorced, and a white wedding is out of the question, if we can even have a church wedding at all."

He held up his hand, halting her tense litany. "What did you just say?" he asked politely.

She sighed, rubbing her forehead. "You know very well what I said."

"Then let me reassure you on two points, at least. One, we will be married in my family church, and no one will think anything of the fact that you've been married before. Two, you will definitely wear white."

"That's totally unsuitable."

"Let's talk it over with your mother, shall we? I think she'll agree with me."

"Of course you think that! Has any female ever *not* agreed with you?" she said with a groan.

"You, love," he teased. "Is there anything else bothering you?"

It was obvious that she wasn't getting anywhere with him. She sat down and twined her fingers together, watching him with somber dark eyes. "I've been thinking about my job. I realize that it's only reasonable that I leave the company after we're married, and I certainly haven't been there long enough to get attached to the job, but I do want to continue working somewhere."

He watched her in silence for a moment, as if trying to read her thoughts. "If that will make you happy," he finally said in a gentle tone. "I want you to be happy with our marriage, not trapped in a gilded cage."

She was wordless; he'd never suffered from self-doubt, so how could she tell him that she wasn't worried about herself being happy but rather that he wouldn't be happy with her? He sat down beside her and eased her into his arms, cradling her head against his shoulder. "Don't worry about any of that, love. Let our mothers worry about the wedding, and we'll just enjoy watching them run about. I expect we'll have our share of problems after we're married, but let's not anticipate them, hmmm? They may never materialize."

Whenever he had her in his arms, Claire felt reassured. Her hand drifted across his chest, absently stroking the hard muscles she found there. Beneath her ear his heartbeat picked up a beat in speed.

"I believe we've found another subject that needs discussing," he muttered as he tightened his arms around her. "How likely is it that you're pregnant after last night?"

She caught her breath then concentrated and counted in her mind. "It isn't likely, not right now."

His mouth nuzzled under her ear, finding the soft little

hollow there and filling it with kisses. Claire caught her breath again, her eyes closing as pleasure began heating her blood. Her breasts tautened, aching for his touch, and his uncanny sense of timing told him exactly when to cup his palm over her.

"I'll be more cautious until after we're married, then, but I damned well refuse to do without you for six weeks." His mouth was at the corner of hers, his breathing mingling with hers. Blindly Claire turned her head until the contact was complete, her arms sliding around his neck.

Much later he swore softly as he got out of bed. "I'm not fond of this business of leaving you in the middle of the night," he said in sharp displeasure. "Why don't you move in with me?"

Claire drew the sheet up to cover her, a little alarmed by the thought of living with him. Of course they would live together after they were married, but she would have six weeks to get used to the idea. She had lived alone and liked it for quite some time now. The loss of privacy wouldn't be an easy thing to handle. "Where would I put my furniture?"

"Don't be logical," he said in frustration, buttoning his shirt. "Bloody hell, we do have some details to work out, don't we? Would you prefer to live in my apartment, or should we go house hunting?"

"I've never seen your apartment," she pointed out.

He shrugged. "I suppose we should begin looking for a house, as we'll need one eventually."

For the children he planned, she thought. She lay on the bed watching him dress, her body nude and still throbbing from the power of his lovemaking, and she thought of being pregnant with his children, of nursing them and watching them grow. "How many children do you want?" she whispered.

He looked down at her, seeing her soft, slim body outlined by the sheet, and the dark wells of her eyes. His hands stilled on the buttons. "Two, I think. Perhaps three. How many do you want?"

"That doesn't matter. I would be content with one, or half a dozen." No, the number wasn't important at all.

Slowly he began undoing his buttons and stripped off his shirt again. Tossing it aside, he unzipped his pants and stepped out of them. "You make me react like a teenager," he said, his eyes narrow and bright. Lowering himself onto the bed with her again, he forgot the irritation of living apart, and Claire forgot to worry. When he was making love to her, nothing else was real.

Instead of making the long drive to Houston, they flew down that Friday afternoon, and Max rented a car at the airport. It was already night, but the humid heat enveloped them like a wet blanket, and Claire sighed tiredly. It had been a hectic week, though they hadn't really done anything. But, rather than wait for the weekend, Alma had called every night about some detail that had to be discussed immediately.

She closed her eyes, wanting to rest on the drive to her parents' house. As excited as Alma was, Claire had no hope of getting to bed before midnight—there would be endless discussions about subjects they had already discussed endlessly.

"We're here, love," Max said, touching her arm to wake her.

Claire sat up, startled that she had dozed so quickly. She started to get out of the car, then sank back against the seat. "We aren't at Mother's."

"No, we aren't," he agreed, taking her hand and urging her from the car.

"You kept the apartment?"

"It seemed reasonable. I knew I would have to be coming here on business several times a year, and we'll be visiting your parents. Until the original tenant returns, I see no reason to give it up."

Claire was oddly reluctant as they went up in the elevator. She hadn't been in his apartment since the night they had first made love. Her face was burning as he opened the door and she stepped into the elegant black-tiled foyer, with the gilt-framed mirror over the lovely Queen Anne table. She had a vivid memory of her underwear lying discarded on the black tile.

Max dropped their overnighters where he stood and locked the door. His eyes were hot. "We'll go to your parents' house tomorrow."

By now Claire was intimately familiar with that look. She retreated, her heart pounding, and stopped abruptly when she came up against the table.

"Perfect," he crooned, his strong hands closing on her waist and lifting her up.

She buried her hot face against his shoulder. "Here?"

"It's my favorite memory, darling. You were so beautiful…so wild…so ready for me. I've never wanted any woman the way I want you."

"I hated myself for being so shameless," she confessed softly.

"Shameless? You were so beautiful, you took my breath."

Beautiful wasn't a word that Claire was accustomed to hearing in connection with herself, but that night, in Max's arms, she felt beautiful. She would always blush when she remembered that foyer, but thereafter it was with excitement and remembered pleasure, never again with embarrassment.

"I don't see why you shouldn't wear white," Alma said, making a note in a thick notebook she'd already half-filled with reminders. "This isn't the fifties, after all. Not white-white, of course, that's not your color, but you've always looked beautiful in a creamy golden-white."

Alma and Martine had a full head of steam going, making plans enthusiastically. It was her wedding, but Claire was the only calm one. Since she'd arrived that morning, she had listened to the constant chatter, letting them discuss every detail to death before they remembered to ask either her or Max's opinion. Occasionally she looked at Max, and the amusement in his eyes helped her to remain rational.

"The wedding will have to be in England," Alma pronounced, pursing her lips thoughtfully. "I checked, and it's impossible to reserve a church here that's large enough to hold that many people on such short notice. Max, are you certain there won't be any problem in getting your church?"

"I'm positive."

"Then it's England, and let your mother know. Better yet, give me her number and I'll call her. This schedule is going to be murder. Claire, you have to have your dress made here; there won't be time after we get to England. And we'll have to find one of those big garment boxes for shipping the dress over, but I suppose the dressmaker can help with that."

"I could buy a ready-made dress in England," Claire suggested.

"And take the chance of not being able to find what you want? No, that would be awful. Let's see, we'll need to be there at least three days early. Make that a week. Will that inconvenience your family, Max?"

"Not at all. There are so many of us, a few dozen more won't even be noticed. If you don't mind, I'll handle the plane reservations for the group. Do you have a list of everyone?"

Alma scurried around for her list of guests and wrote out another copy of it for Max. He glanced at it, then folded it and put it away in his pocket, not at all dismayed by the prospect of organizing the transportation of so many people to another country. Knowing what she did about executives, Claire thought that his assistant would probably inherit the burden.

"I have a few names to add to the list, but they'll be flying out from Dallas. I'll arrange for everyone to connect in New York."

Rome and Sarah would probably be attending, Claire realized. She had seen the length of the list and was surprised that so many people would travel so far to see a wedding. Even Michael and Celia were going, and she would have thought they would never want to travel again after moving from Michigan to Arizona in a van.

She scarcely had time to wave at Max before she was whisked away to the fabric store to pore over pattern catalogs and bolts of cloth. From there they went to the dressmaker's, and Claire was measured for what seemed like hours. Then Alma insisted that they find the shoes to go with the gown, since it was almost June and that led to a tooth-and-nail battle over anything connected with weddings.

By the time they returned home, Claire was exhausted. Alma and Martine were still going strong, high on adrenaline, and she wondered what kept them from collapsing. Max was waiting for her, and he looped a sheltering arm over her shoulders to hug her to him.

"Shall we leave?" he asked quietly.

She closed her eyes. "Please. I'm so tired I can't think."

Alma started to protest that Claire could spend the night with them then glanced at Max and swallowed the comment. Claire belonged with him now; he had made that plain, though there were still five weeks until the wedding. For all his golden beauty there was a strength in Max that wouldn't permit any interference between him and the woman he'd chosen.

"This is so exhausting," Claire sighed as he drove them back to the apartment. She slipped off her shoes and wiggled her toes, wondering if they would ever feel normal again. "I think digging ditches wouldn't be as tiring as shopping. I can work all day and do chores at night without feeling half as wiped out as I am now. The terrible thing is, I'll have to come back every weekend for fittings!"

"But I'll be with you," Max said. "If it gets to be too much for you, we'll leave it and go back to Dallas."

"Then everything won't get done."

"I would rather have something left undone than to have my wife collapsing of exhaustion."

His wife. More and more Claire was coming to believe that it was really so, that it was really going to happen. She looked at the pearl-and-diamond ring on her left hand then at Max. She loved him so much that it swelled within her like a tide, relentless and eternal.

When they were in bed, she curled her arm around his neck and pressed against him, sighing as her tired muscles relaxed.

Max cuddled her, loving the feel of her body in his arms, right where she belonged. As usual when he was near her or thought about her, he wanted to make love, but she was too tired. He kissed her forehead and held her until she was asleep.

"Just five more weeks, love," he whispered into the darkness. She would be his wife, and he would no longer have this unreasoning fear that she was going to slip through his fingers like mist melting away before the sun.

Chapter 12

Claire managed a tight smile for the airline attendant as she refused a refill of her tea. They would be landing at Heathrow within the hour. She was relieved that the long, monotonous flight was nearly at an end but she tensed inside whenever she thought of meeting Max's family. She had spoken to his mother on the telephone and felt the warmth of the older woman's greetings, but she wondered how she would get through the ordeal of actually meeting all of them. She had memorized the names of his brother and sisters, as well as that of their spouses and the swarms of children, but that was only scratching the top of the list. There were aunts, uncles, cousins, in-laws, grandparents, great-aunts and uncles, as well as their children and spouses. Such a large family was beyond her experience.

Alma and Harmon were sitting directly ahead of them. It was exactly a week before the wedding, and Alma had been working on her ever-present list most of the flight. Martine and Steve and the children would be flying over in three days, followed the next day by the remainder of the guests. Rome and Sarah were attending, with Missy and Jed. Sarah had suggested leaving the children with a sitter, but Claire had become inordinately fond of the two little imps and wanted them present. After all, her wedding would be swarming with children; what difference would two more make? Rome and Sarah would be bringing a young friend, Derek Taliferro, who was home from college for the summer and who spent a lot of time with the Matthews. Claire had met Derek only twice, but had liked him on sight, and that was unusual for her. She was usually far more cautious with strangers, but there was something about Derek that relaxed her. He was inordinately handsome, with curly black hair and calm golden-brown eyes that reached deep into her mind, yet his handsomeness would normally have made Claire distrust him. But the tall, muscular youth had such enormous self-possession and purpose about him, and he was so tender with the children, who adored him, that instinctively she trusted him, too. For all his lack of years Derek was more of a man than most males who were twice his age. Max and Rome treated him as an equal, and they weren't ordinary men themselves.

Claire glanced quickly at Max, wondering if he had any doubts surfacing about the wedding as it drew closer, but she could read nothing in his expression. For all the passionate hours she had spent in his arms, she still sometimes felt as if he were a stranger to her, a handsome, aloof stranger who gave her his lust but not his thoughts. He was affable, charming, attentive, but she always felt as if he were holding something back from her. She loved deeply but had to keep her love hidden, because he didn't seem to want that sort of devotion from her. He wanted her companionship, her body beneath his in the night, but he didn't seem to want her emotions. He asked for none, and he gave none.

That was the real basis for her unease, she realized. She could have faced an army of relatives with poise if only she were certain of Max's love. All those people would be watching her, measuring her, just as she had been watched when she had married Jeff. How would she fit in with such a family, who were so far-flung and numerous, but oddly close for all that? It had never been easy for her to make friends, and his entire family all seemed to be so warm and outgoing. How could they understand her difficulty in warming up to people? Would they think her cold and unfriendly? Her hands were icy, and she clenched them together in an effort to warm them.

The seatbelt sign flashed on over their heads, and a huge knot formed in Claire's chest, making it necessary for her to breathe in swift, shallow gulps. Max didn't notice her anxiety; he was looking forward to seeing his family again, anticipation making his eyes gleam like jewels set in a golden idol's head.

Heathrow was sheer pandemonium, with the summer crowds thronging the airport. Max didn't turn a well-groomed hair at the hurly-burly. He secured a porter with a lifted finger, and just as the last of their luggage came around on the carousel, a joyous, lilting cry of "Max! *Max!*" soared above the noise.

He turned and a grin split his face. "Vicky!" He held out his arms and a tall, blond woman hurled herself into them. He hugged and kissed her enthusiastically, rocking her in his arms. Then he freed one arm to reach out and pull Claire to him. "Claire, this hoyden is my youngest sister, Victoria. Vicky to those of us familiar with her unruly behavior. Vicky, Claire Westbrook."

"Who became instantly famous when she snared the *in*famous Maxwell Conroy," Vicky teased, then enveloped Claire in a warm hug. Claire smiled quietly, thinking that she liked this unpretentious young woman. The family resemblance was strong—Vicky was tall, with the same golden hair, but her eyes were cerulean blue, and her face wasn't as sculptured. Still, she was a striking woman.

Introductions were made to Alma and Harmon; then Victoria led the way out of the air terminal. "How did you end up with the welcoming duties?" Max asked. His left arm was around Claire, and Victoria clung happily to his right.

"Oh, I'm not the lone delegate," Victoria said lightly. "Mother is waiting in the car. She didn't want to brave the hordes, but she couldn't wait for us to get home before she met Claire."

The knot in Claire's chest, which had subsided a bit on meeting Victoria, now rose to lodge in her throat. Max's mother! From the way he talked about her, Claire knew that he adored his mother, and it went without saying that she adored him. What woman wouldn't?

"We brought two cars, because of all the luggage," Victoria explained, smiling at Claire and her parents. "Mother will insist on Claire and Max going with her, if you don't mind. I'm really a safe driver."

"Really?" Max inquired, looking astonished.

"Of course we don't mind," Alma said.

As they approached the parking area, a man in a dark suit opened the door of a black four-door Jaguar, and a tall slender elegantly-dressed woman got out. "Max!" she called, waving her hand. Then dignity was forgotten as she raced to meet him. Max laughed and left Claire and Victoria to sprint across the tarmac. He scooped the woman up in his arms and hugged her tightly.

"So much for our famous British reserve," Victoria observed humorously. "Everyone is always so happy to see Max again that we make absolute fools of ourselves, but there's no resisting him, is there?"

"None at all," Claire replied, watching him. Was that his *mother?* That lovely, too-young woman, with a sleek knot of blond hair just beginning to fade in color?

Before she could get herself under control and readjust her expectations from a gray-haired proper matron to the sleek reality, Max was walking toward her with his mother on his arm. "Mother, my future wife, Claire Westbrook. Darling, this is my mother, Lady Alicia Conroy, dowager countess of Hayden-Prescott."

Lady? *Countess?*

Claire was numb. Somehow she managed to smile and murmur something appropriate. The general enthusiasm of the all-around greetings continued as Alma greeted Lady Alicia, with whom she had had several long telephone conversations. Max's mother was smiling and gracious and seemed genuinely delighted by the occasion. It was several minutes before all the luggage had been packed into the cars and everyone sorted out, Alma and Harmon into Victoria's blue Mercedes, and Max and Claire, with Lady Alicia, into the Jaguar, which was driven by the chauffeur, Sutton.

"Has the mob begun arriving yet?" Max asked, smiling at Lady Alicia and an answering twinkle lit her green eyes.

"Not yet. We expect another few days of relative quiet, though of course those within easy traveling time will have to come over for tea. Did you expect it to be otherwise?"

"I hoped, but no, I didn't *expect* it. Would it be possible for me to reserve any of Claire's time during the next week?"

"Highly doubtful," Lady Alicia said briskly, though the twinkle remained. "There's entirely too much to be done. There hasn't been such excitement in the family since the war ended—even Great-Aunt Eleanor will be attending, and you know she seldom gets out."

"I would be honored, but I know she isn't venturing out on my account."

"Of course not, everyone knows *you*. It's Claire they're interested in."

Claire didn't want everyone to be interested in her; she hated being an object of curiosity. She would become awkward and silent, afraid of doing anything for fear of making a mistake. What had Max done to her? It had been difficult enough to imagine facing an enormous family; why hadn't he told her that he was a member of the British aristocracy? She should have guessed. Would the average Englishman have quite that degree of mixed elegance and arrogance? His accent, his insouciant sophistication, his rather formal manners, all indicated a circumstance of birth and breeding that was far from the ordinary.

"You're very quiet, love," Max said, reaching out to take one of her hands and frowning when he felt its chill. It was, after all, the middle of summer, and was an unusually warm day for London. "Suffering from jet lag?"

"I do feel…disoriented," she replied quietly.

"There's no wonder at that," Lady Alicia said. "I always need a long nap after a trip, and I've never been quite so far as the States. Don't worry, dear, there's no one descending on us today to meet you, and even if there were, I would send them away."

Lady Alicia was warm and friendly, and it was soon plain that Max had inherited his wry humor from her. On closer inspection it was possible to place her age at perhaps sixty, but it was a very young sixty. Her skin was smooth and virtually unwrinkled, except for the laugh lines at the corners of her eyes, and her hair was still thick, though fading in color. She enjoyed life and enjoyed her family. Love was plain in her eyes when she looked at Max.

Claire listened to them talk, answering whenever she was asked a direct question, but for the most part she was quiet, wondering what else she should expect.

The estate was almost two hours' drive from London, but

finally the Jaguar slowed, then turned left through a set of gates guarded by a thatch-roofed gatehouse. Victoria and Claire's parents followed closely behind in the Mercedes. "We're almost there," Max said. "You can just see the chimneys now. By the way, Mother, where have you put us?"

"Claire and her parents are to be with me at Prescott House," Lady Alicia said serenely. "You'll have your old room at Hayden Hill."

He didn't like that. His eyes narrowed and darkened to green, but he held his tongue. Claire was grateful that he hadn't demanded that they be given a room together, though he was possessive enough and arrogant enough to do exactly that. His fingers tightened momentarily on hers, and she realized that he had sensed her feelings.

Then they rounded a curve, and Hayden Hill came into view. It wasn't a castle, but it was one of the old, enormous manor houses, with chimneys sticking into the sky like sentinels, the yellow brick mellowed with age to a dull gold color. The lawn was immaculately manicured, the hedges sculptured, the rose beds perfectly tended. This was where Max had grown to manhood, and Claire felt the gulf widening between them.

They drove past Hayden Hill down a narrow, paved lane. "My house is just down here," Lady Alicia explained. "It's the traditional dowager house, and I decided to honor tradition by moving into it when Clayton married."

"Not to mention escaping the bloody rows Clayton and Edie used to have when they were first married," Max added, his eyelids drooping.

Lady Alicia smiled at Claire. "My eldest son was very much the earl when he and Edie married," she explained placidly. "It took her the better part of a year to instruct him on the finer points of marriage."

Prescott House was less than half the size of Hayden Hill, though built in a similar style and with the same mellowed brick, but Claire soon found that it possessed eighteen rooms. Both Hayden Hill and the dowager house had been built in the late 1700s, after the original manor house had been destroyed by fire but both had been extensively modernized as time passed. Therefore, unlike many of the old manor houses, Hayden Hill and Prescott House both had efficient wiring and plumbing, while modern insulation and heating made it possible for the enormous fireplaces to be used for pleasure rather than for actual heating purposes. There was even a fireplace in Claire's bedroom, and when she was finally alone, she ran her hand lightly, dreamily, over the polished wood of the mantel. It was a beautiful room, with white lace curtains and a matching bedspread. A rose-colored carpet covered the wooden floor. The furniture was rosewood, and the bed was an enormous four-poster, so high off the floor that she had to mount steps to crawl onto it. A private bath and wardrobe adjoined.

How could Max not have mentioned all of this? It wasn't as if it were an insignificant detail. She had worried about living up to the Halseys, and now she had fallen in love with a man who made the Halseys look like Johnny-come-latelies.

She took a quick shower, unable to stand the grime of travel a moment longer. A thick, fleecy toweling robe hung on a hook behind the door, and Claire wrapped herself in it rather than try to hunt hers out of the pile of luggage. Leaving the bathroom, she stopped short when she saw Max lounging in the reading chair. He looked up, that intent look coming into his eyes when he saw her shiny face and warm, damp body wrapped in the robe.

"My mother can have the most perverse sense of humor at times," he said, holding out his hand to her. "Come here, love, and let me hold you for a little while before I'm banished to Hayden Hill."

She put her hand in his and found herself gathered close, then perched on his lap. Sighing, Claire put her head on his shoulder and felt his arms close around her with steely strength.

"You've been quiet since we left New York," he murmured. "Is something wrong, or is it just jet lag?"

While he held her, nothing was wrong, but she couldn't spend the rest of her life in his arms. "No, there's nothing wrong."

He slipped his hand inside the robe and cupped her breast, stroking her flesh with gentle fingers. "Shall I leave you to your nap, then? Your mother and father have already gone to their room. The telephone is ringing constantly, but Mother is fending everyone off."

She clutched at his shoulders. "Don't go, Max, please. Hold me for a little while longer."

"All right, love." His voice was low. He tipped her face up and kissed her slowly, his tongue probing into her mouth, and his hand was no longer quite so gentle. "This is going to be an endlessly long week," he said, moving his lips down her throat. "I may kidnap you one afternoon and take you to a place where we can be alone."

If only he could kidnap her and take her away now. If only the wedding were behind them and they could return to Dallas.

It only got worse. Sometimes it seemed as if she never had a moment to herself, and every day there were more and more people to meet. Max's wedding was an excuse for a party every night as the celebration escalated. Alma was in her element, and Harmon was perfectly comfortable with the life of an English country gentleman. Then Martine and Steve arrived with the children, and they were exuberantly welcomed. Martine got on like wildfire with Max's outgoing sisters, Emma and Patricia and Victoria, and Prescott House rang with their chatter and laughter.

There were lunches, afternoon teas and endless visits sandwiched between appointments with the photographer, the caterer and the florist. The gowns were pressed and ready, and the tuxedos had arrived from the drycleaners. The most amazing thing to Claire was that no one had had to rent one. It was a gracious, cushioned life, marching to a well-ordered beat, with privileges taken for granted.

There was no time to see Max alone, but becoming acquainted with his background told her more about him than what she had learned before. He had been born superior and saw nothing unusual about his life, even though he was the family maverick. He was a Conroy of Hayden-Prescott. The earldom was a rich one, and his family estate had not been opened to tourists in an effort at survival. Max's inheritance made him independently wealthy; it was only his own restless genius and drive that sent him first to Canada then to the States to take on the challenge of high-level corporate dealings. Centuries of aristocratic breeding ran in his veins.

She couldn't fit into his world. A man in his position needed a wife who was comfortable in society, and Claire knew that she would always prefer a far more private life. She had driven herself into the ground trying to be suitable for the Halseys and had failed. How could she possibly measure up to the standards of the Conroys of Hayden-Prescott? They were the elite, and she was an assistant from Houston, Texas.

The celebrations going on around her took on an unreal, circus quality, and she went through the motions, doing as she was told, going where she was guided, while the certainty grew inside her that it was all a mistake. Max would soon come to see how unsuitable she was, and he would be impatient. She knew all the stages well, having suffered through them before. First he would be impatient because she wasn't living up to expectations; then would come indifference, when it no longer mattered. And, finally, he would pity her. She didn't think she could bear that, to have him pity her. Isolated from him, without even the reassurance of his passion, Claire withdrew as she had always done in an effort to protect herself. Their marriage wouldn't have a firm base even under the best of circumstances, with only a lopsided love holding it together. Max's reasons for proposing to her weren't clear. Perhaps he thought she would be suitable; perhaps he was ready to begin his own family. But he hadn't proposed out of love. Even during all the times when they had made love, with passion burning so high between them that sometimes she felt she would shatter in his arms, he'd never said anything about love.

She had to call it off before it went any further. When she thought of what she was about to do, of the scandal it would cause, Claire went cold, but she couldn't see any other alternative. The marriage simply wouldn't work, and it would destroy her if one day Max despised her for her inability to be what he wanted, what he expected, what he *deserved.*

She reached that conclusion the day before the wedding, but she had no opportunity to talk to him. They were always surrounded by family, both his and hers, and Rome and Sarah had arrived to add to the crowd. The wedding rehearsal went off without a hitch. Everyone was in high spirits, laughing and joking, and the ancient enormous stone church echoed with their joy. Claire watched it all with dark, stricken eyes, wondering what they would all think of her when they knew the wedding had been called off.

Dear God, she couldn't just leave him standing at the altar. His fierce pride would never forgive her for that, and she couldn't live if he hated her. Determined to talk to him, Claire threaded her way through the crowd and caught his sleeve. "Max?"

He smiled down at her. "Yes, love?" Then one of his

cousins hailed him, and she lost his attention. Her nails bit into her palms as she stood beside him, trying to smile and act normally when she felt brittle inside, as if she would shatter at the slightest touch.

"Max, it's important!" she said desperately. "I have to talk to you!"

Max looked down at her again, and this time he saw her pale, taut face, the tension in every line of her body. He covered her hand with his, holding her fingers to his arm. "What is it? Is something wrong?"

"It's private. Can we go somewhere we can talk?" Her eyes begged him, and automatically he put his arm around her as if he could shield her from whatever was bothering her. "Yes, of course," he said, turning to walk with her to the door.

"Oh, no, you two lovebirds!" someone called. "You can't sneak out on the night before your wedding!"

Max looked over his shoulder. "Don't be ridiculous," he said, ushering Claire out the door. "Of course I can."

He led her outside into the cool English night, and the darkness folded around them as they walked down the lane toward Prescott House, leaving behind the brilliantly lit church. Their steps crunched on the loose gravel, and Max pulled her closer in an effort to keep the chill from her bare arms. "What is it?" he asked quietly.

She stopped and closed her eyes, praying for strength to get through this. "It's all a mistake," she said in a muffled tone.

"What is?"

If only he didn't sound so patient! Tears blurred her eyes as she looked up at him in the darkness. "This is," she said, waving her hand at the church behind them. "All of it. You, me, the wedding. I can't go through with it."

He drew in a sharp breath, and tension invaded his muscles. "Why is it a mistake? I thought everything was going along well. My family likes you, and you've given the impression that you like them."

"I do." Tears were making her voice ragged, and she wondered how long she could hold out before dissolving into sobs. "But can't you see what a mismatch we are? I told you the first time we went out together that I'm not in the same league with you, but I didn't know how right I was! I don't fit in here! I can't be more than what I am, and I'll never be the aristocratic wife you need. Your…expectations are too high." She choked and couldn't say anything else, but perhaps it was just as well. Wordlessly she pulled off the pearl-and-diamond ring and extended it to him. He didn't take it, only stared down at it as she held it out in her shaking hand.

Claire couldn't hold back the sobs any longer. Grabbing his hand, she put the ring in it and folded his fingers over it. "It's for the best," she wept, backing away from him. "I love you too much to disappoint you the way I would."

She fled down the dark lane, too blinded by tears to be able to see where she was going, but she knew that Prescott House was down the lane, and she would eventually get there. Misery choked her; she didn't hear the running footsteps behind her. A hard hand grabbed her, swinging her around, and a small scream broke from her throat. She had a glimpse of his face, hard and furious, before he tossed her over his shoulder and started back up the lane.

"Max—wait!" she gasped, startled out of her tears. "You can't—what are you doing?"

"Taking my woman away," he snapped, his long legs eating up the distance as he strode toward the church.

People were milling around in front of the church, chatting before going on to Hayden Hill for the after-rehearsal party. When Max strode into view, there was a moment of dead silence, and Claire buried her face against his back.

"I say," his brother Clayton drawled. "Isn't there time enough for that tomorrow?"

"No, there's not," Max snapped, not even looking around. "I'm taking your car."

"So I see," Clayton said, watching as Max opened the door of a Mercedes and put Claire inside. Claire dropped her face into her hands, so miserable that embarrassment was only a small part of her woes.

Rome Matthews grinned, thinking of a time when he had carried his woman away from a party.

Standing on the steps, elegant in an oyster-white linen suit and pearls, Lady Alicia watched her son drive way with his intended bride. "Do you suppose," she mused, "there's any point in waiting for them? No, of course not. We'll have the party without them," she decided.

Max drove for a long time, his temper crackling around him like a visible flame. Claire sat silently, her eyes burning, wondering if he were taking her anywhere in particular, or if he were simply driving aimlessly, but she didn't dare ask him. She had the answer to her question when he pulled into the courtyard of a small inn.

"What are we doing here?" She gasped as he got out of the car and reached in to pull her out. Roughly he put the pearl ring back on her finger.

He didn't reply but pulled her into the inn. It was small and rustic, just the sort of inn that had lined England's roads for centuries. It was a pub on the bottom, with rooms on top. Max signed the register, paid the landlord and towed Claire after him up a narrow flight of stairs, while the landlord watched them with mild curiosity. Stopping before a door, Max unlocked it and pulled Claire inside, then turned to lock the door again.

"Now," he said, his voice almost guttural with rage. "Let's talk about this. To begin, the only standards and expectations you are measuring yourself against are your own. No one else expects or wants you to be anything other than yourself. I don't want you to be perfect. That would be bloody hell for me to try to live up to, because I'm not perfect. I don't want a china doll who never makes mistakes—I want *you*. As for that garbage about the aristocratic wife I deserve—" He broke off, his fists clenching with rage. Claire found that she had backed across the room, her eyes enormous as she stared at him. She couldn't believe the fury that burned in him. His eyes were like lasers, searing her.

He began unbuttoning his shirt with rough movements. "I'm a man, not a title, and the bloody damned title isn't mine anyway. My brother is the earl, and thank God he's healthy, with two sons to inherit before it would come to me. I don't want the title. I have American citizenship now. I have a job with a lot of damned responsibility that keeps me interested the way an earldom never would, and I have a family I love. I also have the woman I love, and I'll be bloody damned to hell and back before I let you walk out on me now." He pulled his shirt off and tossed it aside then unbuckled his belt and unzipped his pants.

"If you don't want to get married, all right," he bit out, stripping naked. Claire stared at him, her mouth going dry. "We'll just live together, but don't ever think that we *won't* live together, married or not. You're the only woman I've ever met who can drive me so wild that I lose control, and you're the only woman I've ever met whom I love so much I ache with it. I nearly ruined it in the beginning by not being completely honest with you, and you stopped trusting me. You've never trusted me again, have you? Too bloody damned bad, because I'm not letting you go. Is that clear?"

Claire swallowed, looking at him. He was so beautiful that she hurt. "Do you know how many 'bloody damns' and 'bloody hells' you've just said?" she whispered.

"What the bloody hell difference does it make?" he asked, stalking across the floor to grab her and toss her onto the bed.

She bounced and grabbed at the covers to keep from flying off. "You never told me before that you loved me." Her voice sounded strange, too high and tight.

He glared at her, reaching behind her for the zipper on her dress. "Is that an unforgivable sin? You never told me that you love me, either, until you blurted it out at the same time you said you couldn't marry me. What do you think that did to me? I've been trying for weeks to make you trust me again, wondering if you'd ever love me, and you throw it at me like that."

He pulled her dress off, and Claire put her hands on his chest, her heart pounding so hard that she could barely think. "Max, wait. Why are we here?"

"It's obvious, isn't it? I'm having my wedding night, even if you're determined not to have a wedding. I love you, and, I repeat, I'm not letting you go."

"What will everyone think?"

"I don't care." He stopped, looking down at her with burning eyes. "I love you. You're more important to me than anyone else on this earth, and I'd walk on live coals to get to you."

He had managed to strip her completely, and his gaze wandered down her slim body. He had been rough before, but his touch now was so gentle that it was almost like a whisper of wind as he parted her legs and eased into her. Claire accepted him, her body arching in pleasure, her hands clinging to him. She loved him so much that she thought she would burst with it, and it was in her eyes as he propped himself on his elbows over her.

"Let's try this again," he whispered. "I love you, Claire Westbrook, for all the things you are. You're gentle and loving, and you have dreams in your eyes that I want to share. Will you marry me?"

She would never have believed that she could soar so high. With her arms locked around his neck, straining up to put her mouth to his, Claire looked up into those brilliant sea-colored eyes and said, "Yes."

She walked down the aisle of the huge, drafty old church with her cream-colored satin gown rustling and the veil trailing behind her. Her father's arm was steady under her hand. Familiar and beloved faces turned toward her as she walked: the faces of the many people she had met this past week, all beaming at her; Sarah Matthews, pale and serene, with her children beside her; Derek Taliferro, his golden eyes wise beyond his years, smiling as he watched her. Alma, smiling and crying at the same time and still looking lovely while she did it. Lady Alicia, her eyes brimming with pride. At the altar, waiting for her, were Martine, and Max's sisters, four heads in varying shades of blond. Rome Matthews stood beside Max, his dark eyes seeking out his wife where she sat in the pews, and a silent message passed between them. Clayton also stood there, and two of Max's cousins.

And Max. Tall, impossibly handsome, and so beloved that it hurt her to look at him. His image was blurred by the veil she wore, but he watched her, and there was a moist glitter in his eyes, like that of the sea.

Her father gave her hand to Max, who moved to stand by her side. The pearl on her hand gleamed in the golden candlelight of the many tapers that flickered throughout the church.

   Max pressed her hand warmly, and she looked up at him.
His eyes were steady. Hers were dark, secretive pools, but
there were no more secrets between them. Turning toward the
altar, they began speaking their vows.

* * * * *

For M.S.R., always.

FOR THE BABY'S SAKE

USA TODAY Bestselling Author

Christine Rimmer

CHRISTINE RIMMER

came to her profession the long way around. Before settling down to write about the magic of romance, she'd been an actress, a salesclerk, a janitor, a model, a phone sales representative, a teacher, a waitress, a playwright and an office manager. Now that she's finally found work that suits her perfectly, she insists she never had a problem keeping a job—she was merely gaining "life experience" for her future as a novelist. Those who know her best withhold comment when she makes such claims; they are grateful that she's at last found steady work. Christine is grateful, too—not only for the joy she finds in writing, but for what waits when the day's work is through: a man she loves who loves her right back, and the privilege of watching their children grow and change day to day. She lives with her family in Oklahoma. Visit Christine at www.christinerimmer.com.

Chapter 1

Clay Barrett watched his cousin, Andie McCreary, push her food around on her plate. He knew she was trying to make it appear that she was eating, but he wasn't fooled. He'd also noticed that she'd refused both wine and a cocktail.

"Everything all right?" their waitress asked.

Andie shot the waitress a smile, one that tried its best to be bright. "It's wonderful. Thanks." Then she bent her head earnestly over her plate and pushed the food around a little more.

Clay cast about for the right opening. "You know, it's worked out surprisingly well, your running the office. I'll be frank. I didn't expect it to."

Andie looked up at him, her brown eyes unnervingly direct. "I know you didn't. You let me stay on when you took over because Uncle Don asked you to give me a chance."

Her frankness surprised him a little, but he recovered quickly and admitted in a cautious tone, "That's true."

Don and Della Barrett had adopted Clay when Clay was

ten years old. The love and gratitude he felt toward them was the cornerstone on which his life was built. There was very little he could refuse either of them.

Andie added pointedly, "But you *kept* me on because I run Barrett and Company better than you ever thought it could be run."

"Right again." Clay tried a smile.

Andie didn't smile back. "I'd be difficult to replace."

"No argument."

Andie caught her inner lip lightly between her teeth. It seemed to Clay that he could hear what she was thinking: *are you going to replace me?*

But she didn't say the words aloud. A few other things still remained to be said first. They hadn't quite worked their way around to those things yet. But they would, very soon now.

Andie concentrated on her plate again. Clay looked at the sleek crown of her head and thought of the past, of their rivalry when they were growing up.

Andie had been the family darling, the *lovable* one, the mere fact of her existence enough to get her anything she wanted. Clay was the achiever. He showed his worth by what he did.

Their resentment of each other had been as natural as breathing. They'd disliked each other on sight, from the day the Barretts had adopted Clay. And they went on disliking each other, right up to the day Clay left home, on full scholarship, for UCLA.

When Clay left, he'd been eighteen and Andie had been seventeen. Clay hadn't come back for ten years, except to visit. But then last April his father had suffered a heart attack. At the family's urging Clay had decided to return right away to Northern California to take over his father's one-man accounting and investment-consulting firm.

When Clay stepped in at Barrett & Co., his cousin Andie

had been the office manager there for two years. Clay had been absolutely positive that he and Andie wouldn't last a week as a team.

He'd been dead wrong. In the years that Clay had been away, his willful, unfocused cousin had grown up.

Clay was stunned to discover that Andie was absolute dynamite at her job. She could work circles around any of the topnotch clerks and assistants he'd used in L.A. at the major international firm where he'd been clawing his way up through the ranks for five years.

Andie kept ahead of the work load. She was pleasant and businesslike. The clients adored her. And if she remembered how she and her new boss used to squabble and fight when they were teenagers, she never mentioned it or let it affect their working relationship.

Yes, it *had* worked out. It was still working out, in spite of the change in Andie the past couple of months.

Andie pushed her plate away, giving up the pretense that she would eat the food on it.

The waitress appeared again. "All done?"

Andie nodded. Clay ordered coffee. The waitress looked questioningly at Andie.

Andie shook her head and murmured, "Nothing more for me."

"You can bring the check, too," Clay said.

The waitress went about her business, pouring Clay's coffee and bringing the bill. Andie fiddled with her water glass and watched the busers and the hostess, the waiters and the other customers, anyone but Clay.

Clay studied Andie, noting, as he was always doing lately, the faint shadows, like tender bruises, beneath her eyes, the grim set to her pretty mouth. She seemed thinner than before, and there was a tautness about her.

At the office, she was as wonderfully efficient as always, maybe more so. But the charm and the openness that Clay had believed as much a part of her as her gleaming nearly black hair and her easy, musical laugh, were gone. For the past several weeks, Andie had burned with a determined kind of heat.

And Clay had to face facts here. It was the end of *February,* for God's sake. Tax time was upon them. Barrett & Co. was enjoying a brisk business. And it was going to keep getting busier until April fifteenth. If Andie flaked out on him, Clay was going to have problems.

And if Clay had problems, his father, who only worked a few hours a day now, would be drawn back into the business full-time. Don didn't need that kind of pressure, not anymore. That kind of pressure could cause another heart attack. And another heart attack might be the end of him.

"I know what you're thinking, Clay." Andie's voice was tight.

Clay realized he'd been silent too long. He looked up at the beamed ceiling overhead.

"God, Andie…" He breathed the words softly and in them he heard all of his own worry and frustration.

"I'm not going to let anybody down," she said slowly and evenly, as if she was afraid he might not understand the words. "I swear to you. I can handle this."

The moment of truth was upon them. He demanded, quietly, "And just what is *this?*"

Her mouth twisted. A spark of anger lit her eyes. All at once, the old rivalry was there again, rising up to poison the air between them.

"You know. Don't pretend you don't." She spoke in a low, intense whisper. "I've seen you watching me lately, *measuring* me, putting that razor-sharp mind of yours to work on the changes in me. We might as well be kids again, the way you've been following me with those eyes of yours."

Clay stared at her, understanding exactly what she meant. When they were kids, he *had* watched her. She was always doing things she shouldn't and he was always finding her out. He'd caught her pawing around in Granny Sid's bureau drawers when she was nine, smoking one of her father's Roi Tans when she was eleven and riding on the back of Johnny Pardo's Harley Davidson when she was fifteen.

"I never ratted on you." The childish words were out of Clay's mouth before he knew he would say them. They were words from the old language they had shared growing up, the language of their rivalry and mutual resentment.

Andie answered in the same vein. "You never had to rat. You knew. You knew *everything*. I hated you for that, for watching and knowing all the ways I messed up, while you were so perfect and did everything right."

"Andie…"

"No." She chopped the air with a hand, then dragged in a breath. Her eyes shone with tears that she wouldn't let fall. She looked up at the beamed ceiling, just as Clay had a few moments ago, as if seeking whatever he had sought there.

At last she lowered her chin and met his gaze across the table. "I'm sorry. I promised myself I wasn't going to do that."

"What?"

She sighed and the saddest hint of a smile tugged the corners of her mouth. "Act like a brat." She waved a hand on which a gold bracelet of delicate linked hearts gleamed. "Prove to you that I'm still the flaky little twit I was when we were kids."

"I know you're not." He spoke with firm conviction.

She peered at him sideways and in the dim light, for a single instant, she almost looked mischievous. "Meaning I *was* a flaky little twit back then?"

He looked at her, not speaking, realizing he'd more or less put his foot in it.

She echoed his thoughts. "Cautious Clay puts his foot in it once again." She called him by the name she used to taunt him with back in the old days.

He tried to look accusing. "You set me up for that one."

She let out a teasing chuckle. "I certainly did. And it's all right. You only said the truth. I *was* a flaky little twit when we were kids."

"A very charming flaky little twit."

Two spots of color appeared on her pale cheeks. "Well, thank you very much."

"You're welcome." He felt absurdly satisfied to have heard her laugh, to have been the cause of her blush, however faint.

They were quiet for a moment. But it wasn't a bad silence, Clay thought, with some relief. Somehow, resurrecting their old antagonism had reminded them of what their current professional relationship often made them forget.

Beyond being a boss and an employee, even beyond the actual fact of being cousins, they were *family*. They were *connected*—not by blood, since Clay had been adopted—but through the people they both loved and through a shared past.

"Hell. Andie."

"Go ahead. Ask it." The last traces of her teasing laughter had fled. Her eyes were haunted again, her expression resigned.

There was nothing else to do but say it. "Are you pregnant?"

She sighed and rubbed her eyes. "Yes, I am. Are you going to fire me?"

Chapter 2

Clay glared at her, offended. "I wouldn't fire you just because you're pregnant. What do you think I am?"

But Andie didn't want to fight with him. "Clay, don't get self-righteous on me. Please."

He relaxed a little. "All right. Sorry. Let's try this another way."

"What way?"

"Let me start out right now by saying that I have no intention of firing you."

Her slim shoulders slumped, whether with relief or weariness, Clay didn't know for sure. "That's one problem solved," she said softly. "Thank you."

"Don't thank me. I'm the one who should be thankful that you aren't planning to quit. As you pointed out a while ago, you'd be damn near impossible to replace."

"Oh, Clay." Her expression was very vulnerable suddenly. In a totally spontaneous gesture, she reached across the table and squeezed his hand. "Do you have any idea how much it means to me to hear you say that?"

Her hand was warm over his. Clay liked the way it felt, which shocked him a little, for some strange reason. He must have stiffened, because she quickly took her hand away.

"I've embarrassed you," she said in a tiny voice.

He cleared his throat. "No. No, really. You haven't. Not at all." God, he was babbling like an idiot. He drew in a long, slow breath. Then he reminded himself that there were still some things they had to get clear between them.

He made himself ask, though it came out sounding pompous and ridiculously formal, "So then it's settled that you won't be leaving Barrett and Company?"

"Yes."

"Good. So. Are you planning to get married?"

"No."

"I see." He forced himself to go on, though each word emerged more stilted than the last. "Then as far as the, er, child. What exactly do you plan to do about that?"

That burning intensity came into her eyes again. "I'm going to keep it."

He tried to assimilate what she was telling him. "Raise a baby *alone?*"

She let out a little puff of air, then pointed out in a too- reasonable tone, "I'm a single woman. How else would I raise it?"

He knew he should probably just let it be, yet he heard himself asking, "Do you really believe that's the best choice?"

"It's *my* choice." She looked down at the table and then lifted her head again to face him directly. "I've thought about it a lot, Clay, believe me. It's what I want and the best I can do, given the circumstances." She curled her fingers around her water glass, as if to steady herself. Then she shot Clay a defiant look. "A lot of women raise children alone these days."

"That doesn't mean it's a good thing."

"I didn't say it was *good*. I said it's the way it is."

Right then, the hostess led another couple to a booth near theirs. Both Clay and Andie fell silent for a moment, guarding the privacy of their conversation.

As Clay watched the hostess handing out menus, he reminded himself that he really shouldn't get in too deep here. He shouldn't push for answers to questions he was probably better off not thinking about.

He already had most of the information he required as Andie's boss. She was going to be a mother and she wanted to keep working for him. All he needed to know now was how she planned to manage everything—how much leave she was going to need and when she would need it. The rest was her own personal business.

But he couldn't seem to stop himself. Once the other couple was settled with their menus, he turned to his cousin and asked, "What about the father?"

Her shoulders tensed. "What about him? He's not involved."

Clay leaned forward. He pitched his voice low. "Who is he?"

She flinched, then steadied herself. "It doesn't matter."

"Of course it matters."

"No, it doesn't. As I said, he's not involved."

"Andie, I just want to know who he is."

"I understand that." Her jaw was set. "And I'm not going to tell you."

"Why not?"

"Because it's not really any of your business, Clay. And because it would probably only cause trouble if you knew."

"What do you mean, trouble?"

"I mean, you might get it into your head that you should go after the guy or something. I don't know." She lifted her hands in a helpless gesture. "How should I know what you'd do? I just know that nothing but trouble could come from your knowing the man's name."

"That's not necessarily true."

"I don't want to argue any more about this. I'm not telling you. That's all." She had that stubborn, determined look she used to get when they were kids. Whenever Andie got that look, it didn't matter what a guy did, she wouldn't talk.

Clay tried another tack. "Are you saying that the father wants nothing to do with the child?"

Andie sat back from him, then she lifted her water glass and drank from it. Carefully she set down the glass. "Look. What was between me and him just didn't work out."

"Does he *know* that you're pregnant."

"Yes. He knows."

"How did he find out?"

"I contacted him and told him about it."

"And?"

"I told him I thought he should know, that's all."

"What did he say?"

"What could he say? I told you, it was already over between us. There was no chance of trying again, even for the sake of a child. We just…aren't suited to each other. But I did tell him about the baby, because it seemed like he had a right to know. And he said he'd help out wherever he could, but he didn't want me to involve him."

Clay's chest felt tight. "And that was it?"

He saw the flicker of hesitation in her eyes before she answered, "Yes."

"What else?"

"Clay…"

"Just tell me. What else?"

"You're bullying me."

"What else?"

"All right, all right. He sent some money."

"Money."

"Yes. To help out."

"To help out."

She glared at him. "Is there an echo in here?"

He ignored her sarcasm. "Is he going to give the baby his name?"

Andie looked away, then back. "No. He's not. And that's fine with me."

"But I thought he said he'd help you *wherever he could?*"

"Clay, I—"

"What does that mean, *wherever he could?*"

"Clay, if you don't stop this—"

"Just answer me. What does that mean?"

"I'm not kidding here, Clay."

"He could help you by marrying you. Did he say anything about that?" Clay heard the leashed rage in his own voice. He tried to rein it in. He reminded himself again that the things he was grilling her about didn't really concern him at all. But now that the fact of Andie's pregnancy was out, he was finding it very hard to deal with.

Damn it, she *was* family to him. And she had been used. He just couldn't help imagining the immense satisfaction he'd feel if he could only get his hands on the thoughtless bastard who'd done this to her, the rotten worm who now seemed to think a few lousy bucks would get him off the hook.

Andie was looking at him guardedly.

He asked again, "What about the man doing the right thing and marrying you, Andie?"

"Stop it, Clay."

"Well, what about it?"

"If you don't settle down, I'm going to get up and leave." She spoke softly but very deliberately.

He stared at her. On the table between them, both of his fists were clenched. "I'm sorry." He pushed the words out through his teeth.

She met his gaze, unwavering. "Then relax. Sit back. Take a deep breath or two."

"Fine. I will."

"Good. Then do it."

He closed his eyes and mentally counted to ten. Then he made himself sit back in the booth. He pulled air into his lungs and slowly let it out.

"Better," she said warily.

"Good. Now, what about his marrying you?"

She looked at him for a moment, as if gauging how much to say. At last she allowed, "I told you, it's over between us. It didn't work out. I don't want to marry him. And he doesn't want to marry me."

"Why is that?"

She looked away. "Enough. Stop."

"What?"

"I said, enough. I don't want to talk any more about the father. There's nothing more to say about him. I cashed the check he sent me and that's the end of it. I want nothing more from him. I'm not going to marry him, but I *am* going to raise my baby. The man is out of my—*our*—lives. For good and all."

"There are laws, Andie, that will force the man to take responsibility for—"

She put up a hand. "I don't care about laws. My baby and I will be just fine on our own. We'll manage. If you can't accept that, Clay, then maybe I will have to look for another job."

"More coffee?" The smiling waitress appeared out of nowhere, coffeepot held high.

Clay shook his head tightly. Andie gave the young woman a sheepish smile.

"Well, if you need anything else…"

"We won't," Clay said, not bothering to disguise his impatience. The waitress left them. As soon as she was out of sight, Clay turned to his cousin. "Please don't quit." Somehow he managed a rueful shrug. "I'll do my best to mind my own damn business."

Andie nodded. "Fair enough."

Clay forced himself to stop thinking murderous thoughts about an unknown man and to consider the things they really did have to agree on. "So. Have you figured out how you intend to run my office and also have a baby a few months from now?"

"It's more than a few months away, thank goodness," she corrected him.

"When?"

"I'm due in September. That's seven months."

In his head a voice whispered, *Then she's two months along.* Which meant she'd probably become pregnant over the holidays.

Over the holidays, while Jeff was here…

"My due date is September twenty-fourth," Andie was saying. "I saw a doctor just last week."

God. He didn't want to think it. But the timing was right.

And Clay had seen the signs that Andie and Jeff were drawn to each other. His best friend and his cousin had spent at least one evening alone together, as a matter of fact.

"Clay?" Andie's voice showed concern. "Are you all right?"

"Fine. I'm fine."

No, he told himself firmly, it wasn't Jeff. It *couldn't* be Jeff. He wasn't even going to let himself imagine a thing like that. He reminded himself for the umpteenth time to mind his own business, to stick to the question of how she planned to manage both a job and motherhood.

"Clay?"

He blinked. "Yes. Now, where were we?"

"Are you sure you're—"

"Absolutely." He answered the question before she finished it, then suggested, "Since you've thought this all through, why don't you tell me exactly what you have in mind?"

She actually smiled as she launched into her plans. "All right. I'd like to work as long as I can and then I'll take a short leave, maybe eight weeks at the most, to have the baby. I intend to be back at the office as soon as I can find a good baby-sitter. It should work out just fine. Or at least as fine as something like this *can* work out. I mean, September isn't a half-bad time, really. Things aren't too crazy then. And I can be back before the first of the year, when it all starts picking up again." She tipped her head and regarded him. "So, how does that sound?"

Superimposed over Andie's features he saw Jeff's face, the laughing blue eyes and the devilish grin.

"Clay?" Andie asked anxiously.

He could hear Jeff's voice, back in college, when a woman Jeff didn't even know threw her arms around him at a homecoming game and kissed him right on the mouth. Jeff had winked at Clay over the woman's shoulder. *Hell, bud. I'm fatal to women. What can I say?*

"Clay, does that sound all right?"

Clay blinked and forced himself back to the here and now. "Yeah, Andie. It sounds just fine. And I'm glad to hear you've been to a doctor, that you're taking care of yourself."

"I am. I promise." She gave him a real smile now, and it occurred to him how much he'd missed her smiles the past few weeks. She shifted in her seat. "So, then. Are we done?"

"One more thing."

"Yes?"

"Your parents—have you told them yet?"

"No."

"When will you tell them?"

"Right away."

"And what will you say?"

"Just what I said to you. That I'm going to have a baby and I'm raising it on my own."

The very next night Andie faced her parents.

She had them over to her apartment on High Street and she cooked them pot roast. Her father loved pot roast.

Andie waited until the dinner dishes had been cleared away and her father was on his second helping of chocolate cake before she dared to broach the subject of the baby.

With her stomach feeling queasy and her heart pounding a little too fast, she got up to refill her parents' coffee cups and took her seat again. Then she folded her hands on the tabletop and gave a little cough, because her throat felt so tight.

"Andie?" her mother asked, before Andie had said a word.

Andie met her mother's dark eyes and saw the worry and apprehension there. The past several weeks, her mother had asked her more than once if something was bothering her. Andie had put her mother off with vague replies. She said she was fine, or that she was a little tired. But her mother hadn't been convinced, Andie knew. And now, with that emotional sixth sense a mother often has, Thelma McCreary understood that she was on the verge of finding out what had been troubling her only child.

Andie wanted to break down and cry. But she didn't. Now was not the time for indulging herself. Now was the time to tell the truth and tell it with dignity.

As much of the truth as *could* be told, anyway.

She had considered holding off telling them until she was

in her second trimester. But last night had changed her mind about that. Somehow, the moment she'd told Clay the truth, she'd seen that there was no point in postponing telling the rest of them. The sooner they knew, the sooner they could start to get used to the idea of having a single mother in the family.

Andie looked from her father to her mother, thinking that there were a lot of women in the world who'd give anything to have a close-knit family as she had. But there was a price to pay for being part of such a family. If she were all alone in the world, she wouldn't have to tell painful truths like this to people whose love and respect she craved. If she were all alone in the world, the fact that she was going to have a baby without being married would be nobody's business but her own.

"Andie, what is it?" Andie's mother had set down her fork, leaving her cake only half-eaten.

"Well, I—"

Her father now pushed his own plate away. "All right. What's going on? Something's going on."

"I think," Thelma said rather faintly, "that Andie wants to tell us something."

"What?" Andie's father demanded. "What does she want to say?"

"Just wait, Joe. Let her get to it." Thelma patted her husband's hand.

The wifely gesture sent a sharp pang through Andie. She thought of the tiny baby that slept within her and couldn't help wishing there was a good man like her father at her side.

But there wasn't. She was on her own. That was reality. And she had made her choice.

Andie straightened in her chair. She forced a smile to meet her parents' worried frowns.

"I don't really know how to go about telling you this. I know you're not going to like it, and that it will probably hurt you. And I'm sorry, so sorry. But I've made up my mind."

"What?" Joe impatiently wiped his mouth with his napkin. "You've made up your mind about what?"

"Oh, Dad…"

"What? For God's sake, Andie. Tell us."

"I'm going to have a baby."

There. The words were out.

And Andie felt as if she'd dropped them down a bottomless well.

Her father's face went unhealthily pale. And then beet red. Andie thought of Uncle Don. Of heart attacks and strokes and all the things that happen to men in their late fifties who are a little overweight and a little overstressed and then receive a nasty shock.

Andie looked at her mother. Thelma's eyes were very wide. And then they softened. Great tenderness filled them.

"Oh, honey…" Thelma reached across the table, groping for her daughter's hand.

Andie responded without hesitation. She met her mother's hand halfway and was glad for the unconditional love she saw in her mother's eyes.

"You should have told us right away," Thelma whispered.

"I had to have time to think. I had to be sure."

"I know, I know."

"It's what I want, Mom."

"Of course you do."

Suddenly, Joe found his voice. He used it to point out the obvious. "You're not married, Andrea." He was clearly so upset, he'd called his daughter by the name she was born with.

Still clasping each other's hands, both women looked at him.

"Don't you two give me those looks," Joe said with some

testiness. "I'm stating a fact, here. You don't have a husband, Andie."

"Now, Joe," Thelma began in her most placating tone.

Andie pulled her hand from her mother's warm clasp. "It's all right, Mom."

"But I—"

Andie drew herself up. "No. It's all right." She faced her father. "You're right, Dad. I don't have a husband."

"Are you *going* to have a husband?"

"Joe…"

"Quiet, Thelma." He narrowed his eyes at his daughter. "*Are* you?"

"Maybe someday, yes."

"What about right now, Andrea? It seems to me a husband is something you could use right away. It seems to me that the father of your baby might be a good choice as that husband, as a matter of fact."

Andie felt her skin going prickly and her heart beating a sharp, erratic rhythm in her chest. She told her body to calm down. She reminded herself that she'd never expected this to be easy.

But having known it wouldn't be easy didn't make her like it. She'd hated seeing the disapproval and concern in Clay's eyes and she hated seeing them in her father's eyes, as well.

"Look, this is *my* baby." She tried to keep her voice from rising out of control. "No one else's. The father isn't involved. I'm going to have it alone and I'm going to raise it the very best I can on my own."

"Oh, dear," Thelma said to no one in particular.

"But a baby needs a father," Joe insisted gruffly. "And what about money? It's only fair that the man—"

"Just drop it, Dad. I mean it. I'll manage, as far as money goes."

"What about your job? Clay is counting on you to—"

"I've worked things out with Clay."

There was a tiny pause. Andie saw the flicker of a look that passed between her mother and her father.

Her father said carefully, "You've talked to Clay about this?"

"Yesterday evening, yes."

"And what did he say?"

"He said he wants me to keep working for him. So that means I'll be able to support myself and the baby. It won't be easy, but it will certainly be manageable."

"Well." Her father slid a glance at her mother again, then said to Andie, "At least you still have a job."

"Yes, I do."

Joe scrubbed a hand down his broad, lined face. "Well, that's something. You're lucky there."

"I am not *lucky* there, Dad. I'm good at my job, and Clay doesn't want to lose me."

"Well, certainly. Of course. But I still think the father ought to—"

"That's enough, Dad. Really. I wanted you to know the situation, because I love you both and don't want you to be in the dark about something so important. But it's *my* situation. I'll handle it the way I think best."

"It's crazy."

"Joe, please…"

"No, it's crazy, Thelma. And you know it. Women having babies without a man beside them. It's not right." Joe looked at Andie, a weary look.

A look that hurt. It was a look she used to see on his face all the time, back when she was growing up, back when he'd considered her flighty, willful and irresponsible and was always saying he didn't know what he was going to do with her.

In the past few years, Andie knew, her father's opinion of her had changed greatly. He looked at her with pride now, and he often told her how pleased he was that she had finally grown up.

"It will work out," Thelma said, her voice brittle with forced cheer.

Joe shook his head. "Andie, Andie. What are we going to do with you?"

Chapter 3

That Saturday, Clay's father called him and asked him to dinner.

The first thing Clay noticed when he pulled up in front of the house where he'd grown up was that his mother's little four-by-four compact car wasn't in the driveway where she usually parked it. His Uncle Joe's truck, however, was.

Clay knew right then that dinner wasn't the only thing cooking here. He recognized all the ingredients for a "man-to-man" talk.

His uncle and his father were going to pump him for anything he might know about Andie's predicament. He could feel it coming.

Since there was nothing to do but get it over with, Clay left his own truck and went up the front walk past the snowball bush at the front gate. Right now, in the last third of winter, the bush looked like a dead weed.

There were still patches of melting snow in the yard from the last storm a few weeks before. As Clay picked his way around them, the first flakes of a new storm were beginning to fall.

Inside, there was a cheery fire in the new pellet stove Don had put in two years ago. The walls of the living room were pale blue, instead of the light green they used to be when Clay was growing up.

Not much else had changed, though. The same family pictures decorated the walls and the tall vase with the big fake flower arrangement erupting from it still stood beside the front door. Clay hung his heavy jacket in the coat closet and told his dad he'd love a beer.

They settled in the living room. Don and Joe held down either end of the couch. Clay took the wing chair that had been reupholstered in a pattern of blue flowers to complement the walls.

Apprehensive, Clay refused to speak first. As the two older men tried to figure out how to begin, Clay watched them, very much aware of the closeness between them, of their solidarity as long-time members of the same family.

Their wives were sisters and they were best friends. The four of them—Clay's mother, his aunt, his father and his uncle—had grown up together right here in Meadow Valley. And when it had come time to settle down, Don had married Della and Joe had married Thelma. Joe and Thelma had had one child, Andie. And when Della and Don had realized they would have no children of their own, they had set out to adopt a baby.

But then they'd come to understand how many older, less "desirable" children needed families. They'd been introduced to Clay. And they'd taken him to their hearts.

Joe glanced at his brother-in-law. Almost imperceptibly, Don nodded.

Joe shifted a little and adjusted his belt more comfortably under the paunch he'd developed over the past few years. He cleared his throat.

Clay ached to get this over with. He almost volunteered, *It's about Andie, right?*

But he held the words back. What if it *wasn't* about Andie, after all? Then Cautious Clay would have really put his foot in it, but good.

Clay's father, seeing that his brother-in-law couldn't think how to begin, suggested, "We might as well get it right out there, Joe."

Joe looked down at his beefy hand, which was resting on his knee. "I know, I know."

Don reached out and touched Joe's shoulder. "Do you want me to…?"

Joe nodded. "Yeah, would you?"

Don squared his shoulders and turned his level gaze on his son. "Clay, Andie says she's explained to you about her situation."

Clay looked at his father warily, knowing now that he'd been right all along. It *was* about Andie. Still, he didn't want to reveal anything that she hadn't already disclosed. "What situation?"

"That she's going to have a baby," Uncle Joe said in a rush, as if he had to get it out fast, or it wouldn't come out at all.

Now that it *was* out, Clay allowed himself to nod. "Yes. She's told me."

Clay's father and his uncle exchanged another glance. Then they both stared at Clay, their expressions expectant.

Clay couldn't think of a single appropriate thing to say right then, so he said nothing.

After a moment, his father prompted. "So then what else?"

"I don't know what you mean, Dad."

"I mean, did she tell you anything else?"

"Like what?"

Joe grunted, then muttered darkly, "Like who the hell the father is."

Ignoring the image of Jeff that flashed through his mind, Clay took a long drink from his beer, which he then set down very carefully upon a blue crocheted coaster atop the spindly-legged side table next to his chair. "No, she didn't tell me who the father is."

"It must be someone she really cares for," Joe insisted, looking rather piercingly at Clay. "We all know how she is. She's always been adventurous. But when it comes to men, she's choosy. She's just not the type for any one-night stand. She'd have to love the man first."

Clay had to force himself not to look away, out the picture window, where the snow was now coming down more steadily and the wind was starting to blow the white flakes into flurries.

His mind felt as if it was stuck. Stuck on Jeff.

And all of a sudden, it was starting to seem that there were only two possible ways to get *unstuck.* He could go to Andie again and demand she tell him who the father of her baby was. That might or might not get him an answer, depending on how stubborn Andie was going to end up being about this.

Or he could fly down to Brentwood for a little heart-to-heart talk with Jeff.

Of course, Jeff's new wife, Madeline, whom Clay really liked, would be there. Madeline had loved Jeff since the two of them were children. And now that Jeff was finally settling down and starting a life with her, Madeline was the happiest woman in the world.

"Don't you think so, Clay?" Joe was asking.

"Excuse me. Say that again?"

"I said, don't you think Andie would have to be in love before she would…become intimate with a man?"

Now what the hell was he going to say to that? Clay himself didn't believe in the kind of love his uncle was talking about. *Being in love,* as far as Clay was concerned, meant sexual attraction, plain and simple. It was nature's way of ensuring survival of the species and that was all. In Andie's case, he supposed, nature had done her job pretty well.

"Clay?" Joe was leaning forward, waiting for Clay to give some kind of answer.

"Yes," Clay said at last. "You're right. I'm sure Andie would have to really care for someone first. But honestly, I don't know who the man is. Andie told me she's going to have a baby and that she wants to stay on at Barrett and Company. That's all I know."

"Did she tell you she wants to raise the baby herself?" Joe's disapproval was painfully clear.

"Yes, she said that."

Joe shook his head. "I don't know how she'll manage. She's a good person, Andrea is. She means well. But where does she get her crazy ideas? The past few years, she's finally settled herself into a good job." He saluted Don with a quick nod. "Many thanks to you, Don—and you, too, Clay. Her mother and I are finally thinking we can relax—our Andie is all grown up now. And then, out of the blue, she comes to us and tells us she's going to be a mom—without a husband."

Clay sat up straighter in his chair, a strange emotion gripping him. It took him a moment to realize what he felt. It was defensiveness. For Andie, of all people.

"She's turned out to be damn good at her job," he heard himself saying. "Right, Dad?"

"Definitely," Don agreed without hesitation.

"I'm lucky to have her," Clay went on. Then he found himself paraphrasing Andie's words of the other night. "And since the father refuses to be a husband, then if Andie wants the baby, she has no choice. She has to raise it on her own."

Joe was sitting forward now. "She told you that? That the father didn't want her?"

Clay reached for his beer, found it empty and set it back on the coaster. "Uncle Joe, I respect you more than any man in the world, next to Dad, here. But these aren't questions to ask me. You should be asking Andie."

For a moment, Joe stared at him, a look so intense that Clay felt the short hairs rise on the back of his neck. Then Joe shot Don a speaking glance and Don took over again.

"Son, we've got to ask you…"

"What?"

"Is it you?"

Clay's mouth dropped open. He stared from one man to the other. "Me? The *father,* you mean?" He was baffled—and deeply hurt that his family could ever think he would betray their trust this way.

"God, Clay." Joe looked miserable. "Don't be insulted. We just felt we had to ask. It always seemed to us that there was…a little bit of an attraction between you and Andie."

"Attraction?" Clay repeated the word in total disbelief. "Between me and *Andie?* But we never could stand each other—you all knew that. You were always begging us not to fight, to try and get along with each other."

"Strong feelings are strong feelings," Joe said quietly. "Love and hate can be a lot alike."

Don added, "And since she works for you now, you two are thrown together every day. We couldn't help thinking that maybe you just got a little carried away."

"Not that you're the type to get carried away, Clay," Joe hastened to amend. "You've always been a down-to-earth young man and we all admire that in you."

"But what we're trying to say here," Don chimed in, "is if it did turn out to be you, well, that might not be such a terrible thing at all. You're not a blood relation to Andie, after all."

Clay felt the coiled tension inside him relax somewhat as

he began to understand that they actually *wanted* him to be the one. For a moment, he had the most ridiculous urge to tell them they were right, the baby was his. He'd do the right thing and marry Andie immediately.

But the urge passed quickly, leaving him wondering what the hell his problem was. His cousin, the sworn enemy of his teenage years, was pregnant. And here he was, thinking about marrying her.

And did the family really think that the old animosity between Andie and him covered a mutual attraction? The idea was crazy. Totally crazy.

Clay held up his hands, palms out. "Sorry. It really isn't me."

Clay's father and his uncle seemed to sigh in unison. Clay thought they both looked older suddenly.

After a moment, Joe muttered, "Well, then. That's that, I suppose. But who the hell is it, then?"

Clay's father said, "I noticed she seemed awfully friendly with your buddy, Jeff, over the holidays."

Before Clay could think of what to say, Joe argued, "But I can't believe it could be him. He just got married, after all."

"That's right," Don agreed. "Clay flew down to be his best man." He looked at Clay for confirmation.

"Yeah."

"And that was only a couple of weeks ago, wasn't it?"

"Right," Clay said, trying to sound normal and unconcerned, though his heart was galloping inside his chest. "Just a couple of weeks ago. On Valentine's Day."

In that stuck place in his mind, Clay saw Jeff and Madeline beneath an arbor that was covered in white roses, repeating their vows in clear, firm voices.

He also relived that moment when he'd gotten off the plane and Jeff had been there to meet him. Jeff had looked at him so strangely, he'd thought, a look both skeptical and anxious.

But then Clay had reached out and grabbed Jeff in a bear hug. When they stepped away from each other and Jeff met Clay's eyes again, that strange look was gone.

"No, I'm sure it wasn't your friend," Joe said. "But I just don't know who else it could—"

"Listen, guys," Clay interrupted, thinking he couldn't take another moment of this. "I've told you everything I know. And, like I said before, it's Andie you should be talking to. I just plain don't like this, discussing her behind her back."

His uncle and his father regarded him solemnly.

At last his father conceded, "All right, Clay. If that's how you feel."

Clay stayed for dinner, though it was a rather strained affair. His mother kept looking at him hopefully. But he knew she wouldn't ask him any uncomfortable questions. She would be tactful and wait until she had her husband alone to find out what had transpired between the men. He made it easy on her and left early so she could quiz his father in private.

The storm that had started with a few moist snowflakes drifting quietly down had steadily worsened. By the time Clay left his parents' house, the winds were up and the snow was coming down thick and heavy. The roads were a mess, so it took him nearly an hour to travel the fifteen miles to his two-story house on ten acres out at the end of twisting Wildriver Road.

Once there, he mixed himself a whiskey and soda and went out on the top deck outside his bedroom to watch the black storm clouds rise and roll in the night sky. His house was at a lower elevation than his parents' place in town, so he was pelted with freezing rain rather than snow. Within two minutes, he was drenched to the skin.

But he didn't give a damn. Clay loved storms. He was a

very orderly, controlled man, as a rule. But even as a young child he'd always stepped out to feel the rain on his face when he could, to watch thunderheads gather and lightning fork across the sky.

He loved the wildness of a storm. It soothed something inside him.

His biological mother had loved storms. Somewhere, way back in the farthest reaches of his early memories, he could still see her, wearing a cheap red coat, arms outstretched, head tipped up to the sky. She was spinning in circles, laughing, in the middle of a lawn in front of a building where they had a small apartment. The rain poured down on her face and the wind whipped at her flimsy coat.

She didn't care. She laughed and laughed. "Isn't it fabulous, Clay, baby? Can't you feel it, just moving all through you? Oh, I do love a storm. A storm is just grand!"

Clay lifted his whiskey and soda and saluted the black, heavy sky. Then he took a bracing drink, leaving his head tipped up when he was finished, so the icy rain could sting his cheeks. He watched as a claw of lightning ripped the center out of the night. Thunder roared and seemed to roll off down the hills toward the distant valleys.

Maybe that was the one thing Rita Cox had left to him, he thought as he at last lowered his head. Her legacy to him had been the peace he could find in the untamed heart of a big storm.

She certainly hadn't left him much else. She bore him out of wedlock. The line for *father* on his birth certificate was taken up with one word: *unknown*. If Rita knew whose name should have gone there, she'd never told him.

She'd been a woman who could barely take care of herself, was often ill, moving from job to job. She hadn't been equipped to take care of a little boy. Yet she would never give him up. So sometimes he lived with her and sometimes, when times were bad, he lived in foster care or at a home for dependent children. When he was nine, she'd died of a ruptured appendix.

Her death, he understood later, was his big chance. He was free, then, to be adopted. To find the Barretts. To have a real family at last.

He wondered, standing there, soaked and shivering, holding an empty drink, if he was finally zeroing in on the truth about this whole mess with Andie. If he was finally seeing what bothered him so damn much when he thought about Andie and the baby she insisted she was going to raise alone.

His own memories were the problem. His memories of a mother who wouldn't give him up and yet couldn't take care of him, either.

Clay knew in the logical part of his brain that Andie and Rita were not the same at all. Andie was strong and healthy. She had a steady job that she could and would hold on to. She had a devoted family who, once they accepted that she was determined to raise her child alone, would give her all the love and support in the world.

And yet one aspect of the situation would be exactly the same as it had been for Rita. On Andie's baby's birth certificate, the father's name would be *unknown*.

Clay lifted his head to the streaming sky again. The rain beat on his face. He waited to feel set free, lifted outside himself.

The release didn't come. Somehow, tonight, the storm was bringing him no peace at all.

He tossed his ice cubes over the railing and went back inside to mix himself another stiff one.

The next morning, the sun came out. The world was bathed in that cold, thin brightness that often follows a winter storm.

Clay rose early and showered away the fuzziness from one

too many whiskey and sodas. Sometime deep in the night, he had come to accept what he had to do.

He called an airline that scheduled a lot of flights between Sacramento and L.A. Luck was with him. He gave his credit card number and paid for a seat on an 11:00 a.m. flight.

He threw a few things in an overnight bag and headed for the Sacramento airport. He would arrive in L.A. at a little after noon. And not too long after that, he would be knocking on Jeff Kirkland's door.

Chapter 4

Clay had a little trouble finding Jeff and Madeline's house in Brentwood. He had never been there before. The house had been a wedding present from Madeline's father, who ran a real estate business.

But at last, with the help of a *Thomas's Guide* he bought at a convenience store, Clay drove his rental car onto the right street and parked in front of an attractive Spanish-style house with a big magnolia tree in the middle of its graciously sloping front lawn.

Clay knew he couldn't afford to hesitate, or he just might turn the car around and head back the way he'd come. The moment he turned off the engine, he got out of the car and strode up the curving brick walk that led to the front door.

The door had a little window on top, with miniature wrought-iron bars over it. A few moments after Clay rang the bell, a woman's face appeared behind the bars. Clay didn't recognize her.

"Yes?" Her voice crackled from the little speaker to the right of the door.

"Is this the Kirkland residence?"

"Yes."

Clay realized this must be a housekeeper or a maid. "I'd like to speak with Jeff—or Madeline. I'm Clay. Clay Barrett."

"Just a minute. You wait, please."

The woman disappeared. Clay waited, calculating the days since the wedding. He wondered if Jeff and Madeline were still in the Bahamas.

He was just beginning to believe he'd flown all the way to L.A. for nothing when he saw Madeline's face through the little barred window.

Her gray eyes lit up. "Clay!" He heard her disengage the locks and then she threw back the door and grabbed him in a hug. "What a surprise!" Her delighted laughter chimed in his ear. "This is great. Just terrific."

She straightened her arms and held him away from her. "Jeff's upstairs. Come on in." She pulled him through a small foyer into a big room with a fireplace and glass doors that led out to a shaded patio. Couches, tables and bookcases were stacked every which way and there were packing boxes everywhere.

"Don't mind the mess," she instructed. "We just got back. It was heaven. Heaven, I'm telling you. But now it's move-in time. From heaven straight to hell." She cast a glance at the ceiling and put a hand to the side of her face, as if she was afraid her head might roll off. Then she laughed again.

Clay looked at her, slim and pretty in jeans and a simple cotton shirt. Happiness shone from her, turned her prettiness very close to beauty. He'd known her almost as long as he'd known Jeff, since that first year of college, when Jeff had taken Clay to a party at one of the huge, estatelike houses in the neighborhood where Jeff had grown up. Madeline had been at that party, bright and friendly and so in love with Jeff that it was almost painful to see.

Clay learned soon enough what the story was. Madeline's and Jeff's mothers were best friends. Their fathers were partners in a successful real estate business. As babies, Madeline and Jeff had shared the same playpen. They'd played together as kids and gone steady in high school. All Madeline wanted was to be with Jeff. But Jeff said he had some serious living to do before he was going to be ready to even think about settling down.

Three years ago, both Jeff's parents had died of different illnesses just a few months apart. Madeline had comforted him. They'd moved in together. Jeff had taken his rightful place in the real estate firm.

Jeff and Madeline had finally become engaged a few months before Clay moved back to northern California. The wedding had been planned for New Year's Eve.

And a week before Christmas, Jeff had shown up on Clay's doorstep.

"Hey, bud. Can you spare me a bed for a week or two? I need a little space."

Clay had known instantly what was going on. His best friend was suffering from a serious case of cold feet. "What about the wedding?"

Jeff shook his head. "There isn't going to be one. I called it off."

Clay tried not to be judgmental. Being judgmental with Jeff never did any good, anyway. But he couldn't help pointing out, "You're making a big mistake, my friend. Madeline's the best thing that ever happened to you."

Jeff's square jaw hardened. "Can I stay or not?"

Clay had stepped back to let him in.

"Clay? Yoo-hoo, anybody in there?" Madeline's wide smile was wobbling a little.

Clay blinked. "Oh. Sorry. Just thinking."

"Is this something serious, then?" The smile had faded completely now, to be replaced by an uneasy frown.

"What?"

"The reason you're here."

"No," he baldly lied. "Not at all. Not serious at all. I was… I had to see an old client in Century City. Tax time coming up, you know?"

"Oh. I see." It was obvious she didn't.

"I just thought I'd drop in, on the off chance you two might be around."

She smiled again. "Well. I'm glad you did."

"Yeah." It was Jeff's voice. "Always glad to see a friend."

Clay looked up. Jeff was leaning against an arch that led to a hallway. He wore the bottom half of a pair of cotton pajamas and his muscular arms were crossed over his bare chest. His pose was relaxed. But Clay didn't miss the watchfulness in his eyes.

"There you are, lazybones." Madeline wrinkled her nose at him. "Clay's here."

"I can see that."

Clay remembered his objective. He had to get Jeff alone. "Had lunch yet?"

Madeline chuckled. "Oh, please. He hasn't had *breakfast* yet. As a matter of fact, I was just going to see if I could find some eggs and a frying pan in my disaster of a kitchen. Any takers?"

Both Clay and Jeff were silent, looking at each other.

Madeline glanced from one to the other and back again. "Hey, I swear it won't take long. I'll get Marina to help me."

Jeff shrugged. "Naw. Let's go out." His voice was offhand. His eyes were not. He looked down at his pajama bottoms and the bare feet sticking out of them. "I'll get decent."

Clay valiantly cast about for a way to convince Madeline

to stay behind without making her suspicious about this visit all over again.

Madeline did it for him. "Listen. I adore you both and there's nothing I'd like better than a long, leisurely lunch with the two of you. But look at this place. I've got to get going on it." She gave Clay a soulful look. "Please understand."

Clay tried to look regretful, though what he actually felt was relief. "All right. I'll forgive you. Just this once."

Ten minutes later, Clay and Jeff sat in Clay's rental car. Jeff suggested a place he knew out in Santa Monica. Clay drove in silence, dealing with the traffic and trying to think how he was going to phrase what he had to say.

When they were almost to the restaurant, Jeff spoke up. "I'm not really hungry."

Clay glanced at his friend. "Me, neither."

"Let's go to the beach."

They went on to where the highway met the ocean. Clay found a parking space easily. They walked down to the beach, where the winter wind had a bite to it in spite of the cloudless sky. Overhead, the gulls soared. A few hardy surfers and boogie-boarders tackled some rather puny waves.

Clay and Jeff sat down side by side, wrapped their arms loosely around their drawn-up knees and stared out at the waves.

Jeff said, "I was wondering when you'd show up." His voice was flat, matter-of-fact.

Clay's throat felt tight. "You were?"

Jeff shot Clay a look, then grunted. "Come on. You were bound to figure it out." Jeff gave a humorless laugh. "I told your cousin that. But she still held on to her hopeless idea that you wouldn't have to know."

Clay found he couldn't speak for a moment. Then he asked, "It's true, then?"

Jeff looked down at the sand between his knees. "Yeah."

Clay stared hard at the ocean as the truth came to him. It hurt. Bad. But just knowing wasn't enough. The words had been too vague. It had to be said bluntly so there would never be any doubt concerning it.

Clay said, "You had sex with my cousin."

Beside him, Jeff didn't move. "Yeah."

"Why?"

"Hell. Why? How do I know why? Because it was New Year's Eve, the night I should have married Madeline. And I'd called Madeline. And she wouldn't speak to me. Because I was confused and hurting and wanted to forget it all. Because your cousin was *there,* sweet and pretty and soft. We had too much champagne. And it happened. I know it's hard for someone like you to understand, since control is more or less your middle name. But sometimes, for ordinary guys with weaknesses, things just get out of hand."

"Things get out of hand." Clay repeated Jeff's words with great precision.

"Yes."

For a moment, Clay said nothing. Then he swore low and feelingly. "You're dead right about one thing. I don't understand. You didn't even think to use a condom, did you?"

"No. I didn't. I was a jackass. Believe me. I realize that."

"You were my friend. Staying in my house."

"I know."

"You spent the night with my cousin—because she was *there,* and then you came back here to L.A. and you patched things up with Madeline. You *married* Madeline, even though Andie had called you and told you she was going to have a baby. I was at your wedding. I was your best man. And you never said a damn word."

"Guilty. On all counts."

Clay couldn't bear to look at Jeff, couldn't seem to get his mind around the enormity of Jeff's betrayal. He wanted to hurt Jeff right then. He wanted to do him great bodily harm. At the same time, scenes from their ten-year friendship kept playing in his head.

Though Jeff was silent beside him, it seemed to Clay that he could hear his friend's reckless laughter as Jeff burst into Clay's room at the dorm back in college and dragged him off to a beach party or an impromptu baseball game somewhere.

More than once, Jeff had shaken Clay awake at midnight, demanding he throw on some clothes and go with him to a cantina on Alvarado Street, where there was this little *señorita* who could play eight ball like no one you ever saw. Or he'd haul Clay over to some loft downtown, where he'd introduce him to a punk poet with spiked pink hair. They'd stay up all night, the poet reciting, Clay and Jeff listening, talking, laughing. Having fun.

And later, after college was over, when Clay was killing himself to learn the ropes on the audit staff of Stanley, Beeson and Means, Jeff would climb in the window of Clay's apartment with a six-pack under one arm and five Clint Eastwood videos under the other. He'd refuse to go away until Clay drank half of the beer and watched, at the very least, *A Fistful of Dollars.*

Clay had come to L.A. to prove himself, to learn his trade from the best of the best. He had always intended to return home eventually and put what he'd learned to work in the business he would inherit from his father. But the long years of schooling and apprenticeship had been hard for him. He missed the mountains, missed his family.

Jeff, almost singlehandedly, had made life in L.A. bearable for Clay. Having a friend like Jeff made the drudgery endurable. Life in L.A. was okay.

Jeff was like Andie, Clay realized. Jeff was laughter and adventure and a hell of a lot of fun. But with Andie, Clay had always been outside looking in. With Jeff, it was different. There was no family rivalry with Jeff. There were only good feelings and good times.

And now Jeff had done this. The unforgivable. And the unforgivable had produced new life.

Clay pointed out carefully, "Andie says the baby won't have your name."

Jeff let out a low groan. "Look. Your cousin wants to raise the baby alone. She doesn't *want* me to help her. And things are good now, with me and Madeline. I just don't want to mess that up. Can't you understand?"

"You're saying you don't want Madeline to know."

"Right. It would break her heart."

"You'd deny your own child, just so Madeline wouldn't have to know?"

"Your cousin doesn't want it to be my child."

"That's a feeble excuse. You know it. It *is* your child, no matter what Andie says."

"If she's willing to take full responsibility, then she and I are agreed. It's the way it will be."

"She might change her mind. Women have been known to do that."

"I'll deal with that if and when it happens."

Clay thought of Andie, of the proud set to her chin and the absolute determination in her eyes when she'd said, *"The man is out of my—our—lives. For good and all."*

"You know it's not going to happen, don't you?" Clay taunted. "You'll never have to deal with it. Another woman might change her mind, but not Andie. She's too proud. So you're deserting her *and* your baby, that's what you're doing."

"It's how she wants it."

"That doesn't matter. You're turning your back on your responsibility. You're just walking away."

Jeff grabbed a tiny shell from the sand and tossed it overhand, out toward the waves. Then turned his head and met Clay's eyes. "You set such damn impossible standards. For yourself and everyone else. Well, I can't live up to those standards. That's all there is to it. What the hell else do you want from me?"

"Nothing," Clay said flatly, realizing it was true at the same time as he said it. "I want you out of my life. And my cousin's life. I never want to see or hear from you again. As far as I'm concerned, you're dead."

Clay watched the emotions chase themselves across Jeff's face. Pain. Anger. Sadness. Relief.

Clay turned the knife. "Look. If you don't want Madeline to know, it's the best way."

"I know that, damn you." Jeff stood. He held a hand down to Clay.

Clay stared up at him, not moving. "Well?"

Jeff stuck his hand in his pocket. Overhead, the gulls wheeled. One cried out, a long, lonely sound.

"All right, bud." A faraway smile curved Jeff's mouth. "I'm dead."

Clay got to his feet unaided. The two men stood, one brown haired, one blond, both tall and well built, facing each other on the sand.

Jeff's distant smile turned knowing. "You ain't really all *that* civilized, are you now, bud?"

Clay shrugged, though the violence within him seemed to make the air shimmer in front of his eyes.

"I'll make it easy for you," Jeff said. Then his fist shot out and connected with Clay's jaw.

Chapter 5

There was a moment of stark pain, then an explosion behind Clay's eyes. Clay staggered back.

And then, at last, he was set free to act. His body broke the reins of his iron control.

With a guttural cry, Clay sent his own fist flying. Flesh and cartilage gave way. Jeff grunted in pain.

Clay kicked him before Jeff could recover. Jeff stumbled back. Clay jumped on him and brought him down.

The two men rolled, struggling, over and over in the sand. Above, the gulls cried and soared. The waves tumbled in and slid away again, on and on, without end.

Eventually, when pain and exhaustion finally conquered them both, the two men dragged themselves to their feet and reeled back to Clay's rental car.

Clay drove Jeff to Brentwood and dropped him off under the wide canopy of the magnolia tree in front of the gracefully sloping lawn. Then he went to the airport to wait for a return flight.

It was well after midnight when he finally fell into his bed.

"Good Lord, Clay," Andie demanded when he walked into the office the next morning, "what *happened?*"

He gingerly touched the purple bruise on the side of his jaw. "What, this?"

"Yes. And that and that." She indicated his black eye and the cut on the bridge of his nose.

"I fell off my tractor." Clay owned a miniature tractor the size of a riding mower that he used to move dirt and tree stumps around on his ten acres of land.

Andie wasn't convinced. "Fell off your tractor, right. You'll lose your Eagle Scout badge telling lies like that. Now what is going on?"

Clay lied some more. "Nothing." He had already decided she was never going to know the truth about this. "I went out for a drink last night and I chose the wrong bar, that's all."

"That's not like you, Clay."

"What? Going out for a drink or going to the wrong bar?"

"Neither. It's something else. What?"

"God, you're nosy." He peered at her more closely. "But you're looking good. Really good." It was true. The shadows beneath her eyes were gone and there was color in her cheeks again.

"You're not going to tell me what happened, are you?"

"No, I'm not. As I said, it's nothing. And you *are* looking good."

She was quiet for a moment. He knew she was making up her mind whether to keep after him about the source of his injuries. He was relieved when she gave a small shrug and admitted, "I'm feeling much better. Since we talked last week, a lot of what was worrying me isn't worrying me anymore. It's amazing what a few good nights of sleep will do."

"Well, great." He realized he should probably get his coffee and move along to his own office down the hall. But he didn't move.

While he leaned on the reception counter and grinned at her, Andie mentioned that one of the bigger accounts he'd inherited from his father had left a message on the service. "He said he's dropping in this morning some time."

"Nice of him to let us know."

"I pulled his file. It's on your desk."

"You are incredibly efficient."

"Maybe I should get a raise."

"Maybe I should get to work."

She laughed. "Fine. Get to work. But I'm not giving up about that raise. And Clay…"

"What?"

"Are you sure you're all right?"

"I'm fine. Really. Though I've got to admit I'm kind of dreading facing Mrs. Faulkenberry looking like this." Mrs. Faulkenberry had been coming to Barrett & Co. to have her tax return prepared for as long as Clay could remember. Every year, she brought in her receipts in a shoe box and handed them over to Clay's father personally. This year, she'd agreed to hand over the precious shoe box to Clay. She was due in at one that afternoon.

"Don't worry about Mrs. Faulkenberry," Andie reassured him. "She's seen worse things in her time than a beat up accountant, I'm sure."

"I'll take that under advisement."

"Good." She swiveled in her chair and faced her computer screen again.

Clay looked at her delicate profile for a moment before he finally went to pour himself some coffee and get to work.

When Clay arrived home that night, there was a message on his answering machine from Jill Peters, a woman he'd dated a few times last fall and during the holidays. In fact, Jill had been his date on New Year's Eve, the night Jeff and Andie had—

Clay cut the thought off before it was finished and forced himself to keep his mind on Jill. Jill had tickets to a Kings game for Friday night and wanted Clay to go with her.

Clay played the message twice, thinking that he'd enjoyed being with Jill and realizing that more than two months had slipped by since the last time he'd talked to her. He probably should have called her.

But he hadn't. And now he knew that he was going to get back to her and tell her he appreciated her invitation, but it was no go.

He didn't know why, exactly.

He called her quickly and made his excuses and then wondered for a moment or two what was the matter with him, to turn down a pleasant evening with a nice woman.

But then he shrugged and forgot about it. There was no sense in dwelling on it. It was just one of those things.

He thought of Andie right then, for some reason, and realized he was looking forward to going to work tomorrow. The confrontation with Jeff was behind him and Andie was feeling better. Things should be more pleasant at the office from now on.

And they were. All that week, things went smoothly.

Andie told him in a private moment that she knew her father and his father had ganged up on him.

"But you were steadfast, as always," she jokingly praised him. "You didn't give out or give in."

He actually put on a wise-guy voice. "I told you I was no snitch." He was careful to add offhandedly, "Not that there was anything I could have told them. I mean, what do I know, anyway?"

She gave him an odd, pensive look. "That's right. What do you know, anyway?"

Something tightened down inside him. He felt a twinge of guilt. But what was the point of telling the truth here? Jeff was out of her life and Clay's life, as well. Dragging it all out now would only cause her more pain than she'd already suffered.

One of her sleek eyebrows lifted slightly. "Something *is* bothering you. Isn't it, Clay?"

But then the door buzzer rang, telling them there was someone out front.

"Better see who it is," he said softly.

She gave a little sigh and left.

The subject did not present itself again—not immediately, anyway. And that was fine with Clay.

The work load seemed to get heavier every day. They were managing fine, but there wasn't a lot of time for anything but the job. As the first week of March faded into the second, they fell into the habit of ordering take-out food and eating dinner together right there at the office after the last appointment of the day. Then Andie would get to work on the day's time sheets, while Clay would dig into the next tax summary. They'd say good-night at eight or so and start all over again twelve hours later.

Andie said she didn't mind the long hours at all. She was feeling better every day, and she did need the extra money.

Clay believed she really was feeling better. Her eyes were clear and bright now, and though the soda crackers were still ready at her desk, her appetite had definitely improved. Some evenings, he had to watch out or she was likely to eat half of *his* dinner as well as her own.

It was Wednesday night in the second week of March when Clay's mother called him at home.

"Clay, dear, Saturday is Andie's birthday. Did you remember?"

"Yes, Mom."

Clay *had* remembered. He'd been planning to use the event as an excuse to take Andie out to dinner and present her with a nice big check that would be part bonus and part birthday gift.

But the family, evidently, had plans of their own. "We thought we'd have a little party. Just the family and a few close friends."

"I see."

"You sound guarded, dear."

"I'm not. The truth is, I already had something planned for Andie's birthday, that's all."

"You did?" His mother's voice was suddenly bright.

"It wasn't anything important. I was going to take her out to dinner."

"Why, I think that sounds lovely. Maybe you could do both."

"What do you mean, both?"

"Come to the party *and* buy her a nice meal."

"I'll think about it. Tell me about the party."

His mother launched into the plans. It was to be at Thelma and Joe's on Saturday afternoon. "You will come, won't you, Clay?"

Clay promised to attend.

"And don't tell Andie. It's supposed to be a surprise."

"I won't say a word."

"Good. Come at one-thirty, no later. We want everyone there to yell 'Surprise!' when she walks in."

"I'll be there."

His mother rambled on again, about how Andie's best friend, Ruth Ann Pardo, was going to go to Andie's apartment early Saturday morning, to make sure Andie didn't go anywhere. Then Aunt Thelma was going to call Andie at the right time with a trumped-up emergency and beg her to come right over.

"I think it should work, don't you, Clay?"

"Sure, Mom."

"Oh, and do get her something extra nice. She needs all our love and affection right now." His mother's tone was heavy with meaning.

Clay smiled to himself. Slowly, as Clay had known they would, the family was coming to grips with the reality of Andie's pregnancy. Everyone was still speaking in low tones and oblique phrases about it. But that would pass. By the time the baby actually made his or her appearance, they'd all be lined up at the observation window in the hospital nursery, jockeying for their first glimpse of the newest member of the clan.

He promised his mother he'd get Andie something nice and then he said goodbye.

Clay ended up doing as his mother suggested. He planned to attend the party and he also took Andie to dinner on Friday night and gave her the bonus check.

Her eyes misted over a little when she looked at the amount. "I should tell you it's too much."

"But you won't." He raised his wineglass and toasted her with it. "Because you know it's not only a birthday present."

"It isn't?"

"Hell, no. It's also a bonus check."

"Ah. For the terrific job I'm doing at the office."

"Exactly."

"Then you're right. It's not too much. I'm worth every cent."

Andie ate all of her salmon and had chocolate mousse for

dessert. Clay watched her with satisfaction, thinking that she was doing a pretty good job of eating for two.

When they left the restaurant, which was on one of the two major streets in downtown Meadow Valley, a light snow was falling. Andie put out her hands to catch a few flakes. The bracelet of linked hearts that she always wore gleamed on her wrist as it caught the light of the streetlamp beside her. "Snow. In March."

"It happens. Sometimes as late as April."

"Yes." Her smile was so womanly—knowing, and yet shy. "But spring is near. I can feel it." She flipped up the collar of her winter coat. "Come on. Let's go."

Clay flipped up his collar to match hers and they set off up the sidewalk. When they reached the corner, they instinctively moved closer together against the chill of the wind that swept between the buildings. Since the restaurant's small lot in back was full, they'd both parked on the street.

"I'll walk you to your car," Clay suggested.

Andie sent him a smile that seemed to warm the icy air between them. "Thanks."

Andie's car, a little red compact that had seen better days, was waiting two blocks away. When they reached it, she turned to him.

"Thanks, Clay. It was lovely."

"You're welcome." He stared down at her.

The snow caught on her eyelashes and sparkled like tiny diamonds in her nearly black hair. She always pulled her hair back for work, so it looked like a sleek cap on her head. But it had a lot of curl to it and the moisture in the air was working on it. Little tendrils were curling now around her face.

It occurred to Clay, in a dazed sort of way, that something was happening here.

"Can I drive you to your car?" she offered.

"No. It's okay. The walk will do me good."

"You're sure?"

"Absolutely."

She rose on tiptoe. Her lips brushed his cheek, right above the pale remnant of the bruise where Jeff's first punch had landed.

Clay felt the warmth of her breath, smelled the fresh sweetness of her skin. Inside his trousers, his manhood stirred. The pleasant ache shocked him for an instant.

And then something deep inside him gave way. And it was okay. He could allow himself to desire her.

"Good night, then," she said.

"Yes. Good night."

She ran around to the driver's side, unlocked the door and got in. The car started up with a grumbling whine. She pulled out and drove away. Clay watched her go. She'd disappeared around a corner before he shook himself and started for his own car.

The next day at two o'clock, Clay jumped out from behind his Aunt Thelma's couch and hollered "Surprise!" at the top of his lungs. The only thing that kept him from feeling like a complete idiot when he did it was that everyone else around him was doing the same thing.

If Andie wasn't surprised, she did a good job of acting the part. She jumped backward, put her hand to her throat and squealed, "Omigod!"

And then everyone was laughing and hugging her and shouting, "Happy Birthday!"

Clay stood back from all the commotion a little, watching Andie smile and laugh, seeing how she charmed everyone. And feeling thoroughly charmed himself. "She's a captivator, our Andie is," his great-uncle Jerry whispered slyly in his ear.

Clay gave the old man a smile. "Yes. She is."

Uncle Jerry ran his liver-spotted hand over the crown of his head, as if smoothing his hair back, even though he was totally bald. "If I were thirty years younger…"

"You'd still be married to Aunt Bette," Clay reminded him.

Uncle Jerry guffawed. "Damned if you ain't right, my boy. Damned if you ain't right. And where is that wife of mine, anyway?"

Clay pointed to a chair by the wall, where Great-aunt Bette was sitting with another of the great-aunts. Uncle Jerry tottled off in their direction.

"She *is* looking better, don't you think, dear?" Clay's mother, who'd appeared at his side out of nowhere, asked him in a hushed tone.

Clay nodded.

"Did you get her something nice?"

"Mother."

"What?" Della's eyes widened in an expression much too innocent for a woman who was almost sixty years of age. "What did I do?"

Clay just looked at her, a look of great patience.

"Well, I was just checking."

"I gave her a huge bonus."

His mother beamed. "That's wonderful. She can use that." But then she frowned. "But it's not very personal."

"Mother," Clay said again.

"Oh, all right. All right. I'm minding my own business. Starting now."

"That's good news."

"But Andie *is* looking lovely…"

"Yes, she is."

"And I…oh, never mind." She shook her head distractedly and wandered away to talk to her own mother, Granny Sid Santangelo, who was sitting on the couch, holding forth to anyone who would listen about how things used to be and ought to be again.

For the next couple of hours, Clay wandered from room to room, listening to the conversations, answering his relatives when they asked him questions and following Andie with his eyes.

She was so many things to him. His cousin. The passionate rival of his youth. His crackerjack, indispensable office manager.

And now there was more.

He'd always known she captivated people. People called her appealing and engaging and fun. He'd seen the way she charmed everyone, so they let her get away with things that Clay would never have been allowed to do. He'd resented her for her ability to enchant—at the same time as he'd called himself immune.

But now, he realized as he watched her opening her presents, oohing and aahing over each and every one, he *wasn't* immune. He wasn't quite sure how it had happened— something about the baby probably, and all the buried pain and memories the baby's existence had stirred up.

Whatever. The point was, it *had* happened. It was as if he had spent twenty years keeping an invisible wall between himself and the awareness that she was someone he could desire. And then, last night on a side street in his hometown, he'd suddenly discovered that the wall was gone. He didn't even know exactly when he'd let it crumble. But it wasn't there now.

The facts ran through his mind.

There was no blood tie between them. They were a great team at the office. If they married, the family would be thrilled and the baby would have a father.

Hell, for the baby's sake alone, it was certainly something to consider.

"Deep in thought as usual," a rough voice behind him remarked.

Clay turned, already smiling. "Johnny." Johnny Pardo still wore his hair too long and preferred black leather jackets and battered jeans to respectable clothing, but other than that he was all grown up now. Ten years ago, he'd shocked everyone at Meadow Valley High by marrying Andie's best friend, Ruth Ann Pagneti. Everyone had said that the marriage would never last, that Ruth Ann was a smart-mouthed, sheltered schoolgirl who knew nothing about real life, while Johnny was surly and troubled and would never settle down.

A decade later, they were still going strong. They had two boys. Johnny owned and ran a franchise convenience store and coached little league in his spare time.

"I gotta have a smoke," Johnny growled.

"I thought you quit."

"I did. I quit more than any guy I ever met. Come outside with me. If Ruth Ann sees me, I'm gonna get the look."

"What look?"

"The how-can-you-hurt-yourself-this-way-you're-hurting-all-of-us-who-love-you-too look. I can't take that. I just want a puff or two."

Clay went out in the chilly backyard with Johnny. He watched as Johnny lit up, and tried not to smile at the absurdly ecstatic smile on the other man's face as the hazardous fumes filled his lungs.

"We are talkin' nirvana, man," Johnny remarked. "So what were you thinkin' about in there?"

"Hell. Life."

"That deep, huh?"

"Yeah, I guess."

"Your cousin looks good."

"So everyone keeps telling me."

"You don't think so?"

"No. I think so. I think she looks great."

Johnny blew out smoke through his nose and then chuckled. "Remember that time I took her riding on my motorcycle and you got all hot and bothered about it?"

"I remember."

"I always thought you had a thing for her."

"No kidding?"

"No kidding." Johnny dropped his cigarette to the grass, stepped on it and then carefully stowed the smashed butt in his jacket pocket. Then he launched into one of his favorite subjects: the Bulls and the Suns. A few minutes later, Ruth Ann appeared.

"There you two are. I've been looking all over." She marched up to her husband and put her arm through his. "P.U. Cigarettes."

"Gimme a kiss."

Ruth Ann groaned, but she did lift her mouth. Her husband lightly pecked her lips. She turned to Clay, her dark eyes dancing, her pointed chin high. "He adores me."

"I can see."

"Come on inside now. Both of you. Andie's going to cut the cake."

There were twenty-eight candles on the chocolate fudge cake that Aunt Thelma had baked. Andie's hair was loose, in a dark cloud around her face. She had to gather it up in a fist, and hold it at her neck so it would be safe from the lit candles.

Aunt Thelma urged, "Hurry up, they're melting."

Andie's face glowed as she bent over the yellow flames. She closed her eyes.

"Andie…"

"Shh, quiet, Mom. Let me make my wish."

A hush fell over the room. Clay watched Andie's wish take form as a slow, secret smile made her glowing face shine brighter still.

"There," she said, with quiet satisfaction, her eyes still shut. "I see it. Just the way I want it to be."

"Then hurry…"

"All right, all right." She opened her eyes and sucked in a huge breath. And damned if she didn't get every last candle at one try.

Everyone applauded and Andie cut the cake.

Clay took his piece and sat in the living room near enough to Granny Sid that he had to listen to a long diatribe about the youth of today and how there was very little hope for them. When he'd finished his cake, he got up and solemnly told her that she was absolutely right—things were not what they had once been.

Then he kissed her wrinkled cheek. "See you later, Granny Sid."

Her little black eyes impaled him. "You're a smart boy, Clay."

"Thank you, Granny."

"Maybe too smart for your own good."

"Now what's *that* supposed to mean, Granny?"

"Stop thinking so much," Granny advised. "Give your heart a chance to talk."

He chucked her under her wattled chin. "What would a heart say, Granny, if it could talk?"

Granny cackled. "See there, see what I mean? You don't even believe that a heart can talk, now, do you?"

He considered teasing her some more, but decided to answer honestly. "No, Granny. I'm afraid I don't."

She shook her head. "Then what more can I say? We're talking different languages. But that's all right. You just go on. I know you're in a rush. Young people. Always in a rush." She patted him on the arm, dismissing him as if he were still ten years old and waiting for her permission to go outside and play.

He found his aunt Thelma before he left.

"Great cake, Aunt Thelma."

"Have another piece."

"No, I've got to go."

"What's your hurry?" Andie was suddenly beside him, grinning up at him, her midnight hair a halo around her face, the scent of her like roses and peaches combined. How could he have known her all these years and never noticed the enticing, wonderful way that she smelled?

"I've really got to go." He cringed at the lame sound of his own voice.

Andie leaned closer and whispered in his ear, "You'll be sorry. Aunt Bette's going to be getting out her ukulele any minute now."

The same thing that had happened on the street last night occurred again. He felt himself growing hard. It took all the will he possessed not to turn his head and capture her mouth.

Somehow, he managed to remember himself enough to back away from her a little and give a low groan. "That settles it. I'm outta here."

Thelma patted his shoulder and reached up to kiss his cheek. "Thanks for coming, Clay."

"I enjoyed it." He turned to Andie. "Walk me to my car?"

She blinked and her soft lips parted in mild surprise. The request had been just a fraction out of the ordinary. He was only one guest of many, and she saw him nearly every day.

"Oh, go on with him, honey," Aunt Thelma said.

"All right." Andie's face was composed again. She smiled and hooked her arm through his. "Let's go."

Clay felt the warmth of her against his side. It was good, he decided. It was *right*. It was as it should be.

They walked down to the foot of the street, where Clay's car waited. Whatever snow had clung to the ground from the night before was gone now, melted away to nothing by the afternoon sun. Andie held on to his arm, her step in time with his.

He wondered what the hell to do.

He could kiss her. He could stop right there on the sidewalk and turn her to him. He could pull her soft body close and lift her chin with his hand.

Or maybe he should say something, something that would let her know what he was feeling, something that would communicate to her in just a few words everything that was going through his mind.

They reached the car too soon. He still hadn't figured out quite what to do, or what to say.

He turned and leaned against the passenger door. "Andie, I…"

"What?"

"Well, I…"

"Yes?" She folded her arms over her breasts and shivered a little. But she was wearing a huge, soft sweater and leggings and the sun was out. If she trembled, it wasn't from cold.

"There's something I…"

"What?" She bit the inside of her lip. Her nostrils flared, just slightly. He thought of a soft, vulnerable animal scenting a predator.

"Hell." He only breathed the word.

"What? Clay, what is it?"

He had no words. He wanted to touch her. He dared to reach out and cup his hand over her upper arm. Her sweater was as soft as it looked. Beneath that softness, she was firm and warm. Her arm tensed under his fingers.

"Clay, what?" She backed away, out from under his touch.

"Andie…"

Clay couldn't help himself. He reached out and took her arm in a firmer grip. She stared at him, stunned. He pulled her to him.

She came, falling against him with a tiny exhalation of breath. He felt the soft fullness of her breasts against his chest.

"Clay, what is it?" She lifted her head to search his eyes. "What do you want?"

He said it. "You."

He watched her face, watched for the signs. There would be nothing, of course, if she gave him no sign. But the signs *were* there. She didn't—or couldn't—hide them. There was that little hitch of breath, the quickened heartbeat against his own. And most important, he saw the way her dark eyes went cloudy and her lips grew suddenly soft. He took the signs into himself, hoarding them.

It was okay. She hadn't rejected him.

Very slowly and deliberately he lowered his mouth and tasted her, as he'd wanted to do back there in the house.

She sighed. He felt that sigh all through him, felt her body giving, pressed to his. He thought of roses and peaches again, thought that she tasted just the way she smelled. Her mouth, softly parted, allowed the questing entrance of his tongue.

It was silky and hot inside her mouth. So good, and so exactly what he'd imagined it might be. Yes, he did want her. Badly. He swept the sweet, moist inner flesh of her mouth with his tongue.

She moaned, low and hungrily.

And then she stiffened.

"No." Andie breathed the word against his lips.

She gripped him by the arms and pushed herself away from him.

Clay wanted to grab her and pull her back, to take her mouth again, to savor the taste of her just a little bit more. Desire was an ache in him. But he controlled it. He was good at controlling himself, after all. And he'd found out what he needed to know.

There was a long, gaping moment of silence between them. A bird squawked at them from a wire overhead. On the street, a pickup rolled by. Clay wondered if anyone else had driven by while he was kissing her. If they had, Clay never would have known it. He'd been oblivious to everything but the taste and feel of her.

Andie had her arms folded protectively over her breasts again. Her lips were red and full from the kiss. Her face was flushed.

"Why did you do that?" Her voice was tight.

He felt irritated at her suddenly, for pulling back, for trying to avoid what was going to happen eventually anyway.

"I told you." His voice was harder, perhaps, than it should have been. "Because I want you."

Her mouth had no trace of softness about it now. "Just like that." She flicked a hand in the air. "Out of nowhere. Because you want me."

He looked down at his shoes and then back up at her. "You want me, too."

"Don't change the subject."

"This *is* the subject. I want you. You want me. It's simple, if you'll only—"

"It is not." She tossed an indignant glance heavenward and then glared at him once more. "It's impossible."

"No."

"Good Lord, Clay. We have to *work* together."

"I am very well aware of that."

"You could have fooled me. What's gotten into you?"

You! he wanted to shout at her. *You and your black hair and your wide brown eyes and your scent like flowers and ripe summer fruit.*

But he didn't say that. He said, "I want us to be married."

She stared. "Excuse me?"

"I said, I want to marry you. Right away."

She took another step back from him. "Clay, this is ridiculous. It would never work."

"Oh, yes it will. It will work out just fine."

"Clay." She pitched her voice low, but its intensity made it sound like a shout. "I'm *pregnant,* Clay. And it's not your baby."

"I know. That's one of the reasons, probably the most important reason. For the sake of the baby."

Andie shook her head.

Clay nodded.

She backed away, up the street. "I…this is impossible. I can't talk about this now."

"When, then?"

"Don't do this."

"When?"

She glared at him. "I just…right this minute, I *hate* you, Clay Barrett." She sounded very much as she had when they were kids.

Clay was firm, he did not revert to childish taunts. "But you want me. And you'll marry me."

"Not now. I can't think about this now."

"Fine. Tonight, then. We'll talk about it more tonight."

"Oh, God. Tonight."

"Eight o'clock."

"Where?"

"I'll come to your place." No way he was going to tell her to come to his. In the state she was in, she might not show up.

"I can't…"

"Say you'll be there, Andie. Just say that."

"All right." She gave a little frustrated moan. "Oh, how can you do this to me? Everything was worked out. It was all going just fine."

"Say it."

"Damn you."

"Say it."

"I'll be there." And then she turned and ran up the street, all the way to her mother's house.

Andie moved through the rest of her birthday party in a daze, trying to smile and be gracious as the guest of honor, when all she wanted to do was go home.

Go home to her apartment and close all the blinds and sit on her bed and hug her tattered old teddy bear that she'd had since she was a baby.

Clay had *kissed* her.

A real kiss. A man-and-woman kiss.

It wasn't possible.

But it was true.

And, Lord forgive her, she had *liked* it. Liked it more than any kiss she'd ever had in her life.

And then, after that incredible, unforgivable kiss, he'd told her he wanted to marry her.

Marry her.

All her life she'd thought that her watchful, cautious cousin was like a sleeping volcano. Now and then she'd wondered what it would be like if he woke up some day and started spewing fire.

Well, now she knew.

She'd been licked by the flames, swallowed by the heat. It couldn't be true. But it was. Just as Clay had said. She *wanted* him.

It was just a little eerie, actually. Because when she'd blown out the candles on her cake, she'd wished for a good man to stand beside her.

And then, not half an hour later, Clay had asked her to marry him.

Weird. Very weird.

And impossible. Even if Clay *was* a good man. Even if, as

he'd so blankly pointed out, she desired him, nothing could come of it. Nothing but trouble.

There was her job to consider, a job she needed and loved. For a woman to desire her boss rarely led to anything but heartache and the unemployment line. And worse than the way her job was suddenly in jeopardy, there was the truth about the baby's father. She could never tell Clay the truth about Jeff. It would kill Clay to know that his best friend was the one.

And Andie knew very well that the family was involved in this. She could read them all like the open books they were. Andie was pregnant and Clay was single and reliable and only related to Andie by adoption.

How perfect, they were all thinking, *Clay and Andie can get married and everything will be fine.* Andie was also reasonably certain, judging by a few oblique remarks her mother had made, that they'd even tried to convince themselves that Clay was the baby's father.

Which was ridiculous, if they'd only open their eyes. If Clay had been the baby's father, he would have married her in a minute. If she'd refused him, he would have bullied and prodded, reasoned and pleaded. He would have kept after her relentlessly until she gave in. Clay was like that. He always faced his duty and did the right thing.

And now, with a little subtle goading from the family, Clay had decided that the right thing would be for him to marry her anyway—even though the baby *wasn't* his.

Oh, she could gladly strangle each and every one of her loving relatives.

Oh, go on with him, honey, her mother had said when Clay had made that strange request that she walk him to his car. As if Andie hadn't seen the gleam in her mother's eyes.

It was too crazy. And impossible, just as she'd tried to tell Clay.

But Clay wouldn't listen to her.

That was always the problem. Clay had never listened to her. Once he decided what he thought was right, he acted on it. And everyone else just had to go along.

Well, Andie had never gone along. And she was not going to go along now.

Tonight, when he came to see her, she would be better prepared. They would have a real discussion of this, like the two adults they were now. Somehow, without revealing the awful truth about Jeff, she would make her pigheaded cousin see reason.

And then, please God, they would go back to the way things had been before.

Chapter 6

When Andie opened her door to Clay that night, her eyes were deep and serious. She wore neither lipstick nor a smile.

She stepped back to let him in. When he moved past her, he didn't miss the care she took not to allow her body to touch his.

"You can hang your coat there." She indicated a row of pegs by the door.

Clay hung his coat and followed her into her small living room.

"Can I get you something?"

"No, thanks."

"Sit down." She gestured at the couch.

He sat where she'd pointed. Andie perched on a chair several feet away.

Clay had his arguments all lined up in his head. But he could see she wanted to speak first. He allowed that.

"Clay, I…I'm sorry about the, um, harsh things I said this

afternoon. I didn't mean them. Not all of them, anyway. I *don't* hate you. Not really."

"I know that."

She forced a weak smile. "It was just that you shocked me. That kiss. And then saying you wanted to marry me, out of nowhere like that."

"I understand."

One of her slim hands had found a loose thread on the chair arm. Clay watched as she tugged at it, then realized what she was doing and let the thread go.

She spoke again. "I've thought about what you said this afternoon. I really have."

"And?" His stupid heart was in his throat. He swallowed it down.

"And, well, I really don't see how it could work."

Clay gave himself a moment to let her careful refusal sink in. He didn't like it, didn't like the way it made his chest feel tight and his stomach knot up. But it didn't matter. She would marry him in the end. It was what he wanted and it was the right thing. Whatever it took, he would make it happen.

"Why not?" He was proud of how unconcerned he sounded.

She drew in a long breath. "Oh, Clay. Come on. It has to be obvious."

"Fine. Then state the obvious. Please."

"Well." She gave a little nervous cough. "Okay. If you insist."

"I do."

"First, and most important, we aren't in love."

He looked at her for a long time. "Love."

"Yes. Love."

He considered for a moment, framing his argument. Then he spoke. "Of course there's love between us, Andie. We're family, you and me. We work together and we do it damn well. We can build a good life, help each other, *be* there for each other. And we can give your baby two parents to see it all the way to adulthood. That's all the love there needs to be."

Andie wasn't convinced. "No, Clay. That's not enough."

"What else is there?"

She looked away, then back. "You know."

"Tell me."

"Fine. I will." She pulled herself straighter in her chair. "There's a special kind of love that should be there, between a man and a woman when they decide to marry. It's not there with us. You say you love me. But you're not *in* love with me. Are you?"

He tried to contain his impatience, but it was there in his voice when he spoke. "This is a word game, Andie. Nothing more."

"It's not. I want to be in love with the man I marry."

"You'll have love. The only kind that matters."

"It's not enough."

There was a silence, a heated one. She watched him with grim hostility. And her breathing was agitated. Clay thought that he could make this a hell of a lot easier on both of them if he just got up and went over to her and pulled her into his arms. If he did it slowly, she might accept him.

Or he could give in and tell her in so many words that he was in love with her.

Why not, he thought? Why not just say the words she wanted to hear? He cared for her and was willing to do just about anything to see that she was safe and well provided for.

But somehow, those words just wouldn't come. Because in the sense that she meant *in love,* he would be telling a bald-faced lie. There was simply no such thing as the love she thought she wanted. Love like that was just a pretty word for a natural biological urge.

"Clay, please understand." Her soft voice tried to soothe him.

He only bristled more. "Understand what?"

"Don't be angry."

"I'm not."

"Oh, Clay. If I could only make you see. I've made a lot of mistakes. I know I have. But I've also learned a lot. And I really believe that a very special kind of love is important, between a man and a woman, when they begin a life together."

He decided to leave the issue of love alone for right then, since it seemed to be getting them nowhere. "Okay. And what else?"

"What do you mean?"

"What other issues and questions? What else is bothering you?"

"Well, I…I believe there should be honesty, Clay. That honesty between a man and a wife is second only to love."

He regarded her coolly. "Honesty."

"Clay, don't—"

"You're saying you don't think we're being honest with each other. Am I right?"

"Well, I…"

"Say what you mean to say, Andie. Who's lying and what about?"

"It's not a lie. Not really. It's just…about the baby's father." She looked down at her lap and her misery was painful to see.

Clay felt a twinge of guilt again, as he did every time this subject came up around her. He knew the truth, after all. Her closely guarded secret, to him, was no secret at all. He reminded her, "The man is out of your life, isn't he?"

"Yes."

"And out of the baby's life, too?"

"Yes."

"How big is the chance that later, sometime in the future, he'll change his mind?"

She gave him the answer he knew she would give. "Not big. Very small, actually."

"Then why borrow trouble? I'm willing to accept your word about this. The baby will be *our* baby."

Andie stared up at him, a strange expression on her face, hopeful and disbelieving at once. "You would do that? Claim the baby as yours?"

"Yes."

She looked as though she might cry. "Oh, Clay."

"So marry me."

He waited, his heart in his throat. For a moment he actually thought he had convinced her.

But then she sighed and looked at her lap again. "No. I just can't. I know you can't understand that. But it's the way it is. I can't tell you about the baby's father. And I could never marry a man who didn't know the truth. To start out with something like that between us would doom it all right from the first."

Clay studied her bent head. He thought of Jeff, who was dead to him now. And he thought of how he'd sworn to himself that Andie would never have to learn that he knew about Jeff.

He still saw no real reason to tell her the truth. Jeff was the past. And the past would fade to nothing in time. There was no point at all in dwelling on it, in bringing up all the pain and digging around in it for the sake of some noble concept like *honesty*.

What they needed to do was let it go. He saw that clearly. And she would see it soon enough, he was certain.

He stood. "Look. Andie."

Her head shot up. She stared at him, her eyes wide and wary.

He took a step toward her.

She leaned back in her seat. "I don't think you should…"

"What?"

"I, um…"

He stood over her. "Andie." He reached down and took her

hand. She let him do that, though her apprehension was plain in every line of her slender body.

He gave a tug. She slowly stood. He backed away a little, in order to give her just enough space that she wouldn't feel she had to cut and run.

She swallowed. "What?"

He felt tenderly toward her suddenly. He knew what she was experiencing. Consciousness of him as a man.

It was a strange, disorienting feeling, he knew. They'd been certain things to each other for almost twenty years. But now they were finding that what they shared was like one of those drawings with an invisible figure hidden within it. You could look for years and never see the hidden figure, but once you saw it, you couldn't *un*see it. From that moment on, it would always be there.

Gently he whispered, "I won't accept a no."

Her expression became earnest. "You'll have to. It's the only answer, Clay. I'm sorry. Please understand. We have to go back to the way things were."

He shook his head. "We can't do that."

"But we have to."

"We can't."

"Why not?"

"If you insist on saying no, you'll see why not."

"I think we can."

Because he couldn't stop himself, he touched the side of her face with his hand. Her skin was like the petal of a rose. He wanted her mouth again, to taste her mouth.

"Please don't, Clay."

He dropped his hand. Then he turned away. He took the few steps to the sliding glass door that opened onto her minuscule patio. In the window glass, he saw his own shadowed reflection and that of the room behind him.

He was pushing too fast, he knew. He wanted things settled. And he wanted her. Soon.

She was over two months along. And he was greedy for her.

He knew it was crude and thoughtless of him to feel that way, and he certainly would never tell *her* that. But it was an imperative for him. He wanted to lay a real claim to her, and if they waited too long, the pregnancy could interfere. The thought of having to wait until after the baby came to make love to her set his nerves on edge.

Still, she was not going to tell him yes tonight—that much was painfully clear. He would do them both a service to back off for a while.

She needed to learn firsthand, from day-to-day experience, just what he meant when he said they couldn't go back. Let them work side by side in the office for a few days with this new awareness between them. She'd see soon enough that un-satisfied desire could scrape her nerves raw.

He turned to face her. "Look. I guess there isn't much more to say at this point. Let's leave it for now. You know where I stand on this. I want to marry you. I think we'll be good together as husband and wife. So you think about my offer."

"Clay." She made a small, frustrated sound. "I said no. I meant it. I'm not going to marry you."

"Fine. But there's no law that says you can't change your mind."

"I *won't* change my mind."

"We're talking in circles here."

"Because you won't face the truth." She was glaring at him now, her fists clenched in impotent anger at her sides.

He had the most ridiculous flash of memory at that moment. He saw her at twelve or thirteen, outraged at some imagined injustice he'd done her, her fists clenched at her sides and her face scrunched up in a glare, looking almost exactly as she did right now. Whatever they'd been fighting over, he remembered she'd ended up shouting at him. And he'd shouted right back.

It occurred to him right then that if he didn't get out of there, they would end up yelling at each other like a couple of kids. Either that or he would drag her into his arms and shut her up by covering her mouth with his own. Neither option would be likely to further his case in the long run. He'd better get out of there.

He marched toward her. She cringed back, probably afraid he was going to grab her and do something unforgivable— like kiss her. He couldn't resist tossing her a superior smirk as he strode right by her and out to the little cubicle where his coat was hanging. He grabbed the coat off the hook.

"Good night," he called, triumphantly aloof as he went out the door.

Monday morning at the office, Clay was careful to be strictly professional. He was going to have to wait Andie out. And he was ready for that. They would go on as before, until she realized he was right: they *couldn't* go on as before.

Andie saw his point right away.

But there was no way she was going to admit it to Clay.

And besides, it seemed that they *should* have been able to go on as before. Nothing, really, was any different than it had ever been.

And yet everything had changed in a thousand tiny, irrevocable ways.

Andie was so terribly *aware* of Clay now. And that new awareness affected everything. Clay's mere presence in her place of business messed up her concentration. Even when he was down the hall with his door closed, her silly mind would wander to thoughts of him. All the time now, she'd find herself staring into space with a half-finished letter on the computer screen in front of her, listening with every fiber of her being for the sound of Clay's door being pulled back, for the soft thud of his footfalls as he came out into the hall.

His voice set off alarms inside her. And the sight of him could make her weak.

Clay was a handsome man. She'd always known that. But to Andie, Clay's good looks had been nothing but a fact, like his brown hair and green eyes, his high forehead and his straight nose. She'd never thought twice about them. Not even back in high school, when her girlfriends were always swooning over him.

"Sweet Mother Mary, Clay Barrett's got everything," her best friend Ruth Ann used to sigh. "He's smart, he plays sports, and he's got that dangerous look in his eye." Ruth Ann would give a little shiver. "All that control. That's the thing about Clay Barrett. Just the idea of breaking through all that control."

Andie would groan. "Oh, please…"

"Plus he has A-1 fantabulous buns."

"Pass the onion dip, will you?"

"How can you do that? Ask for the onion dip when we're discussing Clay Barrett's buns?"

"It's easy. Pass the onion dip."

"I don't think you're normal, Andrea McCreary."

"I'm normal." Andie had reached across her friend and scooped up the container of dip. "If you knew Clay like I know Clay, you wouldn't give two bits for his buns."

"Try me. I'd *love* to know him like you know him. And you're not even *really* related to him, even though your mother and his mother are sisters. Mother Mary and Joseph, it's the perfect setup. You go to his house for dinner practically every Sunday."

Andie chose a big chip and plowed it through the gooey dip. "Every other Sunday." She stuck the chip in her mouth.

"Oh. Right. And the rest of the Sundays, *he* goes to *your* house. How can you pass up a chance like that? You could be working your wiles on him."

"My *wiles?*" Andie sneered, then chose another chip, shoveled on the dip and popped the delicious morsel into her mouth. "Um. Heaven."

"Like I said, you're not normal. You eat anything you want and stay disgustingly thin. And you don't have a crush on your gorgeous cousin."

"Look," Andie had said around another mouthful of onion dip, "I don't eat anything I want, believe me. Someday, when I get old, I'll have to take better care of myself. And as far as Clay Barrett goes, it's bad enough I had to grow up with him. God would not be that cruel to make me have a crush on him, too."

Andie groaned when she thought of that long-ago conversation and all the others like it that she and Ruth Ann had shared.

Because all of a sudden, God *was* being that cruel.

And it got in the way of her performance at work, this unforeseen, impossible *crush* she was suffering from. She misplaced folders. She saved letters in the wrong files. She sometimes didn't even hear the little buzzer over the door until the client was standing at the reception counter, clearing his or her throat and waiting for Andie to look up from her computer and notice that someone was there.

And Clay was distant. Distant and irritable. He acted like an adult version of the judgmental tyrant he used to be when they were kids. He watched her. He seemed to be thinking mean things about her. And he rarely cracked a smile.

By the time Andie finally escaped the office at the end of the day and went home, she was a wreck. It was as bad as it had been in January, when she'd realized she was pregnant and didn't have the faintest idea what she was going to do about it.

Every day was hell. But at least in January, Clay had been pleasant and reasonably kind while he watched her all the time.

Now, he remained completely detached. He wanted the work done and he wanted it done now and he had no time for a gentle word or a teasing compliment.

Andie remembered very well now why she'd detested him for all those years. He was absolutely heartless when thwarted. Sometimes, when he barked at her for misplacing a file or not getting a letter or a bill out on time, she wanted to just stand up from her computer and yell at him that he was the meanest man she'd ever met, that she hated him and she quit.

But she controlled herself. She remembered the baby. She remembered that there was someone else to think of now, not just herself. She could ride this out. She knew she could.

However, by Thursday night, just five nights after Clay had insisted she marry him, Andie was so depressed that she wondered how she was going to go on. Ruth Ann called to see how she was doing at a little after eight.

"What is the *matter?*" Ruth Ann demanded immediately.

"Nothing."

"Right. I'll be right over."

"Ruth Ann, really, it's not—" But the dial tone was already buzzing in her ear. Ruth Ann had hung up.

The doorbell rang ten minutes later. When Andie opened it, her friend was grinning on the other side.

But then Ruth Ann frowned. "Saint Teresa, what happened? You looked great, and now you look like somebody killed your cat again."

"Thanks."

Ruth Ann stepped inside the door, kicked it closed with her foot and leaned back against it. "Johnny's watching the kids."

"That was nice of him."

"He said to take as long as I wanted. Who woulda thought

it, huh? Meadow Valley High's most incorrigible bad actor now deserves a medal as a husband and a daddy." She held up a brown bag. "I come bearing ice cream. Peanut butter caramel mocha fudge. It *has* to be a sin, right?"

"I'm just not hungry."

"Something is definitely wrong." Ruth Ann grabbed Andie's arm, pulled her into the kitchen and dished out the ice cream into bowls. Then she sat opposite Andie and commanded, "There. Eat. And tell Ruth Ann all about it."

And Andie did. Ruth Ann listened the way Ruth Ann always listened, with absolute attention, her pointed chin thrust forward, her eyes bright and alert. When Andie was done, Ruth Ann relaxed a little. She took a big bite of ice cream.

"Well?" Andie asked, when Ruth Ann had swallowed and started to take another bite without saying anything.

"Well, what?" Ruth Ann savored that other bite.

"Well, now that you've heard it, what do you think?"

Ruth Ann clinked her spoon on the edge of her bowl. "You don't want to hear what I think."

"Yes, I do. Tell me."

Ruth Ann set down her spoon. "Do what he wants. Marry him."

"What?"

"You heard me. He won't give up. You know how he is. And you've admitted you've finally seen the light about him."

"What light?"

"That he's *sexy,* you idiot. That he turns you on. I always told you—"

"Spare me. Please."

"You want him. Admit it."

"You're beginning to sound a lot like him, Ruth Ann."

"Sometimes the truth is painful to deal with, from any source."

"Ruth Ann. His best friend was the father of my baby. He

doesn't know that. I want a real marriage, if I ever have one. A marriage like you've got. Based on love and trust. I can't marry a man who doesn't already know and accept the truth about my baby."

"Fine. So tell him the truth."

"You *are* kidding."

"No. The way it looks from my chair, you don't have a lot of options. How long do you think you're gonna last, working for him every day and having this unsettled *thing* between you? It's only been, what? Four days, and you look almost as bad as you did before you told him you were pregnant and got that out of the way. You should either quit your job—not a terrific choice, I gotta admit, at this point in your life—or tell him what you're afraid to tell him and then wing it from there. You're in deadlock right now, kiddo. It's an ugly place to be."

"But it will *hurt* him, if I tell him. It will hurt him so badly."

"For a woman who can't stand that man, you sure are worried about how bad you're gonna hurt him."

"I never said I couldn't stand him."

"For all the years while we were growing up, that's *all* you said."

"That was then. Things change."

"Oh, really? And anyway, you should have thought of all this before you spent the night with that Jeff character."

Andie looked down at her bowl of melting ice cream. There was nothing to say to that. Ruth Ann was right.

"Didn't I warn you that you'd end up in trouble with some smooth-talkin' out-of-town guy? You were always too picky, you didn't get yourself any experience and then—"

Andie's head shot up. "Look who's talking. You were a virgin on your wedding night—we both know it."

"I was eighteen on my wedding night and a good Catholic girl. I had a right to be a virgin."

Andie looked down at the table again. "This is a stupid argument. I did what I did. And now I have to deal with the consequences."

Ruth Ann was quiet, then she made a soothing sound. "Well, you're right. You're doing the best you can. I'm sorry if I'm too rough on you."

Andie sighed. "I just don't know what to do. If Clay finds out, he'll kill Jeff."

"It's a thought. I could kill him myself, actually."

"Oh, stop it. I was as much at fault for what happened as Jeff was."

"Fine. I still hate the jerk's guts. Want more ice cream?"

"No, thanks."

"I believe I will have just one more little scoop." Ruth Ann went to the refrigerator and dished herself out another bowlful. "Well, like I said, your options are limited. And you can't control what Clay will do." Ruth Ann closed the carton and put it away. "You sure you can't live with just marrying him and *not* telling him?" She licked the serving spoon, considering. "I mean, after all, things really are *finito* between you and the best friend. It's not like you're pining away for him or anything."

Andie looked at her friend in blank disbelief. "Oh, that's a great idea. And then what will I do when Clay and I are married and the baby's been born and Clay wants us to fly down to Los Angeles and visit his best pal, Jeff?"

"Yuck." Ruth Ann set the serving spoon in the sink and began eating from her bowl. "You're right. Not good. Maybe looking for another job *is* the only real choice, after all."

Andie leaned her chin on her hand. She felt so tired. The last thing she wanted to do was go looking for another place to work. But if she was going to have to do it, she should do it right away. She wasn't showing yet, but she would be soon enough. Who would hire a woman who'd be needing maternity leave right away? She'd probably end up working a series of temp jobs for less pay and no benefits, at least until she'd had the baby and was back on her feet again.

And speaking of benefits, what about her insurance? Could she keep it if she left Barrett & Co.? And if she did, how much would it end up costing her a month? She should look into that. Given that she managed to find another job, any insurance she got from it wouldn't go into effect for a while. And then it probably wouldn't cover her having the baby.

Which would mean the family would end up stepping in to take up the slack. She didn't want them to do that. She didn't want them to end up picking up the tab for a choice that was all her own. She didn't want to burden them, and she didn't want to watch them all shake their heads knowingly and whisper that they'd seen this coming all along.

She wanted them to *admire* her the way they admired Clay. So that her child could be proud of her. So that her child could look at her with confidence and feel safe and protected, the way Andie had been safe and protected while she was growing up.

Oh, it was all just a nightmare. A nightmare, any way she turned.

Everything had been all worked out. Things were going just great.

And then Clay had to go and decide to marry her. And her whole fragile little life was turned upside down all over again.

Andie thought of her savings account, which had been growing steadily the past couple of years. With the money Jeff had sent and the bonus from Clay, she now had very close to twelve thousand dollars. She'd been saving for a house of her own, but of course now that would have to be put off.

Oh, she had been such a foolish dreamer of a girl. She'd wasted too many years, drifting, not applying herself. Having fun.

She hadn't earned the grades in high school to get into a really good college. Yet she hadn't minded, really. Life was easy and every day held something to delight her. In summer, there were trips to the river with her friends and waterskiing at the local reservoir. And in winter, there was snowmobiling and cross-country skiing and warm fires waiting when she came in from the snow. She'd found a job as a waitress that paid well enough. And she'd enjoyed herself thoroughly.

By the time she began to think she should do something with her life, she was in her twenties. She'd buckled down then, going to junior college and then to a business school.

Then Uncle Don's longtime office manager had decided to retire. Uncle Don had offered Andie the job. Andie had hesitated at first. She knew that someday Clay would return and the old animosity between them might ruin things. But Uncle Don had offered to pay her very well. The benefits were great, too. And Clay wasn't going to come home for years, anyway. So Andie had stepped in, surprising everyone with her efficiency and her willingness to work. She'd loved the job, especially after the old office manager left and she could run things all on her own.

Then Uncle Don had suffered his heart attack. Clay had come back ahead of schedule.

Those first months with Clay as her boss had been a rough time for Andie. She'd known she would have to prove herself all over again to him. And she'd done it. Clay had discovered how good she was, in spite of his prejudices against her.

But deep down, she'd resented having to prove her competence to the rival of her teenage years. And maybe what had happened on New Year's Eve was partly because of that.

Because her feelings had grown so tangled since Clay had come home. Because all of her accomplishments the past few years were minor compared to his. Because every time she looked at him, she felt edgy and unhappy and unsatisfied with herself. And yet she hadn't been able to let her feelings out. To do that might have cost her her job.

"Come on," Ruth Ann suggested, cutting through Andie's unhappy thoughts, "let's see if there's a decent tearjerker on cable."

"Oh, Ruthie. Watching a movie is not going to solve my problem."

"No, but your problem is not going to be solved tonight, anyway. So you might as well try to forget it for an hour or two. Come on. A little oblivion is good for a person."

"Oh, Ruthie…"

"Come on." Ruth Ann grabbed Andie's hand and pulled her to her feet. "Get in there and find the viewer's guide. I'll make the popcorn."

Since tearjerkers turned out to be in short supply, they watched *The Terminator*. Ruth Ann sat on one end of the couch, squealing between handfuls of popcorn, as Arnold Schwarzenegger cut a swathe through Los Angeles.

Andie sat quietly, hardly aware of what she was watching. By the time the terminator entered the police station and announced, "I'll be back," Andie had made a decision.

She would talk to Clay tomorrow and tell him she was going to be leaving her job.

Chapter 7

"Close the door." Clay's voice was deadly calm.

Andie shut the door to Clay's office, though there was really no need. It was six-thirty at night and they were alone in the building.

"Now say that one more time, please." He was sitting at the big mahogany desk that had been his father's.

She dragged in a deep breath. "I said, this is not working out for me. I'm giving notice. I'll stay two weeks to help you find someone else and then—"

He stood. "It's the middle of March."

"I know that."

"This is an accounting firm. You'll be leaving at precisely the busiest two weeks of the year."

"It can't be helped."

Clay swore crudely and succinctly. "Oh, yes it can."

"Time is running out for me, Clay. If I want to find

another position before the baby's born, I have to start looking right away."

"You're not quitting. You're going nowhere."

Andie gaped at him. "Pardon me? I don't believe that you said that."

"Believe it. It's true. You're not quitting."

"I am."

"You're not."

"This is ridiculous."

"You're damned right it is. What the hell goes through that mind of yours? You *need* this job—and this company needs you."

"Well, thank you for admitting that I'm needed around here. You could have fooled me the past few days."

"The past few days have been difficult. For both of us. I warned you that they would be." Clay spoke very slowly, like someone trying to reason with an insane person.

Andie leaned back against the door she'd just shut, feeling the tiredness in every inch of her body. "I can't do this. I can't *stand* this. It isn't good for me. And it can't be good for my baby."

"Then marry me."

Tears filled Andie's eyes. She willed them back. She was not going to be some silly, weepy female over this. She'd made the best choice of a bad lot. And he would not dissuade her from what had to be done.

She straightened, pulling her shoulders up. "No, Clay. It won't work."

"It will." Slowly, he came around the desk toward her.

"Clay, don't…"

"Don't what?"

"You know what."

"No. Tell me."

She watched him approaching. Her body, so totally exhausted just a moment ago, was suddenly humming, pulsing with a restless, hot kind of energy.

"Tell me." Clay's eyes were green fire. She couldn't stop looking into them.

Andie swallowed. "I…"

And then he was right there. So close that she could feel his body heat.

"This isn't fair." Her voice held no conviction at all.

"I know." Clay's tone was gentle now. He cupped her chin in his hand. His skin burned her. All her senses centered down to the touch of his flesh against hers. "It's just the way it is. Maybe the way it's always been. Did you ever think about that?"

Andie's mind had slowed; she couldn't think. "About what?"

Clay lowered his head just enough to brush his lips across hers. Down below, she went liquid. It was crazy. She softly moaned.

"About you and me," Clay whispered against her mouth. "Fighting. Enemies for all those years. Your dad said something. Love and hate are very close…."

"You don't believe in love."

"That's right. I don't. I want to kiss you. I want to be inside you."

Andie gasped, both aroused and shocked at the bluntness of his words. "I don't…"

"Yes, you do. You want it. With me. Just like I want it with you. There's no point in your quitting. This will not go away."

"It might."

"It won't. It took too long. Years and years building up. And now it's not something we can get over in a day, or a week, a few months."

"How do you know this?"

"I just do. It will take a very long time, I think."

"It will?"

Clay nodded. And then he wrapped his fingers lightly around her neck. "Your skin is so soft. The other night, I remember thinking it was like rose petals."

"Oh, Clay. This is not how I—"

"Shh. I know. I wasn't going to do this, either. Until I had your agreement to marry me. But here I am. Breaking my promise to myself. I should be ashamed. But I'm not."

He looked so very vulnerable then that she smiled before she could stop herself.

"Ah," he sighed. "A smile. I saw that. I've missed your smiles."

"You have?"

"Absolutely. It's been so grim around here without them."

"But it's because of you that I've been—"

"Shh, don't argue. Don't talk at all."

"But I—"

He didn't let her finish. His mouth closed over hers, taking her denials into himself.

Andie sighed, already open for him. She felt his tongue breach the soft barrier of her lips and she didn't even pretend to evade it. She welcomed it, allowing him to explore her in this intimate way, even daring to meet his tongue with a few shy thrusts of her own.

Clay lifted his mouth enough to whisper, "Yes," and then he slanted his lips the other way and kissed her some more.

His hand strayed downward, to the bow at the collar of her silk blouse. He pulled the ends of the bow and she heard a soft whisking sound as it slithered loose. Then he smoothed the tails open and slipped the collar button from its hole.

Andie's nipples ached, pebbling to attention as he lightly brushed them through her clothing. Her knees could hardly hold her up. She was grateful for the nice solid door to lean against.

Clay slipped the next button free and then the next, his

mouth playing over hers all the while. And then he was pulling the blouse free of her skirt, pushing it gently off her shoulders.

The blouse floated to the floor. He eased down the straps of her slip and then did the same with her bra straps, guiding them off her shoulders. Her bra fell away.

It came to her, distantly, that she was standing in Clay's office naked to the waist. He pulled her close and the tender skin of her breasts was pressed against the wool jacket of his suit. Her nipples, already aching, hardened even more. He rubbed himself against her, imprinting his body onto hers. She felt his desire through all the layers of their clothing.

"Oh, Clay…"

Andie nuzzled her head against the crook of his shoulder, aware of his scent. She put her lips to his strong neck, and parted them just enough that she tasted his skin.

Clay brought his hands between them, feeling for her breasts. He cupped them and rubbed the nipples between his fingers. She let her head fall back as she moaned.

But then, for no reason she could comprehend, he was gripping her shoulders, pushing her away, holding her at arm's length.

"What?" Andie murmured, confused, forcing herself to open her eyes and see what he wanted.

Clay's expression was unreadable. He looked at her face, her neck, her shoulders, her breasts. And then he muttered something so low that she couldn't make out the words.

Andie was dazed, yearning. She reached for him, wondering vaguely what was happening, wanting him close again, wanting his wonderful caresses never to stop.

Clay gripped her shoulders harder, holding her even farther away from him. "Andie."

She blinked. "What?"

"Come home with me tonight."

She blinked again. It was all too fast for her. She had to get away from him, get a moment to collect herself. But there was nowhere to go, so she pressed her body harder against the door. And then she slowly bent to retrieve her blouse and bra.

Clay took a step back, picking up her signal for space and acquiescing to it. He waited while she straightened her clothing and buttoned her blouse.

When she was covered, she met his eyes. "I came in here to tell you I quit. And then, all of a sudden, you were kissing me." Chagrin washed over her. "I let you kiss me."

"You did more than that. You kissed me back. Come home with me."

She looked at him, wanting him. Knowing that what he had said earlier was right. There was a very good chance she would *always* want him. From now on.

What was between them was so powerful. It seemed, in this moment of piercing desire, to have always been. Her battles with Clay were so much a part of who she was that she would not be herself had she not known him, fought him, envied him, raged at him.

"Come home with me. We'll make love. It will diffuse some of the tension, at the very least. And afterward, we'll talk."

"There's nothing to talk about."

"We'll see. But in any case, we'll have tonight."

"I don't see how going home with you could make things anything but worse."

"Who's the cautious one now?" He closed the distance between them again. He put his hands on her shoulders once more and gently rubbed through the silk of her blouse. "It would have happened right here. On the rug. Or against the door. I stopped it. You know I did. Show me the guts I know you have. Make it a conscious choice to come with me now.

Otherwise, next time I won't stop it. I'll let it happen all the way, wherever we are."

Andie started to say, I won't let it happen again. But that would have been such a blatant lie, she couldn't quite get it out of her mouth.

He was right. It *would* happen again. She was absolutely starved for him. All he'd have to do was what he'd done tonight. Get her alone. Approach her slowly and deliberately. She would beg him to kiss her, to touch her, to take her yearning full circle to total fulfillment.

Oh, sweet Lord, it was so strange. So bewildering. Andie had waited all of her life, turned away every man but Jeff Kirkland. She'd *known* that just what was happening now would happen someday, that there would be a man who could set her on fire with just a touch. It was one of the most basic of her girlhood dreams.

She'd never given up that dream. Not until a few months ago, when it had begun to seem somehow childish and unreal. A romantic fantasy that was never going to come true.

It had made her sad, the death of that dream. She had mourned it. She'd even told Jeff Kirkland about it, on New Year's Eve.

Clay demanded, "What are you thinking about?"

Andie sighed. "This is impossible. All of it."

"So forget it. Forget thinking. For now. Come home with me."

Andie searched his green eyes. "Oh, Clay. Please tell me this is not another stupid move I'm making, another one of my crazy mistakes."

"That's easy." His voice was firm. "This is not a stupid move. This is what we both want and what will happen eventually, anyway. Come home with me."

Andie thought about her dream again. That at last, the man in her dream had a face: Clay's face. But in her dream, the man said he loved her. Clay didn't love her, not in the way that she longed to be loved. Clay wanted her and would marry her and would take her baby as his own.

And really, shouldn't that be enough?

Maybe he was right. Maybe it was enough. But why did it feel as if there was some great big hole in the center of all of it, then?

And what about her own heart? Was she in love with Clay?

Oh, sweet heaven, she feared that perhaps she was. Yet something inside her held back from that—from admitting to a woman's love for him.

In her life, he'd always been so powerful. It had seemed to Andie that her cousin always got his way. If she gave him her heart, he'd have everything. She'd be completely at his mercy then, far below him, looking up.

And he was so self-contained. Aunt Della always said that Clay never revealed his heart. Aunt Della thought it was because of the difficulties of his early years, because he'd been hurt and alone and had to turn into himself to survive.

Andie could sympathize with that. But could she live with a man who was like that? How would she ever talk to him about the things that mattered, about the things that hurt?

Like Jeff.

"What are you thinking?"

She veered away from the ugly truth to a more general answer. "A thousand things. You. Me. The family. The family wants us to get together. You know that, don't you?"

He shrugged. "Yes."

"You'd do anything for them, wouldn't you?" She tried not to sound bitter.

Clay was unfazed. "Yes, I would, to a point. But I wouldn't marry a woman I didn't want. Not even for the family's sake."

"For some strange reason, I believe you."

"Because I'm telling the truth. Now, give me your answer. Say you'll come home with me."

"You are relentless."

"No argument. Come home with me."

"Nothing can come of it."

"Think that if you want to. But come home with me."

Andie hovered on the edge of a decision for one more moment, wondering how Clay could be so totally focused, so utterly unswerving in the pursuit of his goal. He simply would not give up.

And she was so tired. She wanted to surrender, to go with him to his house and know what it was at last, to share the greatest intimacy with the man from her dream.

If it all fell apart after tonight—which it was bound to do—at least she would have had that much.

She was slumped rather pitifully against the door. She made herself stand straight.

"Well?"

She gave him what he wanted. "All right, Clay. I'll go home with you."

She watched the heat of triumph flare in his eyes. "Good. Let's get out of here."

Chapter 8

The room lay in shadow. Andrea stood in the door to the hall and looked toward a glass door that led onto a deck. Beyond the deck was the huge, dark, star-scattered sky and the black shapes of distant hills. A sliver of moon hung just above the hills.

It was a beautiful view, Andrea thought. Lucky Clay, to go to sleep every night in a place such as this.

Clay stood behind her. Light as a breath, his hands rubbed her arms. She felt the touch of his mouth at her nape and shivered as his lips caressed her.

Andrea leaned back a little, her body giving a sensual signal to which Clay's arms instantly responded. He pulled her close so she felt him more fully against her and his hands came around her, seeking and finding her breasts.

Andrea moaned. Clay cupped her breasts, felt for the response of the nipples and then rubbed them, so they hardened more through the fabric of her clothing. And then his hands were on the bow at her neck, pulling it loose, slipping buttons free. The front of her blouse fell open. He took it from behind and peeled it away. As he had in the office, he began sliding down straps, getting her underclothes out of his way.

Slowly and with great care, he undressed her. As he removed her clothes, he pressed his body against her back. He kissed her neck and caressed her in long, gentle strokes, making her burn hotter and then hotter still.

The moment came when she was naked. Her clothes were over there and she was over here. Clay turned her so she faced him and then he guided her backward to the bed. He pushed her down. His eyes were burning her again.

Clay backed away from her to turn on a light, just a little one, in a corner. By its soft glow, she could see him. And he could see her. He still wore all his clothes, except for his jacket, which he had shed with his coat downstairs. He approached the bed once more.

When he stood over her, she reached for the buttons of his shirt. But then he knelt on the bed beside her and put his hand on her, there, in her most secret place.

Andrea gasped, shocked. And then she realized how totally she was aroused. She could feel her own wetness. She was like a river down there.

"Yes," Clay said softly. He began to move his hand.

Andrea cried aloud. Her body responded, found the rhythm he was showing her. Nothing else mattered but the magic of his stroking hand. She closed her eyes, sure she would faint, it was so glorious. And all he did was touch her, in this way that should have embarrassed her, but only made her want to beg for more.

Clay said, "You're ready."

Andrea moaned and lifted her hips again. And then his hand went still. She opened her eyes a little and saw that he was pulling off his tie, unbuttoning his shirt.

She rose up enough to help him, though it meant she lost the fabulous intimate caress of his hand. She didn't care. She knew what he hungered for. And she wanted it, too.

It was crucial, essential. He had to be pressed to her, naked as she was. He had to be inside her. Now.

Sooner than now….

Andrea shoved Clay's shirt off his shoulders, helped him tear it off his arms. Swiftly they pulled at his clothes together, getting rid of them, getting them off and away.

And then he rose over her. Oh, he was so wonderful to see. The powerful, sculpted shoulders, the strong arms, the hard, deep chest. His manhood jutted out from the silky nest of brown hair.

Slowly Clay lowered himself upon her. She felt the satiny length of him going in. And it was everything. It was what she had always dreamed. The man of her impossible girlhood fantasies. Made flesh.

He was all the way in. It was the most marvelous, fulfilling ache Andie had ever known. She tried to move.

But he didn't let her. He levered up on his hands and held her fast with his body.

Andie licked her lips. They were so dry. She would die if he didn't let her move.

Clay looked down at her, pushed against her one sweet, tantalizing thrust. He pulled back. And then he groaned. And his face went softer. He slid deep into her once more. She lifted her hips to better receive him.

And at last, he was moving, pushing in and out in long, delicious strokes.

It was such heaven. Oh, she had always known that it could be like this. Her whole body was shimmering. The fulfillment was building.

Andrea longed for the feel of him along the length of her. She lifted her arms, tried to pull him close.

"No," he said. "I want to watch you. I want to see your face." His hips kept moving, the length of him going in and slowly, so slowly, pulling back out.

She felt frantic, so hungry, so needful. She was reaching, reaching…

And he was murmuring things, little hot urgent things. She moved faster. He moved with her, picking up each of her body's signals, before she could send them, it seemed.

She reached for him again. And when he still wouldn't come down to her, she stroked his shoulders and the hot, smooth, powerful flesh of his chest. Her fingers moved over him, swift as the wings of a butterfly, learning every contour, committing him to memory.

She had always known him. She had *never* known him….

And then it happened. A pulsing. An expanding and a rippling outward of sensation. Andrea cried out.

Clay whispered, "Yes."

The pulsing went on, to encompass all that she was, to free her for the briefest eternity from her doubts and her unhappiness and from all that remained unsaid and undecided.

Somewhere in the middle of it, Clay was caught up, too. She felt him push strongly into her, a movement of his own need, his own hunger that had claimed him at last.

He groaned, a sound of both pleasure and pain. He thrust once more. They both held absolutely still.

She dared to look at him. He met her eyes. The pulsing went on and on.

They whispered "Yes" in unison.

A moment. Forever. And then a gentle fading. Stark wonder became a kind of glow.

Clay sighed. He lowered himself carefully upon her. She

welcomed the warmth and hardness of him against her slowing heart.

Gently he rolled to the side, holding her with him, so that they lay facing each other, still joined, arms and legs entwined. He stroked her damp hair and kissed her moist cheek. Andrea cuddled up closer to him, curling her arms against his chest, wrapping him tighter with her legs.

It came to her that something wonderful had happened; she was completely at peace.

Clay said in a whisper that was tired, yet triumphant, "Now you're *both* mine."

She knew what he meant. Both herself and the baby. And she had no desire to argue with him. Perhaps his claim was true. In any case, she understood right then that what had just happened changed everything.

Clay went on gently stroking her hair. For the first time in days Andrea felt totally relaxed. She felt safe. It was okay to give in to exhaustion. She drifted off to sleep.

When Andrea awoke the room was flooded with daylight. She was warm and cozy under the covers. And she was alone.

She sat up and looked for a clock, finding one on the stand on the opposite side of the bed. It was after ten in the morning. She had slept for more than twelve hours.

She stretched and realized she felt quite rested. Her stomach growled. She was starved. She also had to answer nature's call. Badly.

She smiled as she saw the man's robe Clay had left for her at the foot of the bed. Then she tossed back the covers and jumped from the bed, grabbing up the robe and shoving her arms into it as she ran for the master bath.

After relieving herself, she left the private stall that housed the commode and went back out to the main part of the big bathroom. She washed her hands in the sink and stood before the wall-to-wall mirror to run one of Clay's brushes through the wild tangle of her hair.

Her stomach growled again. She really was starved. But aside from hunger, she felt just fine. No queasiness at all. Her morning sickness, which had never confined itself to the morning at all, had been fading for the past week or two. She wasn't the least bit sad to see it go.

Andie turned sideways in the mirror, looking at her stomach. In a feminine gesture as old as motherhood, she put her hand there. It was still flat, nothing showing at all through the heavy bulk of Clay's robe. There was, however, a slight roundness when she was nude.

Nude. Andie blushed a little, thinking of the night before. Clay had been careful with her, in spite of the intensity of what they'd shared. Careful for the baby's sake.

Andie smiled, a dreamy smile. She probably shouldn't feel so wonderful. The only thing that had happened was good sex.

But then, since she'd never had good sex before, she supposed she had a right to feel a little wonderful about it.

"You're awake."

With a small exclamation of surprise, Andie shifted her glance to see Clay in the mirror. He was leaning in the doorway to the bedroom, wearing jeans and a snug, dark blue T-shirt, watching her.

She set down the brush and turned to him, tightening the sash of the robe. "How long have you been standing there?"

He was grinning. "Long enough."

"It's not nice to spy on people."

"I know." He contrived a remorseful expression, though she knew very well he wasn't the least contrite.

"Then why do you do it?"

His beautiful shoulders lifted in a shrug. "Because I've always done it. At least, where you're concerned."

"That's no reason."

"I know."

She planted her hands on her hips, feeling devilish, feeling really good. "How am I going to start an argument with you if you refuse to be goaded?"

He left the doorway then and came toward her. "I don't know. Maybe we'll just have to forget about arguing for now."

Her body seemed to be humming again, the way it had been last night. "That wouldn't be normal. We *always* argue."

He was less than an arm's distance away. He reached out and took the sash of the robe from her fingers. He gave a tug.

She landed against his chest with a soft little sigh. "Don't we?" she prompted, since he had said nothing.

"Don't we what? I forgot what we were talking about." He lowered his mouth and kissed her, slowly, sweetly and thoroughly. Andie forgot what they'd been talking about, too, as she slid her hands up to link around his neck.

When the kiss ended he continued to hold her close, stroking her hair and her back. "Hungry?" He breathed the word against her temple.

She pulled back, though she stayed in the circle of his arms. "Am I ever. I could eat your tractor. Have you eaten?"

"Hours ago."

"You should have woken me up."

"No, I shouldn't. You needed the sleep. Want breakfast?"

"Yes, and a shower."

"In which order?"

"I don't care."

"Go ahead and shower. I'll cook you some eggs."

"Three. Over easy. And toast. With butter and jam."

* * *

Andrea's eggs were waiting when she came downstairs dressed in her rumpled skirt and blouse from the night before.

Clay cast a glance at her clothes. She read the look. He was wondering if she was planning to leave as soon as she ate. But he didn't ask her about it. And she was glad he didn't. Because she didn't know yet just what she was going to do.

"I heated some water," he said. "For your tea."

It touched her that he had noticed she wasn't drinking coffee anymore. But maybe that was silly, for her to be touched about that. Of course Clay would notice. He noticed *everything,* always had.

"Thank you." Andie sat down and spread her napkin on her lap.

"I only have regular tea, though, not that peppermint kind you drink at work."

"Regular tea is fine." She picked up her fork and started to eat. It was so *good.* She forced herself to eat slowly so she wouldn't end up feeling nauseated, after all.

Clay poured the hot water over a tea bag and placed the cup at her side. Then he poured himself some coffee and sat opposite her chair.

After Andie had finished two of the eggs and half of the toast, the sharp edge of her hunger was blunted. She savored the rest of the meal. At last, she pushed the plate away.

"That was wonderful."

He took a sip from his coffee. His eyes were serious.

She knew what was coming. "Oh, Clay."

"We have to talk about it."

"No. We don't. Not right now."

He shook his head. "Andie, Andie. What is it with you? Never do today what you can put off till tomorrow?"

There was a window beside the breakfast table. Andie looked

out over the lower deck, over the hillside that sloped away beneath the house and the gnarled live oaks that clung there.

"Look at me, Andie."

She did as he demanded. And took issue with his analysis of her. "I'm not really like that, not about most things. I'm not a procrastinator anymore. If you're going to judge me, please judge me as I am, not as I used to be."

"Fair enough. But still, about this particular subject you *are* putting me off."

She rubbed her eyes. "Maybe. I don't know. I admit, since last night…"

"What?"

"I feel differently."

He leaned on the table. The intensity in him came at her like waves of heat from an oven. She knew the strength of his will and the way he was holding himself in check. "Differently, how?"

"I feel kind of hopeful."

"About you and me?"

"Yes." She found she was blushing. "I, um, never felt anything like that before."

He was puzzled. "You never felt hopeful before?"

"No. I mean I never felt anything like what happened last night."

"Good."

Andie gave a little cough, because her throat felt dry. "It looks like, if nothing else, we could get along in bed."

Clay nodded, waiting. And when she said nothing more, he prompted, "So what are you saying, then?"

Andrea waved a hand. "Oh, Clay. Maybe I don't know what I'm saying." She thought of those three little words, *I love you,* which he'd never said. She decided she could live without them. She felt, since last night, that he was hers in a deep and complete way. That he'd always been hers. As she was his. She was finally woman enough to accept that.

And to accept him.

And besides, eternal optimist that she was, she could still hope that he might change someday. That he'd allow himself to believe in love and to tell her he loved her. And then she might have the nerve to show her deepest heart to him as well.

"Andie." The sound was impatient. "Talk to me."

"I'm trying."

"Try harder."

"Don't push me."

Only one thing held her back. The truth about Jeff Kirkland. She could marry without words of love. But she could not marry Clay unless he knew the truth about Jeff.

It would hurt him to know. And who could tell exactly how he might react? Knowing Clay, she thought he might insist on confronting Jeff. That wouldn't be good.

But it would be worse for Clay *not* to know. Jeff was his friend. The baby could look like Jeff. Or someday, God help them, Jeff might change his mind and want into the life of the child he'd helped create.

"Andie."

"All right, Clay."

"All right, what?"

"All right, I'll marry you."

He stared at her, exultant. And then his eyes narrowed. "But what?"

"You know me so well."

"But what?"

Andrea closed her eyes, drew in a breath and then gazed at Clay squarely once more. "But we have to talk about the baby's father."

"No, we don't."

"We do. Or there won't be any marriage. You can be as persistent as you want. But I won't back down about this. You have to know."

"What?" The word burst out of him. "What do I have to know? You want to tell me you still *love* him? Is that it? You still *love* the bastard who made a baby with you and then just walked away?"

"No, Clay. That's not what I want to tell you at all."

Now he was the one drawing in a deep breath. Andrea watched him calm himself. "Then what?"

"You have to know who the man was, Clay. I won't marry you with this lie between us."

He looked wary. "Now you *want* to tell me who he was?"

"When before I said I *couldn't,* I know. You'll understand. Once you know."

Clay was watching her very closely. He had the strangest expression on his face.

And all of a sudden, *she* understood. She gaped at him and then she murmured, "You already know."

Chapter 9

"How long?" Andie demanded. "How long have you known?"

"Andie." His voice was coaxing. "Settle down."

She wouldn't be coaxed. "How long?"

"Hell. For a while. A few weeks."

"A few weeks." She repeated his words numbly. Then she shook her head. "All this time. I've been worried, knowing I could never tell you, scared to death you might find out someday. And while I've been stewing, you've known all along."

"Yes."

"That Monday morning three weeks ago, when you came in with your face all battered and tried to tell me you fell off your tractor—"

"I'd been to see Jeff. Yes."

"And he beat you up?"

Clay grunted. "Let's say we beat each other up."

Andie found she couldn't sit still. She stood. "You fought. You had an actual, physical fight."

"Yeah."

"What happened? You tell me. All of it."

Clay shifted in his chair, looking miserable. But he did explain. "Damn it, Andie. I'm not blind. And I can count. As soon as you said the baby was due in September, I started thinking about Jeff. And about New Year's Eve, when we all went to that party at Ruth Ann and Johnny's and you and Jeff left together."

"How did you know I left with Jeff? You and your date were gone long before that."

"Jeff told me. He didn't come back to my place until daybreak. And I asked him where he'd been. He said he took you home."

"And what else?"

"I don't remember exactly. Some story about driving around, thinking. He said he'd made up his mind that he wanted to go back to Madeline, if she'd have him. And he did. He went back to L.A. that day."

Andie still couldn't believe this. "So you suspected it was Jeff from the first?"

"Yeah."

"Why didn't you ask *me?*"

"Come on, Andie. The night you told me you were pregnant, you said you'd never tell me who the father was. I knew I wasn't going to get anything out of you. So I went to Jeff. I flew down there and we drove out to the beach together and I asked him point-blank if the baby was his. He admitted it was true."

"What else?"

"He said you wanted to raise the baby on your own and that that was fine with him. All he really cared about was that Madeline wouldn't have to know."

"And?"

"And so I told him I never wanted to see him again. That he was dead to me. He accepted that. And then he punched me. And we fought."

"*He* punched *you?*"

"It was a favor. Never mind. You'd have to be a man."

"Thank God I'm not. Who else knows?"

He snorted. "Knowing you, probably Ruth Ann."

"Very funny. I mean, who else have *you* told?"

"No one. Come on, Andie. Who would I tell? And why the hell would I *want* to tell anyone?"

Andie was still standing, but she put her hands on the table and leaned toward him. She demanded, "What about the family?"

"The family least of all."

Andie straightened, relieved.

He went on, "I think that the family believes the baby is mine." His eyes made a slow, knowing pass from her face to her belly and back up. "And that's just fine with me. As far as I'm concerned, the baby *is* mine. From last night on."

Andie stared at him. She still hadn't fully absorbed the fact that the secret she'd so carefully kept from him was no secret at all. He'd known all along. He'd already confronted Jeff. The worst had happened and she hadn't even realized it was going on.

Her knees felt funny, as if they might not continue to hold her up. And yet she couldn't stay still. She had to move. Just to give herself something to do, she picked up her dirty plate and flatware and carried it all to the sink.

Hastily, her fingers feeling awkward and thick, she rinsed the plate, the fork and the knife and bent to put them in the dishwasher. When she straightened again, Clay was behind her.

He laid his hands on her shoulders and spoke gently against

her ear. "Look. It's out now. There's no more secret, no more lie. Can't we go on from here?"

"Oh, Clay." She turned until she could see his eyes. "I don't know. He's your best friend."

"He *was* my friend. But some things can't be forgiven. He's dead to me now."

Andie shivered. "I don't know how you can do that—just cut him from your life like that."

He made a scoffing sound. "*You've* done it." He looked at her sideways. "Haven't you?"

"Yes."

"Then why shouldn't I?"

She gently put his hands from her shoulders and moved away. "It's different for me."

"No, it's not." He spoke from behind her.

She turned to face him. "It is. I only knew him for a couple of weeks over a holiday. I behaved…foolishly with him. I only feel relief when I think that I'll probably never see him again. He wasn't my friend. I had no history with him."

"What the hell are you getting at?"

"That Jeff Kirkland is a very special person in your life. And he's not in mine."

"That's ridiculous."

"Oh, Clay. Stop it. You actually had *fun* with him. I saw you. I'd never seen you laugh the way you did with him. It…astonished me. I saw you in a whole new light, during those two weeks when Jeff was here."

"So?"

"So it's my fault that your friendship is destroyed."

"It's not your fault."

"At the least, it's half my fault."

"He took advantage of you. He—"

"No. Don't you dare say that. Don't you dare try to make

me into Jeff Kirkland's victim. I wasn't. I did what I did of my own free will."

"Fine. And so did he. And what he did, I will never be able to forgive. He created a baby, and then he just walked away. A man like that is no man. Even if you don't marry me, it will make no difference as far as my relationship with Jeff is concerned. I'll never see him again."

Andie shook her head. She felt such sadness. "Oh, Clay. If you can't forgive *him,* how will you ever forgive *me?*"

"What the hell's the matter with you? Do you *want* me to forgive him?"

"I don't know." She backed up against the L of the kitchen counter and leaned there. "I just can't help thinking that if I weren't in the picture, Jeff would still be your friend."

"He had choices, Andie."

"So did I."

Clay moved toward her. "We're not getting anywhere with this. It's over. He's out of our lives. The best thing we can do now is go on. Make a good life together, give the baby the chance he or she deserves."

"I just don't—"

"Look around you." He made a wide gesture with his hand. "This house has four bedrooms and a study. And plenty of room outside for kids to grow in. I made some pretty good money those last couple of years with Stanley, Beeson and Means and I've used it wisely, I promise you. Half of all I have will be yours.

"And then there's Barrett and Company. I have expansion plans, sound ones. Next year, I intended to have you hire yourself an assistant. Now, with the baby, maybe we'll do it a little early. You can train the new person yourself and she—or he—can cover for you while you're out having the baby. In two years, we'll be ready to bring in another accountant, an all-around guy like me, but with a strong emphasis in tax accounting. That will free me up a little to court more large accounts."

Andie watched his face. He looked so earnest now, as he talked about the future—a future he was offering to share with her. His generosity moved her deeply. She felt a kind of glowing warmth inside, a tenderness toward him, part admiration, part gratitude, part something she didn't dare give a name.

And within this special tenderness, the sadness remained. Clay had given up his best friend. And he was offering her half of all he had. All because she had been so very foolish and was determined now to raise the child she'd created.

Clay must have seen her remorse in her eyes. He misinterpreted it. "Look. Andie. If you decide you don't want to work anymore, we'll manage. You'll be difficult to replace at the office, but I'd be willing to—"

She would burst into tears if he said one word more. She touched his lips. "Stop. No more. Please."

He wrapped his hand around hers and kissed the finger she'd used to shush him. "What is it? What's the problem?"

"Quit talking. Listen."

"All right. What?"

"I do *not* want to give up my job. I love my job."

"All right. Fine. That's great with me."

"I still hate that you've lost Jeff. I feel guilty about it. I'll probably always feel guilty about it."

"Forget about Jeff."

I will when you do, she thought. But there was no point in belaboring the issue anymore. "All right."

He still held her hand in his. He pressed it against his chest. She felt the beat of his heart. "Marry me."

"All right."

He blinked. "I could have sworn you just said yes."

"I did."

"Are there any more *buts?*"

"No, there aren't."

He wrapped his free arm around her and pulled her close. "You won't regret it."

"I only hope *you* don't."

"I won't." He lifted her captured hand again and kissed her fingers once more. "I want to get going on this."

He sounded just the way he did at the office. The thought made her chuckle. "I imagine you have it all planned out."

"Yes."

"Well? Tell me."

"Tahoe or Reno. Right away, today. And then we'll rush back tomorrow night."

"Because of the work load at the office?"

"Exactly. But we'll have it taken care of. We'll be married, you know."

"Yes, Clay. I know." She thought of glow worms, suddenly. Glow worms and fireflies. That was how she felt right then, like some little creature that glows all by itself. Her mind was swimming.

Her own adopted cousin had turned out to be the man of her dreams. And now they would be married. Clay would be her husband. The doubts that still nagged at her seemed to mean nothing right then. Right then, she just felt wonderful, to think that she would sleep beside him every night. For the rest of their lives.

"And then, at the end of April, we could take a trip," Clay was saying. "By then, things will be quiet at the office and Dad can easily handle things alone. We'll go somewhere tropical, I think. Hawaii, maybe. For two weeks or so. We could spend a lot of time on a beach. And in bed…"

Andie blushed. "I see."

"Well, then. What do you think?"

"I think yes. To all of it."

"Good. Tahoe or Reno?"

"I like Tahoe better."

"Tahoe it is." He was stroking her back. "We should call and get a hotel, shouldn't we?"

"I'm sure."

"And then maybe we should tell the folks."

She thought about the family. They wouldn't like finding out about the wedding after the fact. Her mother and her aunt wouldn't like it at all. On the other hand, if they were told now—

"What?" Clay prompted.

Andie pushed the image of her mother's disappointed face from her mind. "After we get back. We'll tell them then. If we tell them before—"

Suddenly, Clay caught on. "They'll want to come. You're right. It will slow us down."

She reached up and brushed his lips with her own. "Exactly."

He caressed the side of her face, toyed with the shape of her ear. "We should get a move on."

"Yes."

"There's only one problem."

"What?"

"I want to kiss you."

"You do?" Something funny happened in Andie's stomach.

"We only made love once last night. You were so tired."

She nodded. "I was. I conked out."

"But you don't seem tired now."

"Oh, I'm not. I'm not tired now at all."

"We could spare an hour, don't you think?" Clay's voice was low, hoarse. It made her stomach quiver all the more.

Andie pressed herself against him, feeling wild and wonderful—and feeling that way with *Clay,* of all people. It seemed so sinful, to feel wild and wonderful with Clay. So deliciously wicked. All those years he'd been her adversary. And now he was the object of her desire.

"Don't you think we could spare an hour?" Clay asked again.

Andie hastened to agree with him. "Oh, yes. An hour. Yes, definitely."

And then he kissed her.

Andie drank in the taste of him. He swept her mouth with his tongue as he had before. But now she brazenly returned the caress, meeting each hungry thrust with a parry of her own.

Clay's hands were on the tie at her neck again. He worked swiftly, and the wrinkled blouse slid to the floor. Then he unzipped her skirt and pushed it down.

Soon enough, she was naked, just as she'd been last night. Andie quivered as his hands roamed her bare flesh. And he went on kissing her. Would she ever get enough of those kisses of his?

She doubted it. This making love was a miracle to her. She'd waited so long to find out what it was all about.

There was a couch, in the family area beyond the kitchen and the breakfast table. Clay led her there. Or rather, they somehow ended up there, kissing and touching and moving across the floor at the same time.

He pushed her down on the couch and said he loved to look at her. And he *did* look at her. Andie was too dazed with desire to blush.

She wanted to see him, too, she realized. So she pulled at his clothes. At first, he tried to ignore her urging, caught up in his exploration of her as he was. But finally, he gave in. He stood and removed his jeans and his T-shirt, every last stitch, tossing them away as if he couldn't get free of them fast enough.

Andie sighed when she saw him, naked as she was at last. She smiled and held out her arms.

He needed no more encouragement. He came down to her. He kissed her breasts, suckling at them and teasing them lightly with his teeth, so that she wiggled and groaned and heard herself crying, "Yes…"

And then he kissed her belly and stroked it with his hand as well. She reveled in that. It felt so good, so warm and good.

And then he kissed her lower still. She gasped a little, when he parted her, right there on that couch in the dazzling light of day. But she didn't protest. How could she protest such wonder, such searing, glorious pleasure?

His tongue was there, tasting her. She moved against it, tossing her head on the throw pillows.

Her climax was swift and all-encompassing. And as soon as it took her, he rose above her, sliding into her with no other prelude, so that one minute she was empty and the next she was filled.

It seemed she reached consummation again then, immediately, as he moved in and out of her, slowly and deliberately, gentle yet demanding, just like the night before. She held on to him, raising herself to him, offering all that she was.

It went on and on. As before, it was so marvelous. How had she lived so long without this? She didn't know.

When his own culmination came, Andie was right there with him, falling off the edge of the universe all over again. They cried out at the same time.

Then they rested, all tangled up on the couch together, so that it was hard to tell where her body ended and his began.

Lying there, her neck a little cramped and her left leg asleep, Andie felt absolutely marvelous. She stroked Clay's shoulders and back with the hand he wasn't lying on. His skin was moist. As it began to cool, she felt the goose bumps break out on him. Or was it on her?

He murmured, "It's too cold to lie here naked. Come on."

He rose, reaching for her hand. She stared up at him, thinking how great it was just to look at him. "Don't look at me like that," he commanded, "or we'll never get to Tahoe."

They showered together, probably an error in judgment as it led to more lovemaking—and a later start. When they were finally dressed, Clay made some calls and managed to get them a nice room in a good hotel-casino. And then he threw a few things in a bag.

Next, they went to Andie's so she could pack.

Andie had barely spread her suitcase open on the bed in her room when the phone rang. Clay ordered her not to answer it, but she did, anyway.

"Well, there you are," groused Ruth Ann. "I called twice last night. I was getting worried."

Clay was frowning at her. "Who is it?"

Andie whispered, "Ruth Ann." Clay rolled his eyes.

"Hey? You still there?" Ruth Ann demanded.

Andie spoke into the phone. "I'm here."

Ruth Ann grunted. "And where were you last night?"

"I was…busy."

"Gotcha. But that wasn't the question."

Andie muttered her friend's name warningly.

Ruth Ann, as usual, refused to take the hint. "What were you *busy* doing?"

Andie cast about for a good answer. But she took too long.

"Oh, sweet Saint Christopher," Ruth Ann declared. "I know. I can smell it. You've been with Clay."

"Look, Ruth Ann—"

"He's there now, right?"

"Ruth Ann, I—"

"Right?"

"Oh, all right. Yes."

Clay mouthed "Hurry up" at her. Andie signaled she was doing her best. Clay shook his head and then left the room.

Ruth Ann demanded, "It was great, wasn't it?"

Andie sank to the side of the bed. "Is nothing private in this world?"

"Not with me around. Well. Wasn't it?"

"Ruthie."

"Well?"

Andie couldn't suppress a giggle. "Yes."

Ruth Ann made a crowing sound. "I knew it, I knew it. Are you going to marry him?"

"Yes."

"Saint Francis! When?"

"Today."

"Hooray! Although I suppose this means I'm going to have to kiss off my dearest dream."

"What dream is that?"

"Being your matron of honor, you dolt."

"Oh. Right. Sorry."

"But it's okay. The dress always costs an arm and a leg, anyway. I'll save some bucks. I've got two sets of braces to pay for, after all."

"How sensitively put."

"Want me to be there?"

"I do…"

"But then again, you don't. Hey. It's okay. This is a special situation, I know. Where are you going?"

Andie gave her the phone number of their hotel in Tahoe. "We haven't told the folks yet."

"I understand."

"If they get worried and call you, just give them that number. Okay?"

"You bet. And wait. One more thing."

"What?"

"Does he know? Did you tell him about you know who?"

"I didn't have to tell him."

"Huh?"

"He already knew."

Ruth Ann was calling on more saints as Andie hung up the phone.

"What did you tell her?"

Andie looked up to find Clay standing in the doorway. She gave a rueful shrug. "Not much. Most of it she figured out on her own. She knows we're getting married today. And I gave her a phone number. In case our folks call her."

"That's fine." His look said he wanted to say more.

"What? What is it?"

"She knows. About Jeff?"

"Yes. But she'll never tell anyone."

Clay made a low sound—part groan, part sigh. "I know. I grew up with Ruth Ann, too, after all. Remember that time your dad grounded you for a month for burning your report card?"

"I remember," Andie admitted with a sigh.

"You were so outraged at the unfairness of the punishment that you ran away."

"Yes, it's true. I did."

"Ruth Ann knew where you were."

"Yes, but I'd sworn her to secrecy. She never talked, did she?"

"No. Eventually, you came home on your own, as I remember it."

"You remember right. As I said, she never tells my secrets. And I never tell hers."

Clay was silent. Andie understood the silence when he finally spoke.

"When the baby's born, my name goes in the space where it says *father of child*."

Andie swallowed. "Okay."

"Just so you know." Suddenly, his voice was brisk. "Now get packing, will you?"

"Yes, sir!"

Andie packed quickly. They were finally ready to leave around three. The ride to Tahoe was uneventful and they managed to get checked into their hotel by five that night.

Then they went looking for a license. In Douglas County, they discovered, the county clerk kept long hours for the sake of all the couples who wanted to get married the quick and easy way. By seven they had the license in hand.

After that, they did some talking. Arguing, actually. Clay wanted to get to a chapel right away. Andie wanted dinner. Finally, Clay gave in. They decided to go back to the hotel and enjoy the remains of their one evening away. They ate in the hotel's best restaurant.

Then they went to their room, since that was where they really wanted to be, anyway. Andie reached out her arms to Clay. Getting married was the last thing on her mind.

But the next morning, when Andie would have lazed in bed awhile, Clay was up and eager to find a chapel and say their vows. Andie groused a little. He told her they had to get the job done.

And then she laughed at him for being so serious and calling marrying her a "job." He glowered at her for a moment. And then he was laughing, too.

She loved the sound of his laughter. Generally, Clay was not a laughing man. She thought briefly, with that now-familiar stab of regret, of Jeff Kirkland. Jeff was the one who could make Clay laugh like that.

But now she, Andie, was making him laugh. The thought filled her with hope for the future. Maybe her doubts were groundless, after all.

Clay told her she looked misty-eyed.

Andie replied that she had a right to be misty-eyed. It was her wedding day.

"Fine. Be misty-eyed. And get in that shower. I've ordered room service. You've got an hour to eat and get ready. Then we're gone."

"An hour!" She gave a shriek of feminine outrage. "To get ready for my *wedding?*"

"All right, don't have a coronary. You can have an hour and a half."

They bought two plain gold bands right there in the chapel. The vows were quick and simple. Andie recited them with feeling, looking into Clay's eyes. Clay said his part in a firm voice. He promised to love, honor and cherish Andie. And he didn't even stumble over that forbidden word, *love.*

When they left the chapel, it was nearly noon. Andie was hungry.

"Hardly news," Clay remarked dryly, and then put his arm around her and kissed her right there on the sidewalk underneath a fir tree.

They found a coffee shop before they headed home. As soon as her stomach was full, Andie began to fret about the family.

"They're probably worried about us." Andie poured the last of her hot water over a soggy tea bag. "Now that I think about it, we really should have left a message, called one of them or something, don't you think?"

"And said what?"

She scrunched up her nose at him, since no immediate answer came to mind. If they'd told the truth, half the family would have followed them up here to witness the event. And if they'd lied, Andie would have felt like a louse.

"Andie, they probably don't even know we're gone. And

we'll be home soon, long before they have a chance to start worrying."

"I've got a great idea." Andie pressed on the tea bag with her spoon, to get whatever was left in it out. "Let's call them."

"What?"

"Let's call them." She set the spoon aside and sipped the lukewarm brew. "We can call them from here. You call your folks and I'll call mine. Then by the time we get home, they'll already have been mad at us for not telling them and they'll be on to the good part."

"The good part?" Clay looked doubtful.

Andie pushed her cup away. "You know, where they smile and exchange significant looks and say they're sure we'll be happy together. What they'll really be thinking, of course, is that it's about time. But they would never, ever say such a thing. Well, except for Granny Sid. She might say it."

Clay chuckled. "Yeah. She just might."

With her finger, Andie traced a jagged heart that someone had carved into the tabletop. "I love them. I really do."

"Then why the long face?"

"Oh, I don't know."

"Yes, you do."

"Sometimes I just wonder, that's all."

"What?"

"What it would be like not to have to worry how the family will take it every time I make a major step in my life." She gave a wry chuckle. "I used to try not to care what they thought, when we were kids."

"Did you ever."

"But trying not to care never really worked. In my heart, I still *did* care. And I'd feel awful when Mom looked bewildered at something I'd done and Dad shook his head and said he didn't know what to do with me. Then on top of feeling awful, I'd have to pretend it didn't matter to me at all. It just wasn't any fun, trying not to care. So I gave it up and just let myself feel wretched when they'd shake their heads over me."

"Hey." His voice was teasing.

She looked up from the raggedly carved heart. "What?"

"They're going to be happy that we're married. I know they are."

"Yes, but your mother and my mother are going to be hurt that we didn't tell them first. But you don't have to worry about that."

"Why not?"

"Because they're not going to be unhappy with you. You're only a man. How could you be expected to know that one way for a girl to really annoy her mother and her aunt is to get married without even telling them, without giving them any chance at all to make a big fuss over the arrangements? *I'm* the one who's supposed to know that."

Clay just stared at her, flummoxed. "Well, I'm sorry. I guess."

"Oh, how can you be sorry? It doesn't even make any sense to you."

"Well, that's true."

"So don't be sorry. *I'm* not even sorry. After all, I was the one who made the choice not to call them before we left. And I did it knowing that Mom and Aunt Della would be peeved."

"Well, if you don't want *me* to be sorry, and *you're* not sorry, either, then why are we talking about this?"

"Because I want to call them before we go home. And I want you to understand *why* I want to call them."

"Well, I still don't understand that."

"I know. So just let me do it, okay? Just…humor an emotional pregnant lady."

"Okay. Fine. Do it."

Andie looked down at the jagged heart again, considering. "Well, maybe calling them wouldn't be such a good idea, after all. Maybe it shows more consideration to tell them face-to-face."

Clay dared to agree. "I think you're right there."

"So, okay then, we'll go see them. Yours first and mine second as soon as we get home."

"Sounds good."

"Or maybe, we should see *mine* first…"

Clay groaned under his breath and suggested they ought to be on their way.

Thelma McCreary jumped up from her chair. "You're *what?* I don't believe it. Say it again."

Andie gripped Clay's hand a little tighter. He gave her a reassuring squeeze. "We're married, Mom. We got married this morning in Tahoe."

"You and *Clay?*"

Andie sighed and smiled. "Yes, Mom. Me and Clay."

Tears rose in Thelma's brown eyes. "Oh, honey." And then she was reaching out.

Clay let go of Andie's hand so she could rise and be enfolded in her mother's arms. As Thelma hugged Andie and sniffled in her ear, Clay received similar treatment from Joe, though the hug was heartier and there were no tears.

"Well, this *is* good news," Joe announced, after everyone had switched places and Joe had hugged Andie while Thelma hugged Clay. "This is *wonderful* news. Thelma, get out that bottle of champagne we've been saving and I'll—Thelma?"

Thelma choked back a sob, grabbed for a tissue from a side table nearby and blew her nose. "Yes, Joe. All right."

"Thelma, what in the world is the matter?"

"My baby. Married at last."

"Yes, well," Joe blustered, "it's about time, now, isn't it?"

Clay looked at Andie and both of them tried not to laugh. "It's about time" was Granny Sid's line, after all.

"Oh, it's wonderful. It truly is." Thelma dabbed her eyes again. "Have you told Della and Don?"

"Not yet." Clay shot another glance at Andie, a weary one. In the car, she'd changed her mind five times about whom they'd tell first. "We'll do that next."

"Well, I suppose you want to get right over there," Joe said. "But we've got time for a toast, don't we?"

"Sure. Plenty of time."

"I'll get the champagne, then." Thelma bustled toward the kitchen. She turned in the arch to the dining room. "Andie, honey. Why don't you come and give me a hand?"

Andie, who'd just sat back down, rose again. She knew what was coming when her mother got her alone. She tried not to sound grim. "All right, Mom."

In the kitchen, Andie stood on a stool to bring down the crystal flute glasses from their high cupboard. She included a glass for herself to be sociable, though she knew she wouldn't actually drink any of the champagne.

"Will you rinse and wipe them, please? It's been a while since we've had champagne."

"Sure." Andie took the glasses to the sink and set about cleaning them up.

Her mother produced a bottle of champagne from somewhere in the depths of her refrigerator. "I suppose I might as well open it. Your father's too rambunctious about it. Last time the cork hit my favorite lamp and blew a hole in the shade."

"Uh-huh." Andie set the last glass to drain and reached for the towel. Out of the corner of her eye, she saw her mother sink to a chair. She turned. "All right. Say it."

Thelma waved at the air in front of her face with the hand

that wasn't clutching the champagne. "Oh, it's nothing. Nothing. I'm so happy for you."

"Look, Mom. Just say it, okay?"

"Well."

"Go on."

"I know it's selfish."

"I'm listening."

"You're my only child."

"That's true."

"And, well, it would have been nice to have been there, that's all. It would have been nice to have been included."

"You're mad at me."

"No, not mad. Hurt. A little. I'm sure Della will feel the same."

"Mom. When we made the decision, we didn't want to wait, you know? With the situation the way it is, with the baby and all."

Her mother gave a delicate little cough. "Yes. Of course, you're right, honey. I'm being selfish. I said I knew I was. But you're still my only child, as Clay is Della's. And now the only wedding we ever might have planned has already taken place."

"So then, you not only wanted to *be* there, you wanted to plan it all."

"Well, yes. Yes, I did. What's wrong with that?"

"There's nothing wrong with that, Mom. It just didn't turn out that way."

"It will take me a while to reconcile myself with this."

"I know, Mom."

"I think you should hug me and tell me how much you love me."

Andie took the champagne bottle from her mother's hand and set it on the floor. Then, kneeling, she wrapped her arms around her mother.

"I love you, Mom."

Her mother held her close and sobbed, "I love you, too. And I'm happy, really. Very happy."

"I'm glad."

"What's the holdup in there?" Andie's father called from the other room.

Thelma yanked out a counter drawer beside her and found a tissue. She blew her nose. "Woman talk! We're coming!" Then she looked at her daughter again. "What about you? Are *you* happy?"

Andie nodded.

"I'm glad. That *is* what really counts." Thelma dried her eyes. "Della will sulk, too, you know."

"I know."

"Want me to call her?"

"No way. She doesn't get to plan the wedding. She should at least get to tell me how much my lack of consideration has injured her."

At last, Thelma smiled. "Every year you become more understanding of your elders—did you know that?"

"It's called growing up, Mom."

"Whatever. It's lovely to see." Thelma picked up the champagne bottle and stood. "Now, let's get the cork out of this thing and get back in there before Clay and your father come looking for us."

"Good idea." Andie grabbed the towel and began polishing the glasses.

"Honey?"

"Um?"

"Clay is a good man."

"I know."

"I think things will be good, for both of you, now you've worked out whatever was…holding you back."

"So do I, Mom."

"And maybe I'm old-fashioned, but I think it's important for a child to have both of its parents, and for the parents to be husband and wife."

"I know you do, Mom."

"Honey…"

"What?"

"Oh, never mind. Just don't forget that I love you and you can talk to me."

"I won't. And thank you."

"I'm coming in there!" Joe called.

"Don't you dare! We'll be right there!" Thelma popped the champagne cork. It flew up in the air and made a dent in the ceiling. She wrinkled her nose at her daughter. "He'll never notice it, if you don't say anything."

Andie hung up the towel. "I promise, Mom. Not a word. Ever."

Chapter 10

Andie awoke to the sound of thunder. Outside, she could hear the heavy pounding of rain. It pattered on the deck and beat on the roof before it tumbled down the gutters to the ground below. She looked at the clock: past two. She was alone in the bed.

There was a frigid draft coming from somewhere. She shivered and saw that the glass door to the deck was open a crack. Her robe was thrown across the chair by her side of the bed. She reached for it and wrapped it around herself. Then she rose and padded across the hardwood floor to the glass door.

She looked outside, scanning the deck for Clay as she started to push the door closed. Lightning streaked across the sky. She saw him, as the thunder boomed.

He stood at the railing, his body held very erect, his face tipped up to the pouring rain. He was naked. The rain streamed down his face, slicked his hair to his scalp and ran down his body in a thousand tiny rivulets. His face, in profile, was transfixed, pure, strong, very male.

Andie gasped. He took her breath away. She'd known him for nearly twenty years. But did she really know him at all? All those years she had taunted him for lacking a spirit of adventure, for being Cautious Clay.

And all this time, he'd been someone who stood naked in freezing rainstorms. It was humbling, she realized. How little we know of those who fill our lives.

As she watched, he turned his head slowly to meet her eyes through the glass of the door. It was as if he had felt the intensity of her gaze. Water ran in his eyes now and dripped off his chin and nose. He stared at her over his shoulder, his eyes far away, defiant. Lightning flashed and thunder cracked once again. And then he turned fully toward her and walked to where she waited beyond the glass door.

She pulled it open enough that he could step through and then closed it behind him to keep out the rain and the biting wind.

She could feel the coldness, the wetness of him as she turned from the door to face him. "What were you doing out there?" There was nothing of the worried wife in her voice, only her curiosity, her wonderment.

He shrugged. "I've always loved storms. My mother—not Della, the other one, Rita—she loved storms."

Andie opened her robe. "You're cold. Come here."

He took one step. She enfolded him, wrapping her robe and her arms around him. He sighed and she gasped as his body met hers. He was cold, so cold. She shivered as she gave him her body's heat.

He started kissing her before she had warmed them both. And then she forgot her shivering. He stepped back and scooped her against his chest and carried her to the bed.

They had been married a week. To Andie, it seemed that what they shared now had always been. He touched her and found her ready. He slid inside. Andie welcomed him with a lifting of her hips and a gratified sigh.

After their pleasure had crested and receded, she pulled the blankets up to shelter them.

"What was she like, your natural mother?"

He turned her and wrapped himself around her back, spoon fashion. Andie thought he wasn't going to answer her, but then he said, "She was a dreamy kind of person. It seemed to me like she was always off in her own world somewhere. I guess that's not surprising. For her, the real world wasn't too great. She was sick a lot. And she had trouble holding a job."

"Did you feel that she loved you?"

"Yes," he said after a moment. "I think she loved me. And she did the best she could."

"You never knew your father, right?"

"Don Barrett is my father." His voice was flat.

"I meant your natural father."

"I know what you meant. And you're right. I never knew him. I never even knew who he was. He was gone long before I was born."

"Do you ever wonder about him?"

"No."

She wanted to see Clay, so she rolled over and lifted up on an elbow. His face was in shadow. She thought of switching on the light but didn't. There was something safe and intimate about the dark. Maybe in the dark he would confide in her a little.

"What is it?" His voice was guarded.

"I just can't believe that you never wonder what he was like."

"I did wonder. When I was a kid. But I got over it."

"It just seems to me like something you would always wonder about."

"That's probably because *you* would always wonder, if you were me."

"That's true."

"But you're *not* me, Andie."

"Well, I know that. Whew. Do I ever."

He chuckled then and seemed to relax a little. He even took her hand and caressed it thoughtfully, toying with the gold bracelet of linked hearts she wore. "Look. Don and Della are all the parents I'll ever need. That is honestly and truly the way I feel."

"Do you hate your natural father?"

Clay sighed and stopped stroking her hand. "No, Andie. I don't hate him."

"There are agencies, aren't there, who will track down birth parents?"

"Yes, there are. And a lot of them operate using illegal means. They break confidentiality laws right and left."

"Yes, but—"

"Stop. Listen. I happen to believe that this country's adoption laws are humane laws, in most cases. I know there are people obsessed with finding kids or parents they lost. But I'm not one of them. I'm honestly not. So get that idea out of your head."

"What idea?" She tried not to sound guilty.

"I know you, Andie."

"What is that supposed to mean?"

"It means if you get it in your head to track down my birth father, you'll be doing it for *yourself,* not for me. The man is a complete stranger to me. I don't have any desire to meet a stranger who says he's my father."

"But it's natural, isn't it, to want to know where you came from?"

"For some people, I'm sure it is. For me, it's a moot point. I needed to *belong,* to be included in a real family. I wanted a true home, a place where they would always take me in if I needed them, no matter what. And I got what I needed when your aunt and uncle adopted me."

Andie leaned closer to him, trying to see what was really in his eyes. "Are you sure?"

"I am positive."

She plopped back onto her pillow and stared up at the shadowed ceiling. "I believe you."

He grunted. "You sound so disappointed."

She pulled the covers up around her chin again and rubbed her toe along Clay's leg. During the past week she'd discovered that one of the loveliest things about married life was the feel of Clay beside her in their bed.

He moved his leg toward her, a silent reply to her caressing toe. "Well? *Are* you?"

"What?"

"Disappointed."

She confessed, "I am, I guess. A little."

"Why?"

"Oh, I suppose it just occurred to me, right now while we were talking, that I could do this wonderful thing for you, find your *father* for you. It was going to be terrific. You were going to be so grateful. You'd never again bark at me at work because you couldn't find some file you needed. And at home, you'd look at me with adoration, because I'd reunited you with your past."

"I already look at you with adoration."

But not with love, she thought, before she could stop herself. She pushed the thought away, turned toward him and snuggled up close. "Good. Keep it up."

"I aim to please."

Ruth Ann demanded, "You're going to have to go into more detail about this. I don't get what you're saying."

It was Sunday afternoon. They were in the living room of

Andie's apartment, packing books and knickknacks to take to the house on Wildriver Road. Andie had put off the job of closing up the place longer than she should have. Now the month was almost over and she had to be out in three days. As they packed, they'd been talking. And now Andie was trying to define her vague worries about her relationship with Clay.

"It's hard to explain. It's all so new between us."

"So try, anyway."

Andie scooped up another handful of books and stacked them in a box.

Ruth Ann, as usual, would not be evaded. "I said, try anyway."

"Oh, Ruthie…"

"Come on."

"Well, he's got this thing."

"What thing?"

"About love."

"What about love?"

"He doesn't believe in it, not in man-woman love, anyway."

Ruth Ann reached a top shelf and took down more books. She handed them to Andie. "Explain."

Andie bent to put the books in the box with the others. "He believes in the love you have in families, you know, the urge to care for each other and help each other in life. But he doesn't believe in being *in* love. He says that's only sex."

Ruth Ann leaned on the bookcase and let out a disgusted groan. "Men."

"So even if he ever got to the point where he might be in love with me, he's not going to be in love with me, because he doesn't believe in it. You know?"

"Blessed Saint Anselm, my head is spinning."

"And I want his love."

"Not unreasonable. Do you love him, er, I mean, are you *in love* with him?"

Andie turned her attention to a pair of carved mahogany bookends that her father had bought her two birthdays ago. She began carefully wrapping them in tissue.

"Well. Are you?"

"It's too soon to tell."

Ruth Ann collected another stack of books. "You want my advice?"

"Yeah. I suppose."

Since Andie was still busy with the bookends, Ruth Ann climbed off her chair and boxed the handful of books herself. "Come on. Fake some enthusiasm, or I won't tell you what I think."

"All right. I do. I want your advice."

"He's acting like a man. But *you're* acting like a woman. I don't know which is worse."

"What's that supposed to mean?"

"It means that until you're at least sure you're *in love* with him, why borrow trouble? Are you having the best time of your life or what?"

"Yes. Yes, I am."

"Then cheer up." Ruth Ann climbed up on the chair again. "There'll be plenty of time to suffer if things ever really go wrong."

Just then, the door burst open.

"Hey, Mommy. Lookit this." A big brown box with two little sneaker-clad feet sticking out from under it staggered into the living room. "I'm a box. Pack me." The box fell over, giggling hysterically.

Ruth Ann rolled her eyes and grabbed another handful of books as her younger son, Kyle, wriggled his way out of the box.

Clay came in then, carrying a stack of boxes. Andie got up and went to meet him. "Hello, there."

He returned her smile. "Hiya." They kissed around the stack of boxes.

Behind them, Ruth Ann made some knowing remark about newlyweds.

Andie asked, "How'd you guys do?"

Clay set the boxes down on the table in the little dining nook right off the living room. "Not bad for a Sunday. We hit the jackpot at Grocery Superstop."

"Yeah, did we ever," Kyle put in. "We had so many boxes, I had to ride with one on my head the whole way home. It was really funny, wasn't it, Clay?"

Clay smiled at the boy. "A riot. Come on. Help me get the rest from the car."

"You bet." Swaggering just a little with the importance of this grown-up job he was doing, Kyle followed Clay out.

"Clay's good with kids," Ruth Ann said when the boy and the man were gone. "Kyle was really irked this morning when he heard he was going with me instead of to the batting cages with Johnny and Butch." Butch was Ruth Ann and Johnny's older boy. "Kyle hates to be stuck with the women. I was sure I was going to have nothing but trouble from him all day."

Andie chuckled. "I'll bet. But the minute he saw Clay he perked right up."

"Exactly. And now he's just thrilled to be driving from one store Dumpster to another, scavenging for packing boxes."

"Yeah, it worked out fine."

Ruth Ann suddenly looked reproachful. "Clay's going to be great with the baby, Andie."

"I know that."

"And you're nuts about him, even if you're not willing to admit it's love yet."

"I know. And stop looking at me like that."

"You should get down on your knees every day, I'm telling you, and thank the good Lord."

Andie met her friend's gaze. "I do, Ruthie. Believe me. I do."

"So do what I told you. Stop worrying. Let yourself be happy."

"I'll do my best, Ruthie. I swear I will."

Over the next few months, Andie took her friend's advice seriously. She stopped borrowing trouble, stopped worrying that Clay's heart would forever be closed to her. Instead, she concentrated on making a good life with him.

And it worked. Life was good. She and Clay put in killing hours at the office through the first half of April and didn't mind them a bit. After all, when they went home, they had each other.

Then the office settled down. Uncle Don took over while Andie and Clay went to Hawaii for the honeymoon they hadn't had time for until then. For nine whole days, they did nothing but bask in the sun, swim in the surf, eat, sleep and make love. After the lovemaking, Clay would often lie with his head against the new roundness of Andie's belly and tell her that he could feel the baby move.

She laughed. "But it's only like moth wings, even to me."

"I can feel it," he assured her. "There. There it is."

When they returned, they signed up for natural childbirth lessons. Clay was eager to be her birthing coach. He went with her to her obstetrician and asked more questions than she ever would have thought of. And then, the next Saturday, he drove her down to Sacramento to one of the huge superbookstores there. He bought out what seemed like half the section on pregnancy and childbirth.

And then at home, while Andie planned how she'd make the small bedroom next to theirs over for the baby, Clay pored over all the baby books he'd bought.

"This is fascinating," he told her. "You should read this. It tells about the baby's development inside the womb, week by week."

Andie was trying to choose curtains. "Just read me the good parts," she suggested vaguely.

He took her at her word. "Let's see. We're at eighteen weeks. Right about now, the baby has eyebrows, hair on its head and lanugo. That's fine hair all over the body. This lanugo may help in temperature regulation, or it may be an anchor for the vernix caseosa, which is a waxlike substance that protects the baby from immersion in the amniotic fluid."

"How charming," Andie remarked with a shudder.

"It's a miracle," Clay said with such a great show of solemnity that she knew he was at least partially teasing her.

She pointed at a crib set in one of her catalogs. "What about these?"

"Too froufrou."

"What does that mean?"

"It means that I really hate ruffles. A kid could suffocate in all those ruffles."

"Okay, how about these?"

"Better. Much better."

A week later, he read her some more. "Okay, nineteen weeks. 'First sucking motions likely. Can grip with hands. The ability to blink develops, though the eyelids are still fused…'"

And then the week after that: "'Twenty weeks. The baby's about ten inches long. Eight to nine ounces in weight…'"

Andie got to where she'd groan a little when he brought out his favorite book and opened it to the page that described the baby's current development. But it was a happy groan. It was wonderful to see him so involved, to really start to believe in the amazing thing that had happened: the baby she'd been sure she was going to be raising alone had a father after all.

At the end of May, they hired another secretary at the

office. Her name was Linda Parks. She was a single mother, in her forties and in need of a dependable job with good benefits. She was also a crack typist and knew both the spreadsheet and word processing programs that Barrett & Co. used. Linda had worked in another accounting firm in Oakland, from which she came highly recommended. She'd moved to the foothills seeking a safer environment for her children.

Linda learned quickly. By the middle of June, since business was only moderate, Andie was able to leave Linda on her own at the office for several hours a day. Clay kept busy, even though it wasn't nearly the rat race at work that it had been at the beginning of the year.

He did the social scene more, took clients to lunch and played golf. When Andie kidded him about partying on company time, he reminded her that the only way to build the client base was to do a little wining and dining. She laughed and said she knew that very well. Couldn't he stand a little teasing? He gave up looking wounded and admitted that he supposed he could.

June became July. In her seventh month, Andie grew ripe and round as a peach.

Clay went on reading about the baby's growth.

"'Week twenty-six. The baby's eyelids can open and close. Increased muscle tone. Sucking and swallowing skills continue to develop...'"

The baby's room was all ready. The curtains and all the bedding were yellow, with little bears and balloons on the wallpaper. The crib, bureau and changing table had been Andie's when she was a baby. They'd been stored in the attic at her mother's. Somehow, over the years, the wood had become worn and scratched. Clay refinished the furniture himself, insisting that Andie stay well away from the fumes of the stripping compound.

He continued with the progress reports.

"'Huge changes taking place in the nervous system. The brain grows greatly during this month. Some experts believe this is the beginning of true consciousness…'"

In mid-July, Andie and Clay began their childbirth classes. Once a week, they went to a room at the public library and joined six other couples learning relaxation techniques, practicing breathing, seeing graphic films of real births.

At home, Clay read, "'By twenty-eight weeks, all the baby's senses are in working order…'"

Clay talked to the baby all the time. Sometimes he called it "he," sometimes "she." Andie asked him which he'd prefer. He said he didn't care. She knew he told the truth.

He read on. "Conscious relaxation, deep breathing and meditative states in the mother stimulate the baby's entire body and developing mind. Music and gentle, repetitive sounds are good for the baby's hearing. When the mother sunbathes, gets massaged, swims, walks, or even showers, the baby's touch perception and balance are improved."

By August, Andie was becoming increasingly uncomfortable. To her it seemed she lumbered around like an elephant, though her weight was in the average range for a woman in her eighth month. She felt hot all the time, too. And everything she ate seemed to hover somewhere up around her breastbone. And she dreamed of the night she'd be able to lie on her back without feeling dizzy—or on her stomach without feeling giddily numb, as if she were trying to rest on a basketball.

Clay's response to her complaints was to read to her from his library of baby books, explaining that she couldn't lie on her back because it pressed on the vena cava, a major vein. And her stomach now literally *was* shoved up between her lungs, so it made sense that food felt as if it got stuck there. And the reason she felt hot all the time was because her heart had expanded in size and her capillary action was greatly increased.

Andie groaned and threw a pillow at him. She had lots of pillows. She had to arrange them strategically under various parts of herself at night so she could sleep. It was getting to the point that she wasn't even interested in making love anymore, which would have seemed impossible just a few weeks before.

Clay, through it all, was patient and wonderful. She *despised* him for being so terrific. Almost as much as she loved him.

And she did love him, was *in love* with him. Sometime in the past few months, she'd accepted the reality of her love and welcomed it. It didn't even seem to matter anymore that Clay still clung to his frustrating belief that the kind of love Andie knew she felt for him didn't exist.

Probably part of the reason it didn't matter was that she knew he loved her, too. In exactly the same way that she loved him, even if he wouldn't admit to it.

Finally, she told him of her love.

It was a night in the fourth week of August. Andie hadn't been able to sleep. So Clay was rubbing her neck and shoulders, reminding her to breathe slowly and evenly, to picture fields of flowers, to see the color blue.

She thought the words of love and they rose to her lips. She released them.

"I love you, Clay."

He went on working his soothing magic with his hands.

"Did you hear what I said?"

"I heard. Breathe slowly. In and out."

"I'm *in love* with you."

"Relax."

"I mean it."

"Whatever. Keep breathing."

She turned around so she could look at him. The room was

dark. It was hard to see his expression. She switched on the bedside lamp.

"I love you."

Something happened in his face. Something tormented yet hopeful, a passionate expression, swiftly quelled. The look was there and gone so fast that the minute it disappeared, Andie wondered if she had really seen it.

Was it possible that he *wanted* to believe her and didn't dare? Or was her heart making her see things that weren't there? Whatever the truth was, the mysterious expression was long gone. Now he merely looked puzzled and a little concerned.

He lifted a bronze eyebrow. "Do you want me to say I love you, too? Is that it?"

The lifted eyebrow did it. Suddenly, she thought of Mr. Spock of "Star Trek" fame. As Spock would say, "But, Captain, love is illogical…"

Andie burst out laughing.

Clay continued to look perplexed and perhaps a bit pained. "Are you all right?"

"I'm fine." She fell over sideways on the bed, holding her huge middle, still giggling.

"Andie…"

"Never mind." Somehow she collected herself. And then she sat up again and showed her back to him, turning her head so she could smile at him, smoothing her mass of hair out of his way over her shoulder. "Would you rub my neck a little more? It really does feel wonderful."

He looked at her with equal parts wariness and suspicion. And then he shook his head. She thought he muttered something about women under his breath. But then he turned off the light and put his incredible hands to work once more.

Andie sighed; it felt so good. She breathed evenly as he had instructed her to do.

And she smiled to herself, marveling at how downright pig-headed her husband could be. She pondered the idea that she was probably going to live a whole lifetime at his side, during which he would never once utter those three incredible little words.

But she was also thinking that it was okay. She could live without those words. Because she knew, even though Clay refused to give his love a name, that he did love her—was *in love* with her. Clay showed his love every day in ten thousand little ways. It was enough.

Clay's hands strayed. They glided, warm and soothing, over her shoulders and down her arms. "Feel sleepy now?"

"Um…"

He scooted up close behind her and put his arms around her. Then he gently explored her belly. After a few moments, his hands went still. "There. A foot, I think."

She investigated where he was touching. "No." She leaned fully against him, resting her head in the crook of his shoulder, feeling sheltered and protected as she'd never dreamed she would be. "That was an elbow, no doubt about it."

He chuckled. And then he nuzzled her hair aside and kissed her earlobe. "You're so beautiful, Andie."

"There's so much of me. It had better be beautiful."

"I'm not kidding."

"Neither am I. Do you realize that my belly button is an *outie* now? Sometimes it actually shows through my clothes. It's gross."

"You're beautiful."

"You're overworked and losing your mind."

"What we have—it's very good."

A warmth spread through her. This was as close as he would come, she knew, to speaking of his love. "Yes, Clay. It is. It's the absolute best."

Carefully he turned her so that she lay back in his arms.

He supported her with his arm and his thigh so that that major vein he'd told her about wasn't put under pressure. And then he kissed her, a very slow kiss.

When he lifted his head, Andie decided that maybe she still liked sex, after all. His hand strayed, caressing, stroking. Andie sighed. For a magical half hour, she forgot everything but the touch of those hands.

When at last he helped her arrange her pillows, she was truly ready for sleep.

"Clay?"

"Yeah?"

"Thanks, Clay."

"For what?"

"For all of it. For our lives together. For being you."

"You're welcome. Go to sleep."

Smiling, Andie closed her eyes.

The next morning, Madeline Kirkland called.

Chapter 11

They were sitting at the breakfast table. They'd already eaten and Clay was having one last cup of coffee while Andie nursed her peppermint tea. It was a beautiful day, especially now, in the morning, with the air just a tad breezy and the windows open. Later, Andie would close up the house and turn on the air conditioner to fight the fierce heat of the afternoon. But just now, it was lovely.

Andie was planning to stay home all day. At the office now, Linda was managing fine. So Andie had decided to start taking it easier, with the baby due in a month. She had slashed her own hours to twenty a week. It was working out quite well.

"More coffee?" Andie asked.

Clay rustled his paper and grunted. Andie lumbered to her feet and shuffled over to the sink, thinking wryly of beached whales, of grounded hippos, cursing the power of gravity and swearing she wouldn't let it get her down.

The phone rang just as she stuck her mug of water in the microwave to heat. The phone was on the wall, not far from where Clay sat. But he was absorbed in his paper.

Andie waddled on over there and picked it up. "Hello?"

A silence, then a strange woman's voice. "Oh. Hello." The voice hesitated. "Is this Clay Barrett's house?"

Andie smiled. An old girlfriend of Clay's, she thought, someone he hadn't seen in a while who didn't know he'd been married. "Yes, it is."

The woman took in a breath. "Well, I…" The voice trailed off. "I wonder if…" Andie began to think the woman sounded troubled, or under some sort of strain. "Please. This is Madeline Kirkland. I need to… May I speak with Clay?"

As soon as Andie heard the name, she felt dizzy. She gripped the section of kitchen counter right beside her to steady herself. Madeline Kirkland, Jeff's wife. What could she want? What possible reason could she have for calling Clay?

The worst came immediately to mind: that Madeline had somehow found out about the baby.

"Hello, are you there?"

Andie forced herself to speak. "Yes. Of course. Just a minute." She put her hand over the receiver.

Clay had already lowered his paper. He was looking at her, alarmed by what he saw. "Andie, what—?"

"Madeline," she said. "Madeline Kirkland." She held the phone close to her heavy belly, not extending it, almost hoping he'd refuse to take the call.

Clay looked at the receiver, his thought the same as Andie's.

He didn't want to take it. He wanted to shake his head and walk out of the room. If it had been Jeff, he would have.

But it wasn't Jeff. It was Madeline. Innocent Madeline. Clay thought the world of Madeline.

He stood. Andie put the phone in his hand.

"Sit down," he said quietly to his pale wife, before he spoke into the receiver. "Hello, Madeline."

"Clay? Oh, Clay…"

"What is it?"

"Clay, you've been a stranger." Her voice sounded so odd, fiercely controlled yet edged with frenzy. He was positive that somehow she had found out the truth about Jeff and Andie and the baby. "We've missed you, Clay. Very much."

"Well, I…" What the hell could he say? "I've been busy. Really busy. I, um, got married."

"Oh, Clay. You did? Was that her? Did she answer the phone?"

"Yes. I'm sure I've mentioned her. My cousin by adoption. Andie."

"Oh. Yes, I remember. Andie was the one you used to always fight with when you were kids, right?"

"Yes, that's the one."

"Well. Congratulations."

"Thank you."

There was an absolutely deadly pause. Andie was staring at him, agony in her eyes. And he still had no clue what was going on with Madeline.

Madeline said, "Oh, Clay. I don't know how…" And then her voice closed off. She made a painful, choking sound, then managed to control herself. "My mother was going to do this. But I…I thought it would help me. To hear your voice. Jeff loved you so."

Loved. Past tense. "Madeline?"

"Oh, I'm making a mess of this."

"Of what?"

"Of telling you."

"Telling me what?"

"About Jeff. Oh, Clay. He… Jeff died, Clay. Yesterday."

Clay sank to his chair, not even realizing he was sitting down until he was already there.

In his ear, tight and frantic, Madeline kept on. "He bought this new sports car. It was beautiful. But you know Jeff. A new toy. He played…he played too hard with it. He went too fast."

"Too fast?"

"Yes. Down Mulholland. Like some crazy kid. You know Mulholland, don't you, Clay? All those turns. He…" A sound came from Madeline, a keening sound. It started out low and slid impossibly high. Clay waited, while she gathered her forces once more. "He went over the cliff. It was a vertical drop, about two hundred feet. He died instantly, they told me. He didn't suffer any pain."

Beside him, Andie spoke. She asked if he was okay. He waved her away. He couldn't deal with her now. There was a huge something, like a rock, inside his chest. He breathed around it. He did not let himself remember Jeff, on the beach that last time, his hands in his pockets, the gulls wheeling overhead.

"All right, bud. I'm dead…."

"Clay?" Madeline said.

Clay closed his eyes and rubbed at the sockets, rubbed the memory away. He reminded himself that Madeline had just lost the man she'd loved all her life and that Madeline was the one to think about now.

"What can I do?" he asked.

"Oh, Clay…"

"What? Anything. Tell me."

"I knew you'd say that. Thank you."

"What?"

"Okay. Yes, I'll tell you. The funeral's the day after tomorrow. Saturday. At eleven in the morning. It would mean a lot to me if you'd be there."

He answered automatically. "Of course I will."

"And would you be a pallbearer?"

"Yes, certainly."

"Oh, that's good. It will be good. To see your face. To remember the good times."

"Yes. The good times."

"Do you want to stay at the house?"

His numbed mind tried to follow what she was asking him. "The house?"

"The new house. You were there, remember, that last time you dropped in, several months ago? When you and Jeff got mugged at the beach?"

"Oh. Yeah." So that was what Jeff had told her.

"I'm not staying there myself. I just can't, not now. I'm at my parents' house for a while. But if you'd like to—"

"No. Listen. I'll get a hotel room. It's no problem. Where is the funeral and what time do I need to be there?"

Beside him, Andie gasped. Clay realized he'd been doing his best to block her out of his mind. Now she'd heard the word *funeral* and was starting to put things together.

"Jeff? Is it Jeff?" Andie asked. Her eyes were two black smudges in her white, white face.

Clay nodded. Then he stood to take the pencil from the notepad that was hanging on the wall by the base of the phone. Madeline gave him the information he needed and he scribbled it down. Then he promised to be there tomorrow.

"I'll call you," he said, "as soon as I get there."

"You'll call me at my parents' house?" Madeline asked.

"Right. What's the number there?"

Madeline rattled off the number, then went on, "Yes, please call. I'd appreciate that. Things are crazy. I hope we can spend a little time together, but I don't know how things will go."

"I understand."

"It might not seem that I appreciate your being there. But

I do. I really do. He loved you so. You're everything he ever wanted to be—did you know that?"

"No, I didn't."

"It's true. He used to tell me that. That he wished he could be like you. You always worked so hard, knew what you wanted and kept your goals in mind whatever you did. And with you, responsibility was like a sacred trust." Madeline gave a strangled little laugh. "That's how he said it, 'With Clay, responsibility is like a sacred trust.'"

"Look, Madeline, I—"

"I know, I know. I'm babbling. But I can't seem to help it. And I just want you to know these things. I want to say them now, when they're in my head and I have the chance. Because I'm grateful to you Clay, I really am."

"For what?"

"Oh, Clay. I know that whatever you said to him over the holidays last year, whatever happened then, it made all the difference. When he came back, he was changed. He really wanted to marry me then. Always before, there'd been something in him that held back. We had a marriage, we were *together*, for at least a little while. And a lot of that was because of you."

"I understand," Clay said again. What the hell else could he say to something like that?

"Well, I…thanks for listening." Madeline said.

"It's okay."

"I should go."

"Of course."

"But I'll see you tomorrow, or at the funeral."

"Yes. Whatever. You take care."

"I will. Goodbye."

The line went dead. Clay hung the receiver back on the wall.

"Clay?" Andie was looking up at him, her face a blank, her eyes haunted. "Oh, Clay. It's Jeff?"

"Yes."

"Dead?" She said the word on a whisper, as if she hardly dared utter it.

"Yes."

"When?"

"Yesterday. A car accident. He bought a new car and drove it too fast."

"Oh." Andie grimaced, touched her belly.

"What is it?"

"Nothing. The shock."

"Are you sure?"

"Positive." She put her hand against her mouth, shook her head. "Oh, I'm so sorry. It's so awful. That poor woman."

"Yes. She asked me to go to the funeral. I'm going, for her sake."

"Of course."

"I'll fly down tomorrow."

"Oh, Clay. Are you all right?" She reached for his hand.

He moved just enough that she didn't connect. "I'm fine. Really." He looked at his watch. "I should get going."

She stared at him. "Where?"

"To work. I'll be late."

"Work? Now? Clay, I don't think—"

"I've really got to go."

"But—"

"Can you call and get me a flight? Tomorrow afternoon would be best. I could check in at the office in the morning, see that everything's under control and then fly out of Sacramento later in the day. Will you do that?"

"Of course, but don't you think that—?"

"If you can't get an afternoon flight, then do what you can. Morning, if you have to. Or night, if all else fails. And I'd like to return as early as possible Sunday."

"I understand. But, Clay—"

"And also, can you get me a reservation at a decent hotel in Brentwood or nearby? The funeral will be in Brentwood and I'd like to keep surface travel to a minimum. And I'll need a rental car."

"All right. I'll take care of it. But I—"

"I have to go, Andie. I have to get out of here."

"Clay, I really don't think you should drive right now."

"I'll be fine."

"Please, Clay. Stay home for a while. Just let yourself get adjusted to what's happened, before you get into a car." Her voice was reasonable, very controlled. But her eyes were pleading with him.

He understood that she was worried for him and that she probably didn't want to be alone. But he knew he could handle himself all right in a car. And as far as her needs, he just couldn't think about them at the moment. He didn't have anything to give her right now. He was empty inside, except for that huge, rocklike something that filled up his chest.

"I have to go." He moved swiftly, around the table and across the room to the hall. He went to the coat closet, grabbed his briefcase and jacket. Then he fled to the garage.

He flung open the door of the car, tossed his briefcase across the seat and jumped in. He'd backed out of the garage and sent the door rumbling down again with the aid of the automatic opener before he allowed himself to relax a fraction. By then, he was sure that Andie wasn't going to try to follow him.

In the house, Andie sat in the kitchen chair for several minutes before she did anything else. She practiced breathing slowly and evenly. She tried to absorb the enormity of what had just occurred.

Jeff Kirkland was dead. Clay's best friend, the biological father of her child, was gone for good and all.

It didn't seem possible. He was out of their lives, yes. They probably would never have seen him again, anyway. Yet Andie had always assumed he would go on living his own life down there in Los Angeles, married to a woman named Madeline.

But now, fate had played the cruelest of tricks. Now Jeff Kirkland wouldn't go on. And that seemed hideous to Andie. Hideous and wrong.

She couldn't stop thinking about Madeline. Madeline would have to go on. Andie had never even met Madeline. Yet she knew the kind of pain Madeline must be suffering. Madeline was near her own age, a young woman, newly married, just like herself. And now Madeline was a widow.

What would that be like, to be a widow? To live the rest of her life without Clay? Andie thought of sleeping in their bed alone, sitting here at the breakfast table every morning alone. Such thoughts brought with them an empty, vast kind of pain.

"Oh, Clay," she whispered to herself, picturing him barreling along Wildriver Road, attempting the impossible, trying to outrun the anguish of losing his best friend twice. "Be careful, my darling," she whispered fervently. "Keep yourself safe." She closed her eyes and sent a little prayer winging toward heaven, a prayer for his safety, and then another for Madeline, whom she didn't even know.

Andie felt her own guilt in this, the guilt that had always been there since her one foolish night with Jeff Kirkland. What Clay would have to suffer now would be doubly hard because of what she herself had done.

Clay hated deceptions, yet he would go to Jeff's funeral and pretend, for Madeline's sake, that everything was as it had always been. That the dead man had never stopped being his friend.

All because Andie McCreary and Jeff Kirkland had behaved so irresponsibly last New Year's Eve.

Yet how could Andie totally regret her own thoughtless indiscretion? It had brought the baby, who, even now, unborn, seemed such an important and transformative part of her life. And, in a roundabout, crazy way, it had brought her the true love she'd given up on finding.

Sometimes she wondered if, without the baby, she and Clay would ever have found their way to each other. They had such a history of hostility. They had both been so careful, over the years, to shield themselves from any intimate contact with each other. It had taken something enormous, another life coming, to break through all the walls.

For the baby's sake, Clay had given himself permission to pursue her. And because of the baby, she had been vulnerable. The walls had come down.

Would Jeff's death raise the walls all over again?

Andie shook her head. She couldn't afford to think such a thing.

With a little sigh, she rose. There were dishes to put in the dishwasher. And maybe after that, she'd go upstairs and make the bed. Put a load of laundry in the washing machine, dust the glass tables in the living room.

And then, when she was reasonably sure she could talk without bursting into tears, she'd call a travel agent she knew in town and see about making the arrangements for the trip to Los Angeles.

After she made the arrangements, Andie called Clay at the office. Linda said he couldn't come on the line right then. He would get back to her.

Andie was so relieved to hear he was there and safe that she didn't worry too much about his refusal to come to the phone. But then, a few hours later, when she called again and got the same response from Linda, Andie began to believe that Clay was evading her.

But she didn't allow herself to stew about it. He was upset about Jeff. She understood that. And he needed time to accept what had happened. She didn't call him again.

Instead, she called Ruth Ann. Ruth Ann cried when Andie told her about Jeff's death.

"Blessed Mother Mary," Ruth Ann sobbed. "Why am I doing this? I loathed and despised that jerk for what he did to you."

"It's because you have a big heart, Ruthie. And because no man should die when he's young and strong and still has years of life ahead of him."

Ruth Ann sobbed some more and blew her nose. "That's right. That is so right." She sniffed. "How's Clay taking it?"

"Not well, so far. But it was only this morning that we heard."

"He needs time."

"I know."

"Listen, how about if I come over?"

"No, I'm fine. But thanks."

"You sure?"

"Yes."

"Well, you know I'm here. Just call. And I'll be there."

"I know, Ruthie. And it helps. It really does."

After that, Andie called her mother.

"Oh, Andie. Such a young man," Thelma said. "It's a tragedy."

"Yes."

"His poor parents. I think that would be the worst thing. To have a child die before you."

"I believe that both of his parents are dead, Mom."

"Oh. How sad. He seemed like a nice young man, too. I'm so sorry. How's Clay?"

"As well as can be expected. He's at work now."

"Will he be going to the funeral?"

"Yes. Jeff's wife, Madeline, asked him to be a pallbearer."

"And of course he will."

"Yes."

"What about you?"

"Me?"

"Well, with the baby coming and all, I suppose it's wisest if you stay at home."

"No, I'm going." Andie came to the decision just as she said the words. "I don't want Clay to be alone."

Andie expected her mother to argue with her, to launch into all the reasons she should stay home and be careful of her unborn baby. But Thelma surprised her. Her voice was sad and accepting. "I know what you mean. If it were your father's friend…well, I do understand. And you're feeling all right, aren't you?"

"I'm feeling just fine, Mom."

"How long will you be down there?"

"We'll leave Friday and be back by Sunday afternoon." Andie gave her mother the phone number of the hotel. As soon as she hung up, Andie called the travel agent again and managed to add herself to all the reservations. After that, she went to see her doctor, who provided the release form that the travel agent had said she'd need in order to fly this late in her pregnancy.

Clay arrived home at 7:49. Andie forced herself not to run—or in her case, waddle—out to the garage the minute she heard the door rolling open. Instead, she calmly pulled his dinner from the oven where she'd been keeping it warm and set it on the table.

She heard the inside garage door open and close, his footsteps on the hardwood floor. She heard him stop at the coat closet, to get rid of his jacket and his briefcase. At last, he appeared.

"I stopped by Doolin's." Doolin's was a bar in town. "For a drink."

She gave him a warm smile and didn't mention that he'd never stopped by Doolin's before in the five months they'd been married. "I kept your dinner warm."

"I'll wash my hands."

Clay came to the table five minutes later. Andie sat opposite him, sipping a glass of milk as he doggedly ate.

"Did you make the plane reservations?"

"Yes."

"For what time?"

"Two in the afternoon tomorrow. Out of Sacramento, arriving at LAX at 3:10."

"That's perfect. What about the hotel?"

"The Casa de la Reina. Triple A gives it four stars. And it's about two miles from the church."

"That sounds fine. Thanks."

"You're welcome."

She waited quietly as he finished up the meal. He talked of the office, of how well Linda was doing, of a dispute with a new client, a big account that Clay had knocked himself out to acquire, but now was just about to kiss goodbye.

"He wants to make a lot of money, and then pay zero taxes. I told him I'm good, but I won't cheat for him. It went downhill from there."

Andie listened sympathetically and waited for him to talk about what was really on his mind: Jeff.

It never happened. The few hours until bedtime slipped by.

After he brushed his teeth, Clay left the bathroom while Andie was still washing her face. When she returned to the bedroom, the light was off and Clay was a motionless lump on his side of the bed.

Suppressing a sigh, Andie approached her own side. Once

there, she positioned her nest of pillows and then carefully arranged herself so that her upper knee was supported and her stomach rested comfortably on a pillow of its own. Through this procedure, Clay, who usually made a big production of moving her pillows around for her until she had them just right, remained still as a stone.

Andie settled in. She closed her eyes. She told herself to be patient, to give him time.

Yet she couldn't resist asking hesitantly, "Clay, are you awake?"

No answer. But she could feel the tension coming from him. He was not asleep.

"Clay, don't you think we should talk?"

He stirred, rolled over and gently patted her shoulder. "Go to sleep, Andie. Don't worry. Everything will be fine."

And that was all. Andie felt miserable. She hardly slept the whole night.

The next morning was a replay of the night before. Clay was a thousand miles away from her, though he persisted in the fiction that everything was just fine. He rose and showered, shaved and dressed. He ate his breakfast, drank his coffee and then returned to the bedroom to pack his bag.

Then he told her, "I might as well go directly from the office to the airport, don't you think?"

She smiled patiently at him, though she was becoming angry in her heart. "They'll be dropping the tickets off here at the house, by express mail, around eleven."

"You should have had them sent to the office."

"Well, it's a little too late to change things now. But I'd be happy to drive them over."

"Were you planning to come in this afternoon?" Lately, she'd been working from one to five on Fridays. But she wouldn't today, of course, because she was going with Clay.

She shook her head. "Actually, today I was going to call Linda and see if everything seemed under control. If she didn't need me, I was going to stay home."

"Fine, then. I'll come back and get the tickets."

"You're sure?"

"Yes." He kissed her on the cheek, a chaste little peck that made her want to grab him and shake him and demand to know what he'd done with her husband. Because he wasn't her husband, not this cold, distant stranger who seemed to be in such a hurry to get away from her. "Goodbye, then. I'll see you when I come back for the tickets."

Andie opened her mouth to tell him that the tickets weren't the only thing he'd be picking up this afternoon; she was going, too. But somehow, all she said was "Goodbye, Clay."

She reasoned that if she told him now, there would only be a big argument. She would wait until he came back for the tickets to tell him. That would be soon enough for the confrontation.

The minute he was gone, she went in the bedroom to pack her own bag.

"Absolutely not." Clay glared at her. "You are not coming with me."

"Yes, I am, Clay." They were standing in the little service porch area that led out to the garage. Andie's suitcase was at her feet.

"It's not safe for the baby."

"I'm nearly a month from my due date. I've had a textbook pregnancy. The doctor said it should be perfectly safe."

Clay paced in the small space. He walked a few steps down the hall toward the main part of the house and then spun on his heel to confront her again. "What about the family?"

"What about them?"

"They'll be worried if we're both gone."

"I've called them. I've explained everything. I said we'd be back Sunday, which we will."

"You called them."

"That's what I said."

"You told them we were both going without even discussing it with me?"

"You and I haven't done a lot of talking in the past twenty-four hours, Clay."

He ignored that. "And the reservations? The flights and the hotel room?"

"What about them?"

"You made them all for two?"

"Yes, I did."

"I don't believe this. You just assumed you were going."

"No."

"What does that mean?"

"Just what I said. I assumed nothing. I *decided* I was going."

He stared at her for a moment. Then he said in a voice as cold as dry ice, "Well, you decided wrong."

Andie kept her shoulders high, even though her back was aching and the weight of the baby seemed to drag at her. "I'm going, Clay."

"No."

"Why not?"

He leaned against the wall, rubbed his hand down his face. "Don't do this, Andie."

"What?" She bit the inside of her lip. She absolutely was not going to cry. "Don't do what? Don't stick with you when you need me?"

He looked at her some more. His eyes were old. "I do *not* need you."

That hurt. Like a knife to the heart. She winced but refused to wrap her arms around herself and cry out as she longed to

do. Gently she said, "Yes, you do. You need me very badly
right now. And it's my job as your wife to make sure I'm there
when you *admit* you need me."

"This is ridiculous. I'll just leave without you."

"I have my own car. I'll follow you."

Clay looked away down the hall and made a scoffing
sound. "I don't believe you're doing this. I thought you'd
grown up. I thought you were past these selfish, grandstand-
ing displays."

"This is not a display, Clay."

"Isn't it? I'm sorry, but from here, it looks damn dramatic
a real Andie McCreary show. Eight months pregnant and
you're so noble. You'll fly to Los Angeles to be with your
husband, because he *needs* you."

"It's not dramatic. It's not noble. It's just how it is. I'm going."

"No."

"Yes."

He looked so angry for a moment that she thought he was
going to march over to her, grab her and shake her until she
agreed to do things his way. But he didn't. His broad shoulders slumped. "Look. I just want to get through this. I just
want it over with. Can't you understand?"

"Yes. I can. I do."

"Then stay here. Please."

The little section of counter that she used for folding
clothes was at her back. She pressed herself against it, not
resting really, but bolstering herself. She dared to ask, "Why
Clay? Why don't you want me to go?"

He closed his eyes, shook his head. "Oh, come on."

"No. Say it. Tell me."

"It's inappropriate."

"Why?"

"You know why."

"No, I don't."

"For Madeline's sake. It's cruel."

"Oh. I see. It's cruel."

"Don't be snide, Andie. It is. It's cruel."

"I don't see how. Madeline doesn't know the truth about the baby. Does she?"

"No, she doesn't."

"And you never plan for her to know, do you?"

"No."

"Then what she's never going to know won't hurt her. As far as she knows, I'm just your wife from Meadow Valley who's going to have a baby soon. *Your* baby."

There was a silence. Andie watched her husband's face. He looked so tired. The lines around his eyes seemed to have been etched deeper overnight.

He pointed out, "She's a bright woman, you know. She's going to see that you must have been pregnant before we got married."

"So? I got pregnant. And you did the right thing. Happens all the time. That's what the family thinks. Why shouldn't Madeline think the same thing?"

Clay rubbed his eyes so hard that Andie worried he would hurt them. "I don't like it." His voice was bleak. He was still slumped against the wall. He looked so awful, so drained.

Andie's determination slipped a little. Maybe she *was* in the wrong here. Maybe just giving him what he said he wanted— letting him get through this alone—would be the best thing, after all. Perhaps she'd been too hasty in deciding to go with him. She'd do better to give up and agree to stay home.

But her heart rebelled at the thought. This was the first real crisis of their married life. And Clay was a solitary type of man. The coming baby and their newlywed happiness had brought him close to her for a time. But if she let him weather this storm alone, she knew that a precedent would be set. He would never learn that he could turn to her in the difficult times.

No, she had to be there. If, while he was in Southern California, the moment came when Clay was willing to reach out for her, she couldn't afford to be five hundred miles away.

"I'm going, Clay."

"It's a mistake."

"No, it's not."

"There's no reasoning with you, is there, once you've made up your mind?"

"Not about this there isn't."

"You just do what you want to do, no matter who it hurts."

More knives, she thought. Words like knives. "I'm sorry you feel that way."

Clay let out a long, infinitely weary breath of air. "All right, Andie. We'll be late for our flight. Let's go."

Chapter 12

Clay hardly spoke to her during their flight. Andie tried to console herself with the thought that she'd done the right thing. If he really did need her during this awful time, she would be there.

She found the airline seats very uncomfortable. Her back seemed to be aching pretty badly, a low, deep kind of ache that was almost like cramps. She almost told Clay about it, but decided not to. He was so distant and closed off that he was sure to see any physical complaints as more "grand-standing" on her part.

When the steward came by, Andie asked him for a pillow, which she braced behind her back. It seemed to help. By the time they touched down at L.A., she felt better.

Luckily for her poor overburdened body, they had carried their luggage to their seats with them so they didn't have to wait at the baggage carousels. And then the rental car she'd ordered was ready right outside the terminal.

Clay drove them to their hotel. Andie adjusted her seat so that it pushed against the small of her back and then stretched the seat belt over her middle. She looked out the window at the palm trees and the low, red-roofed stucco houses and the towers of glass and steel in the distance.

In spite of the smog that colored the summer air gray, Andie found Los Angeles a beautiful city. It seemed to be exotic, sophisticated and sad all at once.

There were too many people wrapped in rags, pushing shopping carts piled with dirty bags. And yet the variety of humanity was fascinating to see. Barefoot men with shaved heads wearing pink robes strolled down the street beside tattooed homeboys with their billed hats on backward. And everywhere there were expensive cars, showroom perfect, driven by men who wore black-lensed sunglasses and talked very intently on their car phones as they drove.

Their hotel, the Casa de la Reina, was a Spanish-style structure with little courtyards and fountains everywhere. Bougainvillea and fragrant jasmine tumbled down the walls. Their room was on the second floor overlooking the pool.

As soon as the bellman had been tipped and was gone, Clay asked her if she was hungry.

"No. What I'd really like to do right now is put my feet up."

"That makes sense." He actually sounded noncombative, for a change. "I promised Madeline I'd call her when I got in."

Andie slipped off her shoes and sighed. "Go ahead." She climbed up on one of the two king-size beds and began arranging herself against the headboard in a sort of half-reclining posture, with pillows at her back.

"Here. Let me help." Clay grabbed more pillows off the other bed and propped up her knees, a thoughtful little gesture that she would have taken for granted just two days before.

Gratitude and love for him washed over her. She nearly drowned in it. And then the baby punched her in the stomach.

"Oh, you little scoundrel," she groaned, and touched the place where she'd been kicked.

Clay put his hand over hers. "You stop kicking your mom," he said to her stomach.

He was so close that his warmth and that subtle scent that was only him swam around her. She slipped her fingers from beneath his and reached out to cup the back of his neck, a fond gesture and an intimate one. She felt the slight toughness of the skin there, where the sun tanned him, and the blunt hairs at his nape, where his barber tapered them short. She touched the very place where his skull began.

It felt wonderful, just to have her hand on him, just to know, for that moment, that he was right there.

He looked at her. They shared a smile.

And then his glance slid away. "I should call Madeline."

"Of course."

Clay ducked out from under her touch and went to get his address book. Then he sat on the other bed and punched out the number.

Tuning out Clay's side of the conversation, Andie closed her eyes and let her mind float. But then Clay spoke to her.

"Andie?"

"Hmm?" She rolled her head and looked at him. He had his hand over the receiver.

"Madeline wants to get out. To talk. She's at her parents' house. I was thinking we could take her out to dinner."

We. He was including her, a fact that moved Andie deeply. He had made it so painfully clear that he hadn't wanted her here, yet now that she *was* here, he wasn't going to try to cut her out.

Andie considered for a moment and came to a decision. Were things different, were this baby she carried Clay's baby

in every single way, she *would* have come for the funeral—
but she would *not* go to dinner with them tonight. To
Madeline, she was a stranger. And right now, Madeline didn't
need an evening with a stranger. Madeline needed a friend.
Like Clay.

Andie shook her head. "I think I'll take it easy tonight and
order room service. But you go."

He frowned. "Are you sure?"

"Positive."

He looked at her closely. And then he nodded. "All right,
then. I'll go alone." He tried to hide his relief, but she saw it
nonetheless. He turned his attention to Madeline again.

Andie closed her eyes once more, feeling marginally better.
It eased her troubled heart a little to think that, in this at least,
she could do things the way Clay wanted them done.

"Hey, there."

"Huh?" She opened her eyes.

Clay was bending over her. "You went to sleep."

Andie struggled to sit up a bit higher. Her back was
bothering her again and she wanted to find a position that
would ease it.

"No." Clay gently guided her down. "Stay there. I just
wanted you to know I'm leaving."

Her mind felt fuzzy. "I want to turn to my side."

"Okay, then." He helped her to sit. And then he moved the
pillows around. "Try that."

Andie slid down and lay in her favorite sleeping position,
on her side.

"Better?"

"Much." She smiled. "Now what are you doing? Leaving
for dinner?"

"Right."

"Okay. Give my apologies to Madeline. Say I hope to meet her in person tomorrow."

"I will. Shall I order you something before I go? I can tell them to send it up later."

"No. I can do it when I feel like eating. You go on."

He smoothed back a few stray curls, which had clung to her cheek as she slept. "I won't be late."

His touch felt good. And her back seemed to have eased. She yawned. "Take your time." She drifted off again, hardly hearing the door close behind him.

The house where Madeline's parents lived was hidden in a small park behind a locked gate.

"Yes?" asked a disembodied voice when Clay pulled up to the gate.

He saw the speaker then, built into the stone fence at the side of the driveway. "Clay Barrett. I'm here to see Madeline."

"Come right in."

The gate made a clicking sound and swung open. He drove through.

When he saw the house, Clay thought it looked a lot like the Casa de la Reina, where he and Andie were staying. The place was huge and Mediterranean, more of a villa than anything else. Everywhere he looked he saw tropical foliage, wrought ironwork and Mexican tile.

A maid let him in. "Right this way."

He followed obediently, down a hall into a vast, airy room decorated with woven rugs, several groupings of Mission-style furniture and lots of potted palms. Clay thought of the Casa de la Reina again. The room really was like the lobby of a big hotel. An older man and a woman, seated in one of the sets of furniture, turned to look when he entered.

The woman, who had the same blond, fine-boned good

For the Baby's Sake

looks that Madeline possessed, smiled graciously. "You must be Clay Barrett. I'm Madeline's mother, Cybil Shaeffer. And this is my husband, Madeline's father, Jim."

Jim, who looked like an aging movie star right down to the blue blazer and the ascot tie, stood and extended his arm. "Hello, Clay." He was holding a drink in his free hand. The ice cubes in it rattled. "We've heard a lot about you. It's good to meet you, even under these circumstances."

Clay shook the proffered hand. "Yes. Good to meet you, too, Mr. Shaeffer."

"Jim will do."

"Jim, then."

Jim gestured at a wrought-iron cart laden with crystal decanters. "How about a drink?"

Before Clay could answer, Madeline spoke. "Thanks, Dad. But we're leaving."

Clay turned to see her, in the arch to a hallway that began on the other side of the massive room. She wore toreador-length white pants and some kind of gauzy shirt. The straps of her wedge-heeled sandals crisscrossed over her bare ankles. She was pale, and her eyes were tired. The joyful glow that had radiated from her the last time Clay had seen her was gone.

She came toward him. "Hey, bud."

"Hey to you."

Dutifully, she kissed her parents.

"What time will you be home?" her mother asked.

"I don't know for sure, Mom. But don't worry. I'll be fine." She turned to Clay. "Shall we?"

"You bet."

They walked out of the giant room and down the long hall to the front door. Madeline's parents followed them, their shoes echoing on the tiles. They stood waving as Madeline and Clay got in the car.

"Take it easy, now," Cybil warned. "Be careful."

"We will," Madeline called to them. Then she rolled the window up and smiled a wan smile at Clay. "They hover a lot. Since it happened."

"That's normal."

"Yes. But I feel stifled already. And it's only been two days." She snapped her seat belt in place. "Now." Her voice was determinedly bright. "It's hot and it'll be light for hours yet. Can we go somewhere outside and maybe sit under a tree in the shade?"

"You bet."

Clay drove to a wild park he knew of, which was only a few miles to the west along Sunset Boulevard. The park was covered with expanses of dry grass and crisscrossed with hiking trails. Clay stopped by the side of the road and discovered a blanket in the trunk, stowed there courtesy of the rental company. They walked up a hillside and found a shady oak.

Clay spread the blanket and they sat. For a while, neither of them spoke. A hot, languid wind blew across the grass and from somewhere, quail cooed timidly to each other.

"Is this really happening?" Madeline asked at last in a wispy little voice.

Clay looked at her. Then he held out his hand. She took it. "Yes, I'm afraid so," he said.

Madeline gave his hand a squeeze and then pulled free, as if she needed the contact, yet couldn't bear it for too long.

At the edge of the blanket, near where Madeline sat, a purple thistle grew. She touched it, touched the cruel little spikes around the blue flower.

"Will I keep living?" she asked.

He told her the truth. "Yes."

"Did anyone ever die on you, Clay?"

"Just my mother, my biological mother. When I was a kid."

"Were you there when it happened?"

"No. I was in a foster home at the time. There was some mix-up in communication. I didn't find out until she was in the ground."

"What did you feel like?"

"Angry. And lonely. I felt deserted."

Madeline's lips were pursed. "Yes. Exactly." She took in a breath that seemed painful to draw, then let it out slowly. "I'm so mad at him, Clay. So many times he left me. But this time. This way. This is forever. He's gone from the world. I think, in a way, I hate him for this. For this...ultimate recklessness. I just can't forgive it."

He understood that. Not being able to forgive Jeff.

He'd told Andie, "What he did, I'll never be able to forgive."

And Andie had said, "Oh, Clay, if you can't forgive him, how will you ever forgive me?"

"Is that awful to say, Clay?"

Clay forced himself to think of the woman beside him and not his wife. "What? That you can't forgive him?"

"Yes."

"No. It's not awful. It's just...how you feel right now."

Madeline gave him a pitiful little smile. "Thanks, Clay."

"For what?"

"For everything. For being here. For telling me that what I feel is okay."

"Hey. What are friends for?" Strange, he thought, it wasn't that difficult to sit here like this with Madeline, to listen, to say the things she needed to hear. Maybe it was because Madeline wanted nothing from him beyond acceptance and a listening ear. And he wanted nothing from her.

"Clay?"

"Yeah?"

"Clay, did something happen? Did something go wrong?"

"What do you mean?"

"Between you and Jeff?"

It took her words a few seconds to register. When they did, everything changed.

The world became ominous. The drone of insects, harmless until now, suddenly buzzed heavy with threat. The heat of the afternoon, bearable just seconds ago, was now stifling.

"Why do you ask that?" His voice seemed to tread on eggshells, it was so careful.

"Because we never saw you again, after that strange day you and Jeff went out for lunch and Jeff came back alone looking like he'd had a run-in with a meat grinder. And then, you got married. And you never even told us."

Clay looked away, across the grasses. He was stalling for time. He hadn't expected these questions from her, for the truth to rear its ugly head and demand a hearing. If he didn't tell her now, he would have to lie outright.

And yet what possible good could Madeline's knowing the truth do anyone at this point? Jeff was dead. Madeline was in a world of pain. The truth would only make the pain worse.

"Clay? What is it?"

Clay made himself look at her. "It's a long story. My wife…" He sought the right words.

She prompted, "Andie, right?"

"Yes. Andie. I mentioned on the phone today that she was pregnant, remember?"

"Yes. You said she was a little tired and wanted to rest. So she wouldn't be coming with us tonight."

"Right."

"I assumed she was being thoughtful," Madeline said. "You know, letting me have you alone, so I could cry on your shoulder."

Clay thought about that, about Andie's motives. Who could tell about Andie's motives sometimes? She'd insisted on fol-

lowing him here when he'd practically begged her to stay
home. And yet then she'd surprised him, by backing right out
of the picture when it came to this visit with Madeline. He
still didn't understand what she was up to in this situation and
he continued to resent the fact that she'd come.

Deep inside, maybe he was a little afraid she'd come here
to say her own private goodbyes to Jeff. It made a hollow, sick
place inside him, to think that she might still carry on some
senseless fantasy about Jeff.

Though who could tell what went through Andie's mind?
Clay certainly couldn't. Just two nights ago, she'd said she
was in love with *him*. And though he didn't believe in such
foolishness, it had still been satisfying to hear. He'd thought
how good they had it, and even told her as much. And then
Madeline called the next day.

And the world had fallen apart.

"Clay?"

He blinked. "I'm sorry."

Madeline's gray eyes were full of understanding. "Don't
apologize. It's a tough time for you, too."

"Yeah, it is."

"You were saying about your wife, Andie, and about her
pregnancy?"

"Right. Well, see, she was pregnant when we got married."

Madeline gave a tremulous little smile. "Oh. I get it." She
actually chuckled. "Clay Barrett, you devil. You led your
cousin astray."

"Er, right."

"So you're saying it all happened sort of quickly, the
wedding, I mean?"

"Right. She didn't want to marry me at first."

"Ah. A woman with a mind of her own."

"Is she ever. And then, when we finally worked things out,

we just wanted to have it taken care of. We went to Tahoe and did it the quick way, over a weekend."

"I see." Madeline looked knowing, but then she frowned. "But there were all those months. You never called."

"I know. It was inexcusable."

"It's not like you."

"My life, it just changed completely." In his mind, he saw Andie, laughing, holding her big stomach, rolling on the bed the other night, after she told him she loved him. Yearning welled in him, a slow, deep ache. How had it happened that she'd become so important, that she'd filled up his life? "I hope you can understand. Lately, it's just seemed like there's me and Andie and the baby. And nothing else matters. That's selfish, I know."

"Yes." Madeline's voice was soft. "Selfish. And completely understandable." She patted his hand. "It's okay. And I'm looking forward to meeting this special woman of yours tomorrow."

"I'm glad." And he was.

He was also massively relieved. Looking into Madeline's eyes, he saw that his half-truths had been believed. She wouldn't have to know about Jeff's worst betrayal, after all.

Madeline wore a dreamy, faraway look now. "You know, what I really want to do is reminisce."

"About Jeff?"

"Yes. Is that shameless and self-indulgent?"

"Absolutely. Do it."

She closed her eyes. "I will. Do you remember the time when…?"

Madeline launched into a long story from the past, during their college days, when Clay and Jeff had first been friends. Clay let her tell the whole story, only stopping her when she left something out. And then he told a few old stories of his own.

Eventually, they got up and shook out the blanket and went back to the car. Madeline gave him directions to a little restaurant she knew of out at the beach. They ate dinner and watched the surf. Madeline cried and had to ask the waiter for tissues. It was near nine o'clock when they got in the rental car again.

After Clay drove through the gates and pulled up in front of her parents' house, Madeline asked him to come in.

"No, I think I'll go on back to the hotel."

Madeline leaned across the console and kissed him on the cheek. "Say hello to Andie."

"I will."

"There'll be food and, you know, people getting together, here tomorrow. After the interment."

"We'll come. Our return flight isn't until Sunday, anyway."

"Good." She leaned back against the seat. "Thanks, Clay. This helped."

"Any time."

She straightened and opened the door. He watched her run up the tile steps. Before she went inside, she turned and waved. He waved back. And then she was gone.

Twenty minutes later, Clay sat in a chair in the room at the Casa de la Reina, watching Andie sleep. The empty bed stretched between them. But his eyes had adjusted to the night. He could see her just fine. Her hair was a tousled cloud all around the side of her face and her skin looked like cream, except for the dark smudges beneath her eyes.

She'd probably tired herself out, he realized, with all the tension over the past couple of days. She was eight months' pregnant and looked like nine to him, her belly big and round, so heavy under the sheet. He sometimes thought, lately, that it must hurt her skin, to stretch that much. She rubbed creams there, he knew, to try to keep the marks to a minimum. Still, she would have a few when this was over, after the baby was out in the world.

Her arm, still slim and shapely, lay above the sheet. She wore the gold bracelet of linked hearts that she wore all the time since he'd returned from living in L.A. That bracelet seemed a part of her, a part of all that was Andie. And now that he thought of it, he didn't even know where she'd gotten it.

An old boyfriend, maybe.

It was petty of him, but he didn't like that. Didn't like to think of Andie and anyone else. Not even some long-ago high school crush.

And not Jeff. Jeff, least of all.

Jeff, who hadn't mattered, who'd been a ghost to both of them two days ago. Jeff who now, with his death, seemed to hover nearby every moment of the day and night.

Clay couldn't get his mind clear—that was the problem. He thought of Madeline, and there was hurt and sympathy. Jeff, and there was pure pain. And Andie, and there was agony.

It was all roiling around inside him. He didn't know how to get it to straighten itself out.

"Clay?" Andie's voice was sleepy, full of dreams.

He wanted to cherish her, keep her close, keep her safe. And to be inside her. He always wanted that, even now, when she was so big, when they probably shouldn't, when it might hurt the baby.

Although the doctor said it was okay and so did the books, as long as everything was all right with her.

"What are you doing, sitting there in the dark?"

"Watching you." When he made love with her, he knew he was the only one. There were no ghosts between them then. No doubts. Nothing but the two of them and a universe of pleasure.

"Is everything all right?"

"It's fine." He was hard. Aching. Wanting. And yet angry,

too. He feared her, feared her power to empty out his life to nothing, if she should ever choose to leave him. And he still didn't understand why she was here, in L.A., for the funeral of the man who had used and discarded her and the baby. Not that he wanted to understand. He didn't. He was too afraid that understanding would end up hurting worse than not knowing at all.

With a little groan at the effort, she levered up on an elbow and turned on the lamp between the beds. "How did it go?"

"Fine. Where did you get that bracelet?"

"This?" She held up her right arm.

"Yeah."

A musing smile lifted the corners of her mouth. "Ruth Ann."

"What?"

She chuckled. "Well, half Ruth Ann. I saw it in the window at that jeweler's at Main and Mill streets. Ruth Ann was with me. I had half the money for it. She paid the other half. For my eighteenth-birthday present."

He grunted. "Ruth Ann." No long-lost boyfriend, after all. He wondered what was wrong with him, since Jeff had died. Always suspecting the worst. It wasn't good. "Did you eat?"

"Yep. Hours ago."

"Are you all right?"

"Yes. I'm fine. Why?"

He stood, the wanting intensifying, his hardness straining the placket of his trousers. He watched her eyes change, watched the softness and the knowing come over her.

"Oh, Clay."

"Is it a bad idea?"

He could see by her expression that she knew exactly what he meant: to make love. "No. It's just…"

"What?"

"Clay, we need to talk."

He was halfway around the end of the empty bed. He stopped there. "About what?"

She lifted her hands, a helpless gesture. "About everything. About how badly you're hurting. And how you're pushing me away."

Talking about all that was the last thing he wanted to do. He felt his desire fade to nothing, just at the thought. "It will be fine, Andie. Just let it be."

"But Clay…"

"I just need time, that's all. It will pass. In time."

"I don't know, Clay. I don't think it will. I think we have to get it out, all of it. We have to talk about Jeff, *really* talk about him. You have to let yourself admit that you didn't actually manage to cut him out of your heart and your life the way you thought you had. You have to forgive him. And then you have to forgive me."

He said nothing for a moment. His anger was a cold thing now. Then he muttered, "That's a hell of a lot that *I* have to do."

A tear spilled over her lower lid and slid down her cheek. "Clay. Please, Clay…"

"Don't." He pointed a rigid finger at her. "Just don't. I can't take it now, Andie." He started walking again, but this time he kept on going, right past her bed, into the bathroom.

"Where are you going?"

"I'm tired, Andie."

"You're running away."

He closed the bathroom door on her voice and twisted the privacy lock. He half expected her to follow him, to pound on the door, make an Andie McCreary type of scene. But all was quiet in the other room.

He took a quick shower and brushed his teeth. When he

went out to the main room again, she'd turned off the light and lay on her side, facing the wall.

He didn't disturb her. Instead, he climbed into the empty bed, turned on his side away from her and closed his eyes.

As it had been the night before, his sleep was troubled. He heard Andie every time she shifted her weight in the other bed. He wanted to be there with her, beside her, to feel her leg brush his now and then and her body's warmth radiating toward him beneath the sheet whenever either of them moved.

But it was a thousand miles to that other bed. He certainly couldn't make it there in the space of a single night.

Three times, she got up and went to the bathroom. He wanted to ask if everything was okay. But he didn't. He stayed quiet. He wondered if morning would ever come. Eventually, he drifted into a shallow sleep.

Andie was already in the shower when Clay awoke. He opened his eyes and dreaded the moment when she would emerge from the bathroom.

The moment came. She appeared in a cloud of warm steamy air, wrapped in her robe that now barely covered her stomach, drying her hair with a towel.

She looked so terribly vulnerable, her body ungainly, her hair hanging in wet ropes, her skin soft from her shower. He thought again about how he wanted to protect her, to keep her and the baby safe from any harm.

And how he hadn't been doing a very good job of that the past few days.

He made himself speak. "Andie, I…"

"Please." She held up her towel for silence and she granted him a rueful smile. "Don't worry. I promise I absolutely will not bug you until we've made it through the church and the cemetery and all that stuff. I know that you've got enough to deal with right now."

His throat closed off for a moment, in gratitude and tenderness. Gruffly, he answered, "Thanks."

She lifted her shoulders in a resigned little shrug. "'S all right. What's for breakfast?"

"Room service?"

"Sounds fine."

"What do you want?"

She thought for a moment, tipping her head sideways and rubbing the ends of her hair with the towel. "Two poached and an English muffin. Tea and tomato juice. In about an hour. I want to do my hair and put on my tent." She indicated the maternity dress that was hanging in the closet area. It was navy blue, with a wide sailor collar.

Clay called the number on the room menu and ordered the food. Then he went to the bathroom to clean up himself.

Andie dried her hair and put on her makeup while Clay shaved. Then they dressed in their funeral finery. The breakfast came right on time.

After they ate, they drove together to the church. Clay wanted to be there early, to find out where he was supposed to sit or stand, what he was to do as pallbearer.

The church was a huge gothic-looking structure made of gray stone. When they'd parked the car, they went in through the massive front door. The church was quiet, hollow sounding inside. Andie sat in one of the pews while Clay went to find someone to tell him what to do.

After a while, when the baby started shifting around, Andie grew uncomfortable. So she stood and walked around a little, exploring the small sanctuaries in nooks along the side walls and studying the stained-glass windows. Up in front, the

closed coffin, pristine white, was already in place. There were
flowers everywhere.

Clay came and found her eventually, to explain that he would
be expected to ride in one of the limousines of the cortege to
the cemetery. They could make a place for her, too. But Andie
told him she would prefer to take the car and follow along.

"Are you sure?"

"Yes. Don't worry. I'll be fine."

By then, it was about ten. Clay said he had a few minutes, so
they sat down together. Andie looked at the coffin and all the
flowers and tried to do what people did in churches, feel peaceful
and serene, lifted above the everyday trials of the world. She
didn't really succeed. There was too much on her mind.

Also, that uncomfortable, cramping feeling was back
again. It seemed to be very low down, very deep inside. More
and more she was feeling as if it wasn't her back at all. She
was even starting to wonder if it could be contractions.
Perhaps those contractions Clay had read to her about, the
ones that took place in the last month before delivery. Braxton
Hicks contractions, Andie thought they were called.

But whatever they were, they weren't that difficult to handle.
She just had to relax, not let things get to her. And Monday
morning, bright and early, she would give her obstetrician a call.

"Andie?" Clay's voice was very low, yet still it echoed a
little in the big empty church.

"Um?"

He took her hand, squeezed it, but said nothing more. She
looked at him, wondering what he hadn't said. A few days
ago, she would have asked him what was on his mind. But
not today. Not after last night and the way he had locked
himself in the bathroom to get away from the truth.

Things were so tenuous between them. And this wasn't the
time or the place to speak of their problems, anyway.

Andie closed her eyes, tipped her head up, let the rainbow of light that came through the stained-glass window above the altar bathe her face. They sat that way for a while, holding hands, saying nothing and Andie felt a little better.

Then Clay whispered to her that he'd meet her at the cemetery after the burial. From there they would drive to Madeline's parents' house for the reception.

Andie whispered back, "Okay." Clay rose and disappeared down the aisle.

Slowly, the pews filled up around her. Andie got up once before the service started to look for a bathroom. She managed to relieve herself and find another seat just in time.

The service was short. The minister read from the psalms and talked about Jeff. Around her, Andie heard people sniffling and those tight little sounds that happen when someone is trying not to cry out loud.

When it was over, Clay and five other young men surrounded the coffin. They lifted it between them and carried it down the aisle. The ushers led the family members out and then the rest of the mourners followed.

To Andie, the ride to the cemetery took forever, much longer than the service had taken. Driving was becoming more difficult all the time now, with her huge stomach nearly pressing against the steering wheel. And the line of cars was long and slow.

But at last, she arrived at the place where Jeff would be buried. She found a parking space with reasonable ease and joined the others, who had regrouped around the grave site. There were some folding chairs set up, in two groups beneath a pair of canopies. By then, all the chairs were taken.

Being as big as a house had advantages, though. An older gentlemen who spoke with a charming Irish brogue gave Andie his seat. She thanked him and sank gratefully into it.

Andie watched Clay, who was standing right by the grave where the coffin was already set. He was looking around, his expression tense and concerned. She didn't realize he was looking for her until their eyes met. His face smoothed out. She gave him a smile and a tiny wave.

The minister spoke again, reciting more verses from the Bible. And then a slim blond woman stepped forward. Madeline. She put a single rose on top of the huge bouquet that was already covering the coffin. They lowered the coffin into the ground. Madeline threw a handful of dirt on it. The minister said words of benediction.

Slowly, the mourners began to move away, singly and in groups. Andie sat in her chair, waiting for Clay. Finally he came. She led him to the car and they drove to the reception.

"Are you all right?" Clay asked her when they'd driven through a wrought-iron gate and parked in the driveway that was lined with cars.

Andie looked at him, thinking, *That's all we do lately— ask each other if we're all right.*

Down inside that tightness came. Like a hand in there, turning to a fist. Not that hard to bear, but definitely worrisome. She breathed deeply. The tightness eased.

"Andie?"

She gave him the answer he wanted to hear. "I'm fine. Let's go in."

The big house was full of flowers and people. Andie left Clay soon after they were shown in the door. She found a bathroom and felt better after she'd used the toilet and rinsed her face.

Then she waddled her way down several hallways to the big living room, where most of the people were. The nice older man who'd given her his chair at the cemetery introduced himself. His name was Bob and he was a great-uncle of Madeline's, on her father's side. He asked Andie if she'd like something to drink.

Andie smiled gratefully and requested some mineral water. The man disappeared down a hallway. Andie found a vacant chair of dark rich wood with studded leather cushions. It seemed suitable to be the throne of a Spanish grandee. She lowered her bulk into it.

As she waited for her mineral water, Andie watched the people. Most of them seemed older and, judging by their jewelry and clothing, quite well-to-do. There were a few children, dressed in somber colors but irrepressible nonetheless, as children usually are. They played tag in the long hall that Andie could see to her left, and giggled and chased each other around the heavy, dark furniture. Every once in a while, an adult would grab a little arm and tell the pint-size culprit to settle down. For a few moments, there would be sedate good behavior. And then the fun would start again.

"Hello."

Andie turned from watching a little girl playing peekaboo behind an areca palm to see the woman she knew to be Madeline standing by her chair.

"You're Andie, aren't you?"

Andie started to stand. "Yes, I—"

"No. Don't get up." Madeline was looking at Andie's stomach. "Please."

Andie chuckled. "Great idea." She sank back into the chair. "Madeline?"

"Yes."

Andie stuck out a hand. "Glad to meet you."

"Me, too."

Their hands clasped briefly, then both let go. At the same time, they both began, "I've heard so much about—" And then they laughed, in unison.

Madeline said, "Thanks for lending me your husband's shoulder last night."

"I hope it helped."

"It did."

They looked at each other, strangers yet connected. They didn't know what to say to each other, but both felt the link. Andie decided she liked Madeline's eyes. There was great kindness in them. Goodness seemed to radiate from her.

Andie thought of Jeff. A fool, to have chanced losing this woman, she thought. The ultimate fool to have thrown it all away in the end for a fast ride in a new car.

Graceful and slim, Madeline pulled up a nearby hassock and perched on it. Andie watched the lithe movement longingly. Would she ever be thin again?

Madeline leaned close. "I have to tell you. When Clay said you two had gotten married, I wasn't surprised."

"You weren't?"

"No. Sometimes he used to talk about you, his willful and troublemaking cousin Andie. I thought then that his feelings about you were more than cousinly. But I also knew if I pointed it out, he'd glare at me and tell me to mind my own business, that I was way off."

"So you didn't point it out?"

"Right. I'm no fool."

Bob reappeared carrying the promised mineral water. Andie thanked him and took the glass.

"Anything," Bob declared, "for a sweet Irish colleen."

"Uncle Bob," Madeline groaned. "Honestly. He thinks everybody's an Irish colleen."

Andie took a sip of her water. "Well, he's half-right. My mom's Italian, but my dad's Irish."

"Sure, and what did I tell you?" Uncle Bob laid it on thick.

"I'll just bet," Madeline said.

"It's true," Andie assured her. "McCreary. That was my last name, before I married Clay. About as Irish as they come."

Uncle Bob remarked that he believed McCreary was a Scots name. Before Andie could argue with him, Clay appeared.

"*There* you are," Clay said from behind her chair. "I was looking all over."

Andie tipped her head back and smiled up at him. "I was just listening to a little blarney from Uncle Bob here, and Madeline and I—"

Andie cast a swift, conspiratorial glance toward Madeline. What she saw made her look again.

Madeline was on her feet. "McCreary?" she said softly. "Andie for *Andrea?*" Her face was dead white.

"Yes," Andie said. "Andie for Andrea."

"I see," Madeline said. "And just when is your baby due?"

Andie blinked. Madeline looked so strange. "I, um…"

Madeline waved a limp hand in the air. "Never mind. Now I think about it, I don't believe I really want to know." Then her eyes rolled back and her knees buckled.

Somehow Uncle Bob managed to catch her before she hit the tiled floor.

Chapter 13

At once, the whole sprawling room was a beehive of frantic activity.

"Oh, my sweet Lord!" a woman cried.

"What is it? What's happened?"

"It's Madeline. She's fainted."

"What?"

"Step back everyone, give her air."

"Bob, follow me. To her room. This way."

Andie watched, clutching the arms of her chair, as Madeline was carried away.

"What in the world happened?" A painfully slim woman with rather wild-looking, curly gray hair asked Andie.

Clay was the one who answered. "We don't know."

"But what did she say? What were you talking about?" The woman tipped her head to the side, a birdlike movement, curious and alert.

"Nothing, just small talk," Clay insisted.

The woman, however, wasn't taking Clay's word for it. Her little brown eyes were on Andie. Andie struggled to give her some kind of response. "Clay's right. We don't know what happened. She, um, asked me when the baby was due and then…"

The woman finally saw that Andie was almost as distressed as poor Madeline. "There, there, dear." Her voice had become soothing. "Don't *you* go getting all upset. I'm sure she'll be fine. It's just the stress, you know. She loved Jeffrey so."

"I'm sure it must be awful for her," Andie heard herself murmur.

"But she'll survive. Madeline is very strong. Very strong, indeed."

"Yes, I'm sure she is," Andie agreed.

There was a moment of awkward silence, then the woman launched into the amenities. "Oh, I'm sorry. I didn't even tell you who I am. My name is Suzanne. Suzanne Corey. Jeffrey's mother was my cousin." She held out a thin, veiny hand.

Andie took the hand and murmured her own name. "And this is my husband, Clay."

Suzanne nodded at Clay. "You were Jeffrey's friend, right?"

"Yes."

"It's so hard to believe," she said in sad little whisper.

"Yes," Andie agreed.

"He was so young, so vital. And now he's gone. All the Kirklands, gone now."

"Yes," Andie said again, not knowing quite what else to say.

"But Jeffrey was always a little wild. Too much of a risk taker." Suzanne glanced at Clay. "Do you know what I mean?" She went on before Clay could say anything. "He had it all. He was bright and handsome and there was always plenty of money. And everyone loved him. How could we not? He was so very full of life, brimming with it. Always. I'm sure you remember."

"Yes." Clay's voice sounded a little hoarse, Andie thought. "I remember."

"And then there was Madeline. A wonderful girl. They grew up together, did you know?"

"Yes. I know."

"But somehow it wasn't enough. It was just never enough. And it was hard on him, to lose both of his parents so close together, even if he was a grown man. He felt very alone then, I think." Suzanne shook her head. "Poor dear boy."

Right then, a tall man put his arm around Suzanne's narrow waist and bent to whisper something in her ear.

Suzanne nodded, "Yes, I know. All right." She looked at Clay and Andie. "This is my husband, Lou."

Andie and Clay nodded and said hello.

Suzanne smiled fondly at her husband. "Lou says I talk too much." Lou looked down on her indulgently. "And maybe he's right. Well." She was suddenly brisk. "We have to be on our way now. I do hope we meet again."

"Yes, nice to meet you," Lou said. Then he took Suzanne's arm and off they went.

As soon as Suzanne and Lou were out of earshot, Clay bent near Andie's ear and asked, "Are you ready to go?"

Andie was more than ready. But it didn't seem right, somehow. "No. We should stay. We should see that she's okay."

"Do you really think it's necessary?"

"Yes."

He let out a long breath. "All right." In spite of his eagerness to get out of there, she knew he agreed with her. They should stay.

And they did, though each minute seemed like a year. Finally, half an hour later, Madeline returned.

The moment she entered the room, everybody, even the children, grew quiet. Then slowly the conversations began again. Madeline went from guest to guest, touching and hugging, reassuring everyone that she was just fine.

"She's all right," Clay said in Andie's ear.

"Yes."

"I think we should go." There was dread in his voice. He knew, of course, that something had happened, that Madeline had come to some awful realization. And he didn't want to learn what.

Probably because, in his heart, he already knew.

"No." Andie reached up and patted his hand, which rested on the back of her chair. "Wait. She'll work her way around to us."

And slowly she did.

"I'm sorry." Madeline's smile was distant and gracious. "It's a hard time. I hope you understand."

Andie looked in the other woman's eyes, saw denial, saw the desperate plea that she say nothing at all of what they both knew had really happened.

"We do. We understand completely," Clay said.

"Yes." Andie smiled, a smile as distant as Madeline's. She saw a little of the tension leave Madeline's face. "And we really have to be going."

Madeline simulated regret. "Oh, no. Not so soon."

"Yes." Andie levered her heavy body to a standing position. Then she took Madeline's hand. Madeline allowed that, though Andie felt her flinch. "Take care of yourself. Please," Andie said.

"Oh, I will." Madeline's smile looked as if it could break right off her face and fall, shattering into a thousand sharp pieces, to the tiles below.

Clay came around the chair. Dutifully, Madeline lifted her cheek to be kissed. Clay brushed his lips against her skin.

"Keep in touch now," Madeline chided. Both Andie and Clay knew what those words were worth: nothing. Madeline was only making the noises people make when they don't dare say what's really on their minds.

"She knows." Andie waited to say the truth until after they had returned to their hotel room.

Clay tossed his jacket on a chair and yanked his tie off as it were strangling him. "You can't be sure of that."

"I can. I am. And so are you."

"Look. What's the point in talking about this? We don' know *what* she knows. We'll probably never know."

Andie gaped at her husband for a moment, wanting to strangle him. Then she kicked her shoes into the corner of the open closet area and lumbered into the bathroom, closing the door behind her.

When she came out wearing her robe, Clay had changed into jeans, a T-shirt and running shoes. He was sprawled in one of the chairs next to the small table by the window drinking a beer from the beverages that were stored in the half refrigerator beneath the sink of the room's small courtesy bar

Andie hung up her dress and decided she could use a drink too. So she got herself a ginger ale. Then she went to the bed she'd been using and began moving her pillows around.

"You want some help with that?"

Andie turned to look at Clay. "No. I can manage." She crawled up on the bed and settled in, then treated herself to a little ginger ale. After one long refreshing drink, she set the bottle on the stand between the beds and looked at her husband defiantly. "Madeline knows about the baby, Clay. saw it in her eyes."

Clay drank from the beer, draining it. Then he admitted "Maybe. But what can we do about it if she does? There's just no point in stewing about it. Let it be."

"I am not stewing. I just want you to admit that—"

He sighed. "How? How could she know? Nothing at all was said. Except that your maiden name is McCreary and Andie stands for Andrea. How do you figure she *knows* from that?"

"I saw her face. I know she knows. And so do you."

Clay got up, lean, unfettered, his body hard and proud. As she had envied Madeline, Andie envied him. She felt so huge and slow just watching him move. One of those strange, contractionlike cramps gripped her. She grabbed one of her pillows, clutched it against herself, to her heart.

Clay didn't even notice what was happening to her. He was striding to the refrigerator, bending to yank the door open. When he had another bottle in his hand, he straightened with his back to her, shoved the refrigerator door closed with his leg and knocked off the bottle cap with the opener that was built into the side of the counter. By then, the cramp, or whatever it was, had crested and was fading away. Still not facing her, Clay tipped the bottle and drank from it.

Andie stared at his back, wondering if she should tell him what had just happened. But no, it really hadn't been that bad. Like the other contractions, it was one she had ridden out easily. It was nothing to be too concerned about, she was sure. But if she mentioned it to Clay, he'd make a big deal about it. And he'd use it to end this painful—but important—conversation.

Gently Andie reiterated, "Madeline knows the truth, Clay."

That did it. He turned around and faced her. His eyes were like cold green stones. "All right, fine. Madeline knows. Isn't that terrific?"

Andie chose to ignore the sarcasm. "It will take her some time, but I'm sure we'll be hearing from her."

Clay made a disgusted sound. "What the hell are you talking about? We'll never see or hear from Madeline again."

"You're wrong."

He stared at her for a long time. Then he swore and drank some more.

Andie wanted to cry. But she didn't. She dared to try once more. "We have to talk, Clay. We can't go on pretending that nothing's wrong between us."

His hand shot up, palm out. "Stop. Right there."

"But we—"

"No." He turned enough to set his beer down, hard, on the counter, then he glared at her once more. "Listen. You just listen. For a change."

Andie bit her lip. "All right."

"You just had to get me to admit that Madeline knows about the baby. All right. I've admitted it. But why stop there? You're so brave and honest, let's take it all the way. Let's examine *why* she knows."

Andie suddenly found she couldn't look at him. She was still holding the pillow. She clutched it tighter. "I—"

He cut her off before she even started. "Right. Look away."

"I'm not, I—"

"Fine. Then face it. She knows because of *you,* Andie. Because you just *had* to come here. Because you wouldn't do as I asked you to do and stay home where you belong right now."

That hurt. Badly. The pillow Andie hugged brought no comfort against that. Again in her mind, she saw Madeline, pale-faced, slowly sinking to the floor. And Madeline later, with her brittle, ghastly smile, reminding them to keep in touch.

Oh, yes. Clay was right. Andie had begged for honesty. And he was giving it to her. It had been a bad call for her to come here. Those awful moments at the reception never had to happen.

Clay wasn't through. He demanded, "What's going on, Andie? What the hell are you up to?"

She made herself meet his eyes, *willed* him to believe. "

just wanted to be with you. I swear. I wanted to be here for you, in case you needed me."

He grunted. She could see he wasn't buying. How in the world could she convince him that her motives had been true ones when he simply refused to believe her every time she tried to explain? "I want to get something clear right now." Clay leaned back against the counter, his hands behind him, gripping the counter rim. "I want to be sure you hear it. Are you listening?"

"Yes."

"Okay. Look. I *am* angry at you. For coming here. But I want you to know that I can live with that. I'll get over that. If you'll just…get off me for a while. Just let it go. You did what you did and that's that. We have to go on from here. There's no sense in belaboring all of this. As I keep trying to make you see, there is nothing more to talk about."

"But there is. There's—"

"I'm not finished."

"I…okay."

"I don't know what happens with you sometimes. I don't understand why you do what you do. And it doesn't matter."

"Yes, it does. It does matter." She put everything she had into those words.

He only shook his head and looked down at his shoes, waiting for her outburst to end. When she said nothing more he looked up. "Are you through?"

Bleakly, she nodded.

"Okay, then. I don't like that you came here, but you *did* come here. It's done. And as for the rest, well, it's *my* problem and I have to handle it." He rubbed at his eyes, scrubbed his hair back from his forehead. "Jeff is dead. And for some reason, I'm having a little trouble dealing with it. But I *will* deal with it."

"But Clay—"

"No. Hear me out." He waited. She said nothing. He went on. "I want you to know that I believe in your basic integrity, Andie. I swear I do. I know that you've been a good wife to me, that you'll continue being a good wife. We'll get on with our lives. And everything will work out well enough in the end."

He appeared to have finished. For a moment, there was quiet. She asked, her tone carefully controlled, "May I speak now?" He shrugged.

"Thank you. I think you're wrong. Very wrong. I don't believe that everything is just going to work out by itself. I think we have to tell the truth. All the truth. To each other. I think we have to drag it out into the light and look at it and see what it really is."

"What truth? I know the truth. There's nothing more to say about it."

"Yes, there is. And you know there is. I want us to talk, Clay. Really talk. You say that I do things you don't understand. And I say I'm willing to explain those things to you. But you don't want to hear. That doesn't make any sense, Clay. It won't work. You have to know. I have to tell you. About Jeff and New Year's Eve. About what happened, why I—"

"No!" He seemed to realize he had shouted the word, and lowered his voice to a near whisper. "There's no need for that. No need at all."

"But there *is*."

His jaw was set. "I've said all I'm going to say on this subject. Drop it. Just let it go."

She stared at him, thinking about walls, the walls they'd breached for a golden time. The walls that were so high and impenetrable now. Andie felt as if she were clawing at those walls, raking her nails bloody. But they were made of stone, impervious to her feeble efforts to batter them down with her two soft hands.

And she felt so tired. Tired and huge and ponderous. The baby seemed to drain her, to demand everything of her. She didn't have enough of herself left right now to keep battling Clay like this. And it couldn't be good for the baby, all this tension and frustration. She had to take care of herself, not allow herself to become so upset.

She met his eyes. "All right, Clay. Have it your way."

She saw relief on his face—and something else, too. What was it? Disappointment? Despair?

She didn't know, was just too tired to try anymore to keep fighting and find out.

"Are you hungry?" he asked.

"No. I just want a nap. A long nap."

He was suddenly all solicitude, helping her to lie down in the bed, fluffing her pillows. When she was settled, he touched her cheek. "You have to take care of yourself." He echoed her own thoughts.

"I know." She sighed, understanding with a stab of regret that his kindness, his attentiveness, were her rewards for not saying what needed to be said. She thought of all those years they'd been enemies. Had she been wiser then than now, to keep him at bay with hostility? Had something inside her always known how dangerous it would be to give her heart to a man like him, a man who refused even to believe that the very special love she bore him was real?

Gently he asked, "Are you going to be okay?"

"Yes, I'm fine."

"There's a gym in the basement. I thought maybe I'd—"

She completed his sentence for him. "Go work off a little tension?"

"Yeah. More or less."

"Sounds like a great idea. Do some sit-ups for me." She closed her eyes.

His lips brushed her forehead. "I will." He left her and moved around the room, changing into shorts, she imagined, getting ready to go. She heard the door close behind him just as another contraction took hold down inside her. But it faded quickly. Not real labor. Surely not.

Minutes later, she was asleep.

When Clay returned, they ordered room service and watched a movie. The contractions Andie had been experiencing became more frequent and pronounced as the evening went by. It became impossible to hide them from Clay. He wanted to call the doctor in Meadow Valley.

Andie soothed him. They should wait until tomorrow. If the contractions were still happening in the morning, they would get hold of the doctor somehow, and ask his advice before she got on a plane. But it was very possible that a good night's rest would make all the difference. And really, she was getting along in the pregnancy. These were probably the normal contractions that a mother often felt in her last month as her body begin readying itself to give birth.

Rather unwillingly, Clay accepted her judgment about it.

They went to bed at dusk, planning to be up before dawn since their flight was an early one.

But in the middle of the night, Andie awoke from a dream where some awful, cackling, witchlike person was pressing on her stomach. She dragged herself to a sitting position and pushed her hair away from her face.

Clay, who had lain down next to her at bedtime, sat up beside her.

"What is it?"

"Nothing, really. I just…I think I want to go to the bathroom, that's all." She slid off the far side of the bed and edged her way toward the bathroom.

And then something stunning happened. Her uterus contracted, from the top down. It was the most incredible thing she had ever experienced. She could feel it, moving like a living thing, over her extended belly and down to the depths of her.

"Oh!"

"My God. Andie, what—?"

And then something gave. Inside. She looked down. There was liquid trickling between her legs.

Clay was out of the bed and at her side in seconds. He put his arm around her shoulders, pulled her close against his solid strength. "What? Tell me. Please, Andie."

"I think..."

"What?"

"I think my water just broke."

Chapter 14

"What are you telling me?" Clay demanded.

The doctor regarded him warily, probably because he'd sounded so harsh. She was an attractive red-haired woman with a stethoscope around her neck and a white jacket over her clothes. She wore a name tag: Dr. A. F. Johannson, Obstetrics and Gynecology.

Clay reminded himself that he needed this woman on his side. "I'm sorry, Dr. Johannson. I'm...not at my best right now."

The doctor's freckled face relaxed. "I understand. And what I'm telling you is that your wife is in active labor."

Clay blinked and shook his head. He'd known that *something* was happening, of course. He didn't have to be a doctor to understand that the baby was probably coming. But the mad rush through the dark streets to the nearest hospital hadn't left him a lot of room for thinking. And now, actually hearing the word *labor* made it suddenly all too real.

Clay struggled to recall what all those books had told him. "*Active* labor?" he asked rather idiotically.

"Yes," Doctor Johannson replied. And then she began speaking calmly and clearly about the high quality of care the obstetrics wing of this particular hospital would provide, about nonstress tests, about effacement and dilatation, about the baby's presentation and the frequency of Andie's contractions. Clay hardly understood a word of it. All those books he'd read to be prepared for this moment were totally useless to him now that the moment was actually here.

All he could say was, "Is she all right? Is the baby all right? It's early. She's not due for—"

"A few weeks yet—we know. But so far, we're doing just great. The baby seems to be okay and is in a fine position. And Andie's a real trooper."

"A trooper." Clay looked at Dr. Johannson as if he'd never heard that word before.

The doctor gave him an understanding smile. "What I'm saying is, so far, so good."

"Can I go be with her now? I've filled out every damn form they shoved under my nose."

"Yes. She's in our labor room at this point. You may go in there as you are. But when the time comes to move Andie to delivery, you'll have to scrub down and wear a gown."

"Fine. Whatever. Where is she?"

Clay was led down two or three hallways to a big room with several beds in it. There was a woman in one of the beds moaning and crying out in a language Clay didn't understand. Andie lay in another bed, on her side, turned away from him.

He went to her. "Andie?"

She opened her eyes and forced a smile. Her face looked so tired, swollen and oily with sweat. A contraction gripped her. She moaned and her hand clawed for his. He gave it and then somehow managed to murmur something soothing and soft as she ground his bones together with her grip.

When the contraction passed, she panted, "Clay, I'm sorry. You were right. I make such bad, thoughtless decisions. I shouldn't have come here, should I? I should have stayed home, not put myself and the poor baby under such stress."

He agreed with her. In fact, he feared he would always nurse a certain resentment against her for her reckless foolishness in all this. She was just like Jeff, doing what she wanted, no matter what the consequences. But now was not the time to think of all that.

He repeated what the doctor had told him. "They say it's going to be all right, Andie. They say the baby is fine."

"But what if—?"

"Shh." He made his voice tender. "No *what ifs*. The baby is fine and you're fine. That's what matters now. Relax."

"They hooked me up to a monitor before they brought me in here."

"And?"

"They said what you said. No signs of fetal distress."

"See?" He smoothed sweat-damp hair back from her face. "What did I tell you?"

Andie didn't get a chance to answer, because another contraction took her voice away. Her hand was in his. He didn't let go. He concentrated on what he'd learned in their childbirth classes and forgot all the reasons he was frustrated with her.

Andie needed him. And so did the baby. And for now, that was all that mattered.

They stayed in that room for four and a half hours.

For Clay, everything blended together. The whole world centered down to the woman moaning and wailing from the other bed, Andie's clutching hand and those strange, dream-like periods that came between the contractions. Then, Andie would ask Clay to rub her back or she would take sips of water or even stagger to the commode behind the door at one end of the room.

And then, at last, Dr. Johannson returned, examined Andie and said that she could start pushing, something Andie had been begging Clay to let her do for what seemed like half a lifetime. Since this was Andie's first baby, she started pushing right there in the labor room.

When Clay could actually see a tiny bit of the baby's head between contractions, Dr. Johannson, who was sticking close by now, said it was time to for Andie to be moved.

Clay was led away to a place where he could scrub his hands. Then, wearing hospital greens, he was taken to the delivery room where Andie already was.

It was there that he truly began to understand why, for generation upon generation, labor and birth had been the province of women. It was simply too much for the average guy to take.

But somehow Clay did take it. And in the end, he was caught up in the excitement, the sense of exhilaration, as each of Andie's contractions brought the baby closer to the world. The doctor stayed beside Andie, monitoring the baby's heart rate after each contraction.

And Andie seemed changed now, totally exhausted, yet suffused with a hot, powerful kind of energy. When the baby's head had crowned and no longer sank back inside between contractions, things moved with alarming rapidity. At the last minute, tearing seemed imminent, so the episiotomy they'd hoped to avoid was performed, after all. Andie took it well, though Clay found he had to look away.

The rest was fast. The head emerged, red and angry, wet with blood and fluids. The doctor guided the shoulders out. The rest of the baby followed quickly.

It was a *she*. Clay, who had been allowed to catch the tiny body as it emerged, could hardly believe that he was holding her. Her eyes were scrunched closed. And she let out a big, angry wail.

"A girl," said the delivery nurse, who quickly scooped the child away from him. "Skinny, from lack of finishing time. But the lungs are just fine from the sound of that wail."

The afterbirth came as they clamped the cord. Clay only stared, stuck midway between awe and nausea. Then they laid the tiny, messy creature on Andie's breast while down below the doctor went to work sewing up the incision she'd made. "Emily," Clay heard Andie say in a soft voice. "We'll call her Emily." She looked for Clay, found him. "Is that okay with you?"

He nodded, since right then his throat was too tight to allow words to come.

Clay spent the next half hour on the phone, calling Andie's mother and his mother, and, of course, Ruth Ann. He assured them all that both Andie and the new baby were fine and said he didn't know how long it would be until they came home. A few days, at the very least.

His aunt Thelma was ready to hop the next flight south, but Clay convinced her to wait until at least tomorrow when they'd have a better idea of how long Andie and the baby would have to be in the hospital.

When he hung up from the final call, Clay dropped into the plastic hospital chair that was right there by the phone and stared at the wall for a few minutes.

"Hey, fella, you through?"

There was a man standing over him, waiting to use the phone.

"Yeah. Sure. Go ahead." Clay staggered to his feet.

He wandered off down the hall like a man in a trance.

After walking for several minutes, he took an elevator down two floors and then, by instinct perhaps, found himself at the door to the cafeteria.

Clay went through the line and bought scrambled eggs, wheat toast and a big cup of black coffee. He sat down and ate. The toast was slightly soggy and the eggs reminded him of something he used to play with as a kid—Goofy Putty, he thought it was called. But it was eleven in the morning and he hadn't eaten since early last night. After everything that had happened, his body craved fuel.

When the food was gone, he went back to the obstetrics floor. The nurse told him where Andie was, that they'd just moved her to one of the private rooms. The nurse pointed out the room.

Clay went in and found Andie asleep. He stood over her for a few moments, thinking how drained she looked and yet peaceful, too.

Her right hand was outside the blanket, the hearts-of-gold bracelet gleaming there along with the plastic identity band the hospital had snapped on. When they'd first arrived in emergency, the admitting clerk had tried to convince Andie to give the gold bracelet to Clay for safekeeping, or at least allow the hospital to store it in their safe.

"No way," Andie had informed the clerk. "This is my lucky bracelet."

The clerk had given in.

Clay stared at the linked hearts, feeling a little bit guilty. He'd jumped to conclusions about that bracelet at first. In fact, if he hadn't asked her where it came from, he probably would have been eaten up with jealousy when she wouldn't part with it. He'd have been positive that she cherished it because an old flame had given it to her. And in reality, the "old flame" had only been Ruth Ann.

He should be more understanding of her—he could see that. And yet, she *was* reckless. She did throw herself into things, never considering the cost.

Because of her ill-considered decisions, Madeline had been compelled to endure even more suffering. And the baby had been forced into the world ahead of time.

Both Madeline and the baby would survive.

But look at Jeff. A sharp pain twisted inside him at the thought of the dead man. In the end, Jeff hadn't survived the consequences of his own recklessness.

Jeff had been dangerous to know, in the truest sense of the word. He'd left heartbreak in his wake.

And Andie was the same.

A small sigh escaped Andie's lips. She turned her head on the pillow but didn't open her eyes.

Clay watched her, as it seemed he had always watched her, his emotions all tangled and knotted inside him. Bemused. Aching. Confused. Resentful. So many feelings, so much turmoil in his life. Because of her.

Yet to consider his world without her now was to imagine emptiness. A blasted, forsaken terrain.

So he wouldn't consider that. Ever. She belonged with him, and he with her. Eventually, this anger and hurt he felt every time he looked at her would fade. Time would do that.

They didn't need to do any more talking, as she seemed to think. They didn't need to dredge up all the hurtful details of her brief love affair with his ex-best friend.

They just needed to forget it. It was over. That was all.

Clay bent and lightly kissed his wife's forehead. She mumbled something and turned to her side, tugging at the blanket with one hand. He helped her, pulling up the cover and tucking it around her chin.

She murmured something else. It sounded like "Thanks."

"You're welcome." He hardly breathed the words. And then he quietly left the room.

He went to see Emily next. They'd cleaned her up and she was in the nursery. They told him he could look through the observation window. Or, if he would scrub down again and put on another gown, they'd let him in among the rows of tiny beds to hold her.

Clay washed and dressed in green. And then they let him in with her. He stood over her and looked down at her, all swaddled up tight in a white blanket. Then the nursery aide lifted her and handed her over.

She was so light, like a warm puff of air in his arms.

A tiny red fist wearing an armband like Andie's broke free of the blankets and waved at him. Clay touched that fist, so soft and wrinkled and powdery dry with its perfect tiny nails. It instantly opened and closed around his finger in a strong, needful grip.

"Yes," he whispered. "Yes, I'm here. I'll always be here."

And Emily opened her eyes. She looked at him. Something happened in the deepest part of him. It was as if she reached down into him with that tiny perfect hand of hers and took hold of his heart.

He saw Andie in the shape of her jaw and the curve of her mouth. Perhaps he even saw Jeff around the eyes. But those were physical things, insignificant to Clay against the enormity of what he looked at.

He looked at Emily. A person in her own right. And she looked back at him.

He bent close to her so that the baby smell of her surrounded him and he whispered his vow to her. "I won't leave you. I'm right here. You will have what matters. A mother and a father to love you and pay attention to you and teach you what life should be."

She seemed to grip his finger all the tighter. He rubbed her hand against his own cheek. She made a little sound, a gurgling, cooing noise.

Clay looked up. The aide was watching him, a fatuous smile on her face.

"You'll be a good father," the woman said quietly. "I can tell just by watching you. And your daughter is a beautiful child."

Three days later, Andie and Emily were released from the hospital. Before they left, Clay signed the birth certificate as he had sworn he would do. Thelma, who had flown down the day before, was there to help with the mountain of equipment having a new baby seemed to require.

They rode straight to the airport and boarded the plane for home. The flight was uneventful, aside from the fuss the flight attendants made of the newborn.

At home, since Della and Ruth Ann had been hard at work getting things ready, all was in order. It was decided that during these first days, Emily would stay near her mother in the master bedroom. Della had bought a bassinet for this purpose. With great pomp and ceremony, mother and daughter were installed in their beds.

Seeing that the women had everything under control, Clay went to the office to relieve his father, who had stepped in temporarily while they were in L.A. Thelma, who had already decided that she would stay over in one of the spare rooms for a while, made lunch for everyone and began planning the dinner menus for the next week.

Over the days that followed, Andie was grateful for her mother's help and support. Thelma cooked and cleaned and sympathized with her daughter unstintingly when Andie's breasts were sore from nursing and when Andie looked at her pouchy stomach in the bathroom mirror and burst into tears.

"I kept waiting to be thin again," Andie wailed. "And look at me. I'm like an empty paper sack."

"It will go down," her mother assured her.

Andie was shameless. "You promise me, Mom?"

Thelma was, too. "Absolutely. I guarantee it. Especially if you start exercising soon."

"I will. I swear I will."

From the bedroom, Emily started to wail.

Andie groaned, thinking about the pain when that small mouth latched on to her breast.

"You could go ahead and switch to formula," Thelma suggested gently, reading correctly the expression on her daughter's face.

"No, just a few more days and it won't hurt anymore. All the books say so."

On the second Monday in September, when Emily was a little over two weeks old, Thelma went back to her own house. Joe wanted his wife back. Like everyone else, Andie's father adored his granddaughter. But he was tired of sleeping alone and foraging in the freezer when dinnertime came.

Andie was feeling much stronger by then. She took over the maintenance of her own house without much difficulty. She was even able to start dropping in at the office for a few hours twice a week or so, since Thelma was more than happy to keep an eye on Emily for a while.

And Clay was wonderful, he really was. He worked all day. Yet in the middle of the night, when Emily cried, he would get up and check for a full diaper, even rock her before waking Andie for the feeding that was usually required.

Looking back in later years, Andie remembered those first weeks of Emily's life as a stressful yet magical time. A time during which Emily daily performed miracles. She kicked her arms and legs; she gurgled and cooed. Clay swore she smiled though Thelma insisted that was only gas.

Andie would have been happy. She *was* happy. Except for the distance between herself and Clay. A distance that somehow, seemed to inch a little wider every day.

Clay ate breakfast across from her. He went to work and came home right on time—there were no more detours to Doolin's pub. He slept beside her. He was kind and considerate and always ready to do whatever she asked of him.

Except to let her beyond the wall.

Three and a half weeks after Emily's birth, the doctor gave Andie the go-ahead to resume, as he put it, "intimate relations." He even fitted her for a cervical cap, which she went right to the drugstore and bought. She felt so nervous and happy at the prospect of making love with Clay once again.

That night, Andie told her husband what the doctor had said. Clay patted her arm and muttered something about that being fine.

And that was all. The next day he left for Lake Tahoe for a week of continuing-education classes, which were necessary for him to keep his CPA license.

Andie told herself that as soon as Clay returned, they would rediscover the physical side of their marriage.

But when he came back, they rediscovered nothing. Over the next weeks, she tried dropping subtle hints, cuddling up against him, even asking him outright if there was something wrong that he didn't seem to desire her anymore. Clay managed to be vague and distant and neither answer her questions nor respond to her attempts to arouse his interest.

Sometimes Andie dared to imagine that he looked at her with the old hunger in his eyes. But it was always just a glance, quickly masked. It could have been no more than wishful thinking.

There were certainly no other signs that he had any interest in her sexually. Though Clay slept in their bed with her, he kept to his side of it. It almost seemed as if he was making a conscious effort not to let his body so much as brush against hers.

How could she get close to him when he so constantly kept her at bay?

The answer was, she couldn't.

At least, that was what Clay hoped.

Because he was doing just what she suspected. He was keeping clear of her physically. It was driving him nuts, but he was doing it.

Clay was determined to avoid making love with her for as long as he could hold out. Too much happened when he made love with her. He was weakened by the sexual power she had over him.

He knew her too well. With Andie, physical intimacy and emotional intimacy were one and the same. As soon as they made love, she'd be at him, wanting to talk about things he never even wanted to think of again, wanting to root around in the past like a pair of emotional archaeologists at some major dig.

Clay didn't want to do it. He wasn't *going* to do it.

But, damn, he did want her.

If he believed in such things, he would have sworn she was a witch, that she'd put some sort of sex spell on him so he'd finally go crazy from wanting her so much.

And he knew she was exercising to get back in shape. He'd seen the workout pants and T-shirts hanging to dry on the service porch, noticed the stack of exercise DVDs by the TV.

And the exercises were working. Her body was slimmer again. It was taking on its former tight contours. Except for her breasts. They were disconcertingly ripe, heavy and fuller than ever because she was nursing Emily.

The maddening changes in his wife's body weren't all

Clay had to contend with, either. She was spending more time at the office, as well. While she was there, she seemed to make it her personal mission to single-handedly wreak havoc with his concentration.

Clay found that he couldn't walk into the copier room or look for a file without dreading the possibility that he'd have to confront the sight of her, bent over a table stapling papers together. Or standing on tiptoe reaching into a file drawer, the muscles of her calves flexing in a way that sent his libido into hyperdrive.

And then, in bed at night, he didn't know how he bore it. The warmth and scent of her came at him every time she moved. She was so close, just an arm span away. All he had to do was reach for her.

But he refused to reach for her.

It was pure hell. Sometimes he'd lie there, staring at the ceiling, *scenting* her and *knowing* that he wasn't going to last a split second longer. That he was going to roll over and grab her, pull her beneath him and shove himself into her without any preliminary at all.

He'd grit his teeth and turn away, to the very far edge of his side of the bed. He'd think of the shirts he needed laundered, his least favorite client, *anything* to reduce his state of total arousal.

Sometimes Emily, who was now sleeping in her own room, would start to cry. Clay always sighed with relief when that happened.

"I'll go," he'd whisper.

He'd slide out of the bed and pull on his terry robe over the pajama bottoms he slept in nowadays. He'd slip over to the little room next door.

And there he'd find a brief peace, even if it turned out, as it usually did, that Emily was hungry and he couldn't give her what she wanted. There was still that first moment, when he bent over the crib and she blinked and focused in on him, forgetting to wail for an instant.

"What's the problem here?" he would ask.

She'd wail again, flailing her little arms that had grown so fat and round.

He'd pick her up, put her to his shoulder. Every once in a while, that would do it. She'd let out a little burp and snuggle against his neck. But even if burping her didn't work, there was still the chance that changing her was all she needed.

In any case, if she didn't need to be fed, he could sit for a few minutes in the rocker that Granny Sid's mother had brought from the old country. He could hold Emily close and look at the moon out the window.

He could whisper to her how it would be for her, how she would learn to crawl, to walk and to talk. How she'd go to school and take gymnastics or play soccer or maybe even the violin. And how he and her mother would always be there, to teach her about the world and to see that nothing ever harmed her.

Those moments alone with Emily held the greatest peace Clay had ever known. Right now, Emily's wants were so simple, so pure. Food, a dry diaper and a caring touch. Clay could give her those things without much effort at all. Loving Emily was the easiest thing he'd ever done in his life.

Just as what he shared with Emily's mother was the hardest.

The first storm of the season came on a night in late October, nine weeks after Emily's birth.

That night had been a tough one. Another of those nights when Clay lay in bed awake, wanting his wife and yet somehow managing to hold himself away from her.

The gathering storm outside made it all the worse. There was so much electricity in the air, such a heavy *waiting* feeling. Storms always made him want to break free of all the controls he normally put on himself.

After the first few thunderclaps, he'd heard Emily's cry. Andie had stirred. He'd told her to go back to sleep. And he'd come in here, to hold Emily and soothe both her and himself.

He'd rocked Emily and told her all about storms, how he loved them, how one of his two mothers, whose name had been Rita, had loved them, as well. He whispered what he remembered of Rita in the red coat, turning in circles beneath a downpour. He'd said that storms were nothing to be afraid of. A good storm was one of the best things in life.

Now, Emily was asleep over his shoulder. Clay could feel her stillness, the evenness of her breath moving in and out of her little chest.

Outside, rain lashed the window and the sky lit up. Emily didn't even flinch when the thunder crashed.

Slowly, Clay stood from the rocker. He went to the crib and laid the sleeping child down. She cuddled right up, never stirring, as he covered her with the blankets and tucked her in.

He stood watching her through three more thunderclaps. But she simply went on sleeping. Her little body didn't so much as twitch.

Clay tiptoed back to his own room. But when he got there, he couldn't quite bring himself to climb into the bed beside Andie.

He was drawn to the glass door on which the rain was beating, to beyond that door, where the wind and lightning and thunder ruled. He spared a glance for Andie. She seemed to be sound asleep.

And the storm was pulling at him, inviting him out into it. He went, padding across the floor like a man in a trance.

But he was careful. He slid the door open as smoothly as he

could, just wide enough that he could slip through. And he closed it all the way behind him so no icy drafts would wake his wife.

The storm embraced him. He went to the edge of the deck and turned his face to the sky.

In the bed alone, Andie slowly sat up.

She knew where her husband was. She had heard his return, knew that he stood by the bed, felt his hesitation as the storm beckoned to him.

The storm had won. Now he was out in it.

A feeling of sweet anticipation rose inside her. It tingled along each and every one of her nerves.

She probably shouldn't...

Yet when it came to Clay, Andie really had no shame.

She threw back the covers and flew to the bathroom where her clumsy fingers almost defeated her in the insertion of her new contraceptive device. But at last she succeeded. The darn thing was in.

Andie looked at herself in the mirror, a shadowed form. She hadn't dared to turn on the light. It was just possible that Clay might have noticed if she had, since there was one high window over the bathtub that looked out on the deck where he now stood.

Andie wore a modest cotton gown with a button front. The gown was perfect for a nursing mother, but not so great for what she had in mind. She gathered up the hem and pulled the gown over her head, dropping it to the tiles at her feet.

She looked at the dark shape of herself in the mirror. Naked, slim, her hair a black cloud. Her breasts were very full. Her milk could come, she knew, if he kissed her in a certain way. She felt the heat in her cheeks at the thought.

But it couldn't be helped. And surely women had made love with their men for century upon century with milk in their breasts. She'd just have to deal with it when and if the moment came.

On the counter not too far from the sink, there was a monitor, as there was in the master bedroom and in all the major rooms of the house. The monitor picked up noises from the baby's room. It was blessedly quiet right then. And Clay had just been in to check on Emily. The chances of her daughter's interrupting them were minimal.

Andie's heart was beating very fast. What if he rejected her? What if she walked out on that deck stark naked and he turned her away?

Oh, that would be terrible.

But she couldn't let herself think that way. If she thought that way she'd give up trying and worse things might happen if she gave up trying. Sweet Lord, he might never make love with her again.

That awful thought mobilized her. She went out of the bathroom and across the floor of the bedroom. At the glass door she hesitated, pressing her face against the glass to look for him.

She saw him at the railing. He wore his robe and his pajama bottoms, both of which were wet through and clinging to his broad back, his hard, strong legs. He stood with his face turned up, transfixed, beneath the angry sky. His proud, tall body yearned toward the roiling clouds.

Andie's own body relaxed as she watched him. In the space of an instant, everything was changed. All her little fears of rejection, of embarrassment, faded to nothing. The world shimmered under the onslaught of the storm. And she herself was shimmering, needful, hungry for the man outside.

Andie slid the door open, not even bothering to turn and close it behind her. The storm attacked her, pelting her naked body, raising the goose bumps on every inch of her skin.

It was glorious. She lifted her hair and shook it so it fell down her back. And then she tipped her face up, as Clay was doing, letting the rain wash over her, drenching her hair, running down her body in a thousand tiny streams.

When she lowered her face, he was looking at her. His face was naked, washed clean of all pretense. She saw in it the hunger that answered her own.

He said her name, a low, needful sound. And then he covered the distance between them in three long, urgent strides.

Chapter 15

Clay caught Andie's face in his cold wet hands. "You're insane."

"Yes."

"You'll catch pneumonia."

"Or you." She rose on tiptoe, offering her mouth. "Maybe I'll catch you."

He muttered something she didn't really hear, though his meaning was plain. And then he gave her what she craved, his mouth on hers, his tongue delving, his hands everywhere.

Andie held nothing back. She surged up against him, her own hands clutching, grabbing, pushing at his sodden robe. Clay understood what she wanted and helped her, yanking at the soggy terry cloth, shrugging it off, fumbling with the ties of his pajamas and then shoving them down. And at last he was naked, too. No stitch of clothing kept their bodies apart.

The sky opened wider, the rain came down in sheets. Lightning blazed across the heavens and thunder claimed the hills with its roar.

Clay reached down, his wet hands sliding over her, his fingers closing around her thighs from behind. He lifted her, raising her high, sliding her soft, heavy breasts against his chest and then, slowly, he lowered her onto him.

Andie was ready, had been ready forever, it seemed. Clay slipped into her heat and wetness in one smooth, masterful stroke.

She tossed back her head so the water beat on her face. She felt the heavy, sodden coils of her own hair, like silky ropes as they trailed down her back.

"Wrap your legs around me." Clay's voice was harsh, guttural with need.

Andie did as he commanded, encircling him with her thighs, hooking her feet together at the small of his back. Clay staggered away from the railing, clutching her as she clutched him.

And then he turned. Andie felt her back meet the smooth outer wall of the house. Clay used the wall, bracing her against it as he moved in and out of her in long, deep strokes.

Such a sweet, fierce agony, Andie thought in a shattered sort of way. Different than when she'd been pregnant. Now he could be less careful, now he could give the wildness free rein. He seemed to be reaching way up into her, to the very center of her. And she was taking him, all of him, so deep and so good.

Her back scraped the streaming wall. She didn't care. She pushed herself against him, moaning, giving herself up to him. It was a total surrender—one in which he also succumbed.

She stroked his dripping hair, his neck, his shoulders, which bunched and knotted with the strain of keeping her writhing body in place. Everywhere she touched him, the rain ran down in rivulets, making him slick and cold, so hard, so very male.

Lightning flashed again. Thunder clapped.

And then it started.

Her climax came reeling out from that deep place that he was filling so totally. Like a live thing, a flower of sensation, it opened, unfurling petals of wonder along every nerve.

Andie called Clay's name, clutching him even closer, though that didn't seem possible since she held him so tight already. He pressed up, even harder than before. And she felt him spilling as his body jerked and stiffened.

He buried his head against her shoulder. Then he threw it back and groaned his release at the black, roiling sky.

Andie held on, taking all that he gave her, aftertremors shaking her as he finished at last.

And then, the storm still raging around them, they clung to each other, resting against the wall. His head was tucked into the curve of her shoulder, his mouth open against her neck. He kissed her neck, a suckling kind of kiss, as if he could draw back from the pulsing artery there the strength he'd expended in the ecstasy they'd just shared.

Andie twined her fingers in his soaking hair and gave a tug. He groaned as his mouth lost its hold on her flesh. She nuzzled his chin, seeking and at last finding his lips.

The kiss was soft and wet, an endless, tender thing. A caress of aftermath, of fulfillment found, of mutual gratitude at the release that had finally come after these endless weeks of abstinence and denial.

Clay's thighs were quivering; his whole body shook. Andie shook with him. She started to loosen her grip, to slide to the deck floor and relieve him of her weight.

But he grunted a protest into her open mouth. And then he hoisted her, getting a better grip. She instinctively clutched him tighter with her legs. He carried her, reeling more than walking, through the open glass door and back into their bedroom.

He hovered there, by the door, his mouth still locked with hers. She understood what he wanted.

Awkwardly, almost toppling them, she managed to reach out and push the door shut. The keening wind and the beating of the rain receded. When thunder boomed out again, it was muffled, farther away.

Now their breathing and their sighs were the loudest things. The whole dark room was alive with the sounds of their loving. Andie gripped his big shoulders again, wrapped herself around him like ivy on a wall. He took her to the bed, turned and dropped to a sitting position, his feet on the floor.

Now she straddled his lap, facing him, her legs still encircling him. They remained joined, though he was softer inside her. If she lifted just a little, he would slip out.

But he didn't slip out. The kiss went on and on.

He only broke it to nuzzle his way down her cheek, over her jaw, back to her neck and the hot pulse there. His hands came between them. He touched her breasts.

They were hard and full. She knew her milk must be coming, at least a little. But they were both so wet, anyway, it hardly seemed to matter. She didn't even bother to look down and see if it was so.

Clay kissed her neck, licking and sucking, as he fondled her breasts, making them ache and yearn. Down inside her, where he was cuddled limp and safe, she felt herself readying again. And he responded; he grew and hardened, rising, eager for more.

And then he fell backward. He moved up onto the bed, so she could ride him.

And ride him she did. A long, slow time.

It seemed as if this pleasure, this glory, might never have an end. And Andie didn't want it to end. Because now, joined as they were, she could forget all the ways they were so far apart. Here, right now, Clay was open to her. He held nothing back. All the hurts and resentments fled away. No walls existed. They were truly one.

Fulfillment overtook her again, high and pure. Andie rode him harder as it claimed her. And again, as before, he answered with a culmination of his own.

When it was over that time, she fell across him. He stroked her back and coiled her wet hair around his hand.

"Andie, oh, Andie," he breathed against her cheek. "What is it? What is it you do to me?" He sounded lost, almost, and drained and a little sad.

Andie pulled back enough to meet his eyes through the gloom. "I just love you, Clay. That's all. Since the first night you brought me to this house, that's all I've ever done."

He sighed and rolled his head to the side, a gentle rejection of her heartfelt words.

She wouldn't have that. Couldn't bear that. Not after the shattering intimacy they had just shared.

She grabbed his chin in her hand. "Don't do that. Don't turn away from me."

Clay gave in to the pressure of her grip and turned to face her again. But then his strong hand closed around her wrist. "Let go."

Hurt welled in her, sharp and acrid, burning her throat like smoke. This was the ultimate proof of the unscalable wall between them. That he could climb to the heights of heaven with her one moment, and then turn away at the merest mention of the word *love*.

Andie did as he demanded, letting go and sliding off his body at the same time.

"Look, Andie—"

"No." She kept on moving, right off the side of the bed and onto her feet. "Don't say anything more. Please."

"Damn it, Andie…"

She didn't stay to hear the rest. She whirled and made for the bathroom.

She didn't quite make it. Clay got there right behind her

nd slid in front of the door so she couldn't slam it in his old, hard face.

Thwarted, Andie glared at him for a moment. Then she rew in a breath, squared her shoulders and flicked on the ight. Both of them flinched at the sudden, glaring brightness.

The moment her eyes adjusted, Andie marched to the bathtub, ent, engaged the drain lock and turned on the taps. She poured n some bath salts and watched them foam and bubble.

Clay remained in front of the door, leaning there insolently. Even though she was turned away from him, Andie could feel is exasperation with her. Resentment came off him in waves.

"This is ridiculous," he said at last. "I knew you would do his. The minute I touch you again, you're on me. And when don't respond the way you think I should, you stage a stupid, hildish little tantrum."

She whirled on him. "Fine, Clay. Call it that. Cut me to he heart and then, when I get mad about it, call it a tantrum. And call the love we have nothing more than sex. Do vhatever you have to do to keep me on the other side of that vall you've put up."

"You always exaggerate. I've hardly *cut you to the heart.* And if I'm wary of you, well, I'd say with all that's happened, have a right to be wary."

"Fine. So let's talk about it."

"I told you—"

"I know, I know. No talk. None of that. Never again." She pat the words at him, then turned to climb into the tub.

He grabbed her arm. "Damn you. What the hell do you vant from me?"

She looked at his fingers, where they pressed into her ender skin. And then she looked right in his eyes. "I've told ou all along what I want. Honesty. And love. It's kind of funny, when you think about it. Since those are the two things you refuse to give me."

He had loosened his grip on her arm a little, but now he squeezed tight again. "I've been truthful with you."

"Have you?"

"You're damn right I have. And you've always known what I think about love. It's a word, and that's all. It's what people *do* that really counts."

"If it's only what people *do* that matters, Clay, then why are you letting us be torn apart?"

"I'm not letting that happen. You're the one who won't—"

"Oh, stop it. Be honest, please, since you keep insisting that you are. Admit to me that all the time now, you're wondering if I'm still carrying a torch for your dead friend."

That did it. He dropped her arm as if it were red-hot. "I'm not wondering anything of the kind."

"Liar." Now she was the one advancing on him. "You are. Admit it."

"I mean it, Andie. Stop this now."

"I won't. No. I won't stop." She had him right up against the door and she spoke directly into his suddenly pale face. "Oh, I know you, Clay Barrett. And I know the lies you tell yourself. Like you don't care about love, love doesn't matter. You're too down-to-earth and realistic for love. And therefore it shouldn't make any difference if I *think* I love your dead friend. As long as I do what I should do as your wife and Emily's mom. But it *does* make a difference to you, Clay. It's eating you up inside. And until you admit it matters and we can talk about it, we'll just go on being miserable and making each other miserable. And eventually, if you haven't already, you'll start thinking that maybe we'd be better off apart. And then we'll end up—"

"Enough!" The word was a raw, hard shout. He lifted a

and and pushed her gently back from him. "That's not going to happen," he said in a hoarse whisper. "You're my wife, and you'll stay my wife."

Andie shook her head. "Never say never, Clay." All the sorrow of the world was in her voice. "I won't be miserable for the rest of my life. Not even for you."

Right then, from the monitor on the counter, there came a long, angry wail.

Clay sighed. "I'll go."

"No." Andie turned and spun the taps again, this time to the Off position. "I'm sure this time it's food she wants. And anyway, it's my turn." Bending, Andie scooped up the gown she'd left on the floor before she'd followed Clay out into the storm. She pulled it over her head and smoothed it down.

Clay said nothing more as she stepped around him and headed for Emily's room.

The next morning, after Clay left for the office, Andie went out on the deck and found his sodden robe and pajamas. She bent to pick them up and then just stayed there, in a crouch, crying in deep, wrenching sobs.

When the sobs finally tapered off to hiccups and sighs, Andie took the wet things and went inside to put them in the washer. She told herself that maybe she'd feel better now, after having indulged in a good, full-out crying jag.

But she didn't feel better. Especially not when she went to the office and Clay treated her as if he could hardly remember her name.

For the next two weeks, it went on like that. They were like strangers forced to share a life. Andie, not knowing how to reach him, began treating him just as he treated her: with extreme caution.

They were polite and considerate with each other, elaborately so. When they passed each other things at the table, they were scrupulously careful to observe the amenities, to say "please" and "thank you" and "if you wouldn't mind."

Like children who had misbehaved and now wished to show how truly good they could be, they informed each other of their every move.

"I thought I'd go over to the supermarket now."

"Yes, of course. Good idea. Go ahead."

Or...

"Dad wants to play golf this afternoon. I was thinking I'd join him at the course."

"Yes, that's fine. Why don't you, then?"

"I will. I'll do that."

"Good. That's just fine."

It was awful. Andie felt that she lived in some artificial world. A perfect world, where no true emotions were allowed to sully the plastic purity of it all.

It was so bad, so banal, so utterly unreal, that Andie almost found herself regretting what she and Clay had shared on the night of the storm. She almost wished she could turn back the clock, let Clay go out on the deck into the storm alone and stay in bed herself.

Because if they hadn't made love in that shattering, total way, she probably never would have said the things she'd said later. She might have kept to herself those painful truths, truths that cut so close to the bone that now Clay wouldn't come near her, much less take her in his arms.

Each day, Andie woke positive that it couldn't go on like this. Something would happen to turn things around.

But each day would slide by, artificial and stifling as ever.

She talked to Ruth Ann. Ruth Ann said she had to keep trying.

So she did, she tried again, though she felt battered and bloody from all the trying she'd done.

It was Friday night and they were watching television.

"Clay. Clay, could we turn this off?"

"What for?"

"Clay, we need to talk."

He looked at her. A look of such weary patience that all her will to confront him faded to nothing.

She couldn't do it. She was as tired of it as he was. "Never mind," she said.

They watched the rest of the program and then went to bed.

And bed was the worst of all. In bed there were miles, continents, between them.

Andie had a premonition that the day would come when Clay would begin to sleep in one of the spare rooms. He'd wait for some reasonable excuse, of course. That he was keeping her up with his reading, which he often stayed up late to do. Or maybe he'd catch a cold and decide he was disturbing her with his coughing and sniffling. He'd move to another room. And never move back.

Andie thought, *This is how it happens between men and women. The love is there, but some hard truth can't be faced. They live a lie with each other. And all the warmth and closeness slowly dries up and blows away.*

Two weeks after the storm, Andie knew she wouldn't be able to bear this forever. She simply would not become a dried-up woman, living an empty life beside a cold, distant man.

She was better off alone.

It hurt, just thinking it. But sometimes the truth hurt.

She wasn't yet to the point where she was ready to take action. She wasn't ready to pack her suitcase or consider the awful effect her leaving might have on Emily. She wasn't even ready to start scanning Apartment For Rent ads.

But the idea was in her mind. The idea was like a tiny seed that had found fertile soil in the cold silence that lay between herself and her husband. A little sprout was unfurling from the seed, though no one could see it yet; it was still underground.

Soon, Andie started thinking to herself. *Soon something has to give.*

On the second Friday in November, Andie and Clay sat in the family room after Emily was in bed. Clay read a spy novel.

Andie did nothing. She leaned back in her big comfortable chair and closed her eyes.

She thought about how normal they would look to any outsider. A lovely young couple relaxing on a Friday night from the fulfilling demands of their new family and their growing business.

She glanced over at Clay. He was a handsome, successful man. And to any casual observer, she would appear to be his female counterpart. They had a beautiful daughter, a wonderful home. And Barrett & Co. was doing just fine. They had it all.

But together, just the two of them alone, they had nothing. Nothing but walls and distance and lies.

The doorbell rang, cutting through her grim thoughts.

Clay glanced up from his book. "Who's that?"

Andie shrugged. "I don't know."

"Do you want me to get it?"

Andie pushed herself out of the deep, soft chair. "No. Read your book. I'll see who it is."

Andie walked down the hall to the front door, her mind on the walls that were unscalable, the distance so vast it had become immeasurable. And the lies. The lies that were sacred now. Never to be disturbed.

Something has to happen, Andie thought for the hundredth time. She turned the handle and pulled back the door.

Madeline Kirkland was waiting on the other side.

Chapter 16

Madeline shivered a little and stuck her hands deeper into the pockets of her expensive trench coat. "I would have called. But I was afraid you wouldn't see me. So I found my way out here. I figured I'd be harder to say no to face-to-face."

Andie only stared, thinking that Madeline looked thinner, and that she'd cut her hair.

"You look…thinner," Madeline said.

"I was just thinking the same thing about you."

Madeline glanced away, into the darkness beyond the porch, and then back. "Your baby?"

"She was a little early. But she's fine."

"A girl, then?"

"Yes. We named her Emily."

"Emily. I like that." Somewhere off in the oaks, an owl hooted.

"Well?" A laugh that sounded a little like a sob escaped Jeff's widow. "May I come in?"

Andie stepped back. "Yes, of course."

"Is Clay here?"

"Yes, he's here."

"I want…I must talk with you. With both of you."

"All right." Andie closed the door and gestured toward the family room. "Through that way."

Madeline turned where Andie pointed.

"Wait."

Madeline froze, then looked back, a question in her eyes.

"Your coat," Andie said lamely. "Why don't you give it to me and I'll hang it up?"

"Oh. Certainly." Madeline took off the coat and handed it over. Then she squared her shoulders and headed toward the family room.

Clay looked up when he heard the sound of high-heeled shoes on the hall floor.

When Madeline appeared, he stared, just as Andie had done. "Madeline?"

"Yes. It's me." She stood awkwardly before him.

He swallowed. Dread curled in his stomach.

Andie appeared from the hall. "Madeline wants to talk with us, Clay."

"What about?" He tried not to sound harsh, but somehow it came out that way.

Madeline said softly, "I think you know."

Clay set his book down. He understood the urge trapped animals had, to chew off their own limbs in order to escape. But Clay wasn't an animal. He looked from Madeline's grim, set face to Andie's and then he tried one last time to avoid the inevitable. "Are you sure this is necessary?"

"Yes," Madeline said.

"All right."

There was an agonized silence, then Andie indicated the

couch. "Please. Sit down. Can I get you something? Coffee? Are you hungry?"

Madeline sat and shook her head. "Nothing. Really. I'm fine."

Andie sank into the chair she'd left when she answered the door.

Madeline said, "Oh. This is difficult. I don't know quite where to begin."

"Just do it," Andie said. "Start anywhere."

"All right, I…Jeff never balanced his checkbook." Clay stared at Madeline, wondering what in the hell Jeff's checkbook had to do with anything. Madeline went on. "Just think of that. I probably never would have figured out the truth if he hadn't turned over all the money matters to me when we got married."

Beside Clay, Andie made a little noise, a sound of dawning awareness. "You found the canceled check."

Madeline nodded. "I found a check he wrote to someone named Andrea McCreary. I never connected the name with you, Andie, because I don't think anyone had ever mentioned your last name. And Clay never called you Andrea—that I remember. It was always Andie, when he talked about you. But anyway, I found a check for five thousand dollars made out to someone I'd never heard of named Andrea McCreary. I asked Jeff about it. He gave me some story about splitting a commission with another real estate agent. The story didn't make a lot of sense to me, but I let it go. After all, it was a check he had written *before* we were married and how he spent his money then wasn't really any of my business. But it bothered me. It stayed there, unresolved, in the back of my mind."

Madeline looked at Clay. "I didn't put it together until Andie said her maiden name the day of the funeral. And at that moment, it all made hideous sense. The check. And the way you came that day at the very end of February, Clay. You went off with Jeff and he came back with his face all battered.

He said you two had been mugged. But of course you'd had a fight with each other, right?"

Gruffly, he answered her. "Yeah."

"And then there were the half-truths you told me, about Andie being pregnant already when you got married. I assumed you meant she was pregnant by *you,* but you never actually said that in so many words. And then you said you'd never contacted Jeff and me again because you were so wrapped up in your new life. Well, of course, I'm sure that was part of it. But the main reason was that you and Jeff had agreed never to see each other again. Isn't that so?"

"Yeah. It's so."

"I knew it. I knew it all, at that moment when Andie said her maiden name. I saw the truth. And I couldn't face it. Not then, anyway."

Madeline's hand lay along the arm of the couch. She moved it to her lap to join her other hand. She looked down at her folded hands. Clay thought she appeared very demure, almost schoolgirlish, sitting that way, with her slim legs pressed so close together and both of her feet placed primly on the floor.

But then she looked up and he saw a grown woman's agony in her eyes. "But now I see that I *have* to face the truth. That I can't go on without knowing for sure."

Madeline dragged in a breath, looked down at her hands again. "Jeff was...well, you know how he was. He lit up a room when he entered it, but he often left disaster in his wake. When I married him, I knew what he was like. And I accepted him just as he was. We'd grown up together and I...I understood him. He was an only child and his parents spoiled him— and yet also expected so much of him. He could never live up to what they wanted. And then they both died, before he'd come to any sort of peace with them. He was..."

Madeline seemed not to know how to go on. She put her hands to her cheeks, as if to steady the thoughts inside her head. Then she folded her hands in her lap once more and took another long breath. "I guess what I mean is, I *knew* Jeff. I never knew anyone the way I knew him. There was such intimacy between us. And yet—he feared our closeness. Sometimes he'd run away from it. But for me, there was just never anyone else. I could never imagine a world without him in it. But now I have to do more than imagine it. I have to *live* with it. I have to make my own peace with Jeff's memory and go on."

Madeline turned to Andie. "That's why I have to know. I can't seem to get on with my life until I know."

Andie said softly, "It's all right. I understand."

And Madeline asked the question at last. "Is your baby my husband's child?"

Clay felt as if someone had punched him in the gut.

But Andie looked so calm.

And when she spoke, her voice was as composed as her expression. "In all the ways that matter," she said, "Clay is Emily's father. He's the one who's been there from the first. And Emily already knows how important he is in her life." Andie smiled, a bemused, wondering smile. "If you could just see her face, when she hears his voice or when he bends over her crib and she can make out his features. She looks so…happy, so totally trusting and content, when she recognizes him. She's a lucky little girl. To have a dad like Clay."

Andie sat forward a little in her chair. "But I'm not answering the question the way you meant it, I know. And so I'll tell you this. Yes, I spent one night with Jeff Kirkland during the holidays last year. I found out, after it was too late, that Jeff was only trying to forget how much he was missing *you*. It was a…foolish act, by two foolish people. And it had consequences."

"You became…pregnant." Madeline's voice broke on the last word.

"Yes. I became pregnant by Jeff. But I was fortunate. Clay found out and wanted to marry me. So it turned out that Emily got a real father, after all."

Madeline's clasped hands were white at the knuckles, though her face was composed. She coughed. "I see."

No one seemed to know what to say then. Silence echoed in the room.

Madeline opened the small purse she carried and lifted out a handkerchief. She dabbed at her upper lip with it before she went on in a clipped tone. "There's something else. One more thing. There's money from the Kirkland trust for the baby. For Emily. I would be glad to arrange for that money to be put aside for her."

Andie turned then, to look at Clay. "What do you think?"

Clay didn't know what he thought. The world seemed to have spun right off its axis and whirled into a whole new dimension. He was still reeling from the way Andie was dealing with all this. She had so serenely described him as Emily's true father. And she'd mentioned Jeff so frankly and dispassionately—as if she was completely over him, as if whatever she might have shared with him was long, long in the past.

"Clay?" Andie prompted.

Clay did his best to collect his scattered wits. It seemed only fitting that he should approach this situation fairly and rationally—as both Andie and Madeline seemed to be doing. "Well, I think when she's old enough, she should probably be told something about Jeff. And I think it would be right for Jeff to have left her some money."

"All right, then," Madeline said. She stood. "We don't have to go into the particulars of it now, I don't think. But it should be set up so Emily can claim the money when she reaches her majority. And of course the money should also be available for her education."

"Yes," Clay said. "That sounds right."

Andie urged, "Madeline. Stay awhile."

Clay blinked. He wasn't catching on too fast here. He hadn't realized that Madeline was ready to go. But now he could see that she meant to leave right away.

"No." Madeline opened her purse again, put her handkerchief away. "I can't. Not now. I need some time. This was hard. Please understand."

"Yes," Andie said. "We do. We understand. Maybe later, then…"

"Yes," Madeline agreed. "Maybe later. I think someday I'd like that."

Andie rose to her feet and Clay, feeling slow and confused, followed suit. They trailed behind Madeline to the front door, with Andie stopping at the coat closet to retrieve Madeline's coat.

Moments later, Madeline had disappeared down the gravel walk to the driveway. Andie closed the door and leaned back against it.

Clay stared at her, feeling as if he was seeing her for the very first time. Damned if he didn't admire what he saw. "You said we'd be hearing from her again."

"Yes. I did." She pushed herself away from the door. "All at once, I'm beat."

"I know what you mean."

"I think I'll go on upstairs. Will you turn off the lights when you come?"

"Sure. No problem."

Andie left Clay standing there, left him wondering what in the world to do next.

He watched her climbing the stairs. She held on to the

banister the whole way, her exhaustion clear in every line of her slim form.

Eventually, Clay shook himself. He went to the family room and turned off the lights. Then he, too, mounted the stairs.

He checked on Emily. She was sleeping peacefully. He couldn't resist touching her hand. As always, she curled her fingers around his. She gave a little sigh and a trace of a smile curled her tiny mouth.

Emily was a happy baby. She trusted her world and the people in it. So far, Clay realized, he'd done right by his daughter.

But he couldn't be so proud of himself when it came to her mother.

"There was such intimacy between us," Madeline had said about her relationship with Jeff. "And yet—he feared our closeness. Sometimes he'd run away from it…."

Clay sank to the rocker by Emily's crib. It hurt to think of Madeline's words. They were too true. And not only in reference to Madeline and Jeff.

What was that other thing Madeline had said?

It was so close to what Andie had said on the night before Jeff's funeral. That she and Clay had to face the truth between them. They had to drag it into the light and see it for what it was.

Slowly, Clay rose from the rocker. He could hide here in the baby's room no longer. He went looking for his wife.

Chapter 17

Andie was in the shower. Clay could hear the water running behind the closed door of the bathroom.

He sank to the edge of the bed, facing the closed door. He was still sitting there in the same place ten minutes later when his wife emerged wrapped in her robe, rubbing the wet strands of her hair with a towel.

Andie paused there, in the doorway to the bathroom. "Clay? Are you all right?"

"I don't know." He stared at her, and then put his head in his hands and gazed blindly down at the floor between his knees. "I…"

Andie approached the bed, the fabric of her robe whispering as her bare legs moved. Once there, she sank down beside him. "Clay?"

He lifted his head again and looked at her. She was so beautiful, with her shower-pink skin, her wet, shining hair. "Andie, I…I want to ask you…"

"Yes?"

"God. I don't know where to begin."

He watched the hope leap into her eyes. It was so bright that it nearly blinded him.

"It doesn't matter. Begin anywhere." Her voice was carefully controlled. She didn't want to jump to conclusions—he could see that. And yet she sensed what was happening. At last, the moment when he would be honest with her had come.

"I…I've been losing you, haven't I? Little by little, every day."

She nodded. She was biting her lip, her eyes glittering with unshed tears.

"Are you gone all the way yet? Is there any chance that—?"

She could control herself no longer. "Oh, Clay, yes. Of course there's a chance. When there's love, there's always a chance."

"What do I have to do?"

She wiped her eyes with her towel. "You mean this? You really want to know?"

"Yeah. I mean it."

"All right. I'll tell you. You have to ask me that awful question you're so afraid to ask. You have to get it out in the open so we can deal with it."

He looked at her for a moment more. The temptation was very great to pretend he didn't know what question she meant. But then he thought of Madeline. Her life had been shattered, yet still she came around. She sought the truth.

If Madeline could do it, so could he.

He asked the question, "Do you still love him? Do you still love Jeff?"

"At last," she murmured in a wondering voice.

"Well. Do you?"

"I never loved him." Her eyes were brimming again. There was such joy in her face. "I told you months ago I didn't. And I was telling the truth."

Clay was silent. Then he admitted, "I don't…know how to do this, to talk about the things that hurt. Until I was ten, nobody would listen. And then Dad and Mom took me in. They respected my habit of silence. I learned to *do,* and let my actions speak for me."

Andie set her towel aside and reached for his hand, enfolding it in her two softer ones. "I understand, Clay. I really do. And maybe that worked out pretty well, when there was only you. But now, there are the two of us—the three of us, including Emily. And we can't live this way, with all these unsaid things between us. We need to talk about them." She looked down at their hands and then back up at him. "Can we talk now, Clay? Please? Can I tell you all about it? About what an idiot I was, and why it happened, and *how* it happened?"

Clay moved the hand she clasped, enough so that their fingers could entwine. "Yes. Yes, I suppose you'd better," he said. "Talk to me, Andie. Tell me. All of it."

The words came tumbling out.

"It started when you returned from L.A., really. When you came home to take over the business…"

She told him how she'd felt then, so edgy and unsatisfied, yet unable to let her feelings out because she was determined to prove to him that she deserved her job.

"I thought if you ever got wind of how frustrated I was with having to show *you,* of all people, that I was really good at my job, you'd fire me on the spot."

Clay couldn't help admitting, "I might have. At first."

"Exactly. Anyway, I got through those months when you first came back. Things were going better. I knew you'd started to realize that I was an asset to Barrett and Company. Then Jeff came. And he was bright and fun and easy to be with. I understood he'd had some sort of problem, that he'd broken off an engagement. But I didn't really give it a lot of thought. I wasn't really *after* him or anything. I just liked him. He was fun to be around. And then New Year's Eve came. We all went to Ruth Ann and Johnny's. You were dating Jill Peters, remember?"

He thought of Jill, though it was hard to picture her face. "Yes. I remember."

"Anyway, that night it seemed like everyone in the world was coupled up. Except me and Jeff. You and Jill left early."

"She had to work the next day."

"Whatever. You two left early. And I...I imagined that you were going somewhere to be alone together. I suppose I was jealous, though I didn't know it then."

"You were...?"

"Let me finish."

"All right."

"I drank more champagne. And Jeff and I kissed when the clock struck twelve. And he took me home, because I'd had more champagne than I should have. At my apartment, I had another bottle of champagne in the fridge. We opened it. We started talking. And I told him my dream."

"Your dream?"

For the first time, Andie looked away. But after a moment, she collected herself and went on. "Yes. I'd always dreamed that there would be this man. And I'd know him when I saw him. And that we'd make love and it would be wonderful and we'd be together for the rest of our lives."

Andie swallowed. "Jeff was great, he really was. I mean, he didn't laugh at me. He just listened. I started out talking about my dream as if it was something that didn't really matter anymore. I was trying to be sophisticated—you know, a worldly woman who was through with all that girlish sentimental stuff. Jeff and I even shared a toast—to the death of my silly romantic dreams. But then, when I lowered my glass after the toast, I just burst into tears. I was sobbing and sniffling. And I said, 'Oh, Jeff. There isn't going to be any special man, I know that now. It's just a fantasy. And I've been waiting all my life for someone who doesn't exist.'

"Jeff was holding me by then, kind of rubbing my back. My head was bowed, but then I lifted it to look in his eyes. We stared at each other for a moment. And then he kissed me. And after that, it just happened. We lay back on the couch and fumbled with our clothes. And we…had sex. It was awkward and painful—for me at least. And I don't think it was much different for Jeff. And when it was over, we both started apologizing to each other."

Andie gave a wrenching little laugh. "It still amazes me. That from an act so…grim and mechanical, something like Emily came." Andie clutched Clay's hand tightly. The tears still glittered in her eyes. One ran over the rim of her lower lid and trailed down her cheek to drop on their clasped hands. "Oh, Clay. It was such a stupid, reckless act. You can't know the guilt I feel for it. No one can…." Her teeth were clenched. Another tear fell.

Clay pulled her close and rocked her a little, whispering soothing, tender things against her wet hair. Finally, Andie was comforted enough to pull back a little, though she still gripped his hand as if she would never let go.

"And then," she said with a sniffle, "Jeff started talking. He talked about Madeline. I don't really remember exactly what he said. But I could see how much he loved her. And how totally confused he was. And so I called him an idiot. I called him ten kinds of fool. I said, here I was lonely all the time because the love I was waiting for had never come to be. And there *he* was, with exactly the kind of love I would do anything for. And he was throwing it away. I told him to get back to L.A. and get down on his knees and beg that woman to take him back. And he…he said that was exactly what he was going to do."

"And he did," Clay said tenderly. "Do you remember that morning when Madeline called to say Jeff was dead?"

Andie shuddered. "I'll never forget it."

"Well, that morning, she thanked me. For whatever I'd said to Jeff over the holidays. She said it had made all the difference. That when Jeff came back, he was changed. He really wanted to marry her then."

Andie's smile was so sad and soft. "She did?"

"Yes, she did. She told me how grateful she was to me. I didn't argue with her. How could I at a time like that? But I had no idea what she was talking about. Now I do, though. It was what *you* had said to him."

Andie didn't completely agree. "I think what really happened was that he had finally figured it out for himself. I only put in words what he'd already decided. But it is strange. Because I've always felt like I owed Jeff a debt, too. Because of him, because of all that happened as a result of that one night, I finally found what I was looking for." She paused for a moment, and then she gave a low, musing laugh.

"What?"

"Just remembering. I was so full of…silly fantasies then. I was right about that special man. But I was afraid to admit to myself that he was you. I didn't even know what love was. Until I suddenly had to grow up—and until us."

Clay had to clear his throat before he asked, rather stupidly, "You didn't?"

"No, I didn't. Oh, Clay. When will you let me love you? When will you believe that I do know what love is now, and I love *you,* Clay Barrett, more than anyone in the world…except maybe the baby sleeping in the other room?"

Clay took her words into himself. They filled him to overflowing with shining, glorious hope.

But there was another question he'd been holding back, one

that had been eating away at him since the day after he found out Jeff Kirkland was dead.

He dared to asked it: "If you love *me,* then why the hell did you insist on going to *his* funeral?"

Andie let out a heartfelt sigh. "How many times do I have to tell you? I went because of *you.* Because I thought you would need me. And I wanted to be there, if you did. I was sure Jeff would never have told Madeline about the baby. So Madeline shouldn't have had a clue that the baby was his. But she did have a clue. She had that canceled check. And so the truth came out, after all. And all the stress made me go into labor. It was so horrible. I knew I'd made one mistake in judgment after another. And yet you kept insisting that it was all right. But it wasn't all right."

"I know," he whispered softly. "I know."

"Oh, Clay. I've been so *lonely.* It's been forever since you've let me near."

"I *couldn't* let you near."

"Why?"

He thought for a moment before he tried to explain. "Remember when you said I had to forgive Jeff and then forgive you, too?"

"Yes."

"Well, you and Jeff weren't the only ones I had to forgive. There was myself, too. I'd called Jeff dead—and then he *was* dead. And I realized I'd turned my back on him."

"But what else could you have done?"

"I don't know. But sometimes I think there might have been a better choice."

"For a saint, maybe. But, Clay, you're just a man."

"I know." He shook his head. "Do I ever know. But it seemed like I had just messed everything up. And I had let you down, don't you see? In the most important way. For all those years, I watched you. I think I always felt that I was watching *out* for you. And then, one night I *didn't* watch out for you. And my own best friend took advantage of you."

"No, that's not true. Or at least if Jeff did take advantage of me, I did exactly the same thing to him. We took advantage of each other that night. And it really wasn't your fault, not in any way." She let out a rueful chuckle. "In fact, when the truth came out, you went far beyond the call of duty. I mean, you married me yourself and gave Emily your own name."

"But if I had only—"

"What? Not gone out with Jill that night so I wouldn't have been so jealous?"

"You're kidding. You weren't really jealous, were you?"

"I didn't know it then. But yes, you're darn right I was."

Clay thought of Jeff again. And it wasn't as painful as it had been. He was able to explain, "All through college, Jeff was my damn *hero*, did you know that? He was the opposite of me. He was like you, always looking for adventure, always ready to have fun."

"And he was reckless and he could be thoughtlessly cruel, as well. And now he's gone. It's so sad." She laid a hand on the side of his face. "But if you want to talk about heroes, then the real hero was right here all along."

Clay captured the hand that caressed his face. "I'm no hero, Andie."

"Yes, yes you are. You're my hero. The best kind of hero. The kind who never rides off into the sunset, the kind who knows how to change a diaper, and load the dishwasher—and hold the baby for two hours while she's screaming with colic. The kind who also just happens to turn my bones to jelly every time you kiss me…"

"Hell, Andie, I—"

She touched his face again, a tender, knowing touch. "Oh,

Clay. Can't you see? It's love, Clay. Love is the thing that binds it all together. Love is the thing that makes forgiveness possible. And if you hold yourself aloof from love, then one wrong move from someone who matters to you, and it all falls apart. If you don't believe I love you, how can you know I mean the best for you, want to be with you, would never hurt you on purpose? None of the important things between a man and a woman can exist without love, Clay. Not trust. Not forgiveness. And not a future."

"What are you telling me?"

"Only what I've been trying to tell you for months. That I love you. With all my heart. In the very special and specific way that a woman loves the only man for her. Won't you please believe me now?"

He let a heartbeat pass before he answered, "Yes."

Clay had never seen a smile as beautiful as the one she gave him then. And then she leaned her head on his shoulder.

He put his arm around her and spoke against her damp, sweet-smelling hair. "Hell, Andie. I have to say it. If there's any hero around here, it's you."

She lifted her head at that and turned to grant him an impudent grin. "You noticed." Lord, she was adorable.

"Andie…" He tipped up her chin.

Their lips almost met, but she held back at the last possible second. "Say it."

He faked an innocent look. "What, that you're my hero?"

"You know what. Say it now."

He stroked the curve of her back with the hand that wasn't holding her chin. "I want you. Damn. I always want you."

But that wasn't enough for her. She pushed him away. "Say it, Clay. Say it now."

"Come back here."

"Not until you tell me. Not until you say the words.

There are only three—four, including my name. Four simple little words."

"Damn it, Andrea Barrett."

"Those aren't the ones."

He reached for her and caught her. "You're not going to let me off the hook on this, are you?"

"You're right, I'm not."

"All right."

"I'm listening."

He said it, very slowly, so she wouldn't miss a word. "I love you, Andie."

Her smile was as bright as the sun after a wild, dark storm. "And I love you, Clay."

And then there was no more need for words. Their lips met. Their lifetime bond was sealed at last, in the best and truest way—with honesty and love.

* * * * *

We hope you enjoyed reading

ALMOST FOREVER

by

New York Times bestselling author

LINDA HOWARD

This story was originally from
our Silhouette Special Edition® series.

*Look for six new romances each and every month
from Silhouette Special Edition®.*

SPECIAL EDITION

Life, Love and Family.

www.eHarlequin.com

We hope you enjoyed
our bonus book

FOR THE
BABY'S SAKE

by

USA TODAY bestselling author

CHRISTINE RIMMER

This story was originally from
our Silhouette Special Edition® series.

*Look for six new romances each and every month
from Silhouette Special Edition®.*

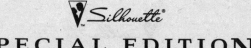

SPECIAL EDITION

Life, Love and Family!

Available wherever books are sold.

www.eHarlequin.com

NYTSSECR10

BESTSELLING AUTHOR COLLECTION

WE HOPE YOU ENJOYED THIS TITLE FROM
THE HARLEQUIN
BESTSELLING AUTHOR COLLECTION.

DISCOVER MORE GREAT ROMANCES FROM HARLEQUIN® AND SILHOUETTE® BOOKS.

Whether you prefer romantic suspense, heartwarming
or passionate novels, each and every month Harlequin® and
Silhouette® have new books for you!

AVAILABLE WHEREVER YOU BUY BOOKS.

*Use the coupon below and save $1.00 on the purchase of
any Harlequin® or Silhouette® series-romance book!*

$1.00 OFF the purchase of any Harlequin® or Silhouette® series-romance book.

Coupon valid until Aug 31, 2010. Redeemable at participating
retail outlets in the U.S. only. Limit one coupon per customer.

5 65373 00076 2   (8100)0 11652

FFUSCPNR

BESTSELLING AUTHOR COLLECTION

WE HOPE YOU ENJOYED THIS TITLE FROM
THE HARLEQUIN
BESTSELLING AUTHOR COLLECTION.

DISCOVER MORE GREAT ROMANCES FROM HARLEQUIN® AND SILHOUETTE® BOOKS.

Whether you prefer romantic suspense, heartwarming
or passionate novels, each and every month Harlequin® and
Silhouette® have new books for you!

AVAILABLE WHEREVER YOU BUY BOOKS.

*Use the coupon below and save $1.00 on the purchase of
any Harlequin® or Silhouette® series-romance book!*

$1.00 OFF the purchase of any Harlequin® or Silhouette® series-romance book.

Coupon valid until Aug 31, 2010. Redeemable at participating
retail outlets in Canada only. Limit one coupon per customer.

52609002

FFCNDCPNR

Choose the romance that suits your reading mood

Passion

Harlequin Presents®
Intense and provocatively passionate love affairs set in glamorous international settings.

Silhouette Desire®
Rich, powerful heroes and scandalous family sagas.

Harlequin® Blaze™
Fun, flirtatious and steamy books that tell it like it is, inside and outside the bedroom.

Choose the romance that suits your reading mood

Home and Family

Harlequin® American Romance®
Lively stories about homes, families and communities like the ones you know. This is romance the all-American way!

Silhouette® Special Edition
A woman in her world—living and loving. Celebrating the magic of creating a family and developing romantic relationships.

Harlequin® Superromance®
Unexpected, exciting and emotional stories about homes, families and communities.

Look for these and many other Harlequin and Silhouette romance books wherever books are sold, including most bookstores, supermarkets, drugstores and discount stores.

SMP60HOMER2

Choose the romance that suits your reading mood

Romance

Harlequin® Romance
The anticipation, the thrill of
the chase and the sheer rush
of falling in love!

Harlequin® Historical
Roguish rakes and rugged
cowboys capture your
imagination in these stories
where chivalry
still exists!

Harlequin's officially licensed
NASCAR series
The rush of the professional
race car circuit; the thrill of
falling in love.

THE HARLEQUIN BESTSELLING AUTHOR COLLECTION

CLASSIC ROMANCES IN COLLECTIBLE VOLUMES
FROM OUR BESTSELLING AUTHORS

Six *New York Times* bestselling authors bring
readers some of their classic romance stories in
the Harlequin Bestselling Author Collection.
Each book also includes a bonus story by
some of our top series authors—
a true treat for romance readers!

Available March 2010
The Best Is Yet to Come by Diana Palmer
Almost Forever by Linda Howard

Available June 2010
Sweet Memories by LaVyrle Spencer
Forever My Love by Heather Graham

Available September 2010
Dream Mender by Sherryl Woods
Part of the Bargain by Linda Lael Miller

Available wherever books are sold.

www.eHarlequin.com